9 PLAYS
BY BLACK WOMEN

EDITED AND WITH AN INTRODUCTION BY

MARGARET B. WILKERSON

A MENTOR BOOK

NEW AMERICAN LIBRARY

A DIVISION OF PENGUIN BOOKS USA INC., NEW YORK

PENGUIN BOOKS CANADA LIMITED, MARKHAM, ONTARIO

(The following page constitutes an extension of this copyright page.)

Library of Congress Catalog Card Number: 86-60744

 MENTOR TRADEMARK REG. U.S. PAT. OFF. AND FOREIGN COUNTRIES
REGISTERED TRADEMARK—MARCA REGISTRADA
HECHO EN DRESDEN, TN, U.S.A.

SIGNET, SIGNET CLASSIC, MENTOR, ONYX, PLUME, MERIDIAN and NAL BOOKS are published *in the United States* by New American Library, a division of Penguin Books USA Inc., 1633 Broadway, New York, New York 10019, *in Canada* by Penguin Books Canada Limited, 2801 John Street, Markham, Ontario L3R 1B4

First Printing, August, 1986

3   4   5   6   7   8   9   10   11

PRINTED IN THE UNITED STATES OF AMERICA

To my family—for believing

> Stan, husband and best friend
> Gladys, Cullen and Darren who kept faith
> with their working mother
> My mother and father, mother-in-law and
> father-in-law, my sisters and all the
> twigs and branches of the Bufords and
> Wilkersons

To black women everywhere in honor of their beauty, wisdom,

> and resilience—and the men whom we love

CONTENTS

ACKNOWLEDGMENTS

For several years, new black writers have been sending their plays to me, asking for evaluative comments or for production leads. I am delighted with this opportunity to bring some of them, the works of black women, into publication. While preparing this anthology, I have come to know many black women who are dedicated to writing for the theatre, and I have been both amazed and gratified by these artists who celebrate life even as they critique it. Unfortunately, space did not allow me to include all of the fine work being written. Hopefully this anthology will stimulate enough interest for other publications to succeed this one. I wish to thank the numerous colleagues and playwrights who sent or recommended scripts to me.

The playscript, however, is only the beginning, not the end of a play. Life is breathed into the text through production, that process of interpretation, collaboration, honing and refining by directors, actors, designers and technicians in concert with the writer. Without the production process, playwrights never know the full social and artistic import of their work. Thus the theatres, both professional and amateur, which have showcased plays in this anthology as well as other plays by black women deserve special praise—among them, the New Federal Theatre, American Place Theatre (Women's Project), New York Public Theater, Negro Ensemble Company, Richard Allen Center for Culture and Art, New Heritage, Frank Silvera Writers Workshop, and many, many others. New York producers like Woodie King, Joseph Papp, Julia Miles, Garland Thompson, the late Hazel Bryant, the late Roger Furman and others consistently nurtured new works such as these.

ix

There are also a number of organizations whose role in producing or awarding prizes to new playwrights deserves special recognition, among them: AUDELCO, th— nedy Center, the American College The— Black Theatre Program and th— American Theatre A— Conference — atr—

A—
ta—
sh—
on—
I a—

I —
sona—
Jack—
Alice—
Sharp—
phone—
certain—
Library—
committ—
it. I also —

ACKNOWLEDGMENTS

For several years, new black writers have been sending their plays to me, asking for evaluative comments or for production leads. I am delighted with this opportunity to bring some of them, the works of black women, into publication. While preparing this anthology, I have come to know many black women who are dedicated to writing for the theatre, and I have been both amazed and gratified by these artists who celebrate life even as they critique it. Unfortunately, space did not allow me to include all of the fine work being written. Hopefully this anthology will stimulate enough interest for other publications to succeed this one. I wish to thank the numerous colleagues and playwrights who sent or recommended scripts to me.

The playscript, however, is only the beginning, not the end of a play. Life is breathed into the text through production, that process of interpretation, collaboration, honing and refining by directors, actors, designers and technicians in concert with the writer. Without the production process, playwrights never know the full social and artistic import of their work. Thus the theatres, both professional and amateur, which have showcased plays in this anthology as well as other plays by black women deserve special praise—among them, the New Federal Theatre, American Place Theatre (Women's Project), New York Public Theater, Negro Ensemble Company, Richard Allen Center for Culture and Art, New Heritage, Frank Silvera Writers Workshop, and many, many others. New York producers like Woodie King, Joseph Papp, Julia Miles, Garland Thompson, the late Hazel Bryant, the late Roger Furman and others consistently nurtured new works such as these.

There are also a number of organizations whose role in producing or awarding prizes to new playwrights deserves special recognition, among them: AUDELCO, the Kennedy Center, the American College Theatre Festival, t' Black Theatre Program and the Women's Program of :. American Theatre Association, Eugene O'Neill Wri Conference, and the many fine college and university t. atre programs around the country. Amateur and sn professional companies such as Kuntu Repertory in C cago and those in my own San Francisco area—Julian T. atre, Lorraine Hansberry Theatre, Oakland Ensembl. Theatre and Black Repertory—continue to include new works by black women in their production schedules.

The fact that this is the first published collection of plays by black-American women made background research particularly challenging, since little attention has been paid to these writers as a group. Thus I am indebted to the careful research done by James Hatch and Ted Shine, who singled out early plays by black women in *Black Theater USA*, Claudia Tate, who conducted wonderful in-depth interviews for *Black Women Writers At Work*, Mari Evans, who compiled critical essays in *Black Women Writers (1950–1980): A Critical Evaluation*, as well as Jeanne-Marie Miller and Nellie McKay, who have written definitive articles. I especially appreciate the generosity of friend and colleague, Winona Fletcher, who shared her new work on Georgia Douglas Johnson and May Miller. Recent books by Angela Davis (*Women, Race and Class*), Paula Giddings (*When and Where I Enter*), and Trudier Harris (*From Mammies to Militants*) provided validation and documentation of black women's history. Jewelle Gresham willingly shared her extensive research for her forthcoming book on black and white women and their history of struggle. I am deeply indebted to these as well as other colleagues.

I also want to thank the writers and agents whose personal enthusiasm for the project kept my spirits high: Elaine Jackson, Aishah Rahman, P.J. Gibson, Beah Richards, Alice Childress, Ruby Dee, Alexis DeVeaux, Saundra Sharp, Victoria Lucas, and my agent, Susan Schulman. A phone conversation with them rejuvenated me in the uncertain hours. I salute Carole Hall, editor at New American Library, who conceived the idea of the book and remained committed to its potential even as we struggled to define it. I also appreciate Robert Nemiroff's cooperation in releasing unpublished Hansberry materials for this volume and the care and concern which he brought to the handling of *Toussaint*. The support of research assistants Kathy Haynes and Maria Roberts, the staff of the Department of Afro-American Studies at U.C. Berkeley, and my department chair, Erskine Peters, helped me to complete the project on time. Invaluable assistance in the preparation of the manuscript was generously provided by Bernisteen Holmes.

I am particularly indebted to the Rockefeller Foundation and the Ford Foundation for fellowships which enabled me to do basic research on black women playwrights during the early stages of this project.

This book was, in some ways, a family affair: my husband, Stan, daughter, Gladys, and sons Cullen and Darren helped with manuscript preparation and also relieved me of my share of family responsibilities when I needed time to write. Their support, both spiritual and material, is a constant source of strength and inspiration.

Finally, I thank all of the playwrights—their families, friends and supporters—who made this anthology possible.

—Margaret B. Wilkerson
University of California, Berkeley

INTRODUCTION

by
Margaret B. Wilkerson

Black women are a prism through which the searing rays of race, class and sex are first focused, then refracted. The creative among us transform these rays into a spectrum of brilliant colors, a rainbow which illuminates the experience of all humankind.

Social, economic and political forces have long demeaned and distorted the life of the black woman, beginning with her enslavement in America. Not only was she a slave, but her children were defined as slaves as well, regardless of their paternity. Today, the enormity of such a fact is almost incomprehensible, for it made the black woman the legal instrument of her people's slavery. An anomaly of the slave system, black women suffered the "equality" of oppression, performing hard labor in the fields and being whipped and flogged along with their men, while enduring those special forms of exploitation reserved for her sex—rape and forced childbearing. Injustice intruded into her most private moments; her survival—and the liberation of her race—depended on her determination to free herself from bondage. While the plight of the slave attracted many whites to the abolitionist movement, the peculiar burden borne by black women caused white women to examine the oppressive nature of their own condition. Thus the women's movement for equality was born out of the black struggle for liberation, with the black woman as midwife. Her presence in both movements, therefore, was not only natural, but inevitable.

The plays selected for this anthology reflect this consciousness of history and reality among black women playwrights. Their characters embody a world in which the personal is political, in which something as intimate as one's hair may indeed declare one's politics. In these works,

cold statistics take on human forms that express the intangible motives for teenage pregnancy and the psycho-
social obsessions that can lead to suicide. Connections are
forged between a black woman's hips and thighs and the
politics of beauty, or between a white man's compassionate
gesture and a black man's rebellion. When the woman's
skin is black, the phrase, "a man-centered woman" takes
on new meaning, and getting an education can become an
impossible burden.

These plays provide a special window on the human
condition and will illuminate any discussion of race, class,
and gender.

The plays date from the 1950s because black women
made major breakthroughs into the professional theatre
during that decade. However, those achievements were
built on traditions developed early in the twentieth century
by women who had little opportunity to see their works
produced.

EARLY PLAYWRIGHTS AND THE
STRUGGLE FOR FREEDOM
(1900–1950)

Like their male colleagues, early black women playwrights were faced with stereotyped images of black figures
on the stage. White-authored entertainment like the minstrel show was the most popular form of theatre in America
for nearly a century. The comic buffoon and the lazy shift-
less Negro in these plays helped to rationalize a system
which oppressed their real life counterparts. Such stereotypes created artistic expectations which black playwrights had to overcome when writing for the stage. For
audiences, even some black ones, were ill-prepared to accept serious portrayals of people presented on stage most
often as objects of ridicule.

Two stereotypes of black women—e.g., the neutered,
domineering mammy who ruled the roost, or the over-
sexed floozy—were particularly insidious, for they masked
the vulnerability of the female to sexual exploitation. The
tragic mulatto embodied another stereotypical notion: that
the "enlightened" white world is a source of fine qualities
(and beauty, of course) and the "savage" black side, of
unruly passions that eventually cause degradation or demise.

Other stereotypes led producers to actively discourage

the portrayal of genuine relationships between black men and women characters. In *Black Manhattan*, James Weldon Johnson explained:

> One of the well-known taboos was that there should never be any romantic love-making in a Negro play. If anything approaching a love duet was introduced in a musical comedy, it had to be broadly burlesqued. The reason behind this taboo lay in the belief that a love scene between two Negroes could not strike a white audience except as ridiculous. The taboo existed in deference to the superiority stereotype that Negroes cannot be supposed to mate romantically, but do so in some sort of minstrel fashion or in some more primeval manner than white people. This taboo has been one of the most strictly observed.[1]

All these onstage stereotypes only reflected the attitudes of American society in the first half of the twentieth century. Blacks and supportive whites pressed unsuccessfully for anti-lynching legislation; the black voter was disenfranchised and the struggle for the right to vote would continue well into the 1960's. Women and men alike suffered under Jim Crow laws which segregated schools, transportation and public accommodations. And black veterans returning home from two World Wars would be denied jobs and beaten in white-instigated riots. The issues confronting blacks during these decades were in no ways subtle; the abuses were blatant, often backed by legislation and states' rights philosophy.

The early works of black women were strong protests against these conditions and were produced largely within the fold—in churches, lodges, and social halls of the sympathetic few.

The National Association for the Advancement of Colored People (NAACP), which had organized interracially to fight for civil rights, recognized the power of live performance and early in its development enlisted the theatre arts in the struggle for black liberation. The first play to be produced by the NAACP's Drama Committee of Washington, D.C., was a "race play," *Rachel*, by Angelina Grimke. It became the first drama of record to be written and performed by blacks in this century. Presented on March 3, 1916, it was later performed in New York City and Cambridge, Massachusetts. A program note recorded the importance of the occasion: "This is the first attempt to use the stage for race propaganda in order to enlighten the American people relative to the lamentable condition of ten millions of Colored citizens in this free republic."[2]

Rachel is a remarkable play for other reasons as well. Written in the sentimental style of the day, the play focuses on Rachel Loving, a caring young woman who manages to maintain positive, hopeful attitudes in the face of racial discrimination until she learns that her father and older brother were lynched. The trauma of this discovery intensifies as Rachel sees the frightening impact of prejudice on black children who become withdrawn and paranoid because of the persecution of their white schoolmates. Unlike the stereotypes of the period, Rachel is neither a superwoman nor of loose character; she is a tender, vulnerable person whom the evils of society overwhelm. Revealing a striking sensitivity to the special way in which racism and sexism affect the black woman, author Grimke has Rachel refuse the marriage proposal of John Strong, a fine young man who loves her and offers her a "little house" with all the protection men were expected to provide for women in that day. However, Rachel refuses, despite her love for him, recognizing that a black man cannot protect her and her children from the assaults of a cruel world. *Rachel*, this first major play by a black woman, boldly depicted a woman who was the antithesis of the prevailing stereotypes, and who refused to pretend that she enjoyed the same privileges as other women in the society.

Later plays during that period would address specific social issues. Alice Dunbar Nelson, the widow of poet Paul Lawrence Dunbar, wrote *Mine Eyes Have Seen* (1918), bringing to the stage the question being hotly debated by black leaders like W.E.B. DuBois and A. Phillip Randolph: Should a Negro soldier fight abroad for freedom that he and his people are denied at home? Although her play was well received in the high school where she taught, no one would publish it.[3] *They That Sit In Darkness* (1919) by Mary Burrill added the voice of poor, black women to the effort to grant women the right to birth control information. Published by *The Birth Control Review*, this play revealed the cycle of poverty, hopelessness and death to which many black women without benefit of contraception were doomed.

Perhaps the most provocative play of this period was *The Purple Flower* (1928) by Marita Bonner. An outstanding graduate of Radcliffe and an English teacher in Washington, D.C., Bonner wrote a compelling allegory which asked: Is the time ripe for revolution? Arguing that neither education nor hard work nor money has brought equality, the play concludes that blood must be shed in order for blacks to gain their rights from the "white devils." In an essay entitled "On Being Young, A Woman and Colored," for which she won first prize in a contest sponsored by the NAACP publication *Crisis*, Bonner revealed her frustration with the limitations placed on black women.

> But—"In Heaven's name, do not grow bitter. Be bigger than they are", exhort white friends who have never had to draw breath in a Jim-Crow train. Who have never had petty putrid insult dragged over them, drawing blood—like pebbled sand on your body where the skin is tenderest. On your body where the skin is thinnest and tenderest.
>
> You long to explode and hurt everything white; friendly; unfriendly. But you know that you cannot live with a chip on your shoulder. . . .
>
> You know, being a woman, you have to go about it gently and quietly, to find out and to discover just what is wrong. Just what can be done. . . .
>
> So—being a woman—you can wait.[4]

Opposed to the "race propaganda" of the NAACP's Drama committee were the devotees of folk plays which emphasized "art" rather than "propaganda." This group later formed the Howard Players, producing such works as *The Death Dance* by Thelma Duncan, a drama of African life. One of the best-known women writers in this genre was Zora Neale Hurston, whose pioneering research as an anthropologist specializing in southern black folklore was a treasure trove of dramatic material. At one point, Langston Hughes and Zora Neale Hurston collaborated on a play, *Mule Bone*, which they hoped would offer an alternative to the problem plays, counter stock comic types of the minstrel tradition and showcase the authentic humor of black folk culture. It was a stormy collaboration which resulted in bitterness between the two famous writers, but the play itself succeeded. The characters were down-to-earth, fun-loving people. The dialogue drew heavily on the verbal improvisation—rhyming, woofing and sounding—which are central to black-American folklore.[5]

The two threads of "propaganda" and "folk art" joined in the plays of Georgia Douglas Johnson, a well-published poet and good friend of black artists and intellectuals such as Langston Hughes, Owen Dodson, Sterling Brown, Alain Locke and May Miller. Lynching informed most of her works—one-act plays taut and spare in dialogue and action based on the very real drama of terrorist acts directed at the southern black community. C. Eric Lincoln in *The Negro Pilgrimage in America* lists 1,886 lynchings between 1900 and 1931, an average of 61 per year or more than one lynching per week for 31 years. The subject matter left no room for humor. In Johnson's *A Sunday Morning in the South*, a young black man is falsely accused of assaulting a white woman. The audience sees his arrest and his family's reaction when they learn a white mob has lynched him. Johnson's presentation is objective; without editorializing, she lets the horrible deed speak for itself. In *Safe*, Johnson depicts a mother who strangles her newborn baby when she hears the pathetic cries of a black man being dragged away by a lynch mob. It is her way of keeping her child "safe." In these and other plays, Johnson's characters are simple people whose dialect and folk customs she skillfully captures. She submitted several of her plays to the Federal Theatre Project, the government sponsored arts program which was part of the Works Projects Administration in the late 1930's, but they were never produced.

Johnson's contemporary, May Miller, used the stage to educate her students about Negro history. As a school-teacher, she had access to a stage where she could produce her works on such subjects as Harriet Tubman and Sojourner Truth. She also co-edited two volumes of plays with Willis Richardson in an effort to promote the works of black playwrights.

Women playwrights before 1950 were full partners in the theatre's protest against conditions for blacks, whether in the form of "race propaganda," folk plays or historical dramas. They also made the unique perspective of black women's reality a part of that protest. Not until mid-century, however, would their voices reach beyond their communities into the highly competitive world of professional theatre.

THEATRICAL BREAKTHROUGHS:
THE CIVIL RIGHTS AND WOMEN'S MOVEMENTS

In 1942 a group of blacks and whites who believed in direct, non-violent action organized as the Congress of Racial Equality (CORE) and staged a sit-in in a Chicago restaurant, signalling a new aggressiveness in the struggle for civil rights and at least two decades of protest, both violent and non-violent, which would rock this nation. A new group of women playwrights would come of age during this period, several of whom were groomed in the progressive youth organizations which helped to fuel the movement. They would converge on New York City, by this time the center of professional theatre in the country, and would be the first black women to be recognized for the quality of their work by the white professional theatre.

In 1950, a strong new voice entered the theatre in Beah Richards, playwright and actress. She would popularize the one-woman show, which may have been the primary vehicle for women playwrights in the early nineteenth century. Richards performed her one-person play, *A Black Woman Speaks* (which is included in this anthology) for a white organization in Chicago, Women for Peace, shocking them with her challenge that white women overcome their racism and sexist bondage. She would go on to tour this play and to win a television Emmy Award twenty-five years later.

Alice Childress, the first black woman to have a play produced off-Broadway, would continue the tradition of her predecessors who wrote about poor, forgotten people—the "losers," according to Childress. But her major characters, most frequently black women, refused to be victims. They were descended from Mildred, the plain-speaking, no nonsense domestic whom Childress had created in the column which she wrote for *Freedom*, the Harlem newspaper founded by Paul Robeson. A prolific writer, Childress created assertive, spunky female characters whom society had rendered powerless. In *Trouble in Mind*, which won an Obie Award for Off-Broadway plays in 1955, a black actress confronts the attitude of white superiority in the theatre, that microcosm of society. Her best-known play, *Wedding Band* (included in this volume) which was televised nationally in 1973, broke theatrical taboos against the portrayal of interracial love. Childress boldly exposes the hypocrisy, deceit and oppression that separate black from white. Her characters are attacked, troubled, hurt and maligned, but never defeated.

Harlem was a center of black culture in these years, nurturing a strong cultural movement. The Committee for the Negro in the Arts produced the work of young black writers, many of whom had been nurtured in turn by the Harlem Writers Workshop. Childress was a member of these groups along with a relative newcomer from Chicago, Lorraine Hansberry.

Hansberry, who had been Associate Editor on *Freedom*, the paper for which Childress had written, made the first major breakthrough into the white-dominated professional theatre in 1959, with her play *A Raisin in the Sun*. Hansberry became the first black and youngest person to win the coveted New York Drama Critics Circle Award. The outstanding cast of the original production made theatre history: Sidney Poitier, Claudia McNeil, Ruby Dee, Diana Sands, Lou Gossett, Glynn Turman, understudies Douglas Turner Ward, Lonne Elder, Ossie Davis, and Beah Richards.

A Raisin in the Sun, destined to become an American classic, could not have been more timely. The Civil Rights Movement had shown whites that they knew very little about the black nation in their midst. The guilt generated by the brutal terrorism against orderly demonstrators in the South turned whites into a ready audience for a play about the black struggle. This play presented a family with which whites were ready to identify. Hansberry's craftsmanship captured the heroism and frustration of a whole era and the heart of a divided nation.

Hansberry's achievement catapulted her to fame. As demonstrations in the South intensified, she became one of several articulate spokespersons for the black struggle. However, this success did not ensure the future of her subsequent works. Her next play, *The Drinking Gourd*, a television drama, was commissioned by the National Broadcasting Company, but was shelved as too controversial to produce. Producer-Director Dore Schary called it, "A powerful, marvelous script that might have been—

with the cast we had in mind and a little luck—one of the great things we've seen on television."[6] The television executives may have found the script potentially offensive because it portrayed slavery as a system which victimized whites as well as blacks and made a heroine of a black woman slave who turns her back on her dying master. *Toussaint*, (a scene from the unfinished script is published in this volume), would have extended the theme of *The Drinking Gourd* to a play based on the successful Haitian Revolution. *The Sign in Sidney Brustein's Window*, which played 101 performances on Broadway, was kept open by the persistent efforts of artists and other loyal supporters but closed on the night of Hansberry's death. Critical response to the play was mixed. In *Les Blancs*, produced posthumously, the audience split along racial lines over this drama about the inevitability of violent revolution in modern-day Africa. Although Hansberry was well-loved by the theatre community and her death at the age of thirty-four was mourned throughout the country, her insistence on the social nature of art, the implicit criticism of American society in her plays, and her uncompromising views on the pervasiveness of prejudice and oppression made her work unpopular in some critical circles.

Nevertheless Hansberry would influence the next generation of black writers. Her success convinced a number of artists that they could seek a career in the theatre and opened doors especially for many actors and technicians. Because she was a young woman, twenty-eight years old at the time that the play went on Broadway, she was a role model to a generation of young black writers. Coining the term "young, gifted and black," she inspired them to write, to expand their horizons, to care about what was happening in the world.

The next decade saw black playwrights "telling it like it is" on stage as never before. As the intransigence of racism became more obvious, the movement and theatre became more militant. Marita Bonner would have fitted well in this era, as poets like Nikki Giovanni and Martie Charles wrote for the theatre, dramatizing the lives of young black women involved in the movement.

In the same year that Le Roi Jones' *Dutchman* poured out the anger of the black male at the symbols of his oppression, another more introspective writer spoke in a different voice. Adrienne Kennedy won an Obie Award

in 1964 for her play, *Funnyhouse of A Negro*. Using sur-
realistic theatre, she externalized the psychological confusion of a young Negro woman who struggles unsuccessfully to reconcile her African and European selves. A cult
play of that period popular among many theatre artists,
the play suggested new ways in which the private and personal dilemmas of blacks could be explored in the public
arena of theatre. Seven years later, in 1971, two popular
plays (J.E. Franklin's *Black Girl* and Elaine Jackson's *Toe
Jam*) would anticipate the explosion of women's theatre
by depicting the intimate problems of growing up black
and female. But the next major breakthrough would have
to wait until 1974.

Just as the Civil Rights Movement had prepared American audiences to receive the honest portrayal of a black
family in the 1950's, so the Women's Movement of the
1970's helped to create an audience eager to validate itself
in Ntozake Shange's play about black women, *For colored
girls who have considered suicide when the rainbow is enuf*.
Shange's play, with its cast of striking black women and
its compelling language, caught fire like no other play since
A Raisin in the Sun. The play not only introduced a new
theatrical form, the choreopoem, to the professional
stage, but presented women's experience with a new in-
timacy and candor. Shange has written that her work "attempts to ferret out what i know & touch in a woman's
body . . ."[7] Created in the women's collectives of the West
Coast, *For colored girls* . . . won an Obie Award in 1974
and quickly became the favorite artistic work of the Wom-
en's Movement. Its frank portrayal of black women's need
for self-affirmation and love generated some debate in black
communities because of the play's implied criticism of black
men. However, the power of Shange's poetry and the mul-
tiple talents of the black actresses combined to create an
irresistible stage production which was both moving and
provocative.

In *spell #7*, which is published in this anthology, Shange
reaches back in theatrical history to find a dramatic device,
the minstrel mask, to express the perceptual and psychological limitations which a racist and sexist society seeks
to impose on women and men.

The work of Hansberry, Childress, Kennedy and Shange
strengthened the social consciousness of black plays, in-
tegrated the social and political with the private and per-

sonal self in new ways, and validated the theatrical richness of women's experience. Their plays pushed beyond the confines of realism to newer theatrical forms more expressive of black reality. As the Civil Rights and Women's Movements changed the face of the country, these writers opened the theatre to new dramatic realities. Contemporary women playwrights would have a solid foundation on which to build.

NEW FREEDOMS, NEW RESPONSIBILITIES

The new generation of black women playwrights represented in this anthology is no longer bound by the restrictions of theatrical realism and cultural inhibitions. They stretch the arts of the theatre to fulfill the demands of their consciousness, their recognition of the self as an integral part of the world, both shaped by and shaping the forces of society. Themes of love and sexuality permeate many of the plays. *Brown Silk and Magenta Sunsets* by P.J. Gibson and *Unfinished Women Cry in No Man's Land While A Bird Dies in A Gilded Cage* by Aishah Rahman (both published in this volume), use music in unique ways to make a statement about the psycho-sexual universe of obsessive women, and the human sexuality behind the statistics of teenage pregnancy.

One of the most significant, new developments among black women playwrights is the treatment of homosexuality. Although an exploitative lesbian liaison is suggested in the 1961 excerpt from Lorraine Hansberry's *Toussaint*, only recently have contemporary writers like Alexis DeVeaux included lesbian and homosexual relationships as a meaningful part of black women's reality. DeVeaux's exploration of the political and sexual needs of black women in *The Tapestry* (published in this volume) lays the groundwork for her later plays, *No* and *A Season to Unravel*, which deal more explicitly with love between women. *Long Time Since Yesterday*, a prize-winning play by P.J. Gibson about black women's friendships, includes a lesbian relationship as a central feature of the plot.

The works of these writers reveal the complex, interior landscape of black women's lives while at the same time looking outward and commenting on the world which impinges on their existence. In this volume, *The Brothers* exposes the emptiness of black women in the middle-class who live on the periphery of their people's struggle for freedom, while *Paper Dolls* by Elaine Jackson uses satire to dissect the international beauty contest—that point at which the personal and political converge in powerful and ludicrous ways.

Among important plays not represented in this book, Saundra Sharp's *The Sistuhs* and Ruby Dee's *Take It From the Top* continue the tradition of socially conscious musicals developed to such a high art by Vinette Carroll in the 1960's and 1970's with *Don't Bother Me I Can't Cope, When Hell Freezes Over I'll Skate*, and *Your Arms Too Short to Box with God*. Other important playwrights not included in this anthology examine the world of women's athletics (Ivey McCray's *Run'ers*), black rural folk culture (J.E. Franklin's *Where Dewdrops of Mercy Shine Bright* and *Under Heaven's Eye . . . Til Cockcrow*), the humor and pathos of black adolescence (Crystal Rhodes' *Stoops*), political repression (Sharon Stockard Martin's *The Moving Violation*, which won a Kennedy Center Black Playwrights Award in 1979), and successful black women (Lee Hunkins' *Hollow Image*, which won the 1979 ABC Theatre Award). Lynda Patton and Ramona Bass and others write for children's theatre, while Vinie Burrows, actress-playwright, carries on the tradition of one-woman shows. These writers along with Pearl Cleage Lomax, Judy Mason, and California Cooper represent only some of the many black women whose plays are being read and produced.

However, this is a chilly period for black women playwrights. A conservative mood has turned the clock back on social and artistic gains for blacks and women. Large numbers of people believe that access to society's benefits has been achieved for all, and that those who are still "locked out" are there by their own fault. But black women are not strangers to hard times. They have continued to write for the theatre, despite limited production opportunities; they continue to speak with authority on the many questions which trouble human beings as individuals and as citizens of America and the world. For they know:

> That no culture can long sustain itself on its own dishonesties; on the residue of its own failure. The very stuff of its art, for instance, tends to shrivel and become sick without the nourishment of genuine exploration of those dishonesties. . . . It is, in fact, the examination of the truths of a civilization which in-

variably offers back to that civilization the rock-like notes of affirmation, significance and beauty.[8] (Lorraine Hansberry)

Black women playwrights continue to offer creative defiance to a world in need of their vision.

NOTES

1. James Weldon Johnson, *Black Manhattan*, New York: Atheneum, 1972, p. 171.

2. Montgomery Gregory, "A Chronology of the Negro Theatre," in Alain Locke, *Plays of Negro Life*, New York: Harper & Brothers, 1927, p. 414.

3. James V. Hatch and Ted Shine, Eds., *Black Theater USA*, New York: The Free Press, 1974, p. 173.

4. Marita O. Bonner, "On Being Young, A Woman and Colored," *Crisis*, December, 1925.

5. Robert E. Hemenway, *Zora Neale Hurston*, Urbana: University of Illinois Press, 1977, p. 148.

6. *Lorraine Hansberry, The Collected Last Plays* edited by Robert Nemiroff, New York: New American Library, 1983, p. 150.

7. Ntozake Shange, *For colored girls who have considered suicide when the rainbow is enuf*, New York: Bantam Books, 1977, frontispiece.

8. Lorraine Hansberry, "Poetry of the Negro" (Album Cover), New York: Glory Records, 1956.

Beah Richards

A BLACK WOMAN SPEAKS

Beah Richards is a writer and actress in the tradition of unsung women who have not only defined themselves through the written word, but have projected their reality through performance. The one-person show has been a popular vehicle in black culture for showcasing individual talent, for coping with the high expense of full-cast productions, and for performing material often unavailable to black performers (e.g., the classics and original works). Ms. Richards represents countless women who have performed their own poetry, prose, and dramas in churches, clubs and lodges—the original homes of black theatre in America.

Ever philosophical about theatre as a mirror of reality, Ms. Richards writes, "Having grown up in a racist culture where two and two are not five, I have found life to be incredibly theatrical and theatre to be profoundly lifeless. Therefore, in order to perceive myself as being at all, it has been mandatory to explore these contradictions and redefine these terms." The Western tendency to separate nature into opposites, the sacred versus the profane, justifies the idea that one can legitimately be master and the other enslaved, Richards argues. "The purity of the white woman and the whiteness of her state of grace are a fundamental arm of the divine right of white to rule."[1] Her famous performance piece, *A Black Woman Speaks*, which won an Emmy Award in 1975, challenges this right with candor and daring.

As the women's movement of the 1970s gathered momentum there was much discussion about the racism within its ranks. The subject still warrants attention as the gains of white women are measured against the losses of black women and their community. It is all the more startling, therefore, to realize that Ms. Richards's cogent piece was first performed in 1950 for a white women's organization in Chicago, Women for Peace. What a shock it must have been for this group to hear Ms. Richards's biting words,

27

which emphasized white women's complicity in the oppression of black women and men.

Although she is represented in this volume as writer, Ms. Richards is better known to the theatre as an actress. Lorraine Hansberry's prize-winning play, *A Raisin in the Sun*, provided her first Broadway vehicle as a standby for the role of Mama, a part she played in the Yale Repertory Theatre's revival of the show in 1983. Her portrayal of Sidney Poitier's mother in *Guess Who's Coming to Dinner* won her an Academy Award nomination as Best Supporting Actress. She has also played featured roles in New York productions of *The Miracle Worker*, *Purlie Victorious*, and Mike Nichols's all-star production of *The Little Foxes* at Lincoln Center. Theatre audiences of the early 1960s remember her best for her performance as Sister Margaret in James Baldwin's *The Amen Corner*, produced by Frank Silvera's Theatre of Being, a vital training ground for black theatre artists.

In 1971, Ms. Richards stunned the Los Angeles theatre community as both writer and actress in her first full-length play, *One Is a Crowd*. Playing the lead role, she made the soliloquy form from her one-woman shows the centerpiece of a compelling drama about a black singer's lifelong pursuit of revenge against a white man whose casual lust had destroyed her family. Written in 1951, twenty years before its first production, this play illustrates Ms. Richards's love for and mastery of language; *One Is a Crowd* is singular in its rich mixture of provocative verse and black idiom. It drew standing ovations and critical raves. Critics called the play "powerful," "unforgettable," and "brilliant." Their praise for Ms. Richards's performance was equally ecstatic: "awesome," "dazzling," "a total performer."

A Black Woman Speaks, the performance piece included in this volume, is a striking example of the singular voice of this black woman. In persistent, uncompromising language, Beah Richards tells her audience what separates black women from white women—and what must change in order for sisterhood (and brotherhood) to become a reality.

NOTES

1. Beah Richards, *A Black Woman Speaks and Other Poems*, Los Angeles: Inner City Press, 1974, v-vi.

A Black Woman Speaks

by
Beah Richards

A Black Woman Speaks was first performed in 1950 for the Women for Peace in Chicago.

It is right that I, a woman
Black,
should speak of white womanhood.
My husbands,
my fathers,
my brothers,
my sons,
die for it,
because of it.
And their blood,
chilled in electric chairs
stopped by hangman's noose
cooked by lynch mobs' fire
spilled by white supremacists' desire
to kill for profit,
gives me that right.

I would that I could speak of white womanhood
as it will and should be,
when it stands tall in full equality.
But then, womanhood will be womanhood,
void of color and class,
and all necessity for my speaking thus will be past.
Gladly past.
But now, since it is deemed a thing apart
supreme!
I must in searching honesty report
how it seems to me.

White womanhood stands in bloodied skirt
and in slavery,
reaching out adulterous hands
killing mine and crushing me.

What then is this superior thing
that in order to be sustained
must needs feed upon my flesh?
How came this horror to be?
Let's look to history.
They said, the white supremacists said,
that you were better than me.
That your fair brow would never know
the sweat of slavery.
They lied!
White womanhood too is enslaved;
the difference is degree.

They brought me here in chains.
They brought you here
willing slaves to man.
You.
Shiploads of women,
each filled with hope
that she might win
with ruby lip
and saucy curl
and bright and flashing eye
him, to wife who had the largest tender.
Remember?

And they sold you here
even as they sold me.
My sisters,
there is no room for mockery.
If they counted my teeth,
they did appraise your thigh.
Sold you to the highest bidder the same as I.
And you did not fight for your right to choose
whom you would wed.
But for whatever bartered price
that was the legal tender,
you were sold to a stranger's bed
in a stranger land.
Remember?
And you did not fight.
Mind you, I speak not mockingly,
but I fought for freedom;

I'm fighting now for our unity.
We are women all.
And what wrongs you
murders me . . .
eventually marks your grave.
So we share a mutual death
at the hand of tryanny.

They trapped me with the chain,
the gun.
They trapped you with lying tongue
for, lest you see that fault,
that villainy,
that robbed you of name, voice, and authority,
that murderous greed that wasted you
and me.
He, the white supremacist, fixed your minds
with poisonous thought:
"White skin is supreme."
And therewith bought that monstrous change
exiling you to things.
Changed all that nature had in you
wrought of gentle usefulness,
abolishing your spring,
Tore out your heart,
set your good apart from all that you could say,
think,
feel,
know to be right.
And you did not fight, but set your minds fast
on my slavery,
the better to endure your own.
It is true . . .
My pearls were beads of sweat
wrung from weary body's pain.
Instead of rings upon my hands
I wore swollen, bursting veins.
My ornaments were the whiplash's scar;
My diamond, perhaps a tear.
Instead of paint and powder on my face
I wore a solid mask

of fear,
to see my blood so spilled.

And you,
women,
seeing, spoke no protest.
But cuddled down in your pink slavery
and thought somehow my wasted blood
confirmed your superiority.
Because your necklace was of gold,
you did not notice that it throttled speech.
Because diamond rings bedecked your hands,
you did not regret their dictated idleness.
Nor could you see that the platinum bracelets
which graced your wrists were chains
binding you fast to economic slavery;
and though you claimed your husband's name,
still could not command his fidelity.

You bore him sons . . .
I bore him sons.
No, not willingly.
He purchased you.
He raped me.
I fought.
But you fought neither for yourselves
nor me.
Sat trapped in your superiority
and spoke no reproach
consoled your outrage with an added brooch.
Oh God, how great is a woman's fear
who for a stone, a cold, cold stone
would not defend honor,
love nor dignity!
You bore the shaming mockery of your marriage
and heaped your hate on me.
A woman too . . .
A slave more so.
And when your husband disowned his seed
that was my son
and sold him apart from me,
you felt avenged.
Understand:
I was not your enemy in this.

I was not the source of your distress.
I was your friend.
I fought.
But you would not help me fight,
thinking you helped only me.
Your deceived eyes seeing only my slavery
aided your own decay.
Yes they condemned me to death and they con-
    demned you
to decay.
Your heart whisked away,
consumed in hate,
used up in idleness
playing yet the lady's part,
exiled to vanity.
It is justice to you to say
your fear equaled their tyranny.

You were afraid to nurse your young
lest fallen breast offend your master's sight
and he should flee to firmer loveliness.
So you passed them,
your children, on to me.
Flesh that was your flesh,
blood that was your blood,
drank the sustenance of life from me,
and as I gave suck, I knew I nursed my own child's
    enemy.
I could have lied!
Told you your child was fed
till it was dead of hunger.
But I could not find the heart to kill orphaned
innocence.
For as it fed it smiled,
burped, and gurgled with content,
and as for color,
knew no difference.
Yes, in that first while
I kept your sons and daughters alive.

But when they grew strong in blood and bone
that was of my milk,
you taught them to hate me.
You gave them the words

"mammy" and "nigger."
So that strength that was of myself
turned and spat upon me,
despoiled my daughters and killed my sons.
You know I speak true,
though this is not true for all of you.

When you made your big push for freedom
my sons fought at your sons' side.
My husbands, brothers too, fell in that battle
where Crispus Attucks died.
And when I bestirred myself for freedom
and brave Harriet led the way,
some of you found heart,
played a part in aiding my escape.
It is unfortunate that you acted not in the way
of JUSTICE!
But to preserve the Union,
and of course, for dear sweet pity's sake;
else how came it to be as it is with me today?
You hated slavery, yet abhorred equality.

I would that the poor among you could have
seen through the scheme
and joined hands with me.
Then we, being the majority,
could long ago have rescued our wasted lives.
But NO!
The rich becoming richer could be content.
While yet, the poor had only the pretense
and sought through murderous brutality
to convince themselves that what was false
was true.
So with KKK and fiery cross
and bloody appetites
set about to prove that
"white is right,"
forgetting their poverty.
Thus the white supremacists used your skins
to perpetuate your slavery.
And woe to me.

Woe to the boy Emmett Till.
And woe to you!

It is no mistake that your naked bodies on the cal-
    endars
announce the fatal dates.
This is what they plan for you.
This is the depravity they would reduce you to.
Death for me,
and worse than death for you.

What will you do?
Will you fight with me?
White supremacy is your enemy and mine.
So be careful when you talk with me;
remind me not of my slavery;
I know it well.
But rather tell me of your own.
Remember, you have never known me.
You've been seeing me as white supremacy
would have me be.
But I will be myself—
FREE!
JUSTICE!
PEACE!
PLENTY!
for every MAN
WOMAN
CHILD
who walks the earth!
This is my fight.
If you will fight with me, then take my hand,
that our land may come at last to be a place of peace
and human equality.

Lorraine Hansberry

TOUSSAINT
Excerpt from Act I
of a Work in Progress

Lorraine Hansberry is the most celebrated of all black women playwrights. Her first and best-known work, *A Raisin in the Sun*, has become an American classic, enjoying numerous revivals during its 25th anniversary season in 1983–84 and frequent productions in high schools, colleges, universities and communities throughout the country.

Her second play, *The Drinking Gourd*, would have received even greater attention, had it been produced. Commissioned by the National Broadcasting Company, it was to be the first episode in a television series designed to commemorate the beginning of the Civil War. The subject: slavery. However, after reading the script, the network executives shelved the play and the project fearing that it might offend large segments of the national audience.

Toussaint was one of Hansberry's favorite projects. In several interviews following the success of *A Raisin in the Sun*, she showed great enthusiasm for this play. It was among the scripts left unfinished at the time of her death in 1965. She began writing it in 1958 as "a drama with music," acccording to Robert Nemiroff, her literary executor. Over the next several years, between work on *A Raisin in the Sun* and the plays which followed it, Hansberry returned to *Toussaint* sporadically to rough out possible themes and plot outlines for what she conceived, alternatively, as an opera (a work on a heroic scale which would require the collaboration of a composer of like-mind and talent) and as a play. She worked slowly because she considered it to be "my epic work"—and therefore her greatest challenge. The notes and sketches she left on her desk were all preliminary, with one exception—the scene published here.

In 1961 she was invited to present and discuss a staged scene from a work in progress on the educational program *Playwright At Work*. She chose *Toussaint* and honed the opening scene for production. It was taped on May 21, 1961, and broadcast nationally the following month on educational television. Hume Cronyn was originally scheduled to play the role of Bayon De Bergier, the plantation manager; however, he took ill and had to be replaced. Given the high quality of this scene, *Toussaint* might have been Hansberry's greatest and most important work. In an interview with Frank Perry following the television performance of the scene, Lloyd Richards, who had directed the Broadway production of *A Raisin in the Sun* as well as the *Toussaint* scene, commented that the excerpt could have gone into rehearsal immediately with only minor changes.

In "A Note to Readers," which precedes the scene in this volume, Hansberry acknowledges her fascination with the historical figure Toussaint, a liberator whom she believed most Americans had never heard of, "despite the fact that in my opinion he was probably greater than . . . Simon Bolivar or even our own Washington." Repulsed by the exotic "romantic racism" which polluted most dramas about the Caribbean, she set out to present the historical achievement of this man who ultimately defeated French colonial rule in Haiti and opened the way to the establishment of a republic.

Hansberry was well prepared to write this play. Having seen the devastating effects of racism and poverty in her native Chicago, she also knew, through her parents' courageous fight against discrimination and her careful study of the past, the resilience of the human spirit and its historical confirmation in the people of Haiti. As a young adult, she had been Associate Editor of *Freedom*, Paul Robeson's progressive newspaper, and was thoroughly conversant with the politics of oppression worldwide. The success of *A Raisin in the Sun* had made her a public figure, giving her an even greater opportunity to use the black struggle for civil rights as a universal metaphor for human dignity and liberation.

Toussaint would have given Hansberry a forum for one of her fundamental ideas about history and human character:

Virtually all of us are what circumstances allow us to be. . . . It really doesn't matter whether you are talking about the oppressed or the oppressor. An oppressive society will dehumanize and degenerate everyone involved . . . and in certain very poetic and very true ways at the same time it will tend to make if anything the oppressed have more stature . . . because at least they are arbitrarily placed in the situation of overwhelming that which is degenerate . . . in this instance the slave society. . . . It doesn't become an abstraction. It has to do with what really happens to all of us in a certain context.[1]

The excerpt from *Toussaint* reveals in one masterful stroke a significant feature of the slave society—the various layers and levels of oppression which such a system nurtures. First, there are the obvious victims as represented by Toussaint himself and his fellow slaves. In an expanded description of the opening scene, a ridiculously large number of servants is shown setting up the dinner table. Forty to serve four was an awful waste of human potential, Hansberry believed. Then there is the slavery of Lucie, the Creole mistress of the plantation, who is "purchased" in that she sells her freedom for empty luxury (much in the same way that Beah Richards so powerfully outlines in *A Black Woman Speaks*—see pages 33–39). Lucie, in turn, exploits both the labor and sexuality of Destine, her body servant, forcing upon her an unwanted homosexual liaison. Finally, there is Bayon, the plantation manager, who is trapped by his own petty bourgeois needs and the demands of an oppressive system. In discussing the scene, Hansberry stated that she was thinking of adding another character to illustrate yet another aspect of this system and its effect on human behavior—a servant who would dress Bayon. Part of the dehumanizing character of this social order, she believed, was the fact that Bayon and Lucie could play out their most intimate revelations before the servant as if he were merely a chair or some other inanimate object.[2] In her notes on the play she wrote, "The master's pride [and] arrogance lead them to discuss [the] French Revolution in front of slaves. . . ."

Although Toussaint does not appear in this first scene, Hansberry gives some clues to the development of his character in a series of three speeches (printed at the end of the scene) which she planned to incorporate "somewhere" in the drama. The speeches reveal Toussaint's political sophistication, a fact which has been obscured by European arrogance. The French underestimate the Haitians because they see them only as slaves, not as free men and women. However, Toussaint soon recognizes that Napoleon Bonaparte, whom he views as "a wise man" like himself, does not make that mistake: "He is different from the others. He is the first of the Europeans to know who I am; and who the blacks of Santo Domingo are." Toussaint realizes that he will be a worthy opponent. The final speech fragment reveals Toussaint's fear that his cause is lost because Napoleon Bonaparte has apparently accepted Toussaint's equality and "has sent all of France for us. They have come to make war on men, not slaves, and we are doomed."

Hansberry may have intended this speech to reflect only a momentary lapse in confidence. Her extensive research on Toussaint (including inspiring passages in W.E.B. DuBois's *Black Folk Then and Now*) revealed that the historical Toussaint ignored Napoleon's command to surrender, freed the slaves, dictated a constitution which made him governor general and established trade relations with the United States and Britain. A year later he would surrender to a large French invasion, and retire with honors, but would later be arrested and would die in a prison in the French Alps. The Haitians continued to revere him as their liberator, the leader who established Haiti as a black-governed French protectorate.

It is impossible to project the ultimate direction and outcome of this tantalizing work. But Hansberry did speak about the purpose of this first scene and thereby offers some clues to her total conception. "[This scene] was an effort to set preliminary character of the two principals and to discover some personal aspects of their lives before we see them in conflict with other people in the play, so that the audience is able at once to begin to relate to them in what may not be entirely sympathetic roles as the play evolves but as human beings . . . which is always a certain measure of sympathy. This is why I want them to be people in our minds first." As in *The Drinking Gourd*, she was writing drama, not history, but drama whose characters an audience would know and recognize—no matter what their historical period.

When Hansberry died in 1965, she left a number of other manuscripts among her papers: fragments of several plays; a novel, *The Dark and Beautiful Warriors*; a playlet entitled *The Arrival of Mr. Todog* which satirized Samuel Beckett's absurdist drama *Waiting for Godot*; a well-crafted screenplay based on *Masters of the Dew* by Afro-Haitian novelist Jacques Romain; notes for a play on the eighteenth-century feminist, Mary Wollstonecraft; and plans for a play on Akhnaton, the Egyptian pharaoh. Five of her plays have been published: *A Raisin in the Sun* (which was made into a film in 1961), *The Sign in Sidney Brustein's Window*, *Les Blancs*, *The Drinking Gourd*, and *What Use Are Flowers?* Robert Nemiroff, her former husband and literary executor, gathered segments of her plays, essays, poems and speeches into a popular production, *To Be Young, Gifted and Black*, which ran longer than any other drama of the 1968–69 Off-Broadway season, toured the country during 1970–71, and was shown as a 90-minute film in 1972. He also produced *Raisin*, a musical based on the prize-winning play in 1974, for which he won a Tony Award. The growing body of scholarship on Hansberry was enhanced by a special issue of *Freedomways* ("Lorraine Hansberry: Art of Thunder, Vision of Light", December, 1979) which featured articles by artists and scholars as well as a comprehensive bibliography of writing by and about this major playwright and her work. The extraordinary quality of Hansberry's work has made her plays essential to courses in American theatre as well as women's studies and black studies.

NOTES

1. Excerpt from unpublished transcript of interview with Lorraine Hansberry by Frank Perry on "Playwright at Work," educational television program, taped May 21, 1961.
2. *Ibid.*

Toussaint

A Drama by
Lorraine Hansberry

Excerpt from Act I of a Work in Progress

An excerpt from Act I of *Toussaint* (A Work in Progress) was first taped for the national educational television program, "The Playwright At Work," on May 21, 1961. Directed by Lloyd Richards, it was broadcast nationally the following month with Bramwell Fletcher as Bayon and Marie Andrews as Lucie. The same scene substantially, with the character of Destine added, was broadcast on WBAI-FM Radio as part of a seven-hour tribute, "Lorraine Hansberry In Her Own Words," January 22, 1967, and February 9, 1967. In that broadcast, Bayon was played by Roscoe Lee Browne, Lucie by Geraldine Page, and Destine by Leslie Rivers.

As published here, the excerpt incorporates some small changes made by the author in rehearsal and restores several key lines and speeches—and the full scene with Destine—which had been cut to fit the television time allotted.

CHARACTERS

BAYON DE BERGIER
LUCIE DE BERGIER, his Creole wife
DESTINE, a servant

A NOTE TO READERS:

I was obsessed with the idea of writing a play (or at that time even a novel) about the Haitian liberator Toussaint L'Ouverture when I was still an adolescent and had first come across his adventure with freedom. I thought then, with that magical sense of perception that sometimes lights up our younger years, that this was surely one of the most extraordinary personalities to pass through history. I think so now.

Since then I have discovered that it has been a widespread obsession. Neither the Haitian Revolution nor the figures of L'Ouverture or Christophe or Dessalines has gone wanting in dramatic or other fictional materials. Those I have troubled to read have offended my early dream. The exotic, the voodoo mysticism, the overrich sensuality which springs to mind traditionally with regard to Caribbean peoples has outlandishly been allowed to outweigh and, to my mind, distort the entire significance and genuine romance of the incredibly magnificent essence of the Haitian Revolution and its heroes.

The people of Haiti waged a war and won it. They created a nation out of a savagely dazzling colonial jewel in the mighty French empire. The fact of their achievement—of the wresting of national freedom from one of the most powerful nations on the face of the earth by lowly, illiterate and cruelly divided black slaves—has, aside from almost immeasurable historical importance, its own core of monumental drama. One need not bow to the impulse to embellish it with romantic racism.

What the Haitian slaves accomplished under the leadership of the Steward of Breda is testimony to purpose and struggle in life. They who were slaves made themselves free. That is not, to argue with current vogues, a tired cliché of romanticism. It is a marvelous recognition of the only possible manner of life on this planet. L'Ouverture was not a God; he was a man. And by the will of one man in union with a multitude, Santo Domingo was transformed; aye—the French empire, the western hemisphere,

the history of the United States*—therefore: the world.
Such then is the will and the power of man. Perhaps that
is the secret of the greatness of humankind.

Lorraine Hansberry
New York City
December, 1958

---

* Lorraine Hansberry is referring here to the fact that it was Napoleon's dis-
astrous defeat in Haiti that caused him to abruptly abandon his plan for massive
development of France's new world empire, and specifically to propose the
Lousiana Purchase—of one-quarter of the future United States, from the Gulf
of Mexico to Canada, the Mississippi to the Rocky Mountains—to President
Jefferson.

"I must warn you that to remain with me means to remain with your race and its cause, to remain in the Land of the Mountains, and to regard the Land of the Mountains as the Mother of the Earth. We must remold human relations here—we must alter human society here—and from here, liberty will go out to the whole world."

Toussaint L'Ouverture
(To his sons during the campaign of LeClerc, 1801)

ACT ONE

SCENE 1

The Great House of a sugar plantation on Santo Domingo in the 1780s—immediately before the outbreak of the Haitian Revolution.

The massed voices of field slaves can be heard, welling up in the distance in a song of fatigue. Their music is an organ-toned plaint which yet awaits a Haitian Moussorgsky. It is, of course, punctuated by the now distinctive rhythms of the island.

> Oh, when will the sun go down!
> Oh, when will the shadows come?
> Shadows of night!
> Shadow of rest!
>
> Oh, when will the night hide the cane?
> Oh, when will the dark hide the sun?
> Night, the friend!
> Friend, the night!

As this strong music fades it is promptly replaced by the fragile tinkle of an 18th-century French minuet being played somewhere in the house on a delicate harpsicord. Exposed to us is the double boudoir of the plantation manager, BAYON DE BERGIER, and his wife. The decor suggests the lush, even vulgar overstatement of too luxurious appointment: thick floor coverings; excessive statuary; extravagant color; cushions and ornate furnishings chosen indiscriminately from prior and contemporary French periods.

A partition marks both the separateness and union of the rooms: the dividing drapes presently being drawn back make it one room. The rear walls give way to tiny balconies de-

signed with exquisite Spanish ironwork. Beyond is the Bay of Cap Francais: a presently serene blue water edged by the curving dark "land of mountains" first called "Haiti," as it will be again in a later century. All is washed in waning late afternoon Caribbean sunlight.

BAYON DE BERGIER *stands, in a state of unfinished dress, at the balcony, with his hands resting heavily on the grill, facing away from us. He is looking out at the Bay and the cane fields below—a slight, weary man who has begun to lose his hair as he moves into his middle fifties. His wife,* LUCIE, *reclines on a chaise, virtually submerged in cushions, so swathed in filmy boudoir fabric that it is difficult, at first, to discern her person from the cushions. But as she talks, now and again, a hand rises and floats through the air. She is many years her husband's junior, in her late twenties or early thirties. Dark, languid, ordinarily indolent in gesture or speech but inclined to outbursts of petulance which punctuate her underlying frustrations.*

LUCIE. (*With dismissive laughter from the depths of the cushions where she absently fingers her long dark hair.*) Oh, Bayon, Bayon, Bayon. The point remains that I am in no mood to hear your dull, tiresome talk of acreage and harvest or an equally dull, tiresome discussion of the present political state of affairs of France. The current palpitations of the Directory don't interest me. Napoleon himself doesn't interest me; the Jacobins don't interest me. (*She turns over slowly on her side and continues.*) I am not interested in one single word your guests will have to say and I won't wish to hear one single word that they have said when they are gone.

BAYON. (*Turning in, wearily, exasperatedly, from the balcony and resuming his dressing.*) Well, my sweet, you will hear it this evening. That is to say, that you will get up now and dress and that you will come downstairs and that you will sit and listen to all of it. (*Coming and hunting about in bureau drawers for items of his costume.*) Not only that, you will listen the entire length of time that their entertainment will require. You will use your most considerable theatrical talents, in fact, to make it perfectly clear to our guests that you have never enjoyed anyone's company quite so

much. You will laugh your most infectious and dis-
arming little laugh all evening at each and every an-
ecdote that M. Petion may care to tell. And you will
stretch your eyes wide with delight at every single item
of Parisian gossip Mme. Petion cares to offer you.
You will do it. You will do all of it. (*Pulling the cord.*)
I will ring for Destine now so that you may get up
and begin your toilette. (*He sighs heavily as he does
so.*)

LUCIE. How you do sigh of late, Bayon. You have turned
into one long sigh.

BAYON. Is it any wonder? (*He wanders back to the balcony,
brushing his side-whiskers and looking out to the
mountains.*) If I could only tell you how tired I am.
(*He says this quietly; rather more to himself than to
her.*)

LUCIE. (*Turning the least little bit.*) What did you say?

BAYON. (*Slightly louder and more emphatic.*) I said if I
could only tell you about my agonies.

LUCIE. (*Throwing up a hand with facetious implication.*)
Oh, Bayon, don't! It's too dreadful when you are
feeling—"agonized." (*He drops his head with the hurt
which she can still achieve with him. He emits yet another sigh. She rises and undulates across the floor to
where his riding boots are and picks them up and turns
them about in her hand musingly; they are caked with
mud and she picks at it thoughtfully.*) It is the measure
of our marriage, Bayon, that you wear the clay from
her grave right into our bedroom now. Remember
when you still cared enough to at least have the mud
meticulously cleaned before you came home to me
after your visits up there? As late as last year we still
had such a fine pretense about it all. I had, I think,
a shred of love left for you because of that. For the
effort. (*She is holding the boots facing his back; he
has bowed his head again.*) Do you still take wild
orange blossoms? I have often wondered about the
specialness of orange blossoms. Did she used to wear
them in her hair?

BAYON. How foolish you are to do this.

LUCIE. And when you put them on her grave, does she
cry out to you in the haunting patois? *"Oh, mon petit,
my strong one! My ivory God! How good that you*

*come to visit me! Do you still love me, my love, my
master!—"*

*(He wheels and comes across to her with fierce violence
and tears the boots from her hand and hurls them the length
of the room. She watches, unmoved, and then saunters to
the balcony herself and looks up to the mountains, continuing her taunting.)*

LUCIE. What made you bury her up there, Bayon? It's so
    far for your visits. Was it some special romantic plea
    on the deathbed perhaps? Ah yes. (*Bitterly affecting
    the mannerisms of an imaginary dying woman, eyes
    half closed and suffering.*) Did she look at you with
    those great dark eyes and say as she lay in your arms—
    (*She points.*) *"Up there, my master! Up there on the
    leeward side of Mont Croix! I would like to be buried
    up there, facing out to the sea which brought you to
    me and near where your God is said to live—"* Was it
    something like that, Bayon?
BAYON. There is nothing for me to say when you are like
    this, Lucie.
LUCIE. When I am like this. (*Turning on him with sudden
    bitter and almost quiet sincerity.*) I do get so close,
    don't I, Bayon? Almost the exact words perhaps?
BAYON. If you wish to torture yourself, Lucie, don't expect
    that I will help you.
LUCIE. You would have given your soul to have been able
    to marry her, wouldn't you?
BAYON. Be still now!
LUCIE. Yes, you're right, Bayon. I am being suffocating.
    It's so hard, but I must learn. I should have taught
    myself long ago not to know—to pretend not to know
    or to care, as is the fashion of the wives of Santo
    Domingo.
BAYON. (*Turning desperately.*) We will forget all of it—
    when we are home—in France.
LUCIE. *I AM home, Bayon.*
BAYON. It would destroy us to stay here.
LUCIE. I know that since she died there is nothing to hold
    you here. But, of late, you seem to forget, my darling,
    I am a *Creole. This* is my home. (*She gestures grandly
    at all of Santo Domingo without the balcony.*) I was—
    as you have said all those times—"spawned" here!

(*Grandly using it.*) That sea there is in my blood; those mountains in my very brain; and those cane fields down there—(*Exultantly.*)—why, Bayon, they are the stuff of this "buccaneer flesh" of mine! (*She runs her hands down the length of herself and turns triumphantly to face him.*) I intend to die here.

BAYON. (*Looking at her sadly and shaking his head.*) The great romance of the Creoles.

LUCIE. (*A new mood; she is swiftly disinterested in the last, bored with it.*) If you like. (*She goes to the chaise and stretches out fully.*) Tell me about the Petions. You knew them in Paris, didn't you?

BAYON. I have never met his wife. I met him once or twice at Noe's.

LUCIE. What is he like? Tell me that and I shall tell you to a detail what his wife is like. I am brilliant at that. You say so yourself.

BAYON. (*Shrugging.*) He is a man. (*Rising and looking about.*) Where are my garters?

(*As he searches for them, she picks them up where he had dropped them and, with a playful, even seductive glint, hides them beneath her body on the chaise.*)

LUCIE. What sort of man?

BAYON. A man, what more? Where are my garters?

LUCIE. (*Teasingly.*) Why are you sullen now, I've changed my mood, why don't you change yours?

BAYON. I am not being sullen; I am looking for my garters.

LUCIE. (*Cat-and-mouse, enjoying the game.*) If you were a true gentleman you would have someone dress you.

BAYON. Well in that respect I shall have to do without being a true gentleman; I cannot bear to have someone hovering around me when I am dressing.

(*He turns and, noting the exaggerated innocence of her expression at last, crosses to her, feels beneath her and, with irritation, produces the garters. She laughs enticingly; he will have none of it.*)

LUCIE. I asked you to tell me about Petion.

BAYON. I have already told you all that you need to know. (*She giggles.*) Marcel Petion is the courier of my employer. He is trusted and respected by Noe.

LUCIE. Ahhh!

BAYON. He has come to survey the plantation, return to France and give his personal estimation to Noe. That is all that matters and need matter. Except that he is to be well entertained. (*Almost pleading.*) I am placing a great deal of hope in his report. If I am to continue for another year I must have a good report. (*Through his teeth, to himself.*) Just one more year . . .

LUCIE. (*Mockingly.*) . . . And then we shall go to live in Paris.

BAYON. (*Looking at her steadily.*) And then we shall go to live in Paris. Now get up and dress. Do none of the servants in this house ever come when they are called! (*He pulls the cord violently.*) If I ran the fields the way you run this house—!

LUCIE. Oh yes, how you love to give orders, Bayon! I think I shall compose a little poem, "When Bayon Gives Orders!" (*She laughs openly at him.*) You do try so hard to be an ominous old *Grand Blanc.* (*She rises and goes closer to him as he, having finished his dressing, takes out a ledger and consults it and scribbles here and there in it.*) Poor little Bayon! No matter what you do you remind me of nothing quite so much as what you are: a poor little petit bourgeois who likes to sit astride his horse out there in the fields play-acting at being master not merely manager of a great plantation, while his so highly esteemed employer esteems nothing at all except the favors of the currently fashionable courtesans of Paris! (*She laughs.*) He is too—(*suggestively*)—occupied to come see for himself how one of his boring old plantations is faring, but instead sends his insignificant little couriers year after year to spy on you. (*She tilts her head a little suddenly, listening to the minuet which has revived below and intruded into their room.*) How badly your Claude plays! But I like it.

BAYON. Yes, you *would* like it. And do not call him *my* Claude. I do not wish to warn you on that again, Lucie!

LUCIE. Poor Lucie! Poor little Creole pig who lacks all sense of the refinements of style which should accompany the playing of a minuet.

BAYON. You have stated the matter as it is.

LUCIE. (*Genuinely angry at that.*) You self-absorbed,

prancing, affected little bourgeois worshipper of the aristocracy! How your insults have ceased to affect me! How pallid they have become. Isn't it depressing! It depresses me horribly. That nothing about you matters, not even your insults, your treasured insults! Or have you forgotten all those succinct little colorful tales of my history told to me in my marriage bed—

BAYON. In the name of God, Lucie, that was ten years ago!

LUCIE. —in the desperate effort to excuse your marriage to yourself!

BAYON. I was beset with problems in those days. I had my own difficulties with myself as you know.

LUCIE. Yes, I know. How could you really be *more* than my father if you had to marry one of his daughters!

BAYON. (*With a sigh.*) I had larger hopes for myself when I was young, that is true. I was brought up that way. I can't apologize for it. My family once fancied that I would marry into a distinguished family. I am sorry that I have hurt you with my regrets.

LUCIE. Hurt me! Do you really think that one may ever forget hearing one's ancestors described as "the baggage of the Paris gutters"? "The prostitutes and refuse of the prisons of France dumped in that Bay out there—"

BAYON. I am asking you, don't start, Lucie—

LUCIE. (*Riding over him.*) "—to begin a new and festering civilization!" How eloquent you were! What graphic rhetoric!

BAYON. (*Slamming the ledger shut.*) I have begged you to forget it!

LUCIE. (*Drawing a finger across her brow.*) It is etched *here*, Bayon!

BAYON. I have told you a thousand times since how unkind of me it was. You should forgive me.

LUCIE. Oh, but tell me, how *does* one forgive hearing how one's own grandmother was—"spawned"? And my father—"the whelp of the discharge of an incoherent panting buccaneer!"

BAYON. Not even among the slaves have I encountered such self-hatred.

LUCIE. Why should the slaves hate themselves. They fetch higher prices on the block!

BAYON. Lucie!

LUCIE. A creature purchased is a creature purchased! To
dress one in laces and sit her at the head of your dining
board is no true index of value! Nor is it an index of
the daily, hourly humiliation of my awareness of the
bastard legions roaming this plantation—opening and
closing doors for me; waiting at my table—*playing
minuets in my own home!* My own daughters have
more cousins and brothers than beaus in Santo Domingo!

BAYON. (*Leaping up and speaking tightly between his teeth
again.*) I will not have this talk in the house! You will
stop it this instant! Suppose the girls should hear—

LUCIE. Hear it! You think they don't *know* it! They are
island-born, Bayon!

(*There is the sudden crack of a whip off-stage and the piercing cry of a human being in terrible pain. The minuet halts
for the merest fraction of a moment, and then resumes as
a second and a third cry are heard.*)

Who is your Toussaint having punished now?

BAYON. (*At the window, casually.*) It looks like Simion.
He is being whipped.

LUCIE. Toussaint is a brute.

BAYON. He is a steward and an excellent one.

LUCIE. What would become of the plantation if he ever
ran away, Bayon?

BAYON. He never will. He is content. He does his work
and I give him plenty of leisure for his walks in the
woods and his little mumble-jumble business. That is
all that he requires for his personal contentment.
Toussaint has his own sense of the order of things.

LUCIE. Yes, I think so. How strange the two of you are
together in the fields. You, in your wide-brimmed hat
astride your horse, *seeming* to command. And he, the
slave, beside you, barefoot in that yellow handkerchief and hideous face—commanding.

BAYON. I have tried to explain to you again and again that
he is not a slave.

LUCIE. Well, is he free?

BAYON. No, he is not free either.

LUCIE. Then he must be a slave. If you are not one then
you must be the other.

BAYON. It is a special situation. You are a woman, you cannot understand it.

LUCIE. (*With deliberate wide-eyed innocence.*) Oh, but explain it to me, Bayon. I will try very hard to understand it. And explain about yourself. Are you a free man, Bayon?

BAYON. Of course I am a free man.

LUCIE. Then why haven't you left Santo Domingo long ago? That is what you have wanted more than anything else for a long time—to be running about Paris. What is it that keeps a *free* man where he does not wish to be? Tell me, what is freedom, Bayon de Bergier?

BAYON. As an abstraction that is something that no one can answer. Least of all, these days, a Frenchman. (*The cries intrude again; but the minuet continues and presently fades under.*)

LUCIE. Do you think he gets pleasure from it?

BAYON. Of course he does.

LUCIE. Personally, I don't think so. I have watched his merciless way with the slaves and I saw no pleasure in it.

BAYON. (*Interested.*) What then?

LUCIE. (*Having won interest is disinterested. With a little laugh.*) A woman's reasoning. It would bore you or make you laugh. (*Mona Lisa.*) I will keep it to myself.

BAYON. Excellent. I know only that I have a steward who knows how to drive men.

LUCIE. (*Turning to him suddenly.*) What did you say?

BAYON. I said that I have a steward who knows how to drive slaves.

LUCIE. But that isn't what you said. You said—"men." Isn't there a difference between slaves and other men, Bayon?

BAYON. (*Impatiently.*) In the sense that I was speaking just then it is all the same.

LUCIE. (*Looking off, remembering.*) I saw him once when he was having Sidelie whipped. He stood quite near, with his arms folded across his chest, watching with the most complicated expression on his face that I have ever seen.

BAYON. Well, he is a weird old buck, if that is what you mean, with his herbs and all.

LUCIE. Could it be possible, Bayon, that if Toussaint knows

how to command men, not merely slaves—since you
use the words the same—that he may command even
you?

BAYON. No—that is not possible. I command. He is my
steward. And one thing is certain—he is content. I
wish the others were as much so; with their running
off and rebelliousness. But Toussaint is a special kind
of black; there is something strange and passive, almost mystical in his acceptance. I once asked him
casually you know, about the insurrections. He waved
it away and seemed very impatient to hear it discussed.
He is—a very wise man.

LUCIE. (*Her own meaning.*) Yes, Bayon, I think so.

(*A knock at the door.*)

BAYON. Now, will you dress, my sweet. (*He has success-
fully changed his mood at last and kisses her on the
forehead perfunctorily and looks at his watch. She looks
closely into his eyes and shakes her head with enormous
perception.*) I shall expect you downstairs in at least
an hour. (*At the door.*) And in *excellent* humor.

(*As he exits, a slender young slave girl enters.*)

LUCIE. (*Her eyes immediately upon the servant.*) Where
have you been! I rang hours ago!

DESTINE. Downstairs, Madame, helping with the table.

LUCIE. Why in the name of God should you be downstairs
helping with the table when I need you here. Get the
rose water and oil (*The woman obeys.*)—my skin
feels like parched leather today. And try to mix it
properly for once! You nearly drowned me last week
it was so full of water and the week before that you
made it so oily that I felt like a greasy pig for days.
(*She arranges herself on the chaise again and drops
her negligee about her shoulders for the massage.*) What
shall I wear. It's too hot for the blue brocade and I
have grown too old for pink faille . . . (*The crack of
the whip is heard again. The servant begins to massage
in the oil, a curiously frozen-faced young beauty with
rigid lips.*) Why don't you ever talk, Destine? I go
mad for someone to talk to . . . a woman. Whatever
her faults, at least Delira used to talk to me . . .

Ungrateful wretch—to run off like that. But then
. . . you will all do it some day, won't you? . . . Run
off to the hills . . . to return with fire and machete?
. . . (*Flowing down into the cushions from the soothing
power of the oil and massage.*) Ah, yes, soothingly
. . . caressingly . . . It is your saving grace, Destine.
You are a savage, but when you are gentle, you are
very gentle, and I need to be treated gently. By someone in this world. I adore it when you show how gentle
you can be. (*Suddenly turning around to face the slave.*)
You despise me, don't you!

DESTINE. (*Continuing to massage, cooly, her face set, a
servant's mask.*) Why should Destine despise such a
kind and a beautiful mistress?

LUCIE. (*Reaching out and seizing the other woman's cheeks
between her fingers.*) You do not think that I am either
kind or beautiful. You fool the others with your grins
and silences, but I am not Monsieur Bergier, Destine!
I can look into those little black eyes of yours and
know all there is to know. You hate me. You hate
my flesh and my scent and it repels you to touch me—
you would like to put those strong fingers around my
neck and choke me until there is no more life left!
You despise me, you despise my children . . . all of
us.

DESTINE. (*Cooly still, continuing her work.*) Madame is
not herself today.

LUCIE. Be still, or I shall have you whipped! You do not
think I am beautiful at all. Above all you do not think
that I am as beautiful as you are with your chiseled
cheekbones and panther eyes! (*She strikes the slave
across the face. The woman sits perfectly still with her
eyes lowered.*) You savage! Don't you know that I am
not some ignorant Frenchwoman—I am a Creole and
I know the blacks! I know you! You dream of mur-
dering me in my bed. I was born knowing. It is the
curse of the Creole that we *all* know . . . I cannot
bear your sullen impertinence day after day! Why,
dear God, have I been so good to you . . . knowing
that you are only waiting—waiting . . . that you are
all only waiting. . . .

DESTINE. I am waiting for nothing, Madame, I am content.

LUCIE. Shut up and finish my massage—don't keep me
lying here half naked! Finish! (*The slave begins to*

smooth the oil on, and we become conscious again of the minuet.) Ahh . . . (*with a sudden change of mood*) . . . How beautiful your hands are . . . (*She catches one of the hands on her shoulder and holds it and looks at it.*) How lovely you are . . . (*Turning to face the slave.*) Your body was molded by the Gods—(*She puts her hands caressingly to the sides of the other woman's body. Her husband re-enters, gets an article he had forgotten, and looks at her with disgust.*)

BAYON. When you are—finished—you will please join our guests downstairs. (*He turns on his heel and exits abruptly.*)

LUCIE. (*Screaming after him.*) My pleasures are my own— monster! monster! . . . (*She stares after him and at last settles back.*) Oh, what does it matter, what does any of it matter . . . That's it . . . soothingly . . . caressingly . . . I must entertain the dull guests from Paris . . . and I am very, very tired. . . .

DESTINE. Yes, Madame. . . .

(*She goes on stolidly massaging the flesh with her face fixed like a mask, as the light converges on mistress and slave, and the minuet and the cries of human pain continue. . . .*)

DIM OUT

Hansberry intended to include these key speeches "somewhere" in *Toussaint*.

TOUSSAINT. We have something in our favor, Biassou. The Europeans will always *underestimate* us. They will believe again and again that they have come to fight *slaves*. (*He smiles at Biassou.*) They will be fighting free men thinking they are fighting slaves, and again and again—that will be their undoing. . . .

*   *   *

TOUSSAINT. (*To Christophe*) You see, Henri, I am a very wise man and we wise men, ha!—we don't make the same mistakes that ordinary men make. Take this, this Napoleon Bonaparte, for instance, this Napoleon Bonaparte and myself; we recognize one another. He is different from the others. He is the first of the Europeans to know who I am; and who the blacks of Santo Domingo are. He is that wise; he is therefore the first enemy of scale I will have matched wits with. This Bonaparte, Henri, he deserves his reputation.

*   *   *

TOUSSAINT. Destine, I am frightened. For the first time. I am frightened. I saw them in the harbor today. He has sent all of France for us and we are doomed. For the first time we have been measured for our worth and he has sent all of France. All the guns of France; all the soldiers, all the generals, surely. We are doomed, Destine. They have come to make war on *men*, not slaves, and we are doomed. . . .

Alice Childress
WEDDING BAND

Alice Childress's composition teachers urged her to write papers about blacks who were " 'accomplishers'—those who win prizes and honors by overcoming cruel odds . . . to inspire the reader/audience to become 'winners.' . . ." She rebelled against this idea, she writes, "and to this day I continue to write about those who come in second, or not at all—the four hundred and ninety-nine and the intricate and magnificent patterns of a loser's life. No matter how many celebrities we may accrue, they cannot substitute for the masses of human beings."[1] The result is a body of works that indeed go against the tide of popularity and at times raise controversy.

Wedding Band is such a work. First produced in 1966 at the University of Michigan, the play focuses on the final days of a ten-year love affair between a black woman and a white man in South Carolina at a time when many states had laws prohibiting interracial marriages and violently discouraged such liaisons. As late as 1973, when the television version of the play was broadcast nationally on ABC with Ruby Dee and J. D. Cannon in the lead roles, eight of the local New York stations refused to carry it.

At first glance, the play may seem atypical of Childress's dramas. The good sense, mother wit, and humanity of the "have-nots" is a strong and persistent theme in her other works. *Trouble in Mind*, for which she won an Obie Award in 1955, features the internal struggles of an interracial cast with the rehearsals of a play that features a lynching. Wiletta, a black actress and central figure in the play, exposes the historical racism of the American theatre, the subtle racism of the white director, and forces the other actors to confront the hypocrisy of their "liberal" attitudes. In *Wine in the Wilderness*, Tommy, a feisty "Sapphire type," gives some bourgeois Negroes an unforgettable lesson in black history, cultural authenticity, and human kindness. In both cases, the black women who are the central characters in these plays represent the ordinary, often uneducated, woman whose knowledge of life gives her a better command of reality and a stronger sense of humanity than those with more training and money. Childress's prototype for these women is Mildred, the black domestic, who is the speaker and subject in "A Conversation from Life," the column that she wrote in the early 1950s for *Freedom*, a progressive newspaper founded by Paul Robeson in Harlem. Mildred, who could have been sister to Langston Hughes's Jesse B. Simple, is a spirited, witty, and plain-speaking woman who takes no nonsense from her white employers. This strong assertion of black consciousness and the implicit criticism of white hypocrisy suggest that racial harmony or interracial cooperation is very difficult, if not impossible, and undesirable. So when *Wedding Band* came along in the 1960s with its implied validation for interracial love, it challenged popular notions of black consciousness and violated white taboos against miscegenation.

A closer reading of *Wedding Band*, however, reveals the breadth of Childress's vision. Interracial love, in the rare instances when it is treated on the American stage or in film, is most often sensationalized with the sense of "forbidden fruit" as the tantalizing element for the audience. Julia and Herman, however, are rather ordinary people who would not warrant a second glance, were it not for their illicit love affair. They meet in sordid, out-of-the-way places like the back-alley community of the play. Whatever glamour may have pertained in the early years of the affair has surely dimmed over the ten-year period of struggle to maintain their relationship. Furthermore, Herman is no noble, exciting man. A common baker, he is a dying man who is tied to his mother's economic apron strings and lacks the courage to marry the woman he loves and move north, where their life may be less complicated. Julia, too, is somewhat different from Childress's other heroines. She is a vulnerable, almost delicate, woman, who has, somewhat passively, structured her life around Herman, moving from one shanty to another.

Yet Childress strikes fire even from these seemingly dull cinders. First, Julia's frustration with her situation bubbles up into a searing condemnation of Herman's vicious mother and an insistent demand that Herman overcome his weakness. Then Herman finds the moral strength to buy their tickets to the North. Finally, in breathtaking, overlapping monologues, Julia and Herman tear at the history and anger that has separated them, and then grope toward a firmer basis for their love. This South Carolina neighborhood is no Catfish Row (as in *Porgy and Bess*) that glorifies the lives of the poor. In the backyard communities where Julia and Herman meet, there is pettiness, racial ugliness, jealousy, and exploitation—from the blacks as well as the whites; but there is also nobility, gentleness, pride, and love.

Childress's play tells more of the truth about black–white relationships than the stage is accustomed to bearing. *Wedding Band* forces the audience to confront fully the historical baggage of racial antipathy. Reconciliation and resolution of interracial strife cannot be achieved without it. Childress also gives the theatre an unusual black heroine whose love makes her defiant. "We are uncommonly and marvelously intricate in thought and action," writes Childress; "our problems are most complex and, too often, silently borne."

In recent years Ms. Childress has become known for her novels (both for children and adults). *A Hero Ain't Nothing But a Sandwich*, which she adapted for film production, was chosen as a Notable Book by the American Library Association and was nominated for both the Newberry Medal and the National Book Award. Many of her plays have been anthologized, and a number of her stories and articles have appeared in *Freedomways* and *Essence*.

NOTES

1. Alice Childress, "A Candle in a Gale Wind," in Mari Evans, Ed., *Black Women Writers (1950–1980): A Critical Evaluation*, Garden City, New York: Anchor Books, 1984, p. 112.

Wedding Band

A Love/Hate Story in
Black and White

by
Alice Childress

Wedding Band was first performed at
the University of Michigan
in December 1966 with a cast headed
by Ruby Dee, Abbey Lincoln, and Moses Gunn.

On November 26, 1972, it was presented by the New York
Shakespeare Public Theater, directed by Joseph Papp and
Alice Childress. The setting was by Ming Cho Lee; costumes by Theoni V. Aldredge; lighting by Martin Aronstein; and produced by Joseph Papp, with Bernard Gersten, the associate producer. The cast was as follows:

Julia Augustine	Ruby Dee
Teeta	Calisse Dinwiddie
Mattie	Juanita Clark
Lula Green	Hilda Haynes
Fanny Johnson	Clarice Taylor
Nelson Green	Albert Hall
Bell Man	Brandon Maggart
Princess	Vicky Geyer
Herman	James Broderick
Annabelle	Polly Holiday
Herman's Mother	Jean David

CHARACTERS
(In Order of Appearance)

Julia Augustine
Teeta
Mattie
Lula Green
Fanny Johnson
Nelson Green
The Bell Man
Princess
Herman
Annabelle
Herman's Mother

ACT ONE

SCENE 1

TIME: *Summer 1918 . . . Saturday morning. A city by the sea . . . South Carolina, U.S.A.*

SCENE: *Three houses in a backyard. The center house is newly painted and cheery looking in contrast to the other two which are weather-beaten and shabby. Center house is gingerbready . . . odds and ends of "picked up" shutters, picket railing, wrought iron railing, newel posts, a Grecian pillar, odd window boxes of flowers . . . everything clashes with a beautiful, subdued splendor; the old and new mingles in defiance of style and period. The playing areas of the houses are raised platforms furnished according to the taste of each tenant. Only one room of each house is visible.* JULIA AUGUSTINE *(tenant of the center house) has recently moved in and there is still unpacking to be done. Paths are worn from the houses to the front yard entry. The landlady's house and an outhouse are offstage. An outdoor hydrant supplies water.*

JULIA *is sleeping on the bed in the center house.* TEETA, *a girl about eight years old, enters the yard from the Stage Right house. She tries to control her weeping as she examines a clump of grass. The muffled weeping disturbs* JULIA's *sleep. She starts up, half rises from her pillow, then falls back into a troubled sleep.* MATTIE, TEETA's *mother, enters carrying a switch and fastening her clothing. She joins the little girl in the search for a lost quarter. The search is subdued, intense.*

MATTIE. You better get out there and get it! Did you find it? Gawd, what've I done to be treated this way! You gon' get a whippin' too.

FANNY. (*Enters from the front entry. She is landlady and
the self-appointed, fifty-year-old representative of her
race.*) Listen, Mattie . . . I want some quiet out here
this mornin'.

MATTIE. Dammit, this gal done lost the only quarter I got
to my name.

(LULA *enters from the direction of the outhouse carrying a
covered slop jar. She is forty-five and motherly.*)

"Teeta," I say, "Go to the store, buy three cent grits,
five cent salt pork, ten cent sugar; and keep your hand
closed 'roun' my money." How I'm gonna sell any
candy if I got no sugar to make it? You little heifer!
(*Goes after* TEETA *who hides behind* LULA.)

LULA. Gawd, help us to find it.

MATTIE. Your daddy is off sailin' the ocean and you got
nothin' to do but lose money! *I'm gon' put you out in
the damn street, that's what!* (TEETA *cries out.* JULIA
sits up in the bed and cries out.)

JULIA. No . . . no . . .

FANNY. You disturbin' the only tenant who's paid in advance.

LULA. Teeta, retrace your steps. Show Lula what you did.

TEETA. I hop-hop-hop . . . (*Hops near a post-railing of
 JULIA's porch.*)

MATTIE. What the hell you do that for?

LULA. There 'tis! That's a quarter . . . down in the hole
. . . Can't reach it . . .

(JULIA *is now fully awake. Putting on her house-dress over
her camisole and petticoat.* MATTIE *takes an axe from the
side of the house to knock the post out of the way.*)

Aw, *move*, move! That's all the money I got. I'll tear
this damn house down and you with it!

FANNY. And I'll blow this police whistle.

(JULIA *steps out on the porch. She is an attractive brown
woman about thirty-five years old.*)

MATTIE. Blow it . . . blow it . . . blow it . . . hot damn—
(*Near tears. She decides to tell* JULIA *off also.*) I'll tear

it down—that's right. If you don't like it—come on down here and whip me.

JULIA. (*Nervous but determined to present a firm stand.*) Oh, my . . . Good mornin' ladies. My name is Julia Augustine. I'm not gonna move.

LULA. My name is Lula. Why you think we wantcha to move?

FANNY. Miss Julia, I'm sorry your first day starts like this. Some people are ice cream and others just cow-dung. I try to be ice cream.

MATTIE. Dammit, I'm ice cream, too. Strawberry. (*Breaks down and cries.*)

FANNY. That's Mattie. She lost her last quarter, gon' break down my house to get it.

JULIA. (*Gets a quarter from her dresser.*) Oh my, dear heart, don't cry. Take this twenty-five cents, Miss Mattie.

MATTIE. No thank you, ma'm.

JULIA. And I have yours under my house for good luck.

FANNY. Show your manners.

TEETA. Thank you. You the kin'est person in the worl'. (LULA *enters her house.* TEETA *starts for home, then turns to see if her mother is coming.*)

MATTIE. (*To* JULIA.) I didn't mean no harm. But my husband October's in the Merchant Marine and I needs my little money. Well, thank you. (*To* TEETA.) Come on, honey bunch. (*She enters her house Stage Right.* TEETA *proudly follows.* LULA *is putting* NELSON'S *breakfast on the table at Stage Left.*)

FANNY. (*Testing strength of post.*) My poor father's turnin' in his grave. He built these rent houses just 'fore he died . . . And he wasn't a carpenter. Shows what the race can do when we wanta. (*Feels the porch railing and tests its strength.*) That loud-mouth Mattie used to work in a white cat-house.

JULIA. A what?

FANNY. Sportin' house, house of . . . A whore house. Know what she used to do?

JULIA. (*Embarrassed.*) Not but so many things *to* do, I guess. (FANNY *wants to follow her in the house but* JULIA *fends her off.*)

FANNY. Used to wash their joy-towels. Washin' joy-towels for one cent apiece. I wouldn't work in that kinda place—would you?

JULIA. Indeed not.

FANNY. Vulgarity.

JULIA. (*Trying to get away.*) I have my sewing to do now, Miss Fanny.

FANNY. I got a lovely piece-a blue serge. Six yards. (*She attempts to get into the house but* JULIA *deftly blocks the door.*)

JULIA. I don't sew for people. (FANNY *wonders why not.*) I do homework for a store . . . hand-finishin' on ladies' shirtwaists.

FANNY. You 'bout my age . . . I'm thirty-five.

JULIA. (*After a pause.*) I thought you were younger.

FANNY. (*Genuinely moved by the compliment.*) Thank you. But I'm not married 'cause nobody's come up to my high standard. Where you get them expensive-lookin', high-class shoes?

JULIA. In a store. I'm busy now, Miss Fanny.

FANNY. Doin' what?

JULIA. First one thing then another. Good-day.

(*Thinks she has dismissed her. Goes in the house.* FANNY *quickly follows into the room . . . picks up a teacup from the table.*)

FANNY. There's a devil in your tea-cup . . . also prosperity. Tell me 'bout yourself, don't be so distant.

JULIA. It's all there in the tea-leaves.

FANNY. Oh, go on! I'll tell you somethin' . . . that sweet-face Lula killed her only child.

JULIA. No, she didn't.

FANNY. In a way-a speakin'. And then Gawd snatched up her triflin' husband. One nothin' piece-a man. Biggest thing he ever done for her was to lay down and die. Poor woman. Yes indeed, then she went and adopted this fella from the colored orphan home. Boy grew too big for a lone woman to keep in the house. He's a big, strappin', over-grown man now. I wouldn't feel safe livin' with a man that's not blood kin, 'doption or no 'doption. It's 'gainst nature. Oughta see the muscles on him.

JULIA. (*Wearily.*) Oh, my . . . I think I hear somebody callin' you.

FANNY. Yesterday the white-folks threw a pail-a dirty water on him. A black man on leave got no right to wear his uniform in public. The crackers don't like it. That's flauntin' yourself.

JULIA. Miss Fanny, I don't talk about people.

FANNY. Me neither. (*Giving her serious advice.*) We high-class, quality people oughta stick together.

JULIA. I really do stay busy.

FANNY. Doin' what? Seein' your beau? You have a beau haven't-cha?

JULIA. (*Realizing she must tell her something in order to get rid of her.*) Miss Johnson . . .

FANNY. Fanny.

JULIA. (*Managing to block her toward the door.*) My mother and father have long gone on to Glory.

FANNY. Gawd rest the dead and bless the orphan.

JULIA. Yes, I do have a beau . . . But I'm not much of a mixer. (*She now has* FANNY *out on the porch.*)

FANNY. Get time, come up front and see my parlor. I got a horsehair settee and a four piece, silver-plated tea service.

JULIA. Think of that.

FANNY. The first and only one to be owned by a colored woman in the United States of America. Salesman told me.

JULIA. Oh, just imagine.

(MATTIE *enters wearing a blue calico dress and striped apron.*)

FANNY. My mother was a genuine, full-blooded, qualified, Seminole Indian.

TEETA. (*Calls to her mother from the doorway.*) Please . . . Mama . . . Mama . . . Buy me a hair ribbon.

MATTIE. All right! I'm gon' buy my daughter a hair ribbon.

FANNY. Her hair is so short you'll have to nail it on. (FANNY *exits to her house.*)

MATTIE. That's all right about that, Fanny. Your father worked in a stinkin' phosphate mill . . . yeah, and didn't have a tooth in his head. Then he went and married some half Portuguese woman. I don't call that bein' in no damn society. I works for my livin'. I makes candy and I takes care of a little white girl. Hold this nickel 'til I get back. Case of emergency I don't like Teeta to be broke.

JULIA. I'll be busy today, lady.

MATTIE. (*As she exits carrying a tray of candy.*) Thank you, darlin'.

TEETA. Hey lady, my daddy helps cook food on a big war boat. He peels potatoes. You got any children?

JULIA. No . . . Grace-a Gawd. (*Starts to go in house.*)

TEETA. Hey, lady! Didja ever hear of Philadelphia? After the war that's where we're goin' to live. Philadelphia!

JULIA. Sounds like heaven.

TEETA. Jesus is the President of Philadelphia.

(TEETA *sweeps in front of* JULIA's *house. Lights come up in* LULA's *house.* NELSON *is eating breakfast. He is a rather rough-looking muscly fellow with a soft voice and a bitter-sweet sense of humor. He is dressed in civilian finery and his striped silk shirt seems out of place in the drab little room.* LULA *makes paper flowers, and the colorful bits of paper are seen everywhere as finished and partially finished flowers and stems, also a finished funeral piece. A picture of Abraham Lincoln hangs on the upstage wall.* LULA *is brushing* NELSON's *uniform jacket.*)

LULA. Last week the Bell Man came to collect the credit payment he says . . . "Auntie, watcha doin' with Abraham Lincoln's pitcher on the wall? He was such a poor president."

NELSON. Tell the cracker to mind his damn business.

LULA. It don't pay to get mad. Remember yesterday.

NELSON. (*Studying her face for answers.*) Mama, you supposed to get mad when somebody throw a pail-a water on you.

LULA. It's their country and their uniform, so just stay out the way.

NELSON. Right. I'm not goin' back to work in that coal-yard when I get out the army.

LULA. They want you back. A bird in the hand, y'know.

NELSON. A bird in the hand ain't always worth two in the bush.

LULA. This is Saturday, tomorrow Sunday . . . thank Gawd for Monday; back to the army. That's one thing . . . Army keeps you off the street.

(*The sound of the* SHRIMP MAN *passing in the street.*)

SHRIMP MAN. (*Offstage.*) Shrimp-dee-raw . . . I got raw
    shrimp.

(NELSON *leaves the house just as* JULIA *steps out on her
porch to hang a rug over the rail.* TEETA *enters* GREEN
house.)

NELSON. Er . . . howdy-do, er . . . beg pardon. My name
    is Nelson. Lula Green's son, if you don't mind. Miss
    . . . er . . . Mrs.?
JULIA. (*After a brief hesitation.*) Miss . . . Julia Augustine.
NELSON. Miss Julia, you the best-lookin' woman I ever
    seen in my life. I declare you look jus' like a violin
    sounds. And I'm not talkin' 'bout pretty. You look
    like you got all the right feelin's, you know?
JULIA. Well, thank you, Mr. Nelson.
NELSON. See, you got me talkin' all outta my head.

(LULA *enters,* TEETA *follows eating a biscuit and carrying
a milk pail . . . she exits toward street.*)

    Let's go for a walk this evenin', get us a lemon phos-
    phate.
JULIA. Oh, I don't care for any, Mr. Nelson.
LULA. That's right. She say stay home.
JULIA. (*To* NELSON.) I'm sorry.
NELSON. Don't send me back to the army feelin' bad 'cause
    you turn me down. Orange-ade tonight on your porch.
    I'll buy the oranges, you be the sugar.
JULIA. No, thank you.
NELSON. Let's make it—say—six o'clock.
JULIA. No, I said no!
LULA. Nelson, go see your friends. (*He waves goodbye to*
    JULIA *and exits through the back entry.*) He's got a
    lady friend, her name is Merrilee Jones. And he was
    just tryin' to be neighborly. That's how me and Nelson
    do. But you go on and stay to yourself. (*Starts toward
    her house.*)
JULIA. Miss Lula! I'm sorry I hurt your feelin's. Miss Lula!
    I have a gentleman friend, that's why I said no.
LULA. I didn't think-a that. When yall plan to cut the cake?
JULIA. Not right now. You see . . . when you offend Gawd
    you hate for it to be known. Gawd might forgive but

people never will. I mean . . . when a man and a
woman are not truly married . . .

LULA. Oh, I see.

JULIA. I live by myself . . . but he visits . . . I declare I
don't know how to say . . .

LULA. Everybody's got some sin, but if it troubles your
heart you're a gentle sinner, just a good soul gone
wrong.

JULIA. That's a kind thought.

LULA. My husband, Gawd rest the dead, used to run 'round
with other women; it made me kind-a careless with
my life. One day, many long years ago, I was sittin'
in a neighbor's house tellin' my troubles; my only
child, my little boy, wandered out on the railroad track
and got killed.

JULIA. That must-a left a fifty pound weight on your soul.

LULA. It did. But if we grow stronger . . . and rise higher
than what's pullin' us down . . .

JULIA. Just like Climbin' Jacob's Ladder . . . (*Sings.*) Every
round goes higher and higher . . .

LULA. Yes, rise higher than the dirt . . . that fifty pound
weight will lift and you'll be free, free without anybody's by-your-leave. Do something to wash out the
sin. That's why I got Nelson from the orphanage.

JULIA. And now you feel free?

LULA. No, not yet. But I believe Gawd wants me to start
a new faith; one that'll make our days clear and easy
to live. That's what I'm workin' on now. Oh, Miss
Julia, I'm glad you my neighbor.

JULIA. Oh, thank you, Miss Lula! Sinners or saints, didn't
Gawd give us a beautiful day this mornin'!

(*The sound of cow-bells clanking and the thin piping of a
tin and paper flute.* TEETA *backs into the yard carefully
carrying the can of milk.* THE BELL MAN *follows humming,
"Over There" on the flute. He is a poor white about thirty
years old but time has dealt him some hard blows. He carries
a large suitcase; the American flag painted on both sides,
cowbells are attached.* THE BELL MAN *rests his case on the
ground. Fans with a very tired-looking handkerchief. He
cuts the fool by dancing and singing a bit of a popular song
as he turns corners around the yard.*)

THE BELL MAN. (*As* LULA *starts to go in the house.*) Stay where you at, Aunty! You used to live on Thompson Street. How's old Thompson Street?

JULIA. (*A slightly painful memory.*) I moved 'bout a year ago, moved to Queen Street.

THE BELL MAN. Move a lot, don'tcha? (*Opens suitcase.*) All right, everybody stay where you at! (*Goes into a fast sales spiel.*) Lace-trim ladies' drawers! Stockin's, ladies' stockin's . . . gottem for the knock-knees and the bow-legs too . . . white, black and navy blue! All right, no fools no fun! The joke's on me! Here we go! (*As he places some merchandise in front of the* WOMEN; *does a regular minstrel walk-around.*) Anything in the world . . . fifty cent a week and one long, sweet year to pay . . . Come on, little sister!

TEETA. (*Doing the walk-around with* THE BELL MAN.)
And a-ring-ting-tang
And-a shimmy-she-bang
While the sun am a-shinin' and the sky am blue . . .
And a-ring-ting-tang
And-a shimmy-she-bang
While the sun am a-shinin' and the sky am blue . . .

LULA. (*Annoyed with* TEETA's *dancing with* THE BELL MAN.) Stop all that shimmy she-bang and get in the house! (*Swats at* TEETA *as she passes.*)

THE BELL MAN. (*Coldly.*) Whatcha owe me, Aunty?

LULA. Three dollars and ten cent. I don't have any money today.

THE BELL MAN. When you gon' pay?

LULA. Monday, or better say Wednesday.

JULIA. (*To divert his attention from* LULA.) How much for sheets?

THE BELL MAN. For you they on'y a dollar. (JULIA *goes to her house to get the money.* THE BELL MAN *moves toward her house as he talks to* LULA.) Goin' to the Service Men's parade Monday?

LULA. Yes, sir. My boy's marchin'. (*She exits.*)

THE BELL MAN. Uh-huh, I'll getcha later. Lord, Lord, Lord, how'dja like to trot 'round in the sun beggin' the poorest people in the world to buy somethin' from you. This is nice. Real nice. (*To* JULIA.) A good friend-a mine was a nigra boy. Me 'n' him was jus' like that. Fine fella, he couldn't read and he couldn't write.

JULIA. (*More to herself than to him.*) When he learns you're gon' lose a friend.

THE BELL MAN. But talkin' serious, what is race and color? Put a paper bag over your head and who'd know the difference. Tryin' to remember me ain'tcha. I seen you one time coming out that bakery shop on Thompson Street, didn' see me.

JULIA. Is that so?

THE BELL MAN. (*Sits on the bed and bounces up and down.*) Awwww, Great Gawd-a-mighty! I haven't been on a high-built bed since I left the back woods.

JULIA. Please don't sit on my bed!

THE BELL MAN. Old country boy, that's me! Strong and healthy country boy . . . (*Not noticing any rejection.*) Sister, Um in need for it like I never been before. Will you 'comodate me? Straighten me, fix me up, will you? Wouldn't take but five minutes. Um quick like a jack rabbit. Wouldn't nobody know but you and me. (*She backs away from him as he pants and wheezes out his admiration.*) Um clean, too. Clean as the . . . Board-a Health. Don't believe in dippin' inta everything. I got no money now, but Ladies always need stockin's.

JULIA. (*Trying to keep her voice down, throws money at his feet.*) Get out of my house! Beneath contempt, that's what you are.

THE BELL MAN. Don't be lookin' down your nose at me . . . actin' like you Mrs. Martha Washington . . . Throwin' one chicken-shit dollar at me and goin' on . . .

JULIA. (*Picking up wooden clothes hanger.*) Get out! Out, before I take a stick to you.

THE BELL MAN. (*Bewildered, gathering his things to leave.*) Hell, what I care who you sleep with! It's your nooky! Give it way how you want to. I don't own no rundown bakery shop but I'm good as those who do. A baker ain' nobody . . .

JULIA. I wish you was dead, you just oughta be dead, stepped on and dead.

THE BELL MAN. Bet that's what my mama said first time she saw me. I was a fourteenth child. Damn women! . . . that's all right . . . Gawd bless you, Gawd be with you and let his light shine on you. I give you good for evil . . . God bless you! (*As he walks down the porch steps.*) She must be goin' crazy. Unfriendly, sick-minded bitch! (TEETA *enters from* LULA's *house.* THE BELL MAN *takes a strainer from his pocket and gives it to* TEETA *with a great show of generosity.*) Here, little honey. You take this sample. You got nice manners.

TEETA. Thank you, you the kin'est person in the world.

(THE BELL MAN *exits to the tune of clanking bells, and* LULA *enters.*)

JULIA. I hate those kind-a people.

LULA. You mustn't hate white folks. Don'tcha believe in Jesus? He's white.

JULIA. I wonder if he believes in me.

LULA. Gawd says we must love everybody.

JULIA. Just lovin' and lovin', no matter what? There are days when I love, days when I hate.

FANNY. Mattie, Mattie, mail!

JULIA. Your love is worthless if nobody wants it.

(FANNY *enters carrying a letter. She rushes over to Mattie's house.*)

FANNY. I had to pay the postman two cent. No stamp.

TEETA. (*Calls to* JULIA.) Letter from Papa! Gimmie my mama's five cents!

FANNY. (*To* TEETA.) You gon' end your days in the Colored Women's Jailhouse.

(PRINCESS, *a little girl, enters skipping and jumping. She hops, runs and leaps across the yard.* PRINCESS *is six years old.* TEETA *takes money from* JULIA's *outstretched hand and gives it to* FANNY.)

TEETA. (*To* MATTIE.) Letter from Papa! Gotta pay two cent!

FANNY. Now I owe you three cent . . . or do you want me to read the letter?

(PRINCESS *gets wilder and wilder, makes Indian war whoops.* TEETA *joins the noise-making. They climb porches and play follow-the-leader.* PRINCESS *finally lands on* JULIA's *porch after peeping and prying into everything along the way.*)

PRINCESS. (*Laughing merrily.*) Hello . . . hello . . . hello.

JULIA. (*Overwhelmed by the confusion.*) Well—Hello.

FANNY. Get away from my new tenant's porch!

PRINCESS. (*Is delighted with* FANNY's *scolding and decides to mock her.*) My new tennis porch!

(MATTIE *opens the letter and removes a ten-dollar bill. Lost in thought she clutches the letter to her bosom.*)

FANNY. (*To* MATTIE.) Ought-a mind w-h-i-t-e children on w-h-i-t-e property!

PRINCESS. (*Now swinging on* JULIA's *gate.*) . . . my new tennis porch!

FANNY. (*Chases* PRINCESS *around the yard.*) You Princess! Stop that!

(JULIA *laughs but she is very near tears.*)

MATTIE. A letter from October.

FANNY. Who's gon' read it for you?

MATTIE. Lula!

PRINCESS. My new tennis porch!

FANNY. Princess! Mattie!

MATTIE. Teeta! In the house with that drat noise!

FANNY. It'll take Lula half-a day. (*Snatches letter.*) I won't charge but ten cent. (*Reads.*) "Dear, Sweet Molasses, My Darlin' Wife . . ."

MATTIE. No, I don't like how you make words sound. You read too rough.

(*Sudden offstage yells and screams from* TEETA *and* PRINCESS *as they struggle for possession of some toy.*)

PRINCESS. (*Offstage*). Give it to me!

TEETA. No! It's mine!

MATTIE. (*Screams.*) Teeta! (*The* CHILDREN *are quiet.*)

FANNY. Dear, Sweet Molasses—how 'bout that?

JULIA (*To* FANNY.) Stop that! Don't read her mail.

FANNY. She can't read it.

JULIA. She doesn't want to. She's gonna go on holdin' it in her hand and never know what's in it . . . just 'cause it's hers!

FANNY. Forgive 'em Father, they know not.

JULIA. Another thing, you told me it's quiet here! You call this quiet? I can't stand it!

FANNY. When you need me come and humbly knock on my *back* door. (*She exits.*)

MATTIE. (*Shouts to* FANNY.) I ain't gonna knock on no damn back door! Miss Julia, can you read? (*Offers the letter to* JULIA.) I'll give you some candy when I make it.

JULIA. (*Takes the letter.*) All right.

(LULA *takes a seat to enjoy a rare social event. She winds stems for the paper flowers as* JULIA *reads.*)

Dear, sweet molasses, my darlin' wife.

MATTIE. Yes, honey. (*To* JULIA.) Thank you.

JULIA. (*Reads.*) Somewhere, at sometime, on the high sea, I take my pen in hand . . . well, anyway, this undelible pencil.

LULA. Hope he didn't put it in his mouth.

JULIA. (*Reads.*) I be missin' you all the time.

MATTIE. And we miss you.

JULIA. (*Reads.*) Sorry we did not have our picture taken.

MATTIE. Didn't have the money.

JULIA. (*Reads.*) Would like to show one to the men and say this is my wife and child . . . They always be showin' pictures.

MATTIE. (*Waves the ten-dollar bill.*) I'm gon' send you one, darlin'.

JULIA. (*Reads.*) I recall how we used to take a long walk on Sunday afternoon . . . (*Thinks about this for a moment.*) . . . then come home and be lovin' each other.

MATTIE. I recall.

JULIA. (*Reads.*) The Government people held up your allotment.

MATTIE. Oh, do Jesus.

JULIA. (*Reads.*) They have many papers to be sign, pink, blue and white also green. Money can't be had 'til all papers match. Mine don't match.

LULA. Takes a-while.

JULIA. (*Reads.*) Here is ten cash dollars I hope will not be stole.

MATTIE. (*Holds up the money.*) I got it.

JULIA. (*Reads.*) Go to Merchant Marine office and push
    things from your end.

MATTIE. Monday. Lula, le's go Monday.

LULA. I gotta see Nelson march in the parade.

JULIA. (*Reads.*) They say people now droppin in the street,
    dying' from this war-time influenza. Don't get sick—
    buy tonic if you do. I love you.

MATTIE. Gotta buy a bottle-a tonic.

JULIA. (*Reads.*) Sometimes people say hurtful things 'bout
    what I am, like color and race . . .

MATTIE. Tell 'em you my brown-skin Carolina daddy, that's
    who the hell you are. Wish I was there.

JULIA. (*Reads.*) I try not to hear 'cause I do want to get
    back to your side. Two things a man can give the
    woman he loves . . . his name and his protection
    . . . The first you have, the last is yet to someday
    come. The war is here, the road is rocky. I am *ever*
    your lovin' husband, October.

MATTIE. So-long, darlin'. I wish I had your education.

JULIA. I only went through eighth grade. Name and pro-
    tection. I know you love him.

MATTIE. Yes'm, I do. If I was to see October in bed with
    another woman, I'd never doubt him 'cause I trust
    him more than I do my own eyesight. Bet yall don't
    believe me.

JULIE. I know how much a woman can love. (*Glances at
    the letter again.*) Two things a man can give . . .

MATTIE. Name and protection. That's right, too. I wouldn't
    live with no man. Man got to marry me. Man that
    won't marry you thinks nothin' of you. Just usin' you.

JULIA. I've never allowed anybody to *use* me!

LULA. (*Trying to move her away Stage Right.*) Mattie, look
    like rain.

MATTIE. A man can't use a woman less she let him.

LULA. (*To* MATTIE.) You never know when to stop.

JULIA. Well, I read your letter. Good day.

MATTIE. Did I hurtcha feelin's? Tell me, what'd I say.

JULIA. I—I've been keepin' company with someone for a
    long time and . . . we're not married.

MATTIE. For how long?

LULA. (*Half-heartedly tries to hush* MATTIE *but she would
    also like to know.*) Ohhh, Mattie.

JULIA. (*Without shame*). Ten years today, ten full, faithful
    years.

MATTIE. He got a wife?

JULIA. (*Very tense and uncomfortable.*) No.

MATTIE. Oh, a man don't wanta get married, work on
   him. Cut off piece-a his shirt-tail and sew it to your
   petticoat. It works. Get Fanny to read the tea leaves
   and tell you how to move. She's a old bitch but what
   she sees in a tea-cup is true.

JULIA. Thank you, Mattie.

LULA. Let's pray on it, Miss Julia. Gawd bring them together, in holy matrimony.

JULIA. Miss Lula, please don't . . . You know it's against
   the law for black and white to get married, so Gawd
   nor the tea leaves can help us. My friend is white and
   that's why I try to stay to myself. (*After a few seconds
   of silence.*)

LULA. Guess we shouldn't-a disturbed you.

JULIA. But I'm so glad you did. Oh, the things I can tell
   you 'bout bein' lonesome and shut-out. Always movin',
   one place to another, lookin' for some peace of mind.
   I moved out in the country . . . Pretty but quiet as
   the graveyard; so lonesome. One year I was in such
   a *lovely* colored neighborhood but they couldn't be
   bothered with me, you know? I've lived near sportin'
   people . . . they were very kindly but I'm not a sporty
   type person. Then I found this place hid way in the
   backyard so quiet, didn't see another soul . . . And
   that's why I thought yall wanted to tear my house
   down this mornin' . . . 'cause you might-a heard 'bout
   me and Herman . . . and some people are . . . well,
   they judge, they can't help judgin' you.

MATTIE. (*Eager to absolve her of wrong doing.*) Oh, darlin', we all do things we don't want sometimes. You
   grit your teeth and take all he's got; if you don't somebody else will.

LULA. No, no, you got no use for 'em so don't take nothin'
   from 'em.

MATTIE. He's takin' somethin' from her.

LULA. Have faith, you won't starve.

MATTIE. Rob him blind. Take it all. Let him froth at the
   mouth. Let him die in the poorhouse—bitter, bitter
   to the gone!

LULA. A white man is somethin' else. Everybody knows
   how that low-down slave master sent for a different

black woman every night . . . for his pleasure. That's why none of us is the same color.

MATTIE. And right now today they're mean, honey. They can't help it; their nose is pinched together so close they can't get enough air. It makes 'em mean. And their mouth is set back in their face so hard and flat . . . no roundness, no sweetness, they can't even carry a tune.

LULA. I couldn't stand one of 'em to touch me intimate no matter what he'd give me.

JULIA. Miss Lula, you don't understand. Mattie, the way you and your husband feel that's the way it is with me 'n' Herman. He loves me . . . We love each other, that's all, we just love each other. (*After a split second of silence.*) And someday, as soon as we're able, we have to leave here and go where it's right . . . Where it's legal for everybody to marry. That's what we both want . . . to be man and wife—like you and October.

LULA. Well I have to cut out six dozen paper roses today. (*Starts for her house.*)

MATTIE. And I gotta make a batch-a candy and look after Princess so I can feed me and Teeta 'til October comes back. Thanks for readin' the letter. (*See enters her house.*)

JULIA. But Mattie, Lula—I wanted to tell you why it's been ten years—and why we haven't—

LULA. Good day, Miss Julia. (*Enters her house.*)

JULIA. Well, that's always the way. What am I doing standin' in a backyard explainin' my life? Stay to yourself, Julia Augustine. Stay to yourself. (*Sweeps her front porch.*)
I got to climb my way to glory
Got to climb it by myself
Ain't nobody here can climb it for me
I got to climb it for myself.

CURTAIN

SCENE 2

TIME: *That evening. Cover closed Scene 1 curtain with song and laughter from* MATTIE, LULA *and* KIDS.

As curtain opens, JULIA *has almost finished the unpacking.
The room now looks quite cozy. Once in a while she
watches the clock and looks out of the window.* TEETA
follows PRINCESS *out of* MATTIE's *house and ties her
sash.* PRINCESS *is holding a jump-rope.*

MATTIE. (*Offstate. Sings.*)
　　My best man left me, it sure do grieve my mind
　　When I'm laughin', I'm laughin' to keep from
　　　cryin' . . .
PRINCESS. (*Twirling the rope to one side.*) Ching, ching,
　　China-man eat dead rat . . .
TEETA. (*As* PRINCESS *jumps rope.*) Knock him in the head
　　with a baseball bat . . .
PRINCESS. You wanta jump?
TEETA. Yes.
PRINCESS. Say "Yes, M'am."
TEETA. No.
PRINCESS. Why?
TEETA. You too little.
PRINCESS. (*Takes bean bag from her pocket.*) You can't
　　play with my bean bag.
TEETA. I 'on care, play it by yourself.
PRINCESS. (*Drops rope, tosses the bag to* TEETA.) Catch.

(TEETA *throws it back.* HERMAN *appears at the back-entry.
He is a strong, forty-year-old working man. His light brown
hair is sprinkled with gray. At the present moment he is
tired.* PRINCESS *notices him because she is facing the back
fence. He looks for a gate or opening but can find none.*)

　　Hello.
TEETA. Mama! Mama!
HERMAN. Hello, children. Where's the gate?

(HERMAN *passes several packages through a hole in the
fence; he thinks of climbing the fence but it is very rickety.
He disappears from view.* MATTIE *dashes out of her house,
notices the packages, runs into* LULA's *house, then back
into the yard.* LULA *enters in a flurry of excitement; gathers
a couple of pieces from the clothesline.* MATTIE *goes to
inspect the packages.*)

LULA. Don't touch 'em, Mattie. Might be dynamite.

MATTIE. Well, I'm gon' get my head blowed off, 'cause I wanta see. (NELSON *steps out wearing his best civilian clothes; neat fitting suit, striped silk shirt and bulldog shoes in ox-blood leather. He claps his hands to frighten* MATTIE.)

MATTIE. Oh, look at him. Where's the party?

NELSON. Everywhere! The ladies have heard Nelson's home. They waitin' for me!

LULA. Don't get in trouble. Don't answer anybody that bothers you.

NELSON. How come it is that when I carry a sack-a coal on my back you don't worry, but when I'm goin' out to enjoy myself you almost go crazy.

LULA. Go on! Deliver the piece to the funeral. (*Hands him a funeral piece.* MATTIE *proceeds to examine the contents of a paper bag.*)

NELSON. Fact is, I was gon' stay home and have me some orange drink, but Massa beat me to it. None-a my business no-how, dammit.

(MATTIE *opens another bag.* HERMAN *enters through the front entry.* FANNY *follows at a respectable distance.*)

MATTIE. Look, rolls and biscuits!

LULA. Why'd he leave the food in the yard?

HERMAN. Because I couldn't find the gate. Good evening. Pleasant weather. Howdy do. Cool this evenin'. (*Silence.*) Err—I see where the Allies suffered another set-back yesterday. Well, that's the war, as they say.

(*The* WOMEN *answer with nods and vague throat clearings.* JULIA *opens her door, he enters.*)

MATTIE. That's the lady's husband. He's a light colored man.

PRINCESS. What is a light colored man?

(CHILDREN *exit with* MATTIE *and* NELSON. FANNY *exits by front entry,* LULA *to her house.*)

JULIA. Why'd you pick a conversation? I tell you 'bout that.

HERMAN. Man gotta say somethin' stumblin' round in a strange back yard.

JULIA. Why didn't you wear your good suit? You know how people like to look you over and sum you up.

HERMAN. Mama and Annabelle made me so damn mad tonight. When I got home Annabelle had this in the window. (*Removes a cardboard sign from the bag . . . printed with red, white and blue crayon . . .* WE ARE AMERICAN CITIZENS . . .)

JULIA. We are American Citizens. Why'd she put it in the window?

HERMAN. Somebody wrote cross the side of our house in purple paint . . . "Krauts . . . Germans live here"! I'd-a broke his arm if I caught him.

JULIA. It's the war. Makes people mean. But didn't she print it pretty.

HERMAN. Comes from Mama boastin' 'bout her German grandfather, now it's no longer fashionable. I snatched that coward sign outta the window . . . Goddamit, I says . . . Annabelle cryin', Mama hollerin' at her. Gawd save us from the ignorance, I say . . . Why should I see a sign in the window when I get home? That Annabelle got flags flyin' in the front yard, the backyard . . . and red, white and blue flowers in the grass . . . confound nonsense . . . Mama is an ignorant woman . . .

JULIA. Don't say that . . .

HERMAN. A poor ignorant woman who is mad because she was born a sharecropper . . . outta her mind 'cause she ain't high class society. We're red-neck crackers, I told her, that's what.

JULIA. Oh, Herman . . . no you didn't . . .

HERMAN. I did.

JULIA. (*Standing.*) But she raised you . . . loaned you all-a-her three thousand dollars to pour into that bakery shop. You know you care about her.

HERMAN. Of course I do. But sometimes she makes me so mad . . . Close the door, lock out the world . . . all of 'em that ain't crazy are coward. (*Looks at sign.*) Poor Annabelle—Miss War-time Volunteer . . .

JULIA. She's what you'd call a very Patriotic Person, wouldn't you say?

HERMAN. Well, guess it is hard for her to have a brother who only makes pies in time of war.

JULIA. A brother who makes pies and loves a nigger!

HERMAN. Sweet Kerist, there it is again!

JULIA. Your mama's own words . . . according to you—
I'll never forget them as long as I live. Annabelle,
you've got a brother who makes pies and loves a nigger.

HERMAN. How can you remember seven or eight years
ago, for Gawd's sake? Sorry I told it.

JULIA. I'm not angry, honeybunch, dear heart. I just remember.

HERMAN. When you say honeybunch, you're angry. Where
do you want your Aunt Cora?

JULIA. On my dresser!

HERMAN. An awful mean woman.

JULIA. Don't get me started on your mama and Annabelle.
(*Pause.*)

HERMAN. Julia, why did you move into a backyard?

JULIA. (*Goes to him.*) Another move, another mess. Sometimes I feel like fightin' . . . and there's nobody to
fight but you . . .

HERMAN. Open the box. Go on. Open it.

JULIA. (*Opens the box and reveals a small but ornate wedding cake with a bride and groom on top and ten pink
candles.*) Ohhh, it's the best one ever. Tassels, bells,
roses . . .

HERMAN. . . . Daffodils and silver sprinkles . . .

JULIA. You're the best baker in the world.

HERMAN. (*As he lights the candles.*) Because you put up
with me . . .

JULIA. Gawd knows that.

HERMAN. . . . because the palms of your hands and the
soles of your feet are pink and brown . . .

JULIA. Jus' listen to him. Well, go on.

HERMAN. Because you're a good woman, a kind, good
woman.

JULIA. Thank you very much, Herman.

HERMAN. Because you care about me.

JULIA. Well, I do.

HERMAN. Happy ten years . . . Happy tenth year.

JULIA. And the same to you.

HERMAN. (*Tries a bit of soft barbershop harmony.*)
I love you as I never loved before (JULIA *joins him.*)
When first I met you on the village green
Come to me e'er my dream of love is o'er

I love you as I loved you
When you were sweet— Take the end up higher—
When you were su-weet six-ateen.
Now blow! (*They blow out the candles and kiss through a cloud of smoke.*)

JULIA. (*Almost forgetting something.*) Got something for you. Because you were my only friend when Aunt Cora sent me on a sleep-in job in the white-folks kitchen. And wasn't that Miss Bessie one mean white woman? (*Gives present to* HERMAN.)

HERMAN. Oh, Julia, just say she was mean.

JULIA. Well yes, but she was white too.

HERMAN. A new peel, thank you. A new pastry bag. Thank you.

JULIA. (*She gives him a sweater.*) I did everything right but one arm came out shorter.

HERMAN. That's how I feel. Since three o'clock this morning, I turned out twenty ginger breads, thirty sponge cakes, lady fingers, Charlotte Russe . . . loaf bread, round bread, twist bread and water rolls . . . and—

JULIA. Tell me about pies. Do pies!

HERMAN. Fifty pies. Open apple, closed apple, apple-crumb, sweet potato and pecan. And I got an order for a large wedding cake. They want it in the shape of a battleship. (HERMAN *gives* JULIA *ring box.* JULIA *takes out a wide, gold wedding band—it is strung on a chain.*) It's a wedding band . . . on a chain . . . To have until such time as . . . It's what you wanted, Julia. A damn fool present.

JULIA. Sorry I lost your graduation ring. If you'd-a gone to college what do you think you'd-a been?

HERMAN. A baker with a degree.

JULIA. (*Reads.*) Herman and Julia 1908 . . . and now it's . . . 1918. Time runs away. A wedding band . . . on a chain. (*She fastens the chain around her neck.*)

HERMAN. A damn fool present. (JULIA *drops the ring inside of her dress.*)

JULIA. It comforts me. It's your promise. You hungry?

HERMAN. No.

JULIA. After the war, the people across the way are goin' to Philadelphia.

HERMAN. I hear it's cold up there. People freeze to death waitin' for a trolley car.

JULIA. (*Leans back beside him, rubs his head.*) In the mid-

dle of the night a big bird flew cryin' over this house—
Then he was gone, the way time goes flyin' . . .

HERMAN. Julia, why did you move in a back yard? Out in
the country the air was so sweet and clean. Makes me
feel shame . . .

JULIA. (*Rubbing his back.*) Crickets singin' that lonesome
evenin' song. Any kind-a people better than none a-
tall.

HERMAN. Mama's beggin' me to hire Greenlee again, to
help in the shop, "Herman, sit back like a half-way
gentleman and just take in money."

JULIA. Greenlee! When white-folks decide . . .

HERMAN. People, Julia, people.

JULIA. When people decide to give other people a job,
they come up with the biggest Uncle Tom they can
find. The *people* I know call him a "white-folks-nig-
ger." It's a terrible expression so don't you ever use
it.

HERMAN. He seems dignified, Julia.

JULIA. Jus' 'cause you're clean and stand straight, that's
not dignity. Even speakin' nice might not be dignity.

HERMAN. What's dignity? Tell me. Do it.

JULIA. Well, it . . . it . . . It's a feeling— It's a spirit that
rises higher than the dirt around it, without any by-
your-leave. It's not proud and it's not 'shamed . . .
Dignity "Is" . . . and it's never Greenlee . . . I don't
know if it's us either, honey.

HERMAN. (*Standing.*) It still bothers my mother that I'm
a baker. "When you gonna rise in the world!" A baker
who rises . . . (*Laughs and coughs a little.*) Now she's
worried 'bout Annabelle marryin' a sailor. After all,
Annabelle is a concert pianist. She's had only one
concert . . . in a church . . . and not many people
there.

JULIA. A sailor might just persevere and become an admiral. Yes, an admiral and a concert pianist.

HERMAN. Ten years. If I'd-a known what I know now, I
wouldn't-a let Mama borrow on the house or give me
the bakery.

JULIA. Give what? Three broken stoves and all-a your
papa's unpaid bills.

HERMAN. I *got* to pay her back. And I can't go to Philadelphia or wherever the hell you're saying to go. I can

hear you thinkin', Philadelphia, Philadelphia, Phil . . .

JULIA. (*Jumping up. Pours wine.*) Oh damnation! The hell with that!

HERMAN. All right, not so much hell and damn. When we first met you were so shy.

JULIA. Sure was, wouldn't say "dog" 'cause it had a tail. In the beginnin' nothin' but lovin' and kissin' . . . and thinkin' 'bout you. Now I worry 'bout gettin' old. I do. Maybe you'll meet somebody younger. People do get old, y'know. (*Sits on bed.*)

HERMAN. There's an old couple 'cross from the bakery . . . "Mabel," he yells, "Where's my keys!" . . . Mabel has a big behind on her. She wears his carpet slippers. "All right, Robbie, m'boy," she says . . . Robbie walks kinda one-sided. But they're havin' a pretty good time. We'll grow old together both of us havin' the same name. (*Takes her in his arms.*) Julia, I love you . . . you know it . . . I love you . . . (*After a pause.*) Did you have my watch fixed?

JULIA. (*Sleepily.*) Uh-huh, it's in my purse. (*Getting up.*) Last night when the bird flew over the house—I dreamed 'bout the devil's face in the fire . . . He said "I'm comin' to drag you to hell."

HERMAN. (*Sitting up.*) There's no other hell, honey. Celestine was sayin' the other day—

JULIA. How do you know what Celestine says?

HERMAN. Annabelle invited her to dinner.

JULIA. They still trying to throw that white widow-woman at you? Oh, Herman, I'm gettin' mean . . . jumpin' at noises . . . and bad dreams.

HERMAN. (*Brandishing bottle.*) Dammit, this is the big bird that flew over the house!

JULIA. I don't go anywhere, I don't know anybody, I gotta do somethin'. Sometimes I need to have company— to say . . . "Howdy-do, pleasant evenin,' do drop in." Sometimes I need other people. How you ever gonna pay back three thousand dollars? Your side hurt?

HERMAN. Schumann, came in to see me this mornin'. Says he'll buy me out, ten cents on the dollar, and give me a job bakin' for him . . . it's an offer—can get seventeen hundred cash.

JULIA. Don't do it, Herman. That sure wouldn't be dignity.

HERMAN. He makes an American flag outta gingerbread.

But they sell. Bad taste sells. Julia, where do you want
to go? New York, Philadelphia, where? Let's try their
dignity. Say where you want to go.

JULIA. Well, darlin', if folks are freezin' in Philadelphia,
we'll go to New York.

HERMAN. Right! You go and size up the place. Meanwhile
I'll stay here and do like everybody else, make war
money . . . battleship cakes, cannon-ball cookies
. . . chocolate bullets . . . they'll sell. Pay my debts.
Less than a year, I'll be up there with money in my
pockets.

JULIA. Northerners talk funny— "We're from New Yorrrk."

HERMAN. I'll getcha train ticket next week.

JULIA. No train. I wanta stand on the deck of a Clyde Line
boat, wavin' to the people on the shore. The whistle
blowin', flags flyin' . . .wavin' my handkerchief . . .
So long, so long, look here—South Carolina . . . so
long, hometown . . . goin' away by myself— (*Tearfully
blows her nose.*)

HERMAN. You gonna like it. Stay with your cousin and
don't talk to strangers. (JULIA *gets dress from her hope
chest.*)

JULIA. Then, when we do get married we can have a quiet
reception. My cut glass punch bowl . . . little sand-
wiches, a few friends . . . Herman? Hope my weddin'
dress isn't too small. It's been waitin' a good while.
(*Holds dress in front of her.*) I'll use all of my hope
chest things. Quilts, Irish linens, the silver cups . . .
Oh, Honey, how are you gonna manage with me gone?

HERMAN. Buy warm underwear and a woolen coat with a
fur collar . . . to turn against the northern wind. What
size socks do I wear?

JULIA. Eleven, eleven and a half if they run small.

HERMAN. . . . what's the store? Write it down.

JULIA. Coleridge. And go to King Street for your shirts.

HERMAN. Coleridge. Write it down.

JULIA. Keep payin' Ruckheiser, the tailor, so he can start
your new suit.

HERMAN. Ruckheiser. Write it down.

JULIA. Now that I know I'm goin' we can take our time.

HERMAN. No, rush, hurry, make haste, do it. Look at you
. . . like your old self.

JULIA. No, no, not yet—I'll go soon as we get around to
it. (*Kisses him.*)

HERMAN. That's right. Take your time . . .
JULIA. Oh, Herman.

(MATTIE *enters through the back gate with* TEETA. *She pats and arranges* TEETA's *hair.* FANNY *enters from the front entry and goes to* JULIA's *window.*)

MATTIE. You goin' to Lula's service?
FANNY. A new faith. Rather be a Catholic than somethin' you gotta make up. Girl, my new tenant and her—
MATTIE. (*Giving* FANNY *the high-sign to watch what she says in front of* TEETA.) . . . and her husband.
FANNY. I gotcha. She and her husband was in there havin' a orgy. Singin', laughin', screamin', crying' . . . I'd like to be a fly on that wall.

(LULA *enters the yard wearing a shawl over her head and a red band on her arm. She carries two chairs and places them beside two kegs.*)

LULA. Service time!

(MATTIE, TEETA *and* FANNY *enter the yard and sit down.* LULA *places a small table and a cross.*)

FANNY. (*Goes to* JULIA's *door and knocks.*) Let's spread the word to those who need it. (*Shouts.*) Miss Julia, don't stop if you in the middle-a somethin'. We who love Gawd are gatherin' for prayer. Got any time for Jesus?
ALL. (*Sing.*) When the roll is called up yonder.
JULIA. Thank you, Miss Fanny. (FANNY *flounces back to her seat in triumph.* JULIA *sits on the bed near* HERMAN.)
HERMAN. Dammit, she's makin' fun of you.
JULIA. (*Smooths her dress and hair.*) Nobody's invited me anywhere in a long time . . . so I'm goin'.
HERMAN. (*Standing.*) I'm gonna buy you a Clyde Line ticket for New York City on Monday . . . this Monday.
JULIA. Monday?
HERMAN. As Gawd is my judge. That's dignity. Monday.
JULIA. (*Joyfully kissing him.*) Yes, Herman! (*She enters yard.*)
LULA. My form-a service opens with praise. Let us speak to Gawd.

MATTIE. Well, I thang Gawd that—that I'm livin' and I
   pray my husband comes home safe.
TEETA. I love Jesus and Jesus loves me.
ALL. Amen.
FANNY. I thang Gawd that I'm able to rise spite-a-those
   who try to hold me down, spite-a those who are two-
   faceted, spite-a those in my own race who jealous
   'cause I'm doin' so much better than the rest of 'em.
   He preparest a table for me in the presence of my
   enemies. Double-deal Fanny Johnson all you want but
   me 'n' Gawd's gonna come out on top.

(ALL *look to* JULIA.)

JULIA. I'm sorry for past sin—but from Monday on through
   eternity—I'm gonna live in dignity accordin' to the
   laws of God and man. Oh, Glory!
LULA. Glory Halleluhjah!

(NELSON *enters a bit unsteadily . . . struts and preens while
singing.*)

NELSON. Come here black woman . . . whoooo . . .
   eee . . . on daddy's knee . . . etc.
LULA. (*Trying to interrupt him.*) We're testifyin . . .
NELSON. (*Throwing hat on porch.*) Right! Testify! Tonight
   I asked the prettiest girl in Carolina to be my wife;
   and Merrilee Jones told me . . . I'm sorry but you got
   nothin to offer. She's right! I got nothin to offer but
   a hard way to go. Merrilee Jones . . . workin for the
   rich white folks and better off washin their dirty draw-
   ers than marryin me.
LULA. Respect the church! (*Slaps him.*)
NELSON. (*Sings.*) Come here, black woman (etc.) . . .
JULIA. Oh, Nelson, respect your mother!
NELSON. Respect your damn self, Julia Augustine! (*Con-
   tinues singing.*)
LULA. How we gonna find a new faith?
NELSON. (*Softly.*) By tellin' the truth, Mamma. Merrilee
   ain't no liar. I got nothin' to offer, just like October.
MATTIE. You keep my husband's name outta your mouth.
NELSON. (*Sings.*) Come here, black woman . . .
FANNY AND CONGREGATION. (*Sing.*)

Ain't gon let nobody turn me round, turn me round,
   turn me round
Ain't gon let nobody turn me round . . .

HERMAN. (*Staggers out to porch.*) Julia, I'm going now,
   I'm sorry . . . I don't feel well . . . I don't know . . .
   (*Slides forward and falls.*)

JULIA. Mr. Nelson . . . won'tcha please help me . . .

FANNY. Get him out of my yard.

(NELSON *and* JULIA *help* HERMAN *in to bed. Others freeze
in yard.*)

END OF ACT ONE

ACT TWO

SCENE 1

TIME: *Sunday morning.*

SCENE: *The same as Act One except the yard and houses are neater. The clothes line is down. Off in the distance someone is humming a snatch of a hymn. Church bells are ringing.* HERMAN *is in a heavy, restless sleep. The bed covers indicate he has spent a troubled night. On the table Downstage Right are medicine bottles, cups and spoons.* JULIA *is standing beside the bed, swinging a steam kettle; she stops and puts it on a trivet on top of her hope chest.*

FANNY. (*Seeing her.*) Keep usin' the steam-kettle. (HERMAN groans lightly.)

MATTIE. (*Picks up scissors.*) Put the scissors under the bed, open. It'll cut the pain.

FANNY. (*Takes scissors from* MATTIE.) That's for child-birth.

JULIA. He's had too much paregoric. Sleepin' his life away. I want a doctor.

FANNY. Over my dead body. It's against the damn law for him to be layin' up in a black woman's bed.

MATTIE. A doctor will call the police.

FANNY. They'll say I run a bad house.

JULIA. I'll tell 'em the truth.

MATTIE. We don't tell things to police.

FANNY. When Lula gets back with his sister, his damn sister will take charge.

MATTIE. That's his family.

FANNY. Family is family.

JULIA. I'll hire a hack and take him to a doctor.

FANNY. He might die on you. That's police. That's the work-house.

104

JULIA. I'll say I found him on the street!

FANNY. Walk into the jaws of the law—they'll chew you up.

JULIA. Suppose his sister won't come?

FANNY. She'll be here. (FANNY *picks up a tea-cup and turns it upside down on the saucer and twirls it.*) I see a ship, a ship sailin' on the water.

MATTIE. Water clear or muddy?

FANNY. Crystal clear.

MATTIE. (*Realizing she's late.*) Oh, I gotta get Princess so her folks can open their ice cream parlor. Take care-a Teeta.

FANNY. I see you on your way to Miami, Florida, goin' on a trip.

JULIA. (*Sitting on window seat.*) I know you want me to move. I will, Fanny.

FANNY. Julia, it's hard to live under these mean white-folks . . . but I've done it. I'm the first and only colored they let buy land 'round here.

JULIA. They all like you, Fanny. Only one of 'em cares for me . . . just one.

FANNY. Yes, I'm thought highly of. When I pass by they can say . . . "There she go, Fanny Johnson, representin' her race in-a approved manner" . . . 'cause they don't have to worry 'bout my next move. I can't afford to mess that up on account-a you or any-a the rest-a these hard-luck, better-off-dead, triflin' niggers.

JULIA. (*Crossing up Right.*) I'll move. But I'm gonna call a doctor.

FANNY. Do it, we'll have a yellow quarantine sign on the front door . . . "INFLUENZA." Doctor'll fill out papers for the law . . . address . . . race . . .

JULIA. I . . . I guess I'll wait until his sister gets here.

FANNY. No, you call a doctor, Nelson won't march in the parade tomorrow or go back to the army, Mattie'll be outta work, Lula can't deliver flowers . . .

JULIA. I'm sorry, so very sorry. I'm the one breakin' laws, doin' wrong.

FANNY. I'm not judgin' you. High or low, nobody's against this if it's kept quiet. But when you pickin' white . . . pick a wealthy white. It makes things easier.

JULIA. No, Herman's not rich and I've never tried to beat him out of anything.

FANNY. (*Crossing to* JULIA.) Well, he just ought-a be and

you just should-a. A colored woman needs money more than anybody else in this world.

JULIA. You sell yours.

FANNY. All I don't sell I'm going to keep.

HERMAN. Julia?

FANNY. (*Very genial.*) Well, well, sir, how you feelin', Mr. Herman? This is Aunt Fanny . . . Miss Julia's land-lady. You lookin' better, Mr. Herman. We've been praying for you. (FANNY *exits to* TEETA's *house.*)

JULIA. Miss Lula—went to get your sister.

HERMAN. Why?

JULIA. Fanny made me. We couldn't wake you up.

(He tries to sit up in bed to prepare for leaving. She tries to help him. He falls back on the pillow.)

HERMAN. Get my wallet . . . see how much money is there. What's that smell?

(She takes the wallet from his coat pocket. She completes counting the money.)

JULIA. Eucalyptus oil, to help you breathe; I smell it, you smell it and Annabelle will have to smell it too! Seventeen dollars.

HERMAN. A boat ticket to New York is fourteen dollars—Ohhhh, Kerist! Pain . . . pain . . . Count to ten . . . one, two . . .

(JULIA gives paregoric water to him. He drinks. She puts down glass and picks up damp cloth from bowl on tray and wipes his brow.)

My mother is made out of too many . . . little things . . . the price of carrots, how much fat is on the meat . . . little things make people small. Make ignorance—y'know?

JULIA. Don't fret about your people, I promise I won't be surprised at anything and I won't have unpleasant words no matter what.

HERMAN. (*The pain eases. He is exhausted.*) Ahhh, there . . . All men are born which is—utterly untrue.

(NELSON *steps out of the house. He is brushing his army jacket.* HERMAN *moans slightly.* JULIA *gets her dress-making scissors and opens them, places the scissors under the bed.*)

FANNY. (*To* NELSON *as she nods towards* JULIA's *house.*) I like men of African descent, myself.

NELSON. Pitiful people. They pitiful.

FANNY. They common. Only reason I'm sleepin' in a double bed by myself is 'cause I got to bear the standard for the race. I oughta run her outta here for the sake-a the race too.

NELSON. It's your property. Run us all off it, Fanny.

FANNY. Plenty-a these hungry, jobless, bad-luck colored men, just-a itchin' to move in on my gravy-train. I don't want 'em.

NELSON. (*With good nature.*) Right, Fanny! We empty-handed, got nothin' to offer.

FANNY. But I'm damn tired-a ramblin' round in five rooms by myself. House full-a new furniture, the icebox for-ever full-a goodies. I'm a fine cook and I know how to pleasure a man . . . he wouldn't have to step outside for a thing . . . food, fun and finance . . . all under one roof. Nelson, how'd you like to be my business advisor? Fix you up a little office in my front parlor. You wouldn't have to work for white folks . . . and Lula wouldn't have to pay rent. The war won't last forever . . . then what you gonna do? They got nothin' for you but haulin' wood and cleanin' toilets. Let's you and me pitch in together.

NELSON. I know you just teasin', but I wouldn't do a-tall. Somebody like me ain't good enough for you no-way, but you a fine-lookin' woman, though. After the war I might hit out for Chicago or Detroit . . . a rollin' stone gathers no moss.

FANNY. Roll on. Just tryin' to help the race.

(LULA *enters by front entry, followed by* ANNABELLE, *a woman in her thirties. She assumes a slightly mincing air of fashionable delicacy. She might be graceful if she were not ashamed of her size. She is nervous and fearful in this strange atmosphere. The others fall silent as they see her.* ANNABELLE *wonders if* PRINCESS *is her brother's child? Or could it be* TEETA, *or both?*)

ANNABELLE. Hello there . . . er . . . children.

PRINCESS. (*Can't resist mocking her.*) Hello there, er . . .
    children. (*Giggles.*)

ANNABELLE. (*To* TEETA.) Is she your sister? (ANNABELLE
    looks at NELSON *and draws her shawl a little closer.*)

TEETA. You have to ask my mama.

NELSON. (*Annoyed with* ANNABELLE'S *discomfort.*) Mom,
    where's the flat-iron? (*Turns and enters his house.*
    LULA *follows.* MATTIE *and* CHILDREN *exit.*)

FANNY. I'm the landlady. Mr. Herman had every care and
    kindness 'cept a doctor. Miss Juliaaaa! That's the fam-
    ily's concern. (FANNY *opens door, then exits.*)

ANNABELLE. Sister's here. It's Annabelle.

JULIA. (*Shows her to a chair.*) One minute he's with you,
    the next he's gone. Paregoric makes you sleep.

ANNABELLE. (*Dabs at her eyes with a handkerchief.*) Cryin'
    doesn't make sense a-tall. I'm a volunteer worker at
    the Naval hospital . . . I've nursed my mother . . .
    (*Chokes with tears.*)

JULIA. (*Pours a glass of water for her.*) Well, this is more
    than sickness. It's not knowin' 'bout other things.

ANNABELLE. We've known for years. He is away all the
    time and when old Uncle Greenlee . . . He's a colored
    gentleman who works in our neighborhood . . . and
    he said . . . he told . . . er, well, people do talk.
    (ANNABELLE *spills water,* JULIA *attempts to wipe the
    water from her dress.*) Don't do that . . . It's all right.

HERMAN. Julia?

ANNABELLE. Sister's here. Mama and Uncle Greenlee have
    a hack down the street. Gets a little darker we'll take
    you home, call a physician . . .

JULIA. Can't you do it right away?

ANNABELLE. 'Course you could put him out. Please let us
    wait 'til dark.

JULIA. Get a doctor.

ANNABELLE. Our plans are made, thank you.

HERMAN. Annabelle, this is Julia.

ANNABELLE. Hush.

HERMAN. This is my sister.

ANNABELLE. Now be still.

JULIA. I'll call Greenlee to help him dress.

ANNABELLE. No. Dress first. The colored folk in *our* neigh-
    borhood have great respect for us.

HERMAN. Because I give away cinnamon buns, for Kerist sake.

ANNABELLE. (*To* JULIA.) I promised my mother I'd try and talk to you. Now—you look like one-a the nice coloreds . . .

HERMAN. Remember you are a concert pianist, that is a very dignified calling.

ANNABELLE. Put these on. We'll turn our backs.

JULIA. He can't.

ANNABELLE. (*Holds the covers in a way to keep his mid-section under wraps.*) Hold up. (*They manage to get the trousers up as high as his waist but they are twisted and crooked.*) Up we go! There . . . (*They are breathless from the effort of lifting him.*) Now fasten your clothing.

(JULIA *fastens his clothes.*)

I declare, even a dead man oughta have enough pride to fasten himself.

JULIA. You're a volunteer at the Naval hospital?

HERMAN. (*As another pain hits him.*) Julia, my little brown girl . . . Keep singing . . .

JULIA.

We are climbin' Jacob's ladder, We are climbin' Jacob's ladder,

We are climbin' Jacob's ladder, Soldiers of the Cross . . .

HERMAN. The palms of your hands . . .

JULIA. (*Singing.*) Every round goes higher and higher . . .

HERMAN. . . . the soles of your feet are pink and brown.

ANNABELLE. Dammit, hush. Hush this noise. Sick or not sick, hush! It's ugliness. (*To* JULIA.) Let me take care of him, please, leave us alone.

JULIA. I'll get Greenlee.

ANNABELLE. No! You hear me? No.

JULIA. I'll be outside.

ANNABELLE. (*Sitting on bed.*) If she hadn't-a gone I'd-a screamed. (JULIA *stands on the porch.* ANNABELLE *cries.*) I thought so highly of you . . . and here you are in somethin' that's been festerin' for years. (*In disbelief.*) One of the finest women in the world is pinin' her heart out for you, a woman who's pure gold. Everything Celestine does for Mama she's really doin' for you . . . to get next to you . . . But even a Saint wants some reward.

HERMAN. I don't want Saint Celestine.

ANNABELLE. (*Standing.*) Get up! (*Tries to move* HERMAN.) At the Naval hospital I've seen influenza cases tied down to keep 'em from walkin'. What're we doin' here? How do you meet a black woman?

HERMAN. She came in the bakery on a rainy Saturday evening.

ANNABELLE. (*Giving in to curiosity.*) Yes?

MATTIE. (*Offstage. Scolding* TEETA *and* PRINCESS.) Sit down and drink that lemonade. Don't bother me!

HERMAN. "I smell rye bread baking." Those were the first words . . . Every day . . . Each time the bell sounds over the shop door I'm hopin' it's the brown girl . . . pretty shirt-waist and navy blue skirt. One day I took her hand . . . "little lady, don't be afraid of me" . . . She wasn't. . . . I've never been lonesome since.

ANNABELLE. (*Holding out his shirt.*) Here, your arm goes in the sleeve. (*They're managing to get the shirt on.*)

HERMAN. (*Beginning to ramble.*) Julia? Your body is velvet . . . the sweet blackberry kisses . . . you are the night-time, the warm, Carolina night-time in my arms . . .

ANNABELLE. (*Bitterly.*) Most excitement I've ever had was takin' piano lessons.

JULIA. (*Calls from porch.*) Ready?

ANNABELLE. No. Rushin' us out. A little longer, please. (*Takes a comb from her purse and nervously combs his hair.*) You nor Mama put yourselves out to understand my Walter when I had him home to dinner. Yes, he's a common sailor . . . I wish he was an officer. I never liked a sailor's uniform, tight pants and middy blouses . . . but they are in the service of their country . . . He's taller than I am. You didn't even stay home that one Sunday like you promised. Must-a been chasin' after some-a them blackberry kisses you love so well. Mama made a jackass outta Walter. You know how she can do. He left lookin' like a whipped dog. Small wonder he won't live down here. I'm crazy-wild 'bout Walter even if he is a sailor. Marry Celestine. She'll take care-a Mama and I can go right on up to the Brooklyn Navy Yard. I been prayin' so hard . . . You marry Celestine and set me free. And Gawd knows I don't want another concert.

HERMAN. (*Sighs.*) Pain, keep singing.

ANNABELLE. Dum-dum-blue Danube. (*He falls back on the pillow. She bathes his head with a damp cloth.*)

JULIA. (*As* NELSON *enters the yard.*) Tell your mother I'm grateful for her kindness. I appreciate . . .

NELSON. Don't have so much to say to me. (*Quietly, in a straightforward manner.*) They set us on fire 'bout their women. String us up, pour on kerosene and light a match. Wouldn't I make a bright flame in my new uniform?

JULIA. Don't be thinkin' that way.

NELSON. I'm thinkin' 'bout black boys hangin' from trees in Little Mountain, Elloree, Winnsboro.

JULIA. Herman never killed anybody. I couldn't care 'bout that kind-a man.

NELSON. (*Stepping, turning to her.*) How can you account for carin' 'bout him a-tall?

JULIA. In that place where I worked, he was the only one who cared . . . who really cared. So gentle, such a gentle man . . . "Yes, Ma'am," . . . "No, Ma'am," "Thank you, Ma'am . . ." In the best years of my youth, my Aunt Cora sent me out to work on a sleep-in job. His shop was near that place where I worked. . . . Most folks don't have to *account* for why they love.

NELSON. You ain't most folks. You're down on the bottom with us, under his foot. A black man got nothin' to offer you . . .

JULIA. I wasn't lookin' for anybody to do for me.

NELSON. . . . and *he's* got nothin' to offer. The one layin' on your mattress, not even if he's kind as you say. He got nothin' for you . . . but some meat and gravy or a new petticoat . . . or maybe he can give you meriny-lookin' little bastard chirrun for us to take in and raise up. We're the ones who feed and raise 'em when it's like this . . . They don't want 'em. They only too glad to let us have their kin-folk. As it is, we supportin' half-a the slave-master's offspring right now.

JULIA. Go fight those who fight you. He never threw a pail-a water on you. Why didn't you fight them that did? Takin' it out on me 'n Herman 'cause you scared of 'em . . .

NELSON. Scared? What scared! If I gotta die I'm carryin' one 'long with me.

JULIA. No you not. You gon' keep on fightin' me.

NELSON. . . . Scared-a what? I look down on 'em, I spit on 'em.

JULIA. No, you don't. They throw dirty water on your uniform . . . and you spit on me!

NELSON. Scared, what scared!

JULIA. You fightin' me, me, me, not them . . . never them.

NELSON. Yeah, I was scared and I'm tougher, stronger, a better man than any of 'em . . . but they won't letcha fight one or four or ten. I was scared to fight a hundred or a thousand. A losin' fight.

JULIA. I'd-a been afraid too.

NELSON. And you scared right now, you let the woman run you out your house.

JULIA. I didn't want to make trouble.

NELSON. But that's what a fight is . . . trouble.

LULA. (*In her doorway.*) Your mouth will kill you. (*To* JULIA.) Don't tell Mr. Herman anything he said . . . or I'll hurt you.

JULIA. Oh, Miss Lula.

LULA. Anyway, he didn't say nothin'.

(HERMAN'S MOTHER *enters the yard. She is a "poor white" about fifty-seven years old. She has risen above her poor farm background and tries to assume the airs of "quality." Her clothes are well-kept-shabby. She wears white shoes, a shirtwaist and skirt, drop earrings, a cameo brooch, a faded blue straw hat with a limp bit of veiling. She carries a heavy-black, oil-cloth bag. All in the yard give a step backward as she enters. She assumes an air of calm well-being. Almost as though visiting friends, but anxiety shows around the edges and underneath.* JULIA *approaches and* HERMAN'S MOTHER *abruptly turns to* MATTIE.)

HERMAN'S MOTHER. How do. (MATTIE, TEETA *and* PRINCESS *look at* HERMAN'S MOTHER. HERMAN'S MOTHER *is also curious about them.*)

MATTIE. (*In answer to a penetrating stare from the old woman.*) She's mine. I take care-a her. (*Speaking her defiance by ordering the children.*) Stay inside 'fore y'all catch the flu!

HERMAN'S MOTHER. (*To* LULA.) You were very kind to bring word . . . er . . .

LULA. Lula, Ma'am.

HERMAN'S MOTHER. The woman who nursed my second
  cousin's children . . . she had a name like that . . .
  Lu*lu* we called her.
LULA. My son, Nelson.
HERMAN'S MOTHER. Can see that.

(MATTIE *and the children exit.* FANNY *hurries in from the
front entry. Is most eager to establish herself on the good
side of* HERMAN'S MOTHER. *With a slight bow. She is carrying the silver tea service.*)

FANNY. Beg pardon, if I may be so bold, I'm Fanny, the
  owner of all this property.
HERMAN'S MOTHER. (*Definitely approving of* FANNY.) I'm
  . . . er . . . Miss Annabelle's mother.
FANNY. My humble pleasure . . . er . . . Miss er . . .
HERMAN'S MOTHER. (*After a brief, thoughtful pause.*) Miss
  Thelma.

(*They move aside but* FANNY *makes sure others hear.*)

FANNY. Miss Thelma, this is not Squeeze-gut Alley. We're
  just poor, humble, colored people . . . and everybody
  knows how to keep their mouth shut.
HERMAN'S MOTHER. I thank you.
FANNY. She wanted to get a doctor. I put my foot down.
HERMAN'S MOTHER. You did right. (*Shaking her head,
  confiding her troubles.*) Ohhhh, you don't know.
FANNY. (*With deep understanding.*) Ohhhh, yes, I do. She
  moved in on me yesterday.
HERMAN'S MOTHER. Friend Fanny, help me to get through
  this.
FANNY. I will. Now this is Julia, she's the one . . .

(HERMAN'S MOTHER *starts toward the house without looking at* JULIA. FANNY *decides to let the matter drop.*)

HERMAN'S MOTHER. (*To* LULA.) Tell Uncle Greenlee not
  to worry. He's holdin' the horse and buggy.
NELSON. (*Bars* LULA'S *way.*) Mama. I'll do it.

(LULA *exits into her house.* FANNY *leads her to the chair
near* HERMAN'S *bed.*)

ANNABELLE. Mama, if we don't call a doctor Herman's
  gonna die.
HERMAN'S MOTHER. Everybody's gon' die. Just a matter
  of when, where and how. A pretty silver service.
FANNY. English china. Belgian linen. Have a cup-a tea?
HERMAN'S MOTHER. (*As a studied pronouncement.*) My
  son comes to deliver baked goods and the influenza
  strikes him down. Sickness, it's the war.
FANNY. (*Admiring her cleverness.*) Yes, Ma'am, I'm a wit-
  ness. I saw him with the packages.
JULIA. Now please call the doctor.
ANNABELLE. Yes, please, Mama. No way for him to move
  'less we pick him up bodily.
HERMAN'S MOTHER. Then we'll pick him up.
HERMAN. About Walter . . . your Walter . . . I'm
  sorry . . .

(JULIA *tries to give* HERMAN *some water.*)

HERMAN'S MOTHER. Annabelle, help your brother.

(ANNABELLE *gingerly takes glass from* JULIA.)

  Get that boy to help us. I'll give him a dollar. Now
  gather his things.
ANNABELLE. What things?
HERMAN'S MOTHER. His possessions, anything he owns,
  whatever is his. What you been doin' in here all this
  time?

(FANNY *notices* JULIA *is about to speak, so she hurries her
through the motions of going through dresser drawers and
throwing articles into a pillow case.*)

FANNY. Come on, sugar, make haste.
JULIA. Don't go through my belongings.

(*Tears through the drawers, flinging things around as she
tries to find his articles.* FANNY *neatly piles them together.*)

FANNY. (*Taking inventory.*) Three shirts . . . one is kinda
  soiled.
HERMAN'S MOTHER. That's all right, I'll burn 'em.
FANNY. Some new undershirts.

HERMAN'S MOTHER. I'll burn them too.

JULIA. (*To* FANNY.) Put 'em down. I bought 'em and they're not for burnin'.

HERMAN'S MOTHER. (*Struggling to hold her anger in check.*) Fanny, go get that boy. I'll give him fifty cents.

FANNY. You said a dollar.

HERMAN'S MOTHER. All right, dollar it is.

(FANNY *exits toward the front entry. In tense, hushed, excited tones, they argue back and forth.*)

Now where's the bill-fold . . . there's papers . . . identity . . . (*Looks in* HERMAN'S *coat pockets.*)

ANNABELLE. Don't make such-a to-do.

HERMAN'S MOTHER. You got any money of your own? Yes, I wanta know where's his money.

JULIA. I'm gettin' it.

HERMAN'S MOTHER. In her pocketbook. This is why the bakery can't make it.

HERMAN. I gave her the Gawd-damned money!

JULIA. And I know what Herman wants me to do . . .

HERMAN'S MOTHER. (*With a wry smile.*) I'm sure you know what he wants.

JULIA. I'm not gonna match words with you. Furthermore, I'm too much of a lady.

HERMAN'S MOTHER. A lady oughta learn how to keep her dress down.

ANNABELLE. Mama, you makin' a spectacle outta yourself.

HERMAN'S MOTHER. You a big simpleton. Men have nasty natures, they can't help it. A man would go with a snake if he only knew how. They cleaned out your wallet.

HERMAN. (*Shivering with a chill.*) I gave her the damn money.

(JULIA *takes it from her purse.*)

HERMAN'S MOTHER. Where's your pocket-watch or did you give that too? Annabelle, get another lock put on that bakery door.

HERMAN. I gave her the money to go—to go to New York.

(JULIA *drops the money in* HERMAN'S MOTHER'S *lap. She is silent for a moment.*)

HERMAN'S MOTHER. All right. Take it and go. It's never too late to undo a mistake. I'll add more to it. (*She puts the money on the dresser.*)

JULIA. I'm not goin' anywhere.

HERMAN'S MOTHER. Look here, girl, you leave him 'lone.

ANNABELLE. Oh, Mama, all he has to do is stay away.

HERMAN'S MOTHER. But he can't do it. Been years and he can't do it.

JULIA. I got him hoo-dooed, I sprinkle red pepper on his shirt-tail.

HERMAN'S MOTHER. I believe you.

HERMAN. I have a black woman . . . and I'm gon' marry her. I'm gon' marry her . . . got that? Pride needs a paper, for . . . for the sake of herself . . . that's dignity—tell me, what is dignity— Higher than the dirt it is . . . dignity is . . .

ANNABELLE. Let's take him to the doctor, Mama.

HERMAN'S MOTHER. When it's dark.

JULIA. Please!

HERMAN'S MOTHER. Nightfall.

(JULIA *steps out on the porch but hears every word said in the room.*)

I had such high hopes for him. (*As if* HERMAN *is dead.*) All my high hopes. When he wasn't but five years old I had to whip him so he'd study his John C. Calhoun speech. Oh, Calhoun knew 'bout niggers. He said, "*MEN* are not born . . . equal, or any other kinda way . . . MEN are *made*" . . . Yes, indeed, for recitin' that John C. Calhoun speech . . . Herman won first mention and a twenty dollar gold piece . . . at the Knights of The Gold Carnation picnic.

ANNABELLE. Papa changed his mind about the Klan. I'm glad.

HERMAN'S MOTHER. Yes, he was always changin' his mind about somethin'. But I was proud-a my men-folk that day. He spoke that speech . . . The officers shook my hand. They honored me . . . "That boy a-yours gonna be somebody." A poor baker-son layin' up with a nigger woman, a over-grown daughter in heat over a common sailor. I must be payin' for somethin' I did. Yesiree, do a wrong, God'll whip you.

ANNABELLE. I wish it was dark.

HERMAN'S MOTHER. I put up with a man breathin' stale whiskey in my face every night . . . pullin' and pawin' at me . . . always tired, inside and out . . . (*Deepest confidence she has ever shared.*) Gave birth to seven . . . five-a them babies couldn't draw breath.

ANNABELLE. (*Suddenly wanting to know more about her.*) Did you love Papa, Mama? Did you ever love him? . . .

HERMAN'S MOTHER. Don't ask me 'bout love . . . I don't know nothin' about it. Never mind love. This is my harvest . . .

HERMAN. Go home. I'm better. (HERMAN'S MOTHER'S *strategy is to enlighten* HERMAN *and also wear him down. Out on the porch,* JULIA *can hear what is being said in the house.*)

HERMAN'S MOTHER. There's something wrong 'bout mismatched things, be they shoes, socks, or people.

HERMAN. Go away, don't look at us.

HERMAN'S MOTHER. People don't like it. They're not gonna letcha do it in peace.

HERMAN. We'll go North.

HERMAN'S MOTHER. Not a thing will change except her last name.

HERMAN. She's not like others . . . she's not like that . . .

HERMAN'S MOTHER. All right, sell out to Schumann. I want my cash-money . . . You got no feelin' for me, I got none for you . . .

HERMAN. I feel . . . I feel what I feel . . . I don't know what I feel . . .

HERMAN'S MOTHER. Don't need to feel. Live by the law. Follow the law—law, law of the land. Obey the law!

ANNABELLE. We're not obeyin' the law. He should be quarantined right here. The city's tryin' to stop an epidemic.

HERMAN'S MOTHER. Let the city drop dead and you 'long with it. *Rather* be dead than disgraced. Your papa gimme the house and little money . . . I want my money back. (*She tries to drag* HERMAN *up in the bed.*) I ain't payin' for this. (*Shoves* ANNABELLE *aside.*) Let Schumann take over. A man who knows what he's doin'. Go with her . . . Take the last step against your own! Kill us all. Jesus, Gawd, save us or take us—

HERMAN. (*Screams.*) No! No! No! No!

HERMAN'S MOTHER. Thank Gawd, the truth is the light.

Oh, Blessed Savior . . . (HERMAN *screams out, starting low and ever going higher. She tries to cover his mouth.* ANNABELLE *pulls her hand away.*) Thank you, Gawd, let the fire go out . . . this awful fire.

(LULA *and* NELSON *enter the yard.*)

ANNABELLE. You chokin' him. Mama . . .
JULIA. (*From the porch.*) It's dark! It's dark. Now it's very dark.
HERMAN. One ticket on the Clyde Line . . . Julia . . . where are you? Keep singing . . . count . . . one, two . . . three. Over there, over there . . . send the word, send the word . . .
HERMAN'S MOTHER. Soon be home, son.

(HERMAN *breaks away from the men, staggers to* MATTIE'S *porch and holds on.* MATTIE *smothers a scream and gets the children out of the way.* FANNY *enters.*)

HERMAN. Shut the door . . . don't go out . . . the enemy . . . the enemy . . . (*Recites the Calhoun speech.*) Men are not born, infants are born! They grow to all the freedom of which the condition in which they were born permits. It is a great and dangerous error to suppose that all people are equally entitled to liberty.
JULIA. Go home— Please be still.
HERMAN. It is a reward to be earned, a reward reserved for the intelligent, the patriotic, the virtuous and deserving; and not a boon to be bestowed on a people too ignorant, degraded and vicious . . .
JULIA. You be still now, shut up.
HERMAN. . . . to be capable either of appreciating or of enjoying it.
JULIA. (*Covers her ears.*) Take him . . .
HERMAN. A black woman . . . not like the others . . .
JULIA. . . . outta my sight . . .
HERMAN. Julia, the ship is sinking . . .

(HERMAN'S MOTHER *and* NELSON *help* HERMAN *up and out.*)

ANNABELLE. (*To* JULIA *on the porch.*) I'm sorry . . . so sorry it had to be this way. I can't leave with you thinkin' I uphold Herman, and blame you.

HERMAN'S MOTHER. (*Returning.*) You the biggest fool.

ANNABELLE. I say a man is responsible for his own behavior.

HERMAN'S MOTHER. And you, you oughta be locked up . . . workhouse . . . jail! Who you think you are!?

JULIA. I'm your damn daughter-in-law, you old bitch! The Battleship Bitch! The bitch who destroys with her filthy mouth. They could win the war with your killin' mouth. The son-killer, man-killer bitch . . . She's killin' him 'cause he loved me more than anybody in the world.

(FANNY *returns.*)

HERMAN'S MOTHER. Better off . . . He's better off dead in his coffin than live with the likes-a you . . . black thing! (*She is almost backing into* JULIA's *house.*)

JULIA. The black thing who bought a hot water bottle to put on your sick, white self when rheumatism threw you flat on your back . . . who bought flannel gowns to warm your pale, mean body. He never ran up and down King Street shoppin' for you . . . I bought what he took home to you . . .

HERMAN'S MOTHER. Lies . . . tear outcha lyin' tongue.

JULIA. . . . the lace curtains in your parlor . . . the shirt-waist you wearin'—I made them.

FANNY. Go *on* . . . I got her. (*Holds* JULIA.)

HERMAN'S MOTHER. Leave 'er go! The undertaker will have-ta unlock my hands off her black throat!

FANNY. Go on, Miss Thelma.

JULIA. Miss Thelma my ass! Her first name is Frieda. The Germans are here . . . in purple paint!

HERMAN'S MOTHER. Black, sassy nigger!

JULIA. Kraut, knuckle-eater, red-neck . . .

HERMAN'S MOTHER. Nigger whore . . . he used you for a garbage pail . . .

JULIA. White trash! Sharecropper! Let him die . . . let 'em all die . . . Kill him with your murderin' mouth—sharecropper bitch!

HERMAN'S MOTHER. Dirty black nigger . . .

JULIA. . . . If I wasn't black with all-a Carolina 'gainst me I'd be mistress of your house! (*To* ANNABELLE.) Annabelle, you'd be married livin' in Brooklyn, New York . . . (*To* HERMAN'S MOTHER.) . . . and I'd be waitin' on Frieda . . . cookin' your meals . . . waterin' that damn red-white and blue garden!

HERMAN'S MOTHER. Dirty black bitch.

JULIA. Daughter of a bitch!

ANNABELLE. Leave my mother alone! She's old . . . and sick.

JULIA. But never sick enough to die . . . dirty ever-lasting woman.

HERMAN'S MOTHER. (*Clinging to* ANNABELLE, *she moves toward the front entry.*) I'm as high over you as Mount Everest over the sea. White reigns supreme . . . I'm white, you can't change that. (*They exit.* FANNY *goes with them.*)

JULIA. Out! Out! Out! And take the last ten years-a my life with you and . . . when he gets better . . . keep him home. Killers, murderers . . . Kinsmen! Klansmen! Keep him home. (*To* MATTIE.) Name and protection . . . he can't gimme either one. (*To* LULA.) I'm gon' get down on my knees and scrub where they walked . . . what they touched . . . (*To* MATTIE.) . . . with brown soap . . . hot lye-water . . . scaldin' hot . . . (*She dashes into the house and collects an armful of bedding* . . .) Clean! . . . Clean the whiteness outta my house . . . clean everything . . . even the memory . . . no more love . . . Free . . . free to hate-cha for the rest-a my life. (*Back to the porch with her arms full.*) When I die I'm gonna keep on hatin' . . . I don't want any whiteness in my house. Stay out . . . out . . . (*Dumps the things in the yard.*) . . . out . . . out . . . out . . . and leave me to my black self!

BLACKOUT

SCENE 2

TIME: *Early afternoon the following day.*
PLACE: *The same.*

In JULIA's *room, some of the hope chest things are spilled out on the floor, bedspread, linens, silver cups. The half-emptied wine decanter is in a prominent spot. A*

*table is set up in the yard. We hear the distant sound
of a marching band. The excitement of a special day
is in the air.* NELSON's *army jacket hangs on his porch.*
LULA *brings a pitcher of punch to table.* MATTIE *enters
with* TEETA *and* PRINCESS; *she is annoyed and upset
in contrast to* LULA's *singing and gala mood. She scolds
the children, smacks* TEETA's *behind.*

MATTIE. They was teasin' the Chinaman down the street
　'cause his hair is braided. (*To* CHILDREN.) If he ketches
　you, he'll cook you with onions and gravy.

LULA. (*Inspecting* NELSON's *jacket.*) Sure will.

TEETA. Can we go play?

MATTIE. A mad dog might bite-cha.

PRINCESS. Can we go play?

MATTIE. No, you might step on a nail and get lockjaw.

TEETA. Can we go play?

MATTIE. Oh, go on and play! I wish a gypsy would steal
　both of 'em! (JULIA *enters her room.*)

LULA. What's the matter, Mattie?

MATTIE. Them damn fool people at the Merchant Marine
　don't wanta give me my 'lotment money.

JULIA. (*Steps out on her porch with deliberate, defiant en-
　ergy. She is wearing her wedding dress . . . carrying a
　wine glass. She is over-demonstrating a show of care-
　free abandon and joy.*) I'm so happy! I never been
　this happy in all my life! I'm happy to be alive, alive
　and livin for my people.

LULA. You better stop drinkin so much wine. (LULA *enters
　her house.*)

JULIA. But if you got no feelin's they can't be hurt!

MATTIE. Hey, Julia, the people at the Merchant Marine
　say I'm not married to October.

JULIA. Getcha license, honey, show your papers. Some of
　us, thang Gawd, got papers!

MATTIE. I don't have none.

JULIA. Why? Was October married before?

MATTIE. No, but I was. A good for nothin' named Delroy
　. . . I hate to call his name. Was years 'fore I met
　October. Delroy used to beat the hell outta me . . .
　tried to stomp me, grind me into the ground . . . callin'
　me such dirty names . . . Got so 'til I was shame to
　look at myself in a mirror. I was glad when he run
　off.

JULIA. Where'd he go?

MATTIE. I don't know. Man at the office kept sayin' . . .
    "You're not married to October" . . . and wavin' me
    'way like that.

JULIA. Mattie, this state won't allow divorce.

MATTIE. Well, I never got one.

JULIA. You shoulda so you could marry October. You have
    to be married to get his benefits.

MATTIE. We was married. On Edisto Island. I had a white
    dress and flowers . . . everything but papers. We
    couldn't get papers. Elder Burns knew we was doin'
    best we could.

JULIA. You can't marry without papers.

MATTIE. What if your husband run off? And you got no
    money? Readin' from the Bible makes people mar-
    ried, not no piece-a paper. We're together eleven years,
    that oughta-a be legal.

JULIA. (*Puts down glass.*) No, it doesn't go that way.

MATTIE. October's out on the icy water, in the war-time,
    worryin' 'bout me 'n Teeta. I say he's my husband.
    Gotta pay Fanny, buy food. Julia, what must I do?

JULIA. I don't know.

MATTIE. What's the use-a so much-a education if you don't
    know what to do?

JULIA. You may's well just lived with October. Your mar-
    riage meant nothin'.

MATTIE. (*Standing angry.*) It meant somethin' to me if not
    to anybody else. It means I'm ice cream, too, straw-
    berry. (MATTIE heads for her house.)

JULIA. Get mad with me if it'll make you feel better.

MATTIE. Julia, could you lend me two dollars?

JULIA. Yes, that's somethin' I can do besides drink this
    wine. (JULIA *goes into her room, to get the two dollars.
    Enter* FANNY, TEETA *and* PRINCESS.)

FANNY. Colored men don't know how to do nothin' right.
    I paid that big black boy cross the street . . . thirty
    cents to paint my sign . . . (*Sign reads . . .* GOODBYE
    COLORED BOYS . . . *on one side; the other reads
    . . .* FOR GOD AND CONTRY.) But he can't spell.
    I'm gon' call him a dumb darky and get my money
    back. Come on, children! (CHILDREN *follow laugh-
    ing.*)

LULA. Why call him names!?

FANNY. 'Cause it makes him mad, that's why.

(FANNY *exits with* TEETA *and* PRINCESS. JULIA *goes into her room.* THE BELL MAN *enters carrying a display board filled with badges and flags . . . buttons, red and blue ribbons attached to the buttons . . . slogans . . .* THE WAR TO END ALL WARS. *He also carries a string of overseas caps [paper] and wears one. Blows a war tune on his tin flute.* LULA *exits.*)

BELL MAN. "War to end all wars . . ." Flags and badges! Getcha emblems! Hup-two-three . . . Flags and badges . . . hup-two-three! Hey, Aunty! Come back here! Where you at? (*Starts to follow* LULA *into her house.* NELSON *steps out on the porch and blocks his way.*)

NELSON. My mother is in her house. You ain't to come walkin' in. You knock.

BELL MAN. Don't letcha uniform go to your head, Boy, or you'll end your days swingin' from a tree.

LULA. (*Squeezing past* NELSON *dressed in skirt and open shirt-waist.*) Please, Mister, he ain't got good sense.

MATTIE. He crazy, Mister.

NELSON. Fact is, you stay out of here. Don't ever come back here no more.

BELL MAN. (*Backing up in surprise.*) He got no respect. One them crazies. I ain't never harmed a bareassed soul but, hot damn, I can get madder and badder than you. Let your uniform go to your head.

LULA. Yessir, he goin' back in the army today.

BELL MAN. Might not get there way he's actin'.

MATTIE. (*As* LULA *takes two one dollar bills from her bosom.*) He sorry right now, Mister, his head ain' right.

BELL MAN. (*Speaks to* LULA *but keeps an eye on* NELSON.) Why me? I try to give you a laugh but they say, "Play with a puppy and he'll lick your mouth." Familiarity makes for contempt.

LULA. (*Taking flags and badges.*) Yessir. Here's somethin' on my account . . . and I'm buyin' flags and badges for the children. Everybody know you a good man and do right.

BELL MAN. (*To* LULA.) You pay up by Monday. (*To* NELSON.) Boy, you done cut off your Mama's credit.

LULA. I don't blame you, Mister. (BELL MAN *exits.*)

NELSON. Mama, your new faith don't seem to do much for you.

LULA. (*Turning to him.*) Nelson, go on off to the war 'fore
somebody kills you. I ain't goin' to let nobody spoil
my day. (LULA *puts flags and badges on punchbowl
table.* JULIA *comes out of her room, with the two dollars for* MATTIE—*hands it to her. Sound of Jenkins
Colored Orphan Band is heard* [*Record: Ramblin' by
Bunk Johnson*].)

JULIA. Listen, Lula . . . Listen, Mattie . . . it's Jenkin's
Colored Orphan Band . . . Play! Play, you Orphan
boys! Rise up higher than the dirt around you! Play!
That's struttin' music, Lula!

LULA. It sure is! (LULA *struts, arms akimbo, head held
high.* JULIA *joins her; they haughtily strut toward each
other, then retreat with mock arrogance . . . exchange
cold, hostile looks . . . A Carolina folk dance passed
on from some dimly-remembered African beginning.
Dance ends strutting.*)

JULIA. (*Concedes defeat in the dance.*) All right, Lula, strut
me down! Strut me right on down! (*They end dance
with breathless laughter and cross to* LULA's *porch.*)

LULA. Julia! Fasten me! Pin my hair.

JULIA. I'm not goin' to that silly parade, with the colored
soldiers marchin' at the end of it.

(LULA *sits on the stool.* JULIA *combs and arranges her hair.*)

LULA. Come on, we'll march behind the white folks whether
they want us or not. Mister Herman's people got a
nice house . . . lemon trees in the yard, lace curtains
at the window.

JULIA. And red, white and blue flowers all around.

LULA. That Uncle Greenlee seems to be well-fixed.

JULIA. He works for the livery stable . . . cleans up behind
horses . . . in a uniform.

LULA. That's nice.

JULIA. Weeds their gardens . . . clips white people's pet
dogs . . .

LULA. Ain't that lovely? I wish Nelson was safe and nicely
settled.

JULIA. Uncle Greenlee is a well-fed, tale-carryin' son-of-
a-bitch . . . and that's the only kind-a love they want
from us.

LULA. It's wrong to hate.

JULIA. They say it's wrong to love too.

LULA. We got to show 'em we're good, got to be three times as good, just to make it.

JULIA. Why? When they mistreat us who cares? We mistreat each other, who cares? Why we gotta be so good jus' for them?

LULA. Dern you, Julia Augustine, you hard-headed thing, 'cause they'll kill us if we not.

JULIA. They doin' it anyway. Last night I dreamed of the dead slaves—all the murdered black and bloody men silently gathered at the foot-a my bed. Oh, that awful silence. I wish the dead could scream and fight back. What they do to us . . . and all they want is to be loved in return. Nelson's not Greenlee. Nelson is a fighter.

LULA. (*Standing.*) I know. But I'm tryin' to keep him from findin' it out.

(NELSON, *unseen by* LULA, *listens.*)

JULIA. Your hair looks pretty.

LULA. Thank you. A few years back I got down on my knees in the courthouse to keep him off-a the chain gang. I crawled and cried, "Please white folks, yall's everything. I'se nothin, yall's everything." The court laughed—I meant for 'em to laugh . . . then they let Nelson go.

JULIA. (*Pitying her.*) Oh, Miss Lula, a lady's not supposed to crawl and cry.

LULA. I was savin' his life. Is my skirt fastened? Today might be the last time I ever see Nelson. (NELSON *goes back in house.*) Tell him how life's gon' be better when he gets back. Make up what *should* be true. A man can't fight a war on nothin' . . . would you send a man off—to die on nothin'?

JULIA. That's sin, Miss Lula, leavin' on a lie.

LULA. That's all right—some truth has no nourishment in it. Let him feel good.

JULIA. I'll do my best.

(MATTIE *enters carrying a colorful, expensive parasol. It is far beyond the price range of her outfit.*)

MATTIE. October bought it for my birthday 'cause he know I always wanted a fine-quality parasol.

(FANNY *enters through the back entry,* CHILDREN *with her. The mistake on the sign has been corrected by pasting* OU *over the error.*)

FANNY. (*Admiring* MATTIE'S *appearance.*) Just shows how the race can look when we wanta. I called Rusty Bennet a dumb darky and he wouldn't even get mad. Wouldn't gimme my money back either. A black Jew. (NELSON *enters wearing his Private's uniform with quartermaster insignia. He salutes them.*)

NELSON. Ladies. Was nice seein' you these few days. If I couldn't help, 'least I didn't do you no harm, so nothin' from nothin' leaves nothin'.

FANNY. (*Holds up her punch cup;* LULA *gives* JULIA *high sign.*) Get one-a them Germans for me.

JULIA. (*Stands on her porch.*) Soon, Nelson, in a little while . . . we'll have whatsoever our hearts desire. You're comin' back in glory . . . with honors and shining medals . . . And those medals and that uniform is gonna open doors for you . . . and for October . . . for all, all of the servicemen. Nelson, on account-a you we're gonna be able to go in the park. They're gonna take down the no-colored signs . . . and Rusty Bennet's gonna print new ones . . . Everybody welcome . . . Everybody welcome . . .

MATTIE. (*To* TEETA.) Hear that? We gon' go in the park.

FANNY. Some of us ain't ready for that.

PRINCESS. Me too?

MATTIE. You can go now . . . and me too if I got you by the hand.

PRINCESS. (*Feeling left out.*) Ohhhhh.

JULIA. We'll go to the band concerts, the museums . . . we'll go in the library and draw out books.

MATTIE. And we'll draw books.

FANNY. Who'll read 'em to you?

MATTIE. My Teeta!

JULIA. Your life'll be safe, you and October'll be heroes.

FANNY. (*Very moved.*) Colored heroes.

JULIA. And at last we'll come into our own.

(ALL *cheer and applaud.* JULIA *steps down from porch.*)

NELSON. Julia, can you look me dead in the eye and say you believe all-a that?

JULIA. If you just gotta believe somethin', it may's well be that. (*Applause.*)

NELSON. (*Steps up on* JULIA's *porch to make his speech.*) Friends, relatives and all other well-wishers. All-a my fine ladies and little ladies—all you good-lookin', tantalizin', pretty-eyed ladies—yeah, with your *kind* ways and your *mean* ways. I find myself a thorn among six lovely roses. Sweet little Teeta . . . the merry little Princess. Mattie, she so pretty 'til October better hurry up and come on back here. Fanny—uh—tryin' to help the race . . . a race woman. And Julia—my good friend. Mama—the only mama I got, I wanta thank you for savin' my life from time to time. What's hard ain't the goin', it's the comin' back. From the bottom-a my heart, I'd truly like to see y'all, each and every one-a you . . . able to go in the park and all that. I really would. So, with a full heart and a loaded mind, I bid you, as the French say, Adieu.

LULA. (*Bowing graciously, she takes* NELSON's *arm and they exit.*) Our humble thanks . . . my humble pleasure . . . gratitude . . . thank you . . .

(CHILDREN *wave their flags.*)

FANNY. (*To the* CHILDREN.) Let's mind our manners in front-a the downtown white people. Remember we're bein' judged.

PRINCESS. Me too?

MATTIE. (*Opening umbrella.*) Yes, you too.

FANNY. (*Leads the way and counts time.*) Step, step, one, two, step, step.

(MATTIE, FANNY *and the* CHILDREN *exit.* HERMAN *enters yard by far gate, takes two long steamer tickets from his pocket.* JULIA *senses him, turns. He is carelessly dressed and sweating.*)

HERMAN. I bought our tickets. Boat tickets to New York.

JULIA. (*Looks at tickets.*) Colored tickets. You can't use yours. (*She lets tickets flutter to the ground.*)

HERMAN. They'll change and give one white ticket. You'll ride one deck, I'll ride the other . . .

JULIA. John C. Calhoun really said a mouthful—men are not born—men are made. Ten years ago—that's when

you should-a bought tickets. You chained me to your
mother for ten years.

HERMAN. (*Kneeling, picking up tickets.*) Could I walk out
on 'em? . . . Ker-ist sake. I'm that kinda man like my
father was . . . a debt-payer, a plain, workin' man—

JULIA. He was a member in good standin' of The Gold
Carnation. What kinda robes and hoods did those
plain men wear? For downin' me and mine. You won
twenty dollars in gold.

HERMAN. I love you . . . I love work, to come home in
the evenin' . . . to enjoy the breeze for Gawd's sake
. . . But no, I never wanted to go to New York. The
hell with Goddamn bread factories . . . I'm a stony-
broke, half-dead, half-way gentleman . . . But I'm
what I wanta be. A baker.

JULIA. You waited 'til you was half-dead to buy those
tickets. I don't want to go either . . . Get off the boat,
the same faces'll be there at the dock. It's that shop.
It's that shop!

HERMAN. It's mine. I did want to keep it.

JULIA. Right . . . people pick what they want most.

HERMAN. (*Indicating the tickets.*) I did . . . you threw it
in my face.

JULIA. Get out. Get your things and get out of my life.
(*The remarks become counterpoint. Each rides through
the other's speech.* HERMAN *goes in house.*) Must be
fine to *own* somethin'—even if it's four walls and a
sack-a flour.

HERMAN. (JULIA *has followed him into the house.*) My
father labored in the street . . . liftin' and layin' down
cobblestone . . . liftin' and layin' down stone 'til there
was enough money to open a shop . . .

JULIA. My people . . . relatives, friends and strangers
. . . they worked and slaved free for nothin' for some-
a the biggest name families down here . . . Elliots,
Lawrences, Ravenals . . .

(HERMAN *is wearily gathering his belongings.*)

HERMAN. Great honor, working for the biggest name families. That's who you slaved for. Not me. The big
names.

JULIA. . . . the rich and the poor . . . we know you . . .

all of you . . . Who you are . . . where you came from . . . where you goin' . . .

HERMAN. What's my privilege . . . Good mornin', good afternoon . . . pies are ten cents today . . . and you can get 'em from Schumann for eight . . .

JULIA. "She's different" . . . I'm no different . . .

HERMAN. I'm white . . . did it give me favors and friends?

JULIA. . . . . "Not like the others" . . . We raised up all-a these Carolina children . . . white and the black . . . I'm just like all the rest of the colored women . . . like Lula, Mattie . . . Yes, like Fanny!

HERMAN. Go here, go there . . . Philadelphia . . . New York . . . Schumann wants me to go North too . . .

JULIA. We nursed you, fed you, buried your dead . . . grinned in your face—cried 'bout your troubles—and laughed 'bout ours.

HERMAN. Schumann . . . Alien robber . . . waitin' to buy me out . . . My father . . .

JULIA. Pickin' up cobblestones . . . left him plenty-a time to wear bed-sheets in that Gold Carnation Society . . .

HERMAN. He never hurt anybody.

JULIA. He hurts me. There's no room for you to love him and me too . . . (*Sits.*) it can't be done—

HERMAN. The ignorance . . . he didn't know . . . the ignorance . . . mama . . . they don't know.

JULIA. But *you* know. My father was somebody. He helped put up Roper Hospital and Webster Rice Mills after the earthquake wiped the face-a this Gawd-forsaken city clean . . . . a fine brick-mason he was . . . paid him one-third-a what they paid the white ones . . .

HERMAN. We were poor . . . No big name, no quality.

JULIA. Poor! My Gramma was a slave wash-woman bustin' suds for free! Can't get poorer than that.

HERMAN. (*Trying to shut out the sound of her voice.*) Not for me, she didn't!

JULIA. We the ones built the pretty white mansions . . . for free . . . the fishin' boats . . . for free . . . made your clothes, raised your food . . . for free . . . and I loved you—for free.

HERMAN. A Gawd-damn lie . . . nobody did for me . . . you know it . . . you know how hard I worked—

JULIA. If it's anybody's home down here it's mine . . . everything in the city is mine—why should I go anywhere . . . ground I'm standin' on—it's mine.

HERMAN. (*Sitting on foot of the bed.*) It's the ignorance . . . Lemme be, lemme rest . . . Ker-ist sake . . . It's the ignorance . . .

JULIA. After ten years you still won't look. All-a my people that's been killed . . . It's your people that killed 'em . . . all that's been in bondage—your people put 'em there—all that didn't go to school—your people kept 'em out.

HERMAN. But I didn't do it. Did I do it?

JULIA. They killed 'em . . . all the dead slaves . . . buried under a blanket-a this Carolina earth, even the cotton crop is nourished with hearts' blood . . . roots-a that cotton tangled and wrapped 'round my bones.

HERMAN. And you blamin' me for it . . .

JULIA. Yes! . . . For the one thing we never talk about . . . white folks killin' me and mine. You wouldn't let me speak.

HERMAN. I never stopped you . . .

JULIA. Every time I open my mouth 'bout what they do . . . you say . . . "Ker-ist, there it is again . . ." Whenever somebody was lynched . . . you 'n me would eat a very silent supper. It hurt me not to talk . . . what you don't say you swallow down . . . (*Pours wine.*)

HERMAN. I was just glad to close the door 'gainst what's out there. You did all the givin' . . . I failed you in every way.

JULIA. You nursed me when I was sick . . . paid my debts . . .

HERMAN. I didn't give my name.

JULIA. You couldn't . . . was the law . . .

HERMAN. I shoulda walked 'til we came to where it'd be all right.

JULIA. You never put any other woman before me.

HERMAN. Only Mama, Annabelle, the customers, the law . . . the ignorance . . . I honored them while you waited and waited—

JULIA. You clothed me . . . you fed me . . . you were kind, loving . . .

HERMAN. I never did a damn thing for you. After ten years look at it—I never did a damn thing for you.

JULIA. Don't low-rate yourself . . . leave me something.

HERMAN. When my mother and sister came . . . I was ashamed. What am I doin' bein' ashamed of us?

JULIA. When you first came in this yard I almost died-a shame . . . so many times you was nothin' to me but white . . . times we were angry . . . damn white man . . . times I was tired . . . damn white man . . . but most times you were my husband, my friend, my lover . . .

HERMAN. Whatever is wrong, Julia . . . not the law . . . *me*; what I didn't do, with all-a my faults, spite-a all that . . . You gotta believe I love you . . . 'cause I do . . . That's the one thing I know . . . I love you . . . I love you.

JULIA. Ain't too many people in this world that get to be loved . . . really loved.

HERMAN. We gon' take that boat trip . . . You'll see, you'll never be sorry.

JULIA. To hell with sorry. Let's be glad!

HERMAN. Sweetheart, leave the ignorance outside . . . (*Stretches out across the bed.*) Don't let that doctor in here . . . to stand over me shakin' his head.

JULIA. (*Pours water in a silver cup.*) Bet you never drank from a silver cup. Carolina water is sweet water . . . Wherever you go you gotta come back for a drink-a this water. Sweet water, like the breeze that blows 'cross the battery.

HERMAN. (*Happily weary.*) I'm gettin' old, that ain' no joke.

JULIA. No, you're not. Herman, my real weddin' cake . . . I wanta big one . . .

HERMAN. Gonna bake it in a wash-tub . . .

JULIA. We'll put pieces of it in little boxes for folks to take home and dream on.

HERMAN. . . . But let's don't give none to your landlady . . . Gon' get old and funny-lookin' like Robbie m'boy and . . .

JULIA. And Mable . . .

HERMAN. (*Breathing heavier.*) Robbie says "Mable, where's my keys" . . . Mable— Robbie— Mable—

(*Lights change, shadows grow longer.* MATTIE *enters the yard.*)

MATTIE. Hey, Julia! (*Sound of carriage wheels in front of the main house.* MATTIE *enters* JULIA's *house. As she sees* HERMAN.) They 'round there, they come to get

him, Julia. (JULIA *takes the wedding band and chain
from around her neck, gives it to* MATTIE *with tickets.*)
JULIA. Surprise. Present.
MATTIE. For me?
JULIA. Northern tickets . . . and a wedding band.
MATTIE. I can't take that for nothing.
JULIA. You and Teeta are my people.
MATTIE. Yes.
JULIA. You and Teeta are my family. Be my family.
MATTIE. We your people whether we blood kin or not.
(MATTIE *exits to her own porch.*)
FANNY. (*Offstage.*) No . . . No, Ma'am. (*Enters with* LULA.
LULA *is carrying the wilted bouquet.*) Julia! They think
Mr. Herman's come back.

(HERMAN'S MOTHER *enters with* ANNABELLE. *The old lady
is weary and subdued.* ANNABELLE *is almost without feeling.* JULIA *is on her porch waiting.*)

JULIA. Yes, Fanny, he's here. (LULA *retires to her doorway.*
JULIA *silently stares at them, studying each* WOMAN,
*seeing them with new eyes. She is going through that
rising process wherein she must reject them as the mold-
ers and dictators of her life.*) Nobody comes in my
house.
FANNY. What kind-a way is that?
JULIA. Nobody comes in my house.
ANNABELLE. We'll quietly take him home.
JULIA. You can't come in.
HERMAN'S MOTHER. (*Low-keyed, polite and humble sim-
plicity.*) You see my condition. Gawd's punishin' me
. . . Whippin' me for somethin' I did or didn't do. I
can't understand this . . . I prayed, but ain't no un-
derstandin' Herman's dyin'. He's almost gone. It's
right and proper that he should die at home in his
own bed. I'm askin' humbly . . . or else I'm forced to
get help from the police.
ANNABELLE. Give her a chance . . . She'll do right . . .
won'tcha?

(HERMAN *stirs. His breathing becomes harsh and deepens
into the sound known as the "death rattle."* MATTIE *leads
the* CHILDREN *away.*)

JULIA. (*Not unkindly.*) Do whatever you have to do. Win the war. Represent the race. Call the police. (*She enters her house, closes the door and bolts it.* HERMAN'S MOTHER *leaves through the front entry.* FANNY *slowly follows her.*) I'm here, do you hear me? (*He tries to answer but can't.*) We're standin' on the deck-a that Clyde Line Boat . . . wavin' to the people on the shore . . . Your mama, Annabelle, my Aunt Cora . . . all of our friends . . . the children . . . all wavin' . . . "Don't stay 'way too long . . . Be sure and come back . . . We gon' miss you . . . Come back, we need you" . . . But we're goin' . . . The whistle's blowin', flags wavin' . . . We're takin' off, ridin' the waves so smooth and easy . . . There now . . . (ANNABELLE *moves closer to the house as she listens to* JULIA.) . . . the bakery's fine . . . all the orders are ready . . . out to sea . . . on our way . . . (*The weight has lifted, she is radiantly happy. She helps him gasp out each remaining breath. With each gasp he seems to draw a step nearer to a wonderful goal.*) Yes . . . Yes . . . Yes . . . Yes . . . Yes . . . Yes . . .

CURTAIN

Alexis DeVeaux

THE TAPESTRY

Alexis DeVeaux is a contributing editor of *Essence*, the popular magazine for black women. A multitalented writer, she has produced works in many genres—poetry, fiction, and non-fiction. Her essays, especially a recent series for *Essence* on international affairs, bear the imprint of her progressive political views and reveal her abhorrence of oppression.

In the Hansberry tradition of activist-artist, she speaks out on a range of political and international issues. She has criticized United States policy in Central America, called for an end to apartheid in South Africa, criticized the subjugation of women in Zimbabwe who helped to win independence, and has expressed contempt for the Duvalier government in Haiti, which spent a pittance on its citizens' education.

Given these views, one might expect her plays to be overtly political tracts. But DeVeaux asserts that one must first understand "what your place as an individual is and the place of the person who is close to you. You have to understand the space between you before you can understand more complex or larger groups." So her fictional works focus on the "inner space of relationships" as a microcosm of community, national, and international relations. DeVeaux is "interested in presenting the black woman in relation to her eros, her sexuality," and seeks to understand its meaning to her political, emotional, and social self.[1] Challenging social labels and taboos, she explores "how the love comes to itself, rather than the gender or the name . . . of the love."[2] Thus lesbian affairs as well as love triangles and parent-child relationships have formed the subject matter of her work.

In "Sister Love," a poem that she wrote for *Essence* in

1983, DeVeaux speaks of a "new world" of relationships, free of sexist, homophobic, classist, and racist labels:

> . . . So I stumble forward and with caution, in search of new worlds/a new path/new context for living and working together. Equally. Whole. Black women and Black men. Not as homosexuals and heterosexuals but as sexual beings. Free from the domination of race, sex and class. This is my naked stance: These are my feminist priorities.[3]

No, a collage of poetry, music and dialogue, explored this theme on the stage and was produced by New Federal Theatre in New York.

In *The Tapestry*, DeVeaux presents the black woman as political, social, and sexual being. Jet, the major character, is at a critical point in her young life; she is studying for her law exams—a moment that brings her career and personal needs into sharp conflict. As she struggles to master the study material as well as the needs of self, she must also cope with the demands of her lover, Axis, and the weakness of her friend, Lavender, which threaten to undo her precarious hold on sanity. Jet also battles chimeras from her mind. How much of her past (family, religion, school) is essential to her future, and how much is unnecessary, destructive baggage? Will she be devoured like the sacrificial chicken of her nightmares? Can she survive the emotional battering of her lover and friend? Jet is no superwoman, but rather her nascence. Perhaps later she will be called "strong" by those unaware of her personal struggle, but in *The Tapestry*, she is in the act of becoming as she battles against her powerlessness in the face of personal relationships and a social and educational system that threaten to overpower her. While her victory is not assured, her final action, when viewed against this tapestry of emotion, becomes an act of courage and will.

DeVeaux draws from a background of involvement in community service. Before receiving her bachelor's degree in 1976 from Empire State College at the State University of New York, she worked extensively in community projects, teaching English and creative writing in the WIN program of the New York Urban league, Project Create, and the Frederick Douglass Creative Arts Center in New York. After serving as a community worker for the Bronx

Office of Probations, she became cultural coordinator of the Black Expo for the Black Coalition of Greater New Haven and in the same year cofounded the Coeur de l'Unicorne Gallery, which exhibited her paintings.

DeVeaux's works for theatre include *Circles*, produced in 1973 in New York City, and *A Season to Unravel*, premiered by the Negro Ensemble Company in 1984. In addition to several children's books, she has also written a biography, *Don't Explain: A Song of Billie Holiday*, published by Harper and Row.

NOTES

1. "Alexis DeVeaux," in Claudia Tate, *Black Women Writers at Work*, New York: Continuum, 1983, p. 55.

2. *Ibid.*, p. 52.

3. "Alexis DeVeaux," by Priscilla R. Ramsey in Thadious M. Davis and Trudier Harris, Eds., *Afro-American Writers after 1955: Dramatists and Prose Writers*, Detroit: Gale Research Company, 1985, p. 93.

The Tapestry

a play woven in 2

by
Alexis DeVeaux

The Tapestry was first produced at the Educational Center for the Arts in association with the Afro-American Cultural Center at Yale University in New Haven, Connecticut, in October of 1975 with the following personnel:

Cast: Jet .... Gwendolen Hardwick
      Axis .... Obaka Adedunyo
      Lavender .... Ejaye Tracey
      Mama .... Pawnee Sills
      Daddy .... Bob Long
      Rev. Paradise .. Akim Babatunde
      Sister Lott .... Marilyn Worrell
      Man .... Skip Waters
      Prof. Wayne .... Skip Waters
      Ticket Seller .... Akim Babatunde
      First Musician .. Ladji Camarr
      Second Musician Obayana Olumide
      Third Musician . Nadi Qamar
Director .... Kalima Soham
Stage Manager .... David Shepperd and Pat White
Lighting Designer ..... Sandra Ross
Electrician .... John Howard Brown
Make-Up and Props .. Carole Byard and
                       Valerie Maynard
Paintings by Adger W. Cowans

The Tapestry was produced for television by KCET-TV (PBS) in New York and broadcast nationally in 1976. It was also produced as a staged reading by Kumoja Players of Richmond, California, for the San Francisco Black Writers Workshop.

People:

JET   a law student of 23 and slim. short
                       hair and beautiful oddly. her speech
                       has a slight southern drawl

AXIS   a musician of 28 and experienced. he
                       always dresses in a dark blue suit and
                       turtleneck sweater. he always carries
                       his saxophone under his arm

LAVENDER   a well-dressed upstairs friend of JETS
                       who is 29. shes a disk jockey at a radio
                       station and quite attractive

CHORUS   reverend paradise
                       momma
                       daddie
                       sister lott
                       man
                       woman

PROFESSOR WANE   (played by man from chorus)

CLIENTS   (played by chorus members)

time: *now*
place: *a black community (urban)*

act one: thursday late afternoon

          JETS *apt*

          and later that evening

          friday morning

          and afternoon

          and later

the weekend passes.

act two: the following monday morning

> *and afternoon*
>
> *and evening*
>
> *with a glimpse of tuesday morning*

the stage:

JETS apt is a one-room studio located uptown in harlem. it is a large room with a window (facing the audience) against the back wall. JETS desk and chair are in front of the window and both face Stage Left. to the Right of the desk and chair is the entrance to the apt. against the adjacent wall a record player sits on the floor surrounded by albums. not far from it is a two-shelf bookcase made of lumber and mortar bricks spilling over with books. a piece of african-design material hangs on the wall above it.

to the Left of the desk is a small kitchen table with two chairs back against the wall and to the Left of the window. three shelves on the wall above it hold various canned goods and boxes of tea. on the adjacent wall a refrigerator is pushed against. not too far from it and also pushed against the wall is a couch-bed covered with african-design material and matching pillows. above it several pictures of african statues are pasted on the wall.

around the corner is the bathroom of which is visible the bathtub toilet washbowl and mirror above it.

there is a small oriental rug on the floor underneath a secondhand coffee table which sits not too far from the couch-bed.

a large hanging plant sits on the window sill. the window looks out to a brick wall.

there is always the smell of incense or incense burning in JETS apt.

her apt is built at Stage Left above the "legal aid office." there is a sign which reads:

legal aid office
waiting room
please take a number

on the back wall and to the Left facing the audience. beneath
the sign there are seven chairs arranged in a three-two-one-
one fashion facing what is the "office area." the waiting
room is divided from the office by a long white line.

the office consists of a bare space furnished only with a desk
and chair a typewriter and stand. in the far Right corner of
the room there is a large grey file cabinet.

stairs from the Right of JETs *apt provide an entranceway to*
the legal aid office and the classroom: Stage Right.

the classroom is a white-walled room furnished with only
a chair back Stage Left and a desk and chair Upstage Right.
the back wall facing the audience has a blackboard or a
piece of one attached to it and there is a large full-length
mirror not far from it.

adjoining the classroom is the radio station: a small space
painted a pastel color consisting of a chair a sofa and a
table and chair. on the back wall facing the audience is a
cork board on which several pictures of black musicians
are tacked not too neatly and a clock above with a large
minute hand.

the room dimensions of the legal aid office the classroom
and the radio station should give the impression of non-
reality/a distortion of perspectives.

ACT ONE

as lights rise several characters appear on stage from various directions of JETs apt. there is no dialogue except for improvised whispered greetings. the characters are all church-going folks and it is apparent from their dress. all carry bibles and all are dressed in sunday clothes. the women carry white paper fans and fan. the men greet with firm handshakes and pats on the back. none are wearing shoes. the atmosphere is one of religious festivity. the preacher enters from the closet. he is also dressed in sunday fashion. he carries a bible bigger than the rest. a white cross is painted on his forehead and he is barefoot. he makes his way toward the bathtub. the congregation members follow him and gather around the tub. the preacher begins to pantomime a sermon to which the congregation members pantomime their responses.

JET enters the apt dressed as for spring weather. she locks the door meticulously. then drops her books on the desk and takes the phone off the hook. she takes orange juice from the refrigerator and drinks while the choir members hum a low sweet tune. the preachers sermon is obviously getting better as the rhythm of their bodies implies. JET enters the bathroom.

JET. (*to herself.*)
    i wish theyd get a church

(*turning on faucet as she reaches for soap and a washcloth speaking louder.*)

    and stop meeting in that mans apt down the hall
    every night of the week
    them and jesus

(*washing her face.*)

remind me of the people in church
at home
every first sunday
seemed like all of savannah was there
down by the ogeechee river
sweating and singing for jesus

(looking in the mirror picking at a pimple.)

and reverend what was his name?
oh yeah   reverend paradise

(REVEREND PARADISE nods his head as if he has just been introduced to someone important)

and sister lott

(she also bows in the same fashion as the REVEREND. JET continues to wash her face and hands as the chorus tune changes into a rendition of "i woke up this morning with my mind set on freedom." they clap their hands and stomp their feet in the rhythm. MOMMA and DADDIE go over to JET and take her by the hands leading her into the tub. gentle. JET is a child now.)

MOMMA.
aint nothing to be scared of baby
we right here with you
DADDIE.
so just put your trust in jesus

(the choir song fades as JET kneels facing REVEREND.)

REVEREND. *(raising his right hand to god.)*
brothers and sisters
hear what i say
hear what i say this great and glorious
morning   yes indeed
for weve come to a river
weve come to a river
and weve stopped at the shore
CHOIR MEMBERS. *(low.)*
yes we did yes we did

REVEREND. (*intermittently clapping his hands.*)
    a band of humble servants
CHOIR MEMBERS. (*low.*)
    yes we are lord yes we are
REVEREND. (*placing his hand gently on* JETs *forehead.*)
    we dont come alone
CHOIR MEMBERS.
    no jesus
    we dont come alone
REVEREND.
    you seen fit to have us
    bring this child to you
CHOIR MEMBERS.
    guide us jesus
    guide us precious lord
REVEREND.
    and so we come to this river
    holy father
    we meet you at the shore

(*pointing to* JET *as he turns his eyes upward*)

    the one youve chosen this day
    kneels before you father
    a witness   yes indeed
CHOIR MEMBERS.
    a witness to his glory
REVEREND.
    waiting to receive the baptismal water

(MOMMA *and* DADDIE *pass to the faucet and gather water
in their hands. the* PREACHER *bends* JET *over backwards as
if he is going to dunk her in the river as* MOMMA *and* DADDIE
splash JETs *face with water. the* CHOIR MEMBERS *hum and
their humming rises with this action.*)

JET. (*snapped from her trance by the feel of the water.*)
    yall crazy or something
    trying to drown me?

(*the action of the* REVEREND *and* CHOIR MEMBERS *freezes
and lights go out on them.* JET *gets out of the tub and dries
her face with the washcloth as she moves to her desk flipping
over the pages of a textbook. there is a knock at the door.*)

JET. (*opening the door and speaking to* LAVENDER.)
    hey whats happening?
    come on in

(*surprised to see* AXIS *behind* LAVENDER.)

    hi   i didnt know that you
AXIS. (*as he follows* LAVENDER *in.*)
    hey there foxy lawyer
    what you doing these days

(*he gently kisses her.*)

LAVENDER. (*looking around the apt.*)
    i know you must be in here studying
    like crazy

(*sniffing.*)

    smells good   what is it?
JET.
    incense
    keeps the spirits watching over me happy
LAVENDER.
    maybe i need to go get some
    cause the spirits looking out for me
    are out to lunch honey

(*she seats herself on the couch-bed.*)

AXIS. (*grabbing* JET *around the waist.*)
    dont you look good
    i hardly get to see you anymore
JET. (*closing the door.*)
    well you know how it is
    hard to study and socialize
    at the same time

(*releasing herself from him she goes to the refrigerator and gets the orange juice. she fills two glasses.*)

AXIS. (*watching her.*)
    all work and no play baby

LAVENDER. (*lighting a cigarette.*)
    could make jack a dissatisfied boy

(*blows out smoke deeply.* JET *pretends not to hear this remark as she hands each one a glass of juice. she sits on top of the desk and puts her feet in the chair.*)

AXIS. (*drinking.*)
    ill be glad when this is all over baby
    dont get me wrong
    you know im a funny man
    i dont like sharing my woman with no law school
    textbooks   *all the time*

(*finishing juice, he places his glass on the kitchen table.*)

LAVENDER.
    so whens the big day?
JET.
    tuesday coming
LAVENDER.
    four more days huh?
JET.
    and then three days of exams
LAVENDER.
    better you than me
    i mean more power to you sister
    but i couldnt stand the grind
    four years at the u of mass was enough
    i should have gone into acting
    like i always wanted to
    my folks thought i was crazy
    said that was a sure way to end up hungry and
    since they was paying for my career
    i didnt have no choice

(JET *goes to the record player and puts on a side:* coltrane plays the blues. AXIS *sits next to lavender placing his horn on his lap.*)

JET.
    yeah but at least you dont have to spend
    all your time reading all of this

(she points to a shelf of extremely fat books.)

LAVENDER. *(sipping juice.)*
    honey if i was you
    id go out this weekend
    and have myself a ball i dont care
    how tired i am
    i still do my wednesday nights
    at the pink seagull having a good time
    with the bar-folks
    what the hell?
    live honey
    cause when it comes to living
    we are some scary folks
JET.
    we are some vulnerable folks
    according to those books
    we dont own nothing
    worth spitting at
    thats why we aint got no say
    no property no justice
    aint that nothing?
    i mean whats more basic?
    when they hand me my papers

(she knocks on wood the coffee table.)

    im going to hand them a new set of rules
AXIS. *(lighting one of* LAVENDERS *cigarettes.)*
    dont count on it baby
LAVENDER.
    youll be fighting something
    with a built in anti-change factor
    rich folks honey
    big money
AXIS. *(intently listening to the music.)*
    how can yall run your mouths
    saying nothing in the presence of a genius?

(closing his eyes to listen better to the music.)

    john coltrane
    that brother was talking
    about things he hadnt even seen yet

(jet and lavender both give him a look)

LAVENDER. you got yourself one music crazy man jet
JET. *(going over to axis sweetly kissing his face and head.)*
    I sure do   dont i?
LAVENDER. first time i met him was at a party
        off campus
        we were both sophomores

(she laughs remembering.)

        axis was standing in a corner
        dancing with his horn

(AXIS's expression and intent on the music does not change but JET continues to play with him and to whisper in his ear. he laughs grabbing and kissing her.)

LAVENDER. *(going to refrigerator.)*
        watching yall is like watching
        a good porno movie
        alone

(bending to peek at refrigerator contents.)

        what you got in here
        to eat jet?
JET. *(removing herself from AXIS's hold.)*
        nothing much
        been so wrapped up in books
        and prep classes
        i havent had time to eat
        much less shop
LAVENDER. *(rummaging in refrigerator.)*
        cheese   squash
        brown rice and peas
        a fish head?
        this vegetarian diet of yours
        sounds like bird food to me

(JET goes to the record and turns it over.)

JET.
        so busy busting my butt

> going to work on top of it
> they dont give up something
> for nothing
> they sure make you pay

(she sits on the couch-bed not far from AXIS. *he takes his horn out of the case and pretends to finger the notes of the music playing while* LAVENDER *resigns herself to another glass of orange juice.)*

AXIS. *(between fingering his horn.)*
> depends on what its worth
> to you baby

LAVENDER. *(sitting at kitchen table.)*
> you cant save the whole race

JET.
> just what my father used to say
> save the race jesus
> save the race

(lights up on the CHOIR MEMBERS *as* JET *goes to the closet and pulls out a pair of oversized rubber boots. she puts them on as the* CHOIR MEMBERS *dance around the tub doing a "shout" in pantomime. they move as if they are walking in mud and are happy to.* AXIS *and* LAVENDER *stare at* JET. *their faces reflect disbelief.)*

JET. *(putting on boots.)*
> the feeling of mud
> gives me the chills
> sinking between my toes
> guts of the river
> like bands of black worms slithering
> i didnt like having to walk
> in that river

LAVENDER.
> jet?
> something wrong?

AXIS. *(staring.)*
> baby?
> whats   uh   going on?
> what you doing you ok?

JET.
> im fine

        i just dont like mud
        on my feet
        thats all
AXIS.
        aint no mud within fifty miles of here
        baby this aint savannah

(laughing.)

LAVENDER.
        you sure those stay-up pills
        you been taking dont make you   hallucinate?
JET.
        yall are making fun of me
        but once you see something
        you always see it

(changing the subject.)

        listen i hate to do this
        cause i really like seeing yall
        but i *have* to get back
        to my books
LAVENDER. *(rising.)*
        try not to work yourself
        to death honey
        dont you let all this studying
        make you lose touch
        with other things

(she gives JET *a big-sister pat on the cheek and then picks up her pocketbook.)*

AXIS.
        i did want to play a section
        from the new piece im working on
        but you too busy to hear it
        at the moment
        i guess ill drop by maxwells house
        and see what he doing

(he carefully replaces the horn in its case.)

JET. (*escorting them to the door.*)
    im sorry i really am but
AXIS.
    all this book worm stuff
    is showing on you baby
    it dont look too good
JET.
    id like to hear your new tune
AXIS. (*going out.*)
    sure baby you will
    be sweet

(*he exits as he gives her a kiss.*)

LAVENDER.
    time for me to go do
    my disk jockey act
    what i should do is   find me a man
    quit my job
    and work on some babies
    see you later honey
JET.
    ok yall   take it easy

(*she starts to close the door behind* LAVENDER *as* AXIS *sticks his face in.*)

AXIS.
    you going to be working
    all night?
JET.
    i do have to get this done

(*coquettish.*)

    why?
AXIS.
    id like to stop by later
JET.
    alone?
AXIS.
    what you mean?
JET.
    nothing

i was just curious i thought maybe
i mean   when you came in
AXIS.
what?   now come on baby
you know aint nothing happening
when i got off the elevator she was
knocking on your door

(changing subject.)

i really want to see you
JET.
in a couple of hours or so?
AXIS.
solid

(kisses her and leaves.)

JET. *(calling down the hallway.)*
and this time call me
if you get hung up
ill leave the phone on the hook

(she shuts the door and goes directly to the phone placing it on the hook. then goes back to the door and carefully locks it. she takes some water and proceeds to water her plant while speaking to it.)

turning brown at the edges
hello? hello?

(lights up on CHOIR MEMBERS *standing in the bathroom in jury fashion and the* REVEREND *is standing near the sink. he taps it with a gavel. the gavel sound is loud and echoes thru the apt.* JET *speaks hurriedly to her plant.)*

its criminal negligence i know
but i really didnt mean
to let you die

(the REVEREND *raps his gavel again.* JET *turns to face him.)*

your honor
may i beg the courts indulgence

to speak in my own behalf?
counsel for the defendant is dying
and is unable at this time
to say a goddamn thing
therefore i submit petition to act
as my own counsel

(CHOIR MEMBERS *crack up laughing pantomime.*)

ladies and gentlemen
i am the only witness to the fact
i have no choice
this is unfair
i must spend all my time   learning
the law is a run on sentence
certain people   your honor   are trained to repeat

(CHOIR MEMBERS *stop laughing and put their hands over
their mouths as little kids do when one of the group says a
"bad word.")*

my plant suffers
i cant give her any attention
i have to attend preparation classes
and so with the courts permission
said defendant did with malice
and willfull knowledge
say fuck yall in the presence of said
witnesses not in the category
of substantive proof
but heard and did not see

(*lights down on* CHOIR MEMBERS *pantomime laughing as*
JET *laughs and sits at her desk opening a book.*)

everybody in savannah
was glad i got that scholarship
being the first to leave home
after a while momma said

(*light up on* MOMMA *sitting on the edge of the tub watching*
DADDIE *coach in pantomime a large black doll to walk to
him. after two tries he picks up the doll playfully kissing
and hugging her as* MOMMA *directs her conversation to* JET.*)*

MOMMA.
        four years is enough baby
        come home help raise your brothers
        and sisters dont you want to get married?
        raise some of your own?

(MOMMA *and* DADDIE *both speak the following lines but*
DADDIE *directs his to the doll.*)

        much education as you got now
        live a little
        dont spend your whole life
        in school daughter

(*light down on them as* JET *intently studies. Light up on*
AXIS *in the street Stage Right. he blows the passage of time
with his horn. when he finishes he tucks his horn under his
arm and heads for* JETS *apt.* JET *pushes herself away from
the desk. rubs her eyes. yawns and stretches.* AXIS *knocks
on the door.*)

AXIS. (*knocking.*)
        jet?
        its me axis
JET. (*opening door.*)
        hello again

(*he comes in and kisses her gently and when she responds
his kiss is more passionate.*)

        you know you got me spoiled jet
        im serious

(*he sits down on the couch-bed and sits* JET *on his lap.*)

        my horn and my woman
        after that nothing matters

(*changing subject.*)

        guess what baby
JET.
        your father finally answered
        one of your letters?

AXIS.
>   no

(he takes a cigarette and a book of matches out his pocket.)

>   my old man and me we two parallel lines
>   we look alike but we dont touch
>   let him stay in san juan with his band
>   anyway maxwell is sold on my idea
>   with him on piano
>   all i need is a bass and a drum
>   and my days of slinging hash on wall street
>   are over
>   maxwell thinks we should hook up
>   with two brothers we met last night
>   in the join lavender works at?

JET.
>   i didnt know they have live music
>   at the pink seagull

AXIS.
>   they do now
>   thanks to lavender
>   she fixed it up
>   nothing to it
>   the dude who runs the place digs her
>   well be playing there saturday night
>   why dont you come with me baby?

JET.
>   id like to
>   but i ought to study as much
>   as i can

AXIS.
>   just for a little while
>   just so you can see
>   what im doing

JET.
>   i wish i could i

AXIS.
>   ok ok   say no more

(they sit in silence a moment as JET *watches him absently rubbing his horn case.)*

>   you know what really turns me on?

JET.
    what?
AXIS.
    i like the way you look
    when youre cooking

(playfully kissing on her neck.)

JET.
    you just like to see me
    so you can watch me cook
    aint that nothing

(she laughs and moves toward the refrigerator.)

AXIS.
    i know you must like it
    cause you swing them wooden spoons
    the way max roach swing drum sticks
JET. *(taking things from the refrigerator.)*
    theres not much
    but theres enough for a salad
AXIS.
    wonderful
    nourish me and leave the fat to other folks
    now all we need is some atmosphere

(he takes out his horn and plays a soft jazz tune as JET gets a large salad bowl and begins to cut up things and place them inside. then she sets the table. she takes a stick of incense off the bookcase and lights it as AXIS leans against the wall, bobbing his head to the music.)

JET.
    is that the new thing youre writing?
    sounds great
AXIS.
    yeah
    just a little thing you know
    its not finished
    you like it?
JET.
    uh huh
    beautiful

(she motions him to sit down as she serves him.)

AXIS. (*eating*)
    oooh its good
    its good baby
JET. (*sitting down*)
    i like to cook when youre around
AXIS.
    id be around more often
    if all you wanted was me
JET. (*defensive.*)
    im not all you want
AXIS. (*throwing up his hands in surrender.*)
    ok ok lets not have the same fight
    again not tonight
    i just want to have a good time
    together

(they continue the meal in silence but from time to time sneak a look at each other so that by the time they are finished eating their attitudes have softened.)

AXIS. (*leaning away from his plate.*)
    that was some meal baby

(he gets up and sits on the couch-bed as JET clears the table.)

    i like a woman who knows how to be a woman
    for a man
    knows what to do to keep him
JET. (*as she puts another record on.*)
    thats a pretty narrow damn
    view of a woman
    if i ever heard one
AXIS.
    what?
    listen baby aint but two roles
    in this universe
    male and female   in that order
    everything else is bullshit
    you hear me?

JET.
>   who elected you
>   the new black jesus?

AXIS.
>   i tell you something serious
>   little girl and you make a joke of it

JET. (*offended.*)
>   how many little girls
>   you know is as serious as i am
>   about anything?

AXIS.
>   if you was really serious
>   youd come over here
>   and give me some serious sugar

(she goes to him after a moment of hesitation. he pulls her close and kisses her long. lights dim on the two of them undressing on the couch-bed as they lie down.)

JET.
>   aixs?
>   i love you

AXIS. (*kissing her.*)
>   i love you too little girl

JET.
>   stop calling me little girl
>   i think

AXIS.
>   shut up   dont think   feel

(the mixed sounds of love as lights dim more and JET and AXIS reach a slow climax.)

JET.
>   oh baby
>   oh baby   do it

(love sounds fade out softly. moments pass. AXIS takes his horn from the floor and blows the passage of time as JET sleeps. lights on stage go from late evening to an early morning suggestion. AXIS puts his horn down and lies next to JET.)

AXIS.
> morning is the best time
> to do it

(he kisses her and she is awakened abruptly.)

JET. *(sitting up staring at him.)*
> let me out

AXIS. *(laughing.)*
> what?
> girl you going crazy on me?
> wake up

JET.
> what?   huh?
> oh   its you

(yawning.)

> a strange dream

(yawning.)

> jesus im still tired
> always tired
> no matter how much i sleep

AXIS.
> i can sure see why
> four years of college and three of law school
> you pushing yourself pretty hard

JET.
> i want to make *life* count
> newspapers lie
> the faces of folks
> have turned to wax
> you know what i mean?
> i want to *do* something about it
> people have to steal just to eat
> and then
> slam
> fifteen years in jail   who cares?
> because its a crime to steal
> from the ones who steal
> from the world

AXIS.
    yeah baby
    i understand what you saying
       i did the college bit too
    but this school thing really seems
    to be wearing on you
    a lot of people
    take a little time off
    and then go back

JET.
    at school they expect me to quit
    they expect it to be too much for me
    i know they do

AXIS.
    yeah but baby
    you got to slow down
    you been so boxed up

JET.
    i was dreaming about boxes
    at the end of a long hallway

AXIS. (*getting up.*)
    i think id better get
    you some tea jet

JET. (*she gets out of bed putting on clothes. she sits at her desk and lights a stick of incense while chanting low.*)
    nine books down and three to go
    spirits watch over me
    help me know

(*aloud.*)

    what time is it?

AXIS. (*putting the cup of tea on her desk.*)
    time spent with you gets shorter
    and shorter
    thats what time it is

(*he begins to put on his clothes.*)

    i hope you know what you doing
    to yourself baby

(to himself.)

>   probably should get in some practice
>   before i hit that wall street scene

(puts his horn in case.)

JET. *(reading as she sips tea.)*
>   what you say?

AXIS.
>   nothing
>   see you later

JET.
>   ok bye

(he runs his hand over her head and leaves. JET studies. on the street AXIS blows the passage of time. light suggests progression from morning to afternoon. JET gets up from her desk and goes to the closet. she removes a jacket and scarf, which she puts on as she gathers her pocketbook and keys and leaves the apt. AXIS's solo ends as JET reaches the legal aid office. in the waiting room all but the first chair is occupied. as JET steps in there is the low sound of circus music playing. JET takes off her jacket and hangs it on the back of her chair. she sifts thru some papers in a folder on her desk. the voice of a ticket seller calling off numbers is heard as a pale blue light descends on the waiting room area.)

TICKET SELLER.
>   num   ber

(low circus music as CLIENTS rise in expectation again.)

TICKET SELLER. *(same voice.)*
>   1998

(CLIENTS sit mumbling. this time louder. a man goes to the line which separates him from JET. he bangs as if banging on a door. one by one the others follow suit. their banging and cursing is pantomime. JET comes to the door/line.)

MAN. *(angry.)*
>   been waiting all morning miss
>   please

LADY. (*coming forth.*)
    do something for me i
JET.
    am only a clerk here i
OTHER MAN. (*desperate.*)
    need your help
    the landlord locked my woman
    and kids out
LADY.
    its not for myself im asking but
JET.
    i only do the typing here
    im not a lawyer
    yet you see
MAN.
    i know she aint the same
    they gave my wife a new drug
    at the hospital
LADY.
    please make them help us
OTHER MAN.
    thats what youre here for
JET.
    im here to do the typing
    i wish i could help but
LADY.
    you just here taking up space

(*circus music continues as* CLIENTS *return to their seats
waving their hands in disapproval at* JET.)

TICKET SELLER. (*same voice.*)
    num   ber

(CLIENTS *rise in expectation.*)

TICKET SELLER.
    1999

(CLIENTS *sit mumbling.* JET *watches over her shoulder as
she returns to the desk but does not sit down. she rips a
piece of paper from the typewriter and throws it in a ball
against the file cabinet while speaking to it.*)

JET.
> whats the difference?
> im not different
> my mother and father birthed me
> to carry on the fucking struggle
> but what difference to you
> do our aches make?

(to CLIENTS.*)*

> listen to me

(to file cabinet)

> ever since the first grade
> you said i was different from the rest
> of them
> smarter

(backing out of the room.)

> and quicker

(she crosses the door/line.)

> oh no
> none of that divide and conquer shit

(she backs into the first chair where CLIENTS *are. lights dim in the office area except for a white spotlight on the file cabinet.)*

TICKET SELLER.
> num   ber

(all rise including JET*)*

> 2000

(all sit mumbling. the funny lady of a circus laughs and fades. lights dim on the waiting room areas as the carnival music blends into alice coltrane. the CLIENTS *and* JET *disperse into the street and go separate ways.* JET *heads for home but changes her mind and heads for the radio station*

where LAVENDER *is sitting at a table reading the back of an album cover and smoking a cigarette. she faces Stage Left and there is a bottle of soda on the table. above the clock is a sign which reads: WBLK-FM. as* JET *peeks in the music of alice coltrane is low but continues.)*

LAVENDER.
    hey girl   come on in
JET.
    hi
LAVENDER. (*putting her cigarette in ashtray.*)
    you look like somebody been
    whipping you or something
JET. (*sitting on sofa.*)
    i feel like a chicken going thru
    her first hurricane

(LAVENDER *removes her earphones and gives a cut signal to the engineer, who is not visible. the music fades out.*)

LAVENDER.
    that was fine ronnie
    give it a little more bass
    on the next cut though   will you?
    i like to hear those drums
JET. (*absently talking.*)
    not knowing what to expect
    dancing in the eye of the storm
LAVENDER. (*to* JET.)
    what you say?

(*to* RONNIE-ENGINEER.)

    after the jingle instead of number three
    lets do *coltrane live at birdland*

(*to* JET.)

    im sorry honey i didnt hear what you said
JET.
    nothing
    just mumble mumble

(*the music is heard low.*)

LAVENDER. (*drinking soda.*)
    what brings you this way?
JET.
    i just came from work
    i figured id walk the five blocks to see you
    i didnt feel like going home to study
    its all getting to me
    i needed a break
LAVENDER.
    i really dont know how you do it jet
    but whatever it takes
    you certainly got it
    wait a minute
    let me do this

(*talks into microphone with a low affected and sensual radio voice.*)

    jimmy garrison on bass
    mccoy tyner on the keys
    elvin jones on the ancestral bells
    and of course   on sax
    john coltrane
    and this is lavender storm
    here with you on WBLK-FM

(JET *roams over to the corkboard as* LAVENDER *is speaking.*)

    lets listen now to miriam makeba
    doing one of my old favorites
    "piece of ground"

(*she removes earphones and lights another cigarette as the music plays.*)

JET.
    it looks different from the last time
    i was here
LAVENDER. (*smoking.*)
    yeah   like my collection?
    i had to do something cause
    it was driving me crazy in here
    staring at the walls and ronnie

in the cube back there
wish he was mine

JET.
    still trying to marry
    every man you meet?

LAVENDER.
    and i aint going to stop
    till i get me one honey
    cause i loves me a fine man

(laughs at herself.)

    my time is getting short
    and i needs me a *constant*
    supply of love
    my security

JET. *(lounging on the sofa.)*
    nothing makes me feel that secure
    not even axis

LAVENDER.
    you got a man
    of your own
    and you aint secure?
    thats more than what most women
    out here got girl
    you better stop looking your gift horse
    in the mouth   let me tell you
    axis is fine and if he was mine

JET.
    would you feel free?

LAVENDER.
    free?
    hell yeah girl!
    id be so damn free
    from all my bar-stool affairs
    just to know theres *one* man around
    to take care of me
    it all boils down to that honey
    a legitimate relationship

(putting on earphones she talks into the mike.)

    WBLK-FM 109.5
    on your fm dial

summers on the way   and if youre one
of those people who likes to look good
in the sun youll be pleased to hear
that the WEAR WHAT BOUTIQUE
has a sale on all the accessories youll need
to make your summer a fly and funky affair
so check out the WEAR WHAT BOUTIQUE
125 street

(she signals to RONNIE *while she talks into the mike.)*

lets change the mood a bit
as we give a listen to miles davis
from his album: *kind of blue*

(a moment of silence passes as the music plays.)

JET.
i want to be defined in my own terms
not somebody elses
i want to leave my mark on the world
make it all worth something
something more than working my way
into old age and a social security check
i see things to be done
so many things
thats why i want to be a lawyer
i was put here to do
LAVENDER.
you was put here
because a woman needs
JET. *(sarcastic.)*
to make babies
and not changes?
live in a too small corner
of the world   and struggle?
that cross has already been carried
and theres already too many
LAVENDER. *(devilish.)*
mothers or martyrs?
youre young
thats why youre so opinionated
JET. *(annoyed.)*
each generation has to raise

    a new question
    tote a new cross
LAVENDER.
    i know what youre saying jet
    i know how you feel
    i feel like that myself sometimes
    but i know how i feel when im happy
    and jesus knows a good man
    can make me feel *real* and happy
    yes indeed   umph umph umph
JET.
    hes losing his patience with me
LAVENDER.
    who?
JET.
    axis   hes not as nice as before
    we used to have more fun
    now hes very demanding
    the more i see him
    the less satisfied he is
    says i dont give him enough
LAVENDER. (*big-sisterly.*)
    if you dont give it to him when he *wants*
    it and as *much as he wants*
    hes going to get it from somewhere honey
    thats a mans nature
    he got to have his stuff
    and if you aint going to treat him right
    you cant expect him to be perfect
JET.
    or faithful
LAVENDER.
    faithful?   girl you been in school
    too long   you better come on out
    and join the rest of us in the maze
    out here sex aint got nothing to do
    with love
    believe me

(*lights a cigarette.*)

    a brother i know once told me
    if he didnt have sex regular
    his thang would shrink

a friend of mines husband
now mind you   she was pregnant
with his kid

JET. (*sitting forward.*)
you believed him?

LAVENDER.
no   but i gave him some anyway
i mean it wasnt no big deal
just a little friendship between friends

JET.
i dont like sleeping with folks
i dont love id rather sleep alone

LAVENDER.
i used to be romantic and idealistic
just like you when i was twenty-three

(*to the* ENGINEER.)

play yusef latiffs "the gentle giant"
next ok? well move right into it

(*to* JET.)

but im six years older than you
more time to get my feathers plucked
to the edge
ill be thirty this year honey
it all went

(*snapping her fingers.*)

just like that
when i was an undergrad
i could recruit more men than the army could
aint that something?
and you think you got problems
listen to me girl
axis is one of them good to screw types
honey the way his pants
be fitting round down the middle snug and

JET.
you supposed to be my friend   lavender

LAVENDER. (*noticing the hard look* JET *gives her.*)
im just kidding you honey

(talking in mike.)

> youve been listening to "gentle giant"
> recorded by yusef latiff
> and this is lavender storm
> on a lovely friday evening
> at WBLK-FM in the big apple
> working hard to please you

(nina simones "work song" plays.)

> feeling sick as a dog
> cramps all over
> must be getting my period
> you got any aspirins jet?

(JET searches in her pocketbook and comes up with a tin of aspirins which she hands to LAVENDER. LAVENDER downs an aspirin with a swallow of soda.)

JET.
> i cant stand cramps
> cant stand the pain
> and the blood
> its a river every month
> theres a flood
> its spiritual

LAVENDER. *(rubbing the small of her back.)*
> call it what you want
> but aint nothing holy about that constant
> toothache in your back for four or five days

(the music changes from nina simone to roberta flack singing "rivers.")

JET.
> i think theres a connection between
> bleeding and vulnerability

LAVENDER.
> oh come on jet

JET.
> no seriously
> what color is associated with blood?

LAVENDER.
> red
> every body knows that

JET.
>and with weakness?

LAVENDER.
>yellow

JET.
>which proves my theory
>that god made women red and yellow
>in the beginning

LAVENDER. (*waving her hand at* JET.)
>you and your textbook theories
>you better get yourself a theory
>for living
>i sure do need to see chin tonight
>but its friday and hes seeing his wife
>*c'est la vie*
>i hate to be home alone weekends
>need a change
>feel like going home and cooking dinner
>for a fine man with a big thang
>between his legs
>big enough to fill this empty feeling
>between mine

JET. (*rising.*)
>i need to go home myself
>finish studying.

LAVENDER. (*finishing soda.*)
>well if i dont find no man to come over
>and eat up this fantastic dinner
>ill give you a ring
>you can stop by for a meal on your study break
>and watch me cry the blues
>itll be late tho   after i leave work

JET. (*going to door.*)
>ok call me
>im glad you were here lavender
>i needed to talk
>take it easy   ill see you
>good luck

(LAVENDER *signals cut to the engineer as* JET *exits. the music of alice coltrane plays and fades as* JET *reaches her apt door. lights down on* LAVENDER.)

JET. (*dropping her pocketbook on the kitchen table and heading for the refrigerator.*)
    bet aint nothing here to eat
    aint nothing never here unless
    axis is

(*she takes a half-filled bottle of orange juice from the refrigerator and a plate of crackers. she stands at the table eating and drinking.*)

    hmmm im so hungry
    tired of eating law books
    for breakfast   lunch   and dinner

(*while eating she goes over to inspect her plant.*)

    still dying
    that brick wall out there aint helping you much
    nothing like city life to kill a plant

(*she puts food back in the refrigerator and lies down on the couch-bed.*)

    hope lavender calls soon
    her cooking is worth going out for
    i should get up and study
    no   ill take a nap first
    that way ill be fresh

(*yawning.*)

    getting nervous
    only three more days til the bar
    so hungry
    suppose i dont pass?
    stop talking nonsense fool
    youll pass   you better

(*singing low.*)

    jesus loves me yes i know
    for the bible tells me so

(lights dim on JET *as she falls asleep. lights up in the street suggest late evening as* LAVENDER *is walking home alone.* AXIS *moves out of the shadows behind her.)*

AXIS. *(almost whispering.)*
    hey fox
LAVENDER. *(startled she turns around.)*
    what the?
    oh   hey axis honey
    you shouldn't creep up on me
    in the pitch black
    might have thought you was a mugger

(coy.)

    out cruising?
AXIS.
    you been looking real good these days fox
    what you been doing?

(stepping back for a better look.)

LAVENDER. *(womanly.)*
    none of your business
    now dont tell me you just happened
    to be on this street at this hour
    that hasnt happened since you started
    seeing jet
AXIS.
    cant a friend walk a friend home
    after   work?
LAVENDER.
    thats very considerate of you
    or do i detect a i-want-me-some-
    company-look in your face
AXIS.
    maybe you do
LAVENDER.
    how about some dinner?
AXIS.
    thats a good place to start

(he steps aside.)

after you

(LAVENDER *walks a step or two in front of him.* AXIS *watches her backside shake and then gently pulls her to him speaking softly.*)
hey   come here

(*he kisses her.* LAVENDER *is not sure at first how to respond but his kiss is insistent and she gives in.*)

LAVENDER. (*pulling away some.*)
you   surprised me
AXIS.
no i didnt

(*he walks her off Stage Right as they exit laughing. on stage the lights dim to a blue spotlight on* JET *in the bed tossing and turning. she mumbles incoherently. the* CHOIR MEMBERS *emerge from the bathroom. they carry picnic baskets and juice jugs. the women fan themselves. all are wearing white gloves and have an air of relaxed festivity. they smile and talk in whispers and sit on the floor in the center of the room. one—a woman—sports a moustache. another—a man—wears a bra over his clothes.* JET *whimpers in her sleep as the* REVEREND *proceeds to distribute black bones to each person from his picnic basket. they smell and eat in the fashion similar to squirrels: quick with small bites. the* REVEREND *is the last to receive a bone and his is the biggest. he eats in the same fashion as the others. there is a low buzzing sound of flies thru out this scene.* JET *tosses and turns. when the* CHOIR MEMBERS *have finished with their bones they stash them in their clothes and proceed to eat on themselves: arms   hands   legs etc. and then they eat each others hands and faces in a very sensual manner. everybody eating on everybody: including man to man and woman to woman. this action continues until all appear to be full. after which they belch and pick their teeth as they begin to clean up their picnic area and file out in the same festive manner as when they came in—humming a gospel tune. as the last one disappears into the dark of the bathroom* JET *bolts straight up in bed. eyes wide. she looks around the room getting up slowly and cautiously. scene black.*)

ACT TWO

monday afternoon. JETS *apt.* JET *is at her desk poring over a stack of fat books. the apt is in a state of total disarray: papers, books, and clothes thrown everywhere.* JETS *physical appearance suggests she has not combed her hair for days and her clothes give the impression that she has not had the time nor the inclination to care for them. her face is tired and gives one the impression she lacks restful sleep. the couch-bed is unmade and blankets and sheets are thrown carelessly over chairs and about the floor. a stack of records are spread out near the record player. several empty bottles of orange juice line the kitchen table along with empty packages of cheese.* JET *pushes herself away from the desk rubbing her eyes and neck. she stands up to stretch.*

JET. *(scratching her butt.)*
    let me see if i got it right now
    land grants   civil law
    corporate law
    landlord-tenant relations

(counting on her fingers she stops trying to remember.)

    section c26-105.2 city building code
    owner responsibility
    states rights
    the supreme court vs the people of georgia
    bet they wont even ask one question about that

(she walks back to her desk and picks up a large book from which she reads aloud.)

    the history of democratic law
    in the united states
    the formation of the constitution and
    colonization of the new world
    good   i know all that

wheres my notes on copyrighting?
what happen to those definitions i had?

*(she searches around the apt to find a small notebook under
the kitchen table.)*

there it is

(she sits on the floor reading aloud.)

law: a rule of conduct or action
prescribed or formally recognized as binding
or enforced by a controlling authority

(closing the book she closes her eyes and repeats it to herself.)

what they mean to say is controlling majority
they aint fooling me one bit
justice?   ha   control
and they expect me to help them do it
well they made a mistake this time
they let the wrong one in

(flipping through the notebook again reciting.)

the action of laws considered as a means
of redressing wrongs   ie litigation
more bullshit
lawful implies conformity
with law of any sort as in divine
canon or common
legitimate implies a legal right
derived from law often without a basis
in actual fact
or one supported by tradition
custom and accepted standards
of authenticity

(standing as she imagines she would before a court of law.)

therefore your honor
42 million people in this country
are illegitimate? is that a fact?
god dont like ugly your honor

what goes around comes around
momma always used to say

(she flippantly tosses the book across the room.)

something foul came out of there   .
beaucoup lies

(she goes into the bathroom and stares at herself in the mirror.)

wonder what momma and daddie doing?
they havent written in a while

(pointing at herself in mirror.)

neither have you

(picking at a pimple.)

oh jesus
i look like i been dragged
thru the valley of hell
by a bunch of carnivorous angels

(she quickly washes her face and brushes her hair.)

wheres the clock?
what day is it?
i gotta get out of here and get to class

(stopping at the refrigerator she takes out a small jar of pills.)

one more for the road jet
ought to keep you from falling asleep
right in the teachers face
ha

(she gulps it down with a swallow of orange juice as she puts the jar back closing the refrigerator.)

wheres the clock?

(she looks around but does not find it. she goes to the window and looks out.)

(mumbling she gathers several notebooks together and puts them in her pocketbook along with pencils and pens. she goes to the closet and takes her jacket searching the pockets for keys. finding them she puts the jacket on grabs her pocketbook and leaves locking the door. she arrives at class where a man is sitting at a too-small desk. he is dressed in a white tuxedo white shirt and bow tie and white shoes. his face is painted red and touches of white suggest a demonic expression. he wears a monocle on his right eye and there is a bright red line drawn from the beginning of his forehead down the back of his bald head to his neck. he is turning the pages of an invisible book and the light in the room is soft red. the PROFESSOR *is a man who carries himself as a member of the upper class would and he is in the habit of removing his monocle and squinting from time to time as he speaks.* JET *noisily comes in and sits in the back of the class as the distance between them is established.)*

JET. *(arranging herself.)*
    sorry im late please excuse me
    i tried to make it on time
PROFESSOR. *(collecting himself he looks up.)*
    i beg your pardon miss
    i am not here as you can see
    why are you?

(low carnival music is heard.)

JET.
    what?
    time for class
    i hate to be absent
    so visible
    im the only one of us here
    havent you noticed?

(taking out pen and notebook.)

    i know you have
    what page are we up to?

PROFESSOR. (*removing his monocle.*)
    you look tired miss
    have you been sleeping?

JET.
    sleeping makes me dream too heavy
    professor wane
    however i am prepared

(*standing she recites.*)

    the constitutional provision
    respecting copyright
    congress shall have the power to promote
    the progress of science and useful arts
    by securing for limited times to authors
    and inventors the exclusive right
    to their respective writing and discoveries
    united states constitution
    article 1 section 8

(*stepping away from her chair a few steps forward.*)

    professor the law is based on
    the intents of the *few* who know
    the nuances of the language
    it is my contention

(*he eyes her sternly as he has not given her permission to take these steps closer.* JET *realizes her transgression and returns to her original position.* PROFESSOR WANE *quite properly replaces his monocle as the carnival music stops.*)

PROFESSOR.
    oh no my dear oh no
    we are not here to reinterpret the law
    we are not interested in these revelations
    of yours

JET. (*still reciting.*)
    revelations   st john the divine
    which god gave unto him
    to shew unto his servants
    things which must shortly come to pass
    blessed is he that readeth
    and they that hear the words of this prophecy
    for the time *is* at hand

(there is the low buzzing sound of flies as the PROFESSOR *stares in disbelief.)*

PROFESSOR. *(opening his imaginary book he quickly flips the pages.)*
    your present state of mind lacks
    the dignity of a well trained student of law
    i strongly urge you to go home my dear
    i am home myself
    you can see   i am not here
    ha   haha   haha

(tucking his book under his arm he salutes her with his monocle in a quick and fancy gesture as he backs toward the full-length mirror. he points to it while speaking to her.)

    step inside the mirrors chamber

(waltzing near it.)

    and take the blues
    in the palm of your hand
    race across the beginning

*(*JET *watches him astonished as he does an exaggerated faggot-dance around the mirror.)*

    stop   maybe you can understand
JET.
    where was yesterday?
PROFESSOR. *(beside mirror.)*
    did it whistle thru your ear
    in a speeding song?
    are you there   are you gone
    cant you tell?

(the buzzing sound of flies fades to carnival music as the PROFESSOR *disappears behind the mirror.* JET *looks around the classroom, turning in different directions.)*

JET.
    where is everybody?
    this is the right room
    what day is it?

(putting her notebook and pen away.)

(the carnival music fades as offstage AXIS *is heard blowing his horn.* JET *wanders out of the class and into the street perplexed. the* CHOIR MEMBERS *including* MOMMA *and* DADDIE *and the* PROFESSOR *all appear in the street from Stage Left. they surround her in a circle. thru out this sequence* AXIS *is barely visible but his music is heard corresponding to drum music and cymbals and to the action of the scene. lights suggest early evening.)*

CHOIR MEMBERS. *(chanting as little children.)*
    little sally walker
    sitting in a saucer   why sally why
    wash your sleepy eye
    turn to the east   my darling
    turn to the west
    turn to the one that you like the best

(the CHOIR MEMBERS *hold hands and begin to sway/dance in place repeating their chant in a rhythm much faster.* JET *slowly responds to the pleasantness of the game. she tries to join the circle but is not permitted to.* AXIS'S *music fades and we see him as lights up on* LAVENDER *and him in the radio station getting up off the sofa. it is clear they have just finished making love and are rearranging their clothes in soft giggles and kisses. they embrace in a long passionate kiss as the action in the street continues.)*

CHOIR MEMBERS.
    turn to the east   my darling
REVEREND. *(laughing loud.)*
    ha ha ha   ha ha
CHOIR MEMBERS.
    turn to the west
REVEREND. *(louder.)*
    hahahahahahaha   haha
CHOIR MEMBERS.
    turn to the one that you like the best

(the REVEREND *laughs uncontrollably as lights dim in the radio station and* AXIS *takes up his horn and joins the street scene while* LAVENDER *fixes herself and primps before a small hand mirror.)*

turn to the one
turn to the one
that you like
the best   thebest   thebest
the best

(the CHOIR MEMBERS *all hurry off stage as* JET *stops spin-
ning around. she opens her eyes to find them gone. she
makes her way home visibly shaken, quickly looking over
her shoulder as she goes. she arrives at her apt door at the
same time* AXIS *does.)*

AXIS.
    hey fox   how you doing?
JET.
    i dont know
    i cant tell

*(she unlocks the door and lets him in. she drops her pock-
etbook to the floor and sinks in a kitchen chair.* AXIS *is
somewhat taken aback by the state of the apt. he clears a
space for himself on the couch-bed and sits down looking
over the disheveled room.)*

AXIS.
    damn baby
    you must really be putting your nose
    to the grind
    never seen your place look like this
JET.
    what time is it?
    you cant stay long
    im really not in the mood for company
AXIS.
    whats wrong with you   cold as ice?
JET.
    nothings wrong
AXIS.
    so why the attitude?
    i just came by to see how you was doing
    and maybe spend some time together

(he rises and moves toward her.)

JET.
> stay over there
> dont   come near me

AXIS.
> whats wrong with you?
> you sick or something?
> come on baby be serious
> grow up for once will you

(JET stares him down eye-to-eye and he retreats.)

> ok ok i wont touch you
> thats what you want isnt it?
> a man who wont need to touch you
> just stand around six feet away
> and admire your brains?
> your sweet nappy brains

(JET takes her jacket off and puts it away in the closet.)

JET.
> thats not what i want

AXIS.
> you dont know what you want
> a simple thing   a man and his woman
> but you make it so goddamn hard
> for us to be together
> why you try so hard to be so different
> from

JET. *(slamming the closet door.)*
> other women you know?

AXIS.
> yeah   thats right
> in all my twenty-eight years i aint never
> met one like you
> you
> never mind   skip it

(he sits down again and takes out a cigarette. looks around for a match.)

> got any matches?

(she goes to her desk and searches under papers to find a book of matches. she gives them to him and he lights his cigarette never once taking his eyes off her.)

aint no point in us kidding each other
things aint been good between us
and they aint getting better
maybe we need to put some distance
between us some breathing room   i mean
we need time to think about it all
i cant think in the city   no more
living in a basement

(a moment of silence passes between them.)

JET.
look axis
i know i havent

AXIS.
maxwell hooked up a couple of one-nighters
in chicago for our new band
a three-week engagement
possibly a month
leaving tomorrow
no telling what we might pick up from there
thats what i came by to tell you
im splitting

(crushes out cigarette in ashtray on coffee table.)

maybe when i get back

JET.
in other words
this is where we shake hands and say *ciao*?

AXIS.
if you want to put it that way
yeah

JET. *(standing.)*
who is it?

AXIS.
what?

JET.
who   is she?

AXIS.
>   oh come off it baby will you?
>   i dont have to go thru this
>   third-degree shit

JET.
>   you been seeing somebody else
>   behind my back
>   i can smell it

AXIS. (*trying to be calm.*)
>   jet
>   you sound like you getting ready to go off
>   on me and i dont want to deal with it
>   no more from you

JET. (*inching closer.*)
>   i bet you been sleeping with her
>   did you before you came waltzing over here
>   tonight? sweet talking and breathing hard
>   one minute and saying so long baby im
>   leaving the next

AXIS.
>   watch yourself
>   you dishing out more than
>   your ears can eat

JET. (*insistent.*)
>   you tell her the same things you tell me
>   when you fall on top of her at night?
>   groping for the wonderland
>   between her legs? do you?
>   do you make her feel like shes more
>   than a good piece of gimme-some-tonight
>   but i dont know if ill be around tomorrow?
>   dont count on me for nothing
>   sis   tah?

(they stand face-to-face confrontation and are nearly screaming at each other.)

AXIS.
>   i sure was wrong about you baby
>   you aint nothing but a goddamn kid
>   youre as far away from being a woman
>   as a pygmy is from heaven

JET.
>   do you pretend with her too?
>   huh axis?

do you tell her how you going to crack the world
open with that pawn-shop horn you stick
under your arm all the time?
or do you just leave the sound of your

*(she illustrates the following words in melodic voice and
quick body movements)*

mu   sic getting mol   dy
in her headlike stink leftovers
in the garbage can as you make it
to the next bed
do you tell her you love her too?

(AXIS *stares at her angrily and it is obvious that he is re-
straining himself from striking her.*)

AXIS.
yeah thats right   thats just what
i tell her and you know why?
because all *she* wants is somebody to love her
a minute of a night   an hour
she dont care   she knows a man needs a woman
to let him be
if hes going to survive balls intact
in this country
somewhere down the line a man in my family
was lynched   did they use a rope?
it dont matter he was the first eunuch
with a snapped neck
he gets to carry the dead weight of all the family
men before me   as far as im concerned
my father was the last one

(picking up his horn in a huff.)

im a whole man you hear me?
i dont take nothing from nobody
i love whoever i goddamn feel like it!

(he unlocks the door and goes out as LAVENDER *stands
about to knock.)*

LAVENDER. (*as he brushes past her.*)
    oh hello   what?
    whats going on?

(JET *angrily moves about the apt picking up papers and books as* LAVENDER *cautiously sits down at the kitchen table.*)

    how are you doing?

(*she takes out a pack of cigarettes. lighting one she places the pack on the table.*)

    tomorrows the big day   huh?

(JET *does not answer but continues what shes doing.*)

    well i just came by to tell you the good news
    i quit my job at the pink seagull

(*waits for* JET *to respond.*)

    finally got tired of it all you know?
    same old same old
    when the partys over everybody goes home
    to their somebody
    makes you stop and think

(*blowing smoke.*)

    im going to start acting again
    get my head together
    might turn out to be something
    never can tell

(*silence.*)

    listen i know its probably none of my business
    but is everything alright between you two?
JET. (*shuffling papers.*)
    no
    everything is *not* alright
LAVENDER. (*smoking as her eyes follow* JET.)
    whats up?

(she reaches for the ashtray on the coffee table.)

JET.
    my man axis has been sleeping
    with somebody else

LAVENDER.
    oh   really?
    did he
    say who?

JET.
    no but i know whoever she is
    she cant be no friend of mine
    she must be a real dog
    i dont have friends who would do this to me

(she sits opposite LAVENDER *at the table.)*

LAVENDER.
    do what?
    you cant expect   i mean
    its not a crime honey

JET. *(self-righteous.)*
    i dont go around sleeping with other womens
    men just for the hell of it

LAVENDER. *(pretending to be nonchalant.)*
    maybe she was in need
    i can understand that
    when the opportunity presents itself
    why not?   whats a little sport?

JET.
    she must be a first class whore

(they sit in a long silence looking away from each other.
LAVENDER *smokes her cigarette and absently taps her lighter*
on the table.)

LAVENDER. *(putting out her cigarette.)*
    am i?

JET.
    you   lavender??

LAVENDER. *(speaking quickly.)*
    listen honey
    it wasnt nothing to it   believe me
    he just needed somebody to fill his gap

it wasnt me he wanted
i could tell

(JET *rises from the table in a huff.*)

JET.
you got to be kidding me
LAVENDER.
didnt you hear what i said?
it wasnt me he wanted
JET.
we been friends for three years lavender
you been like my sister how could you?
i mean   you   me   and   and

(*picking up a pile of papers from the table she throws them across the room.*)

GODDAMN   GODDAMNIT!
the day i moved in this building

(*imitating* LAVENDERS *radio voice.*)

you said knock on your door   anytime
youd help me learn my way
said you always wanted a younger sister
this your idea of help?
sneaking upstairs on the elevator with axis?
LAVENDER. (*coldly offended.*)
i really dont see why
such a little bit of nothing
should make you so upset
JET. (*screaming.*)
youre the one who introduced us!
you brought him over here the same week
i moved in you said
he was a friend of yours from school days
way back when   ha!
LAVENDER. (*standing.*)
its too bad you cant understand nothing
but what you read in those books jet

(*putting away her cigarettes and lighter.*)

now you can deal with it like a woman
or you can do what little girls do
stand outside the closed door
and never have the nerve to face
what you might see behind
its something you got to earn honey
you dont get it just because your chest
was made to wear bras

(she moves to the door as JET *stands holding her head and turning away.)*

JET.
oh lord holy jesus
send me some angels
tell them to bring a miracle

(to LAVENDER.*)*

i thought you was in my corner
i thought you wanted to help me
LAVENDER.
i was   i did
but you can be pretty selfish
and im tired of you leaning on me
whining in my ear every time
you got a problem
how much of a friend was you to me?

(haughtily she unlocks the door.)

so from now on little sister
you can help yourself
dont bother to open the door honey
i can throw myself out

(she slams the door shut.)

JET.
GODDAMNIT
GODDAMN BOTH OF YALL
I DONT NEED NOTHING DRIVING ME CRAZY
SO JUST LEAVE ME ALONE!

(standing in the middle of the room, she looks around at the papers and books on the floor mumbling.)

>   leave me alone
>   leave me
>   jesus somebody please
>   everything is so mixed up
>   jesus

(holding her head.)

>   stop it   stop
>   please stop the tearing in my head
>   oh lord jesus
>   axis
>   lavender
>   please dont

(she sinks to the floor on her knees while holding her head.)

>   leave
>   hurt meeeeee

(a loud moaning scream escapes broken and long as lights up on the CHOIR MEMBERS in the bathroom joined by the PROFESSOR, AXIS and LAVENDER. they are all humming a slow gospel tune, which in time changes to a jazz rhythm. AXIS and LAVENDER are the only two not carrying bibles. all their faces are painted and each is painted a different color. LAVENDER is dressed in a "loose woman" fashion and AXIS is dressed as a ladies man. the PROFESSOR is dressed as before. the REVEREND kneels by the tub from which he extracts a chicken bleeding from the neck and the CHOIR MEMBERS come forth and make sounds as if to suck from its neck. this action is repeated once again in between the humming of their tune.)

>   my head
>   somebodys inside
>   growing
>   pulling out
>   everything i thought was true jesus
>   im not no sacrificial chicken
>   spirits watch over me

(she gets up slowly collecting papers and books and sits on the couch-bed collecting herself.)

im not no sacrificial chicken
spirits i have to be ready
give me what i need
for the morning

(lights down on CHOIR MEMBERS *as* JET *reads over her papers. lights in the apt suggest the passage of night into morning.* JET *changes her clothes gets herself ready and packs her pocketbook. she gives one last look around making sure she has not forgotten anything. she leaves locking the door and heads for the class/exam room. as she reaches the entranceway scene black.)*

THE END

Aishah Rahman

UNFINISHED WOMEN CRY IN NO MAN'S LAND WHILE A BIRD DIES IN A GILDED CAGE

Unfinished Women Cry in No Man's Land While a Bird Dies in a Gilded Cage is an underground classic. It reaches beyond statistics and sociological theories to find the unarticulated, half-understood longings of teenage mothers. Although the play has been well received in various community and university theatres around the country, it is well known only by a small network. The title implies the central conceit of the play: the juxtaposition of the Hide-A-Wee Home for Unwed Mothers (the unfinished women) and Pasha's boudoir, where Charlie Parker (the "Bird"), the brilliant black saxophonist of years past, spent his last days. Many types of girls find themselves in this home: the child of middle-class upbringing who got "caught"; the innocent who was raped; the savvy, street-smart girl who let the music make love to her, as well as the strict nurse who turned her illegitimate child into a "niece." Charlie Chan, that stereotype of Oriental inscrutability, presides over all, a comment on the power of images in our society.

The play focuses on that moment when the girls must decide whether to keep their babies or to give them up for adoption. Despite their fantasies of rescue by "caring" young fathers, they must decide alone. Meanwhile Bird slowly dies in the plush boudoir of his longtime mistress, trapped in a narcotic fog and the lost dreams of his exploited talent. The hauntingly beautiful sound of his saxophone is heard from offstage, occasionally representing the wail of a newborn baby. As relentless as labor pains, the play moves to its climax, forcing an untimely but necessary resolution to the guilt, uncertainty, fear, and pain of these women.

A news report of Bird's death sharply focuses the girls' fear and the enormity of the decision they must make.

Bird's tragic life and music become the metaphor for these girl-women; his notes alone make sense of their inner chaos and give expression to their needs. At the point of giving birth, one of the girls cries: "It's only in the head of a musician that I begin to understand. Only a musician can make sense for me. Only a musician knows how to connect shoes with cardboard to cover holes to P.S. 184 on 116th Street and Lenox Avenue to the red taste of watermelon and mocking white smiles to Anthony's smile and smell of Florida Water to late night loneliness and . . . this . . . [her unborn baby]." Only in the intangible plaint of music does she feel whole, does she begin to overcome her sense of isolation and connect the disparate parts of her life. Music winds its way throughout this drama, sometimes sung, sometimes instrumentalized, but always the language, the communicator. Lyrical and haunting, the play gives voice to the alienation of the young girl prematurely ejected into womanhood.

Aishah Rahman has found theatrical subject matter in famous black women as well as anonymous ones. *Lady Day: A Musical Tragedy* about Billie Holiday, was produced off-Broadway, as were *Transcendental Blues, The Lady and the Tramp*, and *The Tale of Madame Zora*. She is currently working on an opera based on the life of Marie Laveau. Ms. Rahman is an associate professor in the English Department of Nassau Community College in New York and is the director of the Playwrights Workshop at the New Federal Theatre.

Unfinished Women Cry in No Man's Land While a Bird Dies in a Gilded Cage

(A Play in 12 Scenes)

by
Aishah Rahman

Unfinished Women Cry in No Man's Land While a Bird Dies in a Gilded Cage was first originally produced by the New York Shakespeare Festival in June 1977 under the direction of Bill Duke with the cast listed below. (The play has also been produced at the New York University School of the Arts, California State University at Sacramento—University Theatre, and the Mobile Theater of the New York Shakespeare Festival.)

CAST

CHARLIE CHAN, MASTER OF CEREMONY—Kirk Kirksey
WILMA—Latanya Richardson
PAULETTE—Cheryl Tafathale Jones
CONSUELO—Socorro Santiago
MATTIE—Nikki Coleman
MIDGE—Terria Joseph
HEAD NURSE JACOBS—Rosanna Carter
CHARLES PARK, JR., MUSICIAN—Arthur Burghardt
PASHA, A EUROPEAN LADY—Le Clanche Du Rand
MUSICIANS—Sam Burtis, Al Harewood, Dona Summers, Christopher White
DIRECTOR—Bill Duke; Music by Stanley A. Cowell and Bill Duke; Lyrics by Aishah Rahman.
Stage Design by Linda Conaway; Costumes by Judy Dearing; Lighting by Curt Ostermann; Musical Direction by Dona Summers.

AUTHOR'S NOTES

Stylistically, the presentation of this play should be in keeping with Charlie Parker's music. Bird was a genius at improvisation, and harmonically, he would superimpose on certain *fundamental* notes which created polytones. Rhythmically, he would create an opposition of on- and offbeat accentuations and obtain the effect of two streams of rhythms called polyrhythms. Likewise, two streams of consciousness is what I'm aiming for here. The two settings, Hide-A-Wee Home for Unwed Mothers and Pasha's boudoir, should be interplayed and intraplayed with the dramatic image of Bird and Bird's music being the fundamental notes with which both parts bounce off on creating tensions between them while at the same time weaving the seemingly disconnected parts into one "polydrama."

Although a real musician is used as a metaphor, the real is only a takeoff point for the imagination, so please, no imitations of Charlie Parker. The actor who plays Parker should never put a sax to his lips. *A saxophone player offstage who is never seen* must play all the sax music. In order to sustain the metaphor *of birth and art, Consuelo's baby's cry must always be a note from the sax*. It is important to note that tape will not substitute for a live musician in this case because of the urgency and constant playing required of the musician.

MUSICAL NUMBERS

"Charlie Parker Done Died Today" ..... Charlie Chan
"Foolish Women, Wake Up!" .... Nurse Jacobs
"Do You Really Think You Have to Re-
   mind Us?" .... Paulette
"I Tol' You My Mother is From Puerto
   Rico" .... Consuelo
"Your Baby's Awake Again" .... Nurse Jacobs
"Oh Lovely Music Man" .... Wilma
"Beware of Young Men" .... Midge
"Today! What a Beautiful Day" .... Charlie Parker
"A Musician Is Neither a Soldier" .... Pasha

CHARACTERS

CHARLIE CHAN, MASTER OF CEREMONY
WILMA*
PAULETTE*
CONSUELO
MATTIE*
MIDGE*
HEAD NURSE JACOBS
CHARLES PARKER, JR., MUSICIAN
PASHA, A EUROPEAN LADY

Time: 1955
Place: Hide-A-Wee Home for Unwed Mothers
         & Pasha's Boudoir

* All the girls except Consuelo are
   in the last stages of pregnancy.

OVERTURE

A set that represents Hide-A-Wee Home for Unwed Mothers and PASHA's *boudoir. The underlying theme is stark vs. lush and plush. It is an old mansion that is now used as a haven for unwed mothers. Some touches of past grandeur— an ornate chandelier, perhaps a grandfather's clock which never works and has to be manually adjusted to the correct time. Top floors contain the* GIRL's *room. Ground floor is the living room. The house contains a circular staircase. At Extreme Right is a balcony which is the entrance and exit to* PASHA's *boudoir. A lush fragrant love bower.*

AT RISE: *The* GIRLS *are silhouetted in their rooms.* PARKER *and* PASHA *are silhouetted in the boudoir.* CHARLIE CHAN *enters. He is a black man in blackface, a minstrel who acts as Master of Ceremony, commenting between the scenes, always remaining outside of the drama. He is a magic mimetic man. Because he is* PARKER's *alter ego, he should be dressed exactly like* PARKER *except where* PARKER *is impeccably dressed,* CHAN *is ill fitted and tattered. He is wearing a tattered tuxedo, homburg, white gloves.*

CHARLIE CHAN. Ladies and gentlemen . . . Presenting . . . *Unfinished Women Cry in No Man's Land While a Bird Dies in a Gilded Cage* . . . A Polydrama. Dramatis Personae . . . The Innocents . . . WILMA . . . A Black Gal in Conflict ... . PAULETTE . . . Who is Upward Bound . . . CONSUELO . . . A Castilian Puerto Rican . . . MATTIE . . . A Victim . . . MIDGE . . . All-American . . . HEAD NURSE JACOBS . . . CHARLES PARKER, JR., A great Musician and his PASHA . . . a Rich European Lady and . . . yours truly, CHARLIE CHAN, the Invisible Man. Ladies and gentlemen . . . for your entertainment . . . A song of Mourning.
    Charlie Parker done died today
    Charlie Parker done died today
    Charlie Parker done died today

(Piano begins to play a lush romantic tune.)

Lovely tune, isn't it? Let's return to a memory. Think of time as a circle going round and round beginning at this place or any other place where we *think* we began. Where is the past? Up? Down? I wish to relate to you the circumstances of Birth, Death, Musicians and Women on the day that Charlie Parker died. Memory is *not* spontaneous. It is the mind, rooting the soul for self-forgiveness. While they are in this place . . . this home for unwed mothers . . . listening to Bird's music being touched by his sound without understanding the man behind the music . . . without understanding any man because they are from a female world where men are frightening and fascinating, shadowy and intangible, not to be understood, only loved, Bird is dying . . . no, not dying, but disintegrating into pure sound . . . breaking open the shell of life that contained him. Time . . . 8:45 A.M. March 12, 1955. Place . . . Hide-a-Wee Home for Unwed Mothers and Pasha's boudoir. What is the connection between the two events? Simply that it all happened at the same moment. Time stands still. It is only we who are driven in distorted circles and only those of us who have chewed water know it has bones!

ENTIRE CAST.
So part of what I offer you is Fantasy
And part of what I offer you is true
Which is which
Which is which
Is up to you!

SCENE 1

Hide-A-Wee Home for Unwed Mothers. CHAN *is an ever-present hovering spirit, reacting to the interplay of characters even though he is invisible to them. He is fixing the hands of the broken grandfather clock as* NURSE JACOBS *enters.*

NURSE JACOBS. *(Singing.)*
Foolish Women, wake up!
Don't you know what day this is?

What are you . . . deaf in one ear and can't hear out
the other?
Don't you know nothing comes to a sleeper but a
dream?
Better wake up and stop dreaming about the men
Who cast their love like a net, trapped you and disappeared!

(*The* GIRLS *sleepily emerge from their rooms.*)

MIDGE. Why all this noise in the middle of the night. I'm
in a loon house. If I stay here any longer, I'll go out of
my mind.
NURSE JACOBS. Oh pardon. . . . How rude of me to interfere with mademoiselle's repose but let me remind
her highness that she is not at a ritzy resort but at Hide-
A-Wee Home for Unwed Mothers and that it's time to
wake up, wash down and weigh in.
MIDGE. Oh well, a home is not a haven I always say . . .
or even a peaceful hideout.
NURSE JACOBS. (*Taking a head count . . . dispensing towels,
etc.*) Where is Mattie? She still with us? Nobody went
over during the night. Did they?
MIDGE. That's right. Nobody's water broke . . . no babies
murdered into this world. What a dull night!

(*A thin wailing mournful cry like a baby's is played on the
sax.*)

WILMA. Just a crying baby who never sleeps. (*Pokes* CON-
SUELO.) Hey, Connie.
CONSUELO. I told you and I told you. . . . My name is not
Connie. It is Consuelo. Consuelo Maria Maldonando
Harris.
WILMA. Harris? Since when the Harris?
CONSUELO. That's what it will be when my boyfriend comes.
We're going to get married.
WILMA. I tell you, Jim, the bed is the great equalizer.
Don't you know the black boys and the white boys all
hand out the same shit. All right. All right. "Consuelo
Maria Maldonando when my boyfriend comes we're going
to get married Harris." How come I have to have the
room next to you . . . the only girl in the house with a
baby. . . . Can't you do something about that baby of

yours hollering all night long. . . . God! I HATE babies!

NURSE JACOBS. Wilma!

WILMA. I mean I hate the noise they make.

CONSUELO. You won't have to worry about me much longer. My boyfriend is coming for me and the baby today and we're leaving!

PAULETTE. Ha! I hope he does come . . . I really do . . .

WILMA. Hey . . . did anybody hear the news? Charlie Parker died today.

NURSE JACOBS. You have serious things to think about. Today is the day. The day when you have to make a decision about what to do about them babies. So . . .

PAULETTE. (*Singing.*)
Do you really think that you have to remind us what today is?
Just in case you haven't heard
There is a world outside this dump!
Ever since I been in college, I been listening to jazz!
Eric Dolphy, MJQ
And my boyfriend who is going to be a lawyer
Listens to Charlie Parker all the time!

WILMA. (*Mimicking.*) "My boyfriend is going to be a lawyer and he listens to Charlie Parker all the time." I always knew you were an asshole.

PAULETTE. Now you just wait a minute . . .

(MATTIE *slowly emerges from her room. She is younger than the rest but she is tougher. She pops gum, rolls her eyes and is generally "bad." She shifts between saccharin sweetness and quick-as-a-flash anger, but the hostility and toughness is always underneath.*)

MATTIE. Good morning, everybody.

ALL THE GIRLS. (*Mocking her.*) "Good morning, everybody."

MATTIE. (*Hissing at them.*) Shit! Goddam shit. (*Walks over to* NURSE JACOBS *and sulks.*)

WILMA. Hey, Paulette, honey . . . what you doing in a place like this, huh? Slumming? I thought College Queens like you didn't get caught.

PAULETTE. Sugar, I know my brains and looks are a threat to you. I understand the hostility your type feels toward me, but let's try to get along!

WILMA. Aw, love . . . you know . . . your daddy likes my

type. Ask him. Who you think I got inside this belly. It's your brother, bitch!

ALL THE GIRLS. oooooooooOOOOOSOUND! I wouldn't take that!

NURSE JACOBS. Stop it. . . . Stop it, I say.

MATTIE. Don't start again. I don't like it when you fight!

WILMA. Look, Mattie. I'm jumpy today. Don't you know wha's happening? Don't you know what day it is?

MATTIE. Of course I do. What do you think, I'm crazy? Still . . . I like it here.

NURSE JACOBS. Poor lamb . . . it was against her will . . . at least her conscience is clear.

PAULETTE. Her conscience may be clear but her belly isn't. It's full of a baby just like the rest of us.

NURSE JACOBS. It's not the same . . . the rest of you consciously sinned . . .

MIDGE. Love, Nurse Jacobs, is not a sin. . . . It's the most religious act there is.

NURSE JACOBS. Not in my church. . . . You're only supposed to do it to get a family. It's a sin to do it for fun and now you all have this sin on your records.

CONSUELO. I'm telling them I'm keeping my baby. Just like our Holy Virgin . . . Jesus' mother did.

NURSE JACOBS. Watch it about Jesus. . . . He's only trying to teach you girls a lesson.)

WILMA. (*To* CONSUELO.) The only reason why you want your baby is because he looks white like his father and not like a Puerto Rican which is what you are!

CONSUELO. (*Singing.*)

I tol' you, my mother is from Puerto Rico
But my father, he is from Spain.
He is Castilian from Madrid.
And you don't know how *Spanish* people are.
My father, he will kill him if he doesn't marry me.
Because he was the first.
My father, he knows I was a virgin!

MIDGE. It was the first time for all of us. The first time we got caught. That's why we're in this place. They only allow you one mistake. They don't let you back here a second time.

MATTIE. What are we going to do? What are we going to tell them today? When we go downstairs what are we going to do? What are we going to tell them?

MIDGE. Hey hey hey! This day is just like any other to

me. I think I'll play a set of tennis in the morning . . . lunch on the Riviera in the afternoon and dance a wild flamenco in Spain this evening. Oh . . . I don't know . . . to tell you the truth I haven't thought much about it.

WILMA. (*To* MIDGE.) You don't have to give yours up.

MIDGE. I told you, I don't know.

PAULETTE. Oh Midge, you'll probably sign adoption papers today. White girls always do.

MIDGE. Oh . . . I don't know about all that.

WILMA. (*To* PAULETTE.) So what. . . . You're planning to do the same thing. . . . Give up your baby. . . . Does that make you a white girl too?

PAULETTE. All right . . . get off my back . . .

WILMA. I'm just trying to understand how you can be so calm about it . . .

PAULETTE. I see your kind every day, shuffling down the street in bobby sox and two-piece maternity dress, pushing a baby carriage in one hand and a can of beer in the other. My mind is made up. Nobody knows I'm here and no one will ever know. When I leave here it will be just like this place never happened to me and if we should meet on the street just remember to pass me by!

WILMA. What's his name?

PAULETTE. Who?

WILMA. Your lawyer dude . . . the one who digs on Charlie Parker. . . . Your F.O.B. Your Father of Baby?

PAULETTE. His name is Mind Your Own Business.

WILMA. Aw come on . . . don't hide it . . . divide it. . . . Tell us his name. . . . We're all in the same boat paddling down the same river so—

PAULETTE. I could never be like you. You have no class.

WILMA. Pregnant whore.

PAULETTE. Knocked up cow!

WILMA. (*Going toward* PAULETTE *menacingly*.) Ain't you a bodacious bitch. . . . Break bad if . . .

CONSUELO. (*Yelling over their voices*.) I CAN'T hear ANYTHING! (*Then very softly*.) My baby is upstairs. I have to listen in case he cries for me . . . and with all this noise I won't be able to hear when his father comes for me. . . . I can't hear if he rings the door bell or the telephone . . . or he might stand outside and call "Consuelllooooooo, I'm here."

CHARLIE CHAN. (*From the shadows*.) The music world is

still in a state of shock as the news of Charlie Parker's death spread like wildfire. Many of Parker's friends refused to believe it, saying it was only another wild rumor being spread about the legendary Bird.

WILMA. (*Putting her arms around* CONSUELO.) Damn you, Charlie Parker. . . . Today I need you much more than I need your music . . . I was with you when you walked into oceans with your clothes on . . . I wrote love letters to myself and signed them "Bird" and even though I love your music. . . . It's you . . . the MAN that I need. YOU HEAR ME, CHARLIE PARKER. . . . WE NEED YOU!

SCENE 2

PASHA's *boudoir. The omnipresent* CHAN *steps out of the shadows and busies himself setting flowers, dusting and generally setting the scene as* PARKER *enters Upstage. He is intense, a tightly strung instrument, taut and vibrating constantly. There is enough passion in him to give one the feeling of overwhelming strength. Yet his eyes reveal a tender man . . . his physical aura one of intense fire that is burning out. Both bombastic and inward, low-down, funky, yet poetical, intellectual, he has come to* PASHA's *boudoir to die.* PARKER *enters, looks at* PASHA, *lies on her bed without removing his shoes.*

PASHA *is seated, busily tatting. She is old, or better yet, ageless. She is sinister and has a hint of past sensuousness. She is out looking in an old European rich way. One feels the wildness within her which constantly threatens to consume her.*

PASHA.
Ce jardin est rempli de mémoires
Tu m'as marqué avec des piqûres
Comme une abeille passionée qui pique
On dit que tu sois un scorpion de miel

CHARLIE CHAN.
This garden is full of memories
You have left bites on me
Like a stinging scorpion of passion

PARKER.
They say you are a honey bee

Sticking to the flower till it is sucked dry.

PASHA. (*Turning to him angrily.*) Charles, I have wasted my youth, wondering where you are. I sent my servant, scouring the city, searching for you, combing the streets. I have been reduced to leaving messages for you in clubs.

(PARKER *is silently picking a flower from her hair and eating it.*)

PASHA. (*Laughing gaily.*) I see what kind of day this will be. Let's celebrate. We have gin and Bartok . . . what else do we need?

(*Music: A Bartok chorale ever so lightly underneath.*)

CHAN/PARKER. Do you see someone?

PASHA. I have these godawful nights. . . . I am lonely at night without you. Let the night get some rest . . . I know . . . we'll celebrate (*Drinking the gin glass empty.*) this empty glass of gin . . .
　　O! thou round and fragile goblet
　　Thou are more beautiful
　　Than the gin you once contained

(PARKER *attempts to slap* PASHA; *she recoils from him, protecting her face coquettishly.*)

Nooooo. It's crystal. . . . Been in the family for generations. Are you going to beat me . . . ? You're so melodramatic. None of the shadings, the subtleties for you. The trouble with you, my flamboyant, intriguing, devilish madman, is that you never want to sleep. You really must take care of yourself.

PARKER. Zookeeper, I am me. I drink too much, smoke too much, dope too much, fuck too much. Women, that is. I can't stand the smell of men.

PASHA. Where's your wife?

CHAN. (*Answering for* PARKER.) She couldn't take it. . . . She went off.

PASHA. Off where?

PARKER. How the fuck am I supposed to know? She just evaporated like all frail things. Get out!

PASHA. (*Realizing he is ill, going toward him.*) Lie down, baby, I'll call my doctor.

PARKER. (*Pushes her away.*) Why? Does he know where my wife is? I didn't send for you. Get the fuck out of my house.

PASHA. (*Resuming tatting.*) I ain't leaving. I live here . . . remember? Lace. . . . I'm weaving some lace and then I'll fashion a handkerchief from it. After all, every gentleman of color should have a lace mouchoir.

PARKER. (*Caught in a spasm of violent coughing.*) Damn! I sure used up this motherfucker. I might not make the gig.

(PASHA *goes toward him again. He pushes her away.*)

No, please. I came here because you're good for me. You give me what I need and some of what I don't.

(PASHA *begins to sway and dance seductively for him.* PARKER *continues.*)

You are so relaxed, so cool. I like your looseness. It must come from being rich.

PASHA. (*Still dancing.*) Did you know that there aren't too many women who are into jazz. All they want to know is money. But if a man is a serious-minded musician . . . he's got to have time and space to think . . . and he needs a woman like me . . . don't you agree?

PARKER. Fuck you, Pasha! I want a glass of gin!

(PASHA *slowly pours a drink and offers it to* PARKER. *He looks at the drink a long time and slowly pushes her hand away. She immediately understands that it is more than a rejection of the drink but of herself. She furiously takes up her tatting.*)

PASHA. Our child. . . . I'll make us our child.

PARKER. PASHA!

PASHA. Here's the head . . . two holes for the eyes . . .

PARKER. Stop it!

PASHA. (*Tatting furiously.*) Some lungs. Lungs for our child to breathe.

(PARKER *lunges toward her tatting;* PASHA *swiftly moves it deftly out of his reach.*)

No! I will not let you kill this one!

PARKER. You're a witch!

PASHA. (*Holding the tatting, caressing it.*) It's my baby. My
dream. The child that I want. I will make it come true.

PARKER. You are evil.

PASHA. I'm not evil. Why am I left alone night after night
like some dried-up tree? We could have a child if you
would touch me and hold me. Why don't you treat me
like a woman?

PARKER. (*Slowly going toward her.*) Oh for God's sake.
. . . Not now . . . please . . . it's much too late. I came
here because I need a friend. Nooo, you are much more
than that. I came here because I need someone . . . who
loves me and that's all. No needs. Just love. . . . You
do love me, don't you? Pasha. . . . Don't destroy me
with whatever I happen to leave laying around of myself.

PASHA. (*Slowly dropping her tatting to the floor.*) Charles.
. . . Don't be foolish.

SCENE 3

Hide-a-Wee. ALL THE GIRLS *are gathered for daily exam-
ination.*

NURSE JACOBS. (*Examining* MATTIE.) Just what I sus-
pected! You're gaining too much weight. Too much salt.
Lord, today. . . . You're swollen and probably toxic.

PAULETTE. I told you not to eat that whole jar of pickles.

MATTIE. I like 'em.

(ALL THE GIRLS *laugh uproariously.*)

NURSE JACOBS. You think it's funny, don't you. You think
it's funny if she gorges herself with salt and swells up
like a balloon. All right. Everybody off salt.

ALL THE GIRLS. What!

NURSE JACOBS. No more salt on the table. No salt in the
crackers. No salt in the ocean and no salt in your tears.
No more salt, I say! Don't you know it's a mortal sin if
you harm your babies?

CONSUELO. Ay, ay, ay . . . no salt . . . just because of one
person?

NURSE JACOBS. You are your sister's keeper. Especially Mattie.

WILMA. Don't let Mattie fool you. She can take care of herself.

(MATTIE *laughs*.)

NURSE JACOBS. Mattie isn't the only one. After I gave strict orders for your diets, I've seen you sneak french fries and salted peanuts. I think you are purposely trying to cross God by harming your babies. . . . No salt for anyone, I say. . . . Now! You see the shame and burden loose ways bring upon a girl . . . it don't pay to be worthless!

ALL THE GIRLS. (*Chanting and dancing mockingly*.)
    I got it.
    It's in my bed.
    A loaf of bread.
    I got it.
    It's in my stomach.
    I want to vomit.
    I got it.
    You know I got it.
    It's in my booty.
    Tutti Frutti!

NURSE JACOBS. Stop it. Stop this nastiness, I say!

WILMA. Nurse J. . . . Is it true you still a virgin?

(*General laughter*.)

NURSE JACOBS. Is a rudeness you have, talking to me so. Dog my age ain't no pup, you know.

WILMA. I was just wondering if you made of stone . . . that's all. No offense.

NURSE JACOBS. I ain't studying myself with the niggers of this world. Besides, I have God and my Bible!

WILMA. You still a woman . . . and a human being. Every human has feelings. Every woman is flesh.

NURSE JACOBS. See what your flesh and feeling reaped. It ain't *me* having to hide away shame to face people. Now hear me right. I ain't say I not looking for someone suitable. When I finish raising up my niece I hoping to meet some nice retired old gentleman with a nice pension who ain't looking for bed companion and want someone to fetch him a glass of water in his old age. Perhaps me and him could come to an understanding . . .

(ALL THE GIRLS *laugh*.)

Shhhh, hurry up, hurry up. Time is flying and fate will not be kept waiting today. You all know what has to be done. Papers have to be signed. Adoption forms have to be filled out.

CONSUELO. No!

NURSE JACOBS. Look. . . . I just trying to do my job. You from this country, you don't understand. Back home there ain't nothing to do. Here, I take up nurse aid and graduate to head nurse. I happy to be working in this country and I just trying to do my job. So hurry up!

MATTIE. Admit it, Nurse Jacobs . . . you hate all of us.

NURSE JACOBS. Not so, precious lamb. That ain't the truth at all. Don't you know I think of you all as my own daughters?

MATTIE. I don't know nothing except this baby is in my belly and gonna come out my pussy with blood and piss and shit. I'm scared.

MIDGE. Nothing to it, sugar, nothing to it. We're just wonderful vessels of creation for the Lord!

(*Suddenly the wailing cry of the sax.*)

CONSUELO. My baby!

NURSE JACOBS. Your baby's awake again. Consuelo . . . go see to your son. I bet he knows the seriousness of this day.

(GIRLS *and* CONSUELO *laugh defiantly*.)

Laugh, go ahead . . . but remember . . . God is strict, very strict. And before this day is over, I bet you all gonna be laughing on the other side of your faces.

SCENE 4

NURSE JACOBS *is alone onstage*.

NURSE JACOBS. (*To audience.*) I been through this day a hundred times . . . watching hundreds of girls go downstairs and make their decisions to give up their babies or . . . whatever. And I still can't . . . still can't help remembering. Yes! I had a man once. Is Gospel! He broke holes in the air with his laughter! Big-time Calypsonian. Playing from island to island. He, writing me all the time these love letters: "Darlin' . . . I lonely for you. Your heart in front of my eyes all the time. Take care of our green baby growin' inside of you, sweetheart. I missing you in that certain way." Sweet, sweet words. I getting bigger and bigger and happier and happier. I didn't have no shame *then*, only love. I getting ready the marrying things, the white dress, veil, even the eats and drinks and then . . . nothing . . . no sweet words . . . no promises . . . nothing. Nothing slowly stretches into nothing. Saviour in heaven . . . you forgive Mary Magdalene so why not me? I paid my penance for my hour of passion. I work hard . . . keep man outta my life and raise my . . . my . . . "niece." (*Angrily.*) Yes . . . Yes . . . I calling me own *daughter* my niece. You don't understand. Back home we don't have places like this. A girl in trouble has to make her own arrangements. I went to another island . . . bought myself a wedding ring and gave birth to my "niece." It's been hard . . . all these years . . . keeping my daughter a secret . . . raising up me "niece" by myself . . . But I hanging on. . . . Praise God. . . . I hanging on!

SCENE 5

PASHA's *boudoir. As usual* CHAN *watches in the shadows, only emerging to play the servant.*

PASHA. There is no force like desire. It gets rooted in the blood and runs wild. Burning you up! I want my youth. . . . My youth, Parker. . . . I'll tat my youth again . . . then you will look at your Pasha . . . with desire.

PARKER. I dreamed of a giant bird with wings so big they spread out against the sky and blocked out the sun. The bird had a man's face and was really half God and half Man with wings. But the two halves were fighting each other to death. Biting and killing each other right there in the middle of space . . . screeching across the bleeding sky. And it was only when the bird, man god, the whole thing when it would fall to earth and be born again as an ordinary person . . . only then would the sun be able to shine again.

PASHA. Do you ever dream of me?

PARKER. I don't know, Pasha—maybe. . . . But I dream that I am a musician, with money, power, luxury that I earned because of my great music without a boss . . . without anyone to make fun of me or bring me down . . . I give you my dreams as a gift.

(PASHA *holds a golden spoon of drugs under his nose.*)

Tat me a womb, Pasha . . . not attached to any body . . . just some unattached place for me to lay my head. You can do it. You can do anything . . .

PASHA. (*Sarcastically.*) You mean . . . I can give you anything.

PARKER. Yes, you are rich.

PASHA. Yes. I am rich. And wallowing in poverty. Give me a child.

(PARKER *takes the golden spoon.* PASHA *knocks the spoon from his hand.*)

I'm sick of drugs, booze, jazz, all of it. I'm a WOMAN.

PARKER. GET AWAY!

PASHA. Don't push me away . . . LOVE ME.

PARKER. (*Knocking her down.*) BLOODSUCKER! Get the hell away from me!

PASHA. Nigger! You owe me something! I've invested everything I believe in you!

PARKER. You. You don't love me. . . . You want to use me. You want to own me! You want to control me. You want to destroy me.

PASHA. Destroy you? Me? Uh uh, baby. I'm the one that always bails you out. I'm the one that saves your ass! You the one. Don't pull that shit on me. You are the dude that wants to die and is always busy killing himself. I want you to live.

PARKER. (*Laughing sarcastically.*) I can dig it . . . but don't you worry about me killing myself. I'm merely on a path to the sublime. . . . But what would you know about that. . . . You're not a musician. . . . You are just a shell . . . waiting to be filled up . . . (*Falls back exhausted.*)

PASHA. (*Cradling his head.*) Waiting . . . yes, waiting to be filled by you. What's so wrong about that? Just because I want to be a part of you and your music . . . a part of its creation. Don't put me down. Please.

PARKER. I want to separate myself from you and all that ties me to this earth. There is one perfect note. Too perfect for human ears. Yet, *I* keep on hearing it all the time. And when I do every cell of my body wants to break up into tiny parts of that one perfect musical note and float on the ear of every living soul. WHAT A SONG. WHAT A PERFECT COSMIC MELODY I WOULD BE AT THAT MOMENT! Goddam. GET ME MY DRUGS!

PASHA. Why do you put so much effort into being insane?

PARKER. We don't understand each other. We belong in two different worlds.

PASHA. But we're both trapped in this one so would you try not to hate me so much.

PARKER. Me? I love you.

PASHA. You're making fun of me.

PARKER. It's true . . . I do . . . I love your passion for jazz . . . a language you don't understand.

PASHA. I don't understand? Really, Bird. . . . Sometimes you talk to me as if I'm unintelligent.

PARKER. (*Slowly as if teaching a child.*) It's not a question of intelligence. It's a matter of feeling. Of being able to operate *in* things and not *from* things. I'm trying to communicate *feelings*, baby, not *knowledge*.

PASHA. (*Shaking her head in agreement.*) I understand.

PARKER. Do you? Do you really? Who are you? Who do you think I am?

PASHA. Who am I? I am the farmer. You are the seed. I am the farmer that nurtures the seed. You are the genius but I am the power.

PARKER. You . . . are . . . a ho . . . baby. That's all. Clear and Simple. A ho.

PASHA. (*Matter-of-factly correcting his pronounciation.*) A whore . . . not ho. (*Spelling it out.*) W-h-o-r-e!

(*They both laugh.*)

PARKER. When a man loves a woman, he may beat on her, pee on her, adore her, spit on her, cry at the sight of her, torture her, kiss all her toes. When a woman loves a man, she simply wants to become his whore.

PASHA. Why do I have to be whore or saint? Can't I just be ordinary?

PARKER. You're right. You can afford to be ordinary.

PASHA. Damn right, I'm ordinary. Most of my life has been spent doing nothing and being generally in the way. I was bored before. (*Throwing her head back, laughing.*) Did you know that my family owned the original land grant to Manhattan?

PARKER. You mean before the Indians? Damn!

PASHA. You see, darling. We're made for each other. You're a legend. So am I.

PASHA/PARKER/CHAN. (*In unison.*) As one legend said to the other: Shut up and let's get high.

SCENE 6

Hide-A-Wee. WILMA *enters. She is alone Onstage.*

WILMA. (*To audience.*) You know, I first dug Bird 'cause everybody was into him and used to talk about him all the time. Then when I really listened to him. . . . Dudes 'round my way would only take their special woman to dig Bird with. I went down to Birdland one night and everybody was waiting for him and when he finally showed he looked like he slept under the bandstand and hadn't shaved for weeks. I never saw anything like that and I never heard anything like his music. Charlie Parker played in tongues . . . I don't want to give up my baby, but . . . I know that it's a boy in here. S'funny what Bird meant to me. Secretly, I always wanted to be a man 'cause they can do things and go places. Bird is the man I wanted to be. Maybe my son will be like him. Dig that. Maybe I'm giving up a Charlie Parker. Maybe I'm thinking about giving up a Charlie Parker. The baby's father? He's just someone I met at a dance. Tall, dark and good-looking. And I liked the way his smile tasted in my mouth. Anthony. He smiled at me and I smiled back and we wanted each other. He's just a man I gave myself to and I can't blame him for anything. Really.

But I do because I'm here and he's . . . (*Shrugging her shoulders helplessly.*) You know what this is? (*Puts her hands on her stomach.*) It's a curse . . . it got my mother and now it's got me . . . fatherless child, manless woman, it's deep, it's always there waiting no matter how you try to escape. I watched it pick us off like typhoid, one by one. We knew a girl had caught it when her belly got bigger and bigger and her eyes took on a certain feverish look and everybody wondered who's next . . . who's next . . . and now it's my turn . . .

(*Music up.*)

In Anthony's room, in his bed, lying there on my back, I could feel myself far below him, I was on the bottom of an ocean and he was the moon way up over me. A moon I could smell, a moon I could touch but whose face floated in and out of my mind. His body was spread all over, covering me like space. I crouched inside of myself, listening like an animal to our silence. Then, slowly floating in through the open window, very faint at first . . . the sound of Bird's horn . . . tugging at me, taking me back to a memory I was born with. Following the music's heartbeat I took a journey I could no longer avoid and along the way I helped a woman toss her newborn baby overboard a slaveship. I joined hands with my mother as she took *her* mother's hand and I took my place in the circle of black women singing old blues. The man, spread high above me, worked over me, his sweat dripping down in my eyes and my voice screaming higher and higher along with Parker's sax . . . both sounds pouring over me, pulling me, pushing me to a point of passion, a point of pain and then . . . silence . . . and the smell of the rain falling outside as he breaks into my womb and bursts inside of me, over-flowing on the sheets and bed and everything and I knew that the cycle of passion and pain, blood and birth, and aloneness had once again started, inside of me and I lay there wondering how many moons before I could become virgin again!

(*Music up as she listens for a few beats.*)

Hear that? He's not dead. Bird lives . . . Inside here. (*Embracing her stomach.*) Bird's alive. . . . Oh yes, he's alive. (*Bursting into song.*)

    O lovely music man
    women want you for your energy.
    Many love you for your song.
    The whole universe
    swings to your melodies.
    And everybody will listen
    when I shout . . . Bird lives, Bird Lives, Bird Lives!

SCENE 7

Hide-A-Wee. ALL THE GIRLS *are present except Wilma. They are clowning it up.*

ALL THE GIRLS. (*Chanting a 1950s hit.*)
    Earth Angel, Earth Angel
    Will you be mine.
    My darlin' dear
    Love you all the time.
    I'm just a fool
    Just a fool in love.

MIDGE. All right, all right. . . . It's your roving reporter. Tell me, dear. How did you happen to get here?

MATTIE. (*Speaking seductively . . . like a whore talking to a prospective john.*) Psst! Come here . . . I was framed . . . know what I mean . . . I really was. I did it to (*Counting fast on her fingers.*) ten boys including my brother and first cousin and been in love with all of them, you know what I mean. Then one night I ate this really sweet red juicy watermelon . . . know what I mean? But I swallowed some seeds by mistake . . . you know how you do when you eat watermelon and it's so good and cold and juicy you just want to swallow it all and you don't have time to separate the seeds from the juice so I just swallowed it all and next morning I awake and pffft . . . just like that . . . That's why you should always chew your food and spit out the seeds and bones and things like that. Know what I mean?

MIDGE. I said my name is Purity and I am twin sister to the Virgin Mary. I too have been visited by a holy ghost and I shall bring forth a son which shall be called UN-BELIEVABLE.

(*All laugh as* NURSE JACOBS *enters.*)

NURSE JACOBS. Would you look at this. I don't believe my two eyeholes. Time done run out and you still cutting the fool.

(*Music: a long lone cry on the saxophone as* NURSE JACOBS *continues.*)

Consuelo . . . go to your room. Your baby needs changing! Wilma! Paulette! You better go watch Consuelo diaper her baby so you can learn how to be mothers.

PAULETTE. (*Yelling Off-stage.*) I am not going to be a mother. I'm not even going to see my baby.

NURSE JACOBS. You all will see your babies. Maybe now you realize this ain't no joke—ha! (*She exits.*)

MIDGE. None of us had to be here . . . I mean we all could be on the outside now. . . . So we got caught . . . why didn't we get rid of it? I mean . . . why didn't any of us have an abortion?

(*Meanwhile the sax has become more insistent as if to pull* CONSUELO *upstairs. She slowly works her way toward exit while talking.*)

CONSUELO. Shh! Don't say such a thing. Don't you know it's a sin even to talk that way?

MATTIE. My social worker said the state would get me one if I could prove I was raped like I said. Shit! how can I prove that?

CONSUELO. I'd rather go through all this than die on some butcher's table or go to jail. Besides where would I get the money for one anyhow?

MIDGE. I guess underneath I was saying to myself: If I can't have him . . . (*Shrugs her shoulders without completing her sentence. Trying to change mood she sings the following.*)

Beware of young men
in their velvet prime
who give so little
and take so much

and make a girl old
before her time.
Those gay young men
in their velvet prime.

(They laugh as if it is a big joke on themselves. CONSUELO
has almost exited and then she rushes back.)

CONSUELO. I am not here. . . . No. . . . You think you
see me, but I am not here. I am in the lovely island of
Puerto Rico . . . visiting relatives. Let me tell you about
my sweetheart. We would love each other till we would
burst out singing! Our love danced in the air for hours!
And all the time . . . mi madre . . . "Casate con un
hombre Americano, casate con un hombre Americano
. . . marry an American . . . get something out of this
life, make something for yourself." She practically made
the bed for us to lie in. My poor mother . . . when she
was young she gave away my older sister because there
was no money . . . my sister becomes my first cousin.
Then I come along, still no money. This time my father
borrows money from his boss to have me aborted. They
were young. It is a spring afternoon when my mother
knocks the money down to the ground. Neither one of
them picks it up. Now . . . they have to lie about me
. . . telling people I'm in Puerto Rico. So, here I am in
Puerto Rico . . . visiting friends.
MIDGE. I'm beginning to love Latin music. When I first
got to New York a friend of mine took me down to the
Palladium.
CONSUELO. Oh yeah, Tito Puente, Machito, Palmieri
. . . the way some Spanish girls turn on the radio and
listen to music all day long . . . the way I used to move
my body from side to side and stick out my behind makes
me sick. I don't like Latin music much. . . . Now Perry
Como. I love Perry Como, don't you?
MIDGE. *(Laughing.)* PERRY COMO!
CONSUELO. You're always laughing at me. Asking me
questions. But you never talk about yourself, do you?
MIDGE. I hardly know myself, so how can I give anyone
a chance to know me?

(Music: The cry of the sax.)

CONSUELO. I'm coming. I'm coming. (*Reluctantly going toward exit and then turning back.*) Lately, I don't know myself either. You ever read in the newspaper about women who kill babies? I just always have to read cases like that all the way through from beginning to end. Maybe twice even. I read all the details and can't seem to draw myself away from them. I'll kill my baby—NO! I love my baby. Oh, I don't know. . . . He's coming, isn't he? He's coming to take me out of here, isn't he?

MIDGE. Sure, sure, you bet. He's coming. . . . He'll show up.

CONSUELO. But when? It's almost time to . . . (*beat*) change the baby. (*She exits.*)

MATTIE. What about you—What about your F.O.B.?

MIDGE. (*Still clowning . . . the following said with tongue in cheek.*) The father of my baby. Well, it was the first time—

(*Groans from* ALL THE GIRLS, *as* PAULETTE *enters, standing, silently watching* MIDGE.)

Well, it was. . . . If I don't count all those times under the stairs and in the car where everything else happened . . . kissing, sucking, biting . . . letting a dude in just a little bit . . . just the tip but not all the way . . . And I don't count the times when I let a guy in but I was too young to have my period so I couldn't get pregnant yet. . . . But this night was different. There was something inside of me overripe . . . I was one big Yesssss . . . ready to receive him . . .

PAULETTE. (*Sarcastically.*) Yeah . . . yeah . . . yeah . . .

MIDGE. (*Ignoring* PAULETTE.) My stomach was lean and flat.

PAULETTE. Yeah, sure, I bet.

MIDGE. Desire was my name.

PAULETTE. WHY DON'T YOU TELL THEM YOUR F.O.B. IS A BLACK NIGGA!

MIDGE. (*Very quietly.*) Why are you yelling at me?

PAULETTE. I AM NOT YELLING!

MIDGE. Why are you angry?

PAULETTE. I am not angry. . . . Yes, yes, I am angry. You'll go through this day like a breeze and still have a privileged place waiting for *you* on the outside.

MIDGE. What privileged place? The privilege of raising my

black baby by myself. Walking down the street with it, trying to ignore the smirks of both blacks and whites who are offended by my mulatto bastard? 'Cause that's just what people like you will call my baby. Or the privilege of giving it away like it never existed? Look at you all standing around wondering what kind of white girl would end up in a place like this. You think you have a monopoly on pain? How do you think it feels to tell the man you love you're going to have his baby and all he can say is "I'm sorry." And now he's gone. So tell me what's so privileged about that?

(PAULETTE *laughs at* MIDGE *mockingly.*)

MATTIE. But I never even had a boyfriend. Why do I have to have a baby when I never even had a boyfriend?
NURSE JACOBS'S VOICE. (*Over a P.A. system.*) Attention . . . attention . . . girls of Hide-A-Wee. A family from Westchester coming through to inspect the house. Those girls who don't want to be seen may return to their rooms.
MATTIE. They can kiss my ass. What do I care who sees me? I only came here because my probation officer made me. They can put my picture in the *Daily News* for all I care!

SCENE 8

PASHA's *boudoir.* CHAN, *the omnipresent solicitous servant, is hovering about in the background as usual.* PARKER, *restless, half sings, half talks the following:*

PARKER. (*Singing.*)
Today! What a beautiful day.
Sun shining like a soft golden woman.
Today!
Today! What a beautiful day.
Sun shining
Like a soft golden woman
Wrapping herself around
Wrapping herself around me.
OH! Today
What a beautiful day.

Sun shining
Like a soft golden woman
Wrapping herself around.

PASHA. (*Hands* PARKER *a dish and a coke spoon.*) It's here, in this crystal dish, darling.

(PARKER *smiles at* PASHA, *reaches out and then quickly withdraws his hand. Music underneath the following . . . light, airy jazz tune.*)

PARKER. I've found it . . . the unknowable why . . . locked up in my music. Music. My music. O god O god . . . the women I've known. . . . All they ever wanted from me was to stay out of jail . . . and make some money . . . and all I ever wanted to do was fly . . . Pasha . . . please . . . you tell them that I loved them I love them . . .

PASHA. There's a rumor going around that you shoot dope in your dick vein.

PARKER. (*Coughing.*) I am what I am . . . as I was shaped. I'm only sorry I only have one joint!

PASHA. (*Going toward him to help him with his spasm of coughing.*) Why don't you let me call my doctor?

PARKER. (*Summoning all his strength to push her away.*) Will you stop treating me like a dying man? Now listen. . . . I just stopped by to tell you that I'm splitting the scene. I need to be somewhere else. I think I'll hat up and go to Italy . . . Do Europe for a while.

PASHA. (*Dipping spoon in the crystal dish and sniffing coke.*) All right, Charles . . . here's to being somewhere else.

PARKER. (*Doubling over as if in terrible pain.*) KICK ME IN MY ASS! PASHA VON KWONGESTRA, I WANT YOU TO KICK ME IN MY ASS!

PASHA. (*Backing away from him, truly frightened this time.*) Naw . . . NOoooooooooooooo.

PARKER. (*Still bending over, insisting.*) Right here in the crack.

PASHA. No, Bird, no.

PARKER. WOMAN! Do what I tell you. Look at me. (*Stands up suddenly and grabs her.*) LOOK AT ME I SAID. O God, LOOK AT ME! Music is my only motive . . . My only alibi . . . for living. Clubs are named after me. Musicians make it . . . imitating me. And I can't even give it away. I stand around *begging* people to let me

play. I . . . am . . . Charles . . . Parker, Jr. . . . and I
beg people to let me play. KICK ME, Pasha . . . (*Bending over again.*) DAMN YOU . . . KICK MEEEEEEEE.

(*As if jolted by his screaming,* PASHA *gives him a vicious kick that sends him sprawling on the floor. She runs to him and kneels down on the floor caressing him.* CHAN *wipes a tear from his eyes.*)

PASHA. (*Caressing* PARKER *on floor. Singing.*)
    A musician is neither a soldier
    Nor keeps a horse
    Nor has a family
    Yet in the pride of his ancient art
    He remains discontent.
PARKER. (*Rising to his full height.*) C'est un grand malheur de perdre, par notre caractère, les droits que nos talents nous donnent sur la société.
CHAN. Meaning. . . . In this country . . . a nigger ain't shit!
PARKER. (*Making a sound of agony.*) Cha!
PASHA. (*Rising.*) I want you to take some money and go someplace. Ibithia . . . go to Ibithia . . . lay up in the sun, . . . do the Spanish coastline. I'll call my doctor . . . he'll fix up everything . . . I have some friends there . . . they'll let you have a house and a boat . . . take somebody with you . . . your wife . . . I could find her and you two could try to get your thing together . . .
PARKER. (*Putting his finger to her lips to stop her flow of words.*) It's all right, baby. My pain is *not* unbearable . . . I feel good. Really I do. In none of the places inside . . . in none of my secret places inside of me have I condemned myself!

SCENE 9

Hide-A-Wee Home and PASHA's *boudoir.* PARKER *and* PASHA *are in the boudoir as* PAULETTE *enters living room of Hide-A-Wee. The voices of characters weave in and out of one another, overlapping.*

PAULETTE. I am not like them. I am not. I feel so different from them. Oh yes, I know we're all pregnant in here but I'm different. My family expects certain things from me . . . My father . . . has given me everything. . . . I've got a family name to live up to. My mother . . . I used to watch my mother sitting at the dinner table listening to everybody's lives . . . I grew up in my father's house and was never allowed to call him anything but "sir." "Yes, sir." "You do understand that cultured Negroes listen to classical music, not jazz." "Oh, yes, sir." And now it's "You will give up your baby for adoption so you can come home and be my daughter again." You know what . . . I always always felt like his victim. . . . Sometimes I want to keep my baby so I can be free of him . . . free to be what I want to be . . . maybe this dream I keep having would stop haunting me—

PARKER.

Sometimes I wish I could be a thought, a sound
Anything, but flesh . . .

PASHA.

I could be anything you let me be
Anything you need
Come be the child in my womb. . . . Come and be
my seed.

WILMA/PAULETTE.

I want to be free
Not what my body dictates to me

PARKER.

Wish milk could flow from my body
Wish I could cry my tears
Scream out my fears

PASHA.

Once I had a thousand nipples that suckled a thousand
men.

PARKER.

O! to be free. Not a giant, not a God, not a man!

WILMA.

I could be Charlie Parker
Oh the many selves of me
If I could be free, free
To be who I want to be

PAULETTE. (*Reaching out to touch* WILMA.) Wilma.

WILMA. Uh huh.

PAULETTE. Can't you see I'm trying to talk to you?

WILMA. Go ahead, nobody's stopping you.

PAULETTE. I'm, I'm only trying to . . . look, I had this

dream, keep having this dream and you and I are in it, so I thought—look, I know how I've acted but it's just that I can't stand the sight of you or myself or the rest of these pregnant girls. Victims. Helpless victims. Sniveling after a man.

WILMA. What about your F.O.B. Your lawyer dude. Don't you want him? Don't you love him?

PAULETTE. Love? He was exciting but I don't want his baby. I want music and anisette in delicate amber glasses . . . caviar . . . not babies. Babies weigh you down, inside and outside. I bet a woman first used the word, "love." And that's just what "love" is. A woman's weakness. Listen . . . just listen to the sounds outside. . . . Cars, rivers, people, all moving. Going different places. Late at night when all of you are asleep I get up and stand by my window listening to the world. Music and feet and voices and bodies and sights and dreams and shouting mixed up together, calling me. I want to reach out and grab those sounds. I want to go! I want to live! I got visions! I want to do crazy things like walk down the Champs Elysée with a panther on a leash like Josephine Baker. But a man will stop a woman. Someway, somehow, he just manages to pump you full of babies and insecurities and turn you into a rag doll that only lives through him . . .

WILMA. You . . . make . . . me . . . sick! You have a place in this world. You could give your child anything. Everything! Me. . . . I have nothing . . . to hold on to. It all gets destroyed somehow . . . like . . . like . . . Charlie Parker. You did it!

PAULETTE. I don't understand what you're saying.

WILMA. I know you don't. Your kind never does. That's how you killed Bird too. By not understanding. THAT'S RIGHT, YOU AND YOUR WORLD KILLED BIRD!

PAULETTE. Don't say that. Don't ever say that. I loved him too! Bird played for everybody and I heard him too.

WILMA. I just bet you did. Charlie Parker was something we had over white folks and people like you. White boys with millionaire fathers and debutante ball niggas . . . pretending to be so hip. Screaming for the Bird! If you once knew, if one of you knew the pain he was playing about, you couldn't take it. Ya couldn't listen to him. Well, I knew. And I want to take your world and shake it. That's why I can't keep my baby . . . until I make a place for me.

PAULETTE. (*Going to her.*) What are you saying?

WILMA. That I am going to give my baby up for adoption. . . . Maybe.

PAULETTE. Wilma!

WILMA. (*Almost as if arguing to herself.*) I . . . said . . . maybe. After all. I don't have any business keeping this baby. Except that it's a part of me. I keep seeing myself in the future. Each day like a slap in the face. Each year saying to me, "Your son is one year older and you don't know where he is or who's got him or how to try to get him back." Don't look at me like that.

PAULETTE. I am not looking at you.

WILMA. After all . . . you don't know what you are going to do either.

PAULETTE. I do. I have definitely come to a decision. . . . I have decided that I can't sit back and wait for things to happen. This is the last time I will sit and wait. I'll never let this happen to me again. I don't care how many men I have to fight. I will fuck them or fight them with my bare fists. Whatever way I can hurt them best.

WILMA. Tell me.

PAULETTE. What?

WILMA. The dream. You said you had a dream . . .

PAULETTE. Yes . . . I'll tell you.

WILMA. Well, go ahead. I'm waiting.

PAULETTE. I'll try and tell you. It seems like this dream is deep deep inside of me and it comes floating to the top night after night. In this dream I dream that I am making love over and over but I can't see who the man is . . . his face is hidden by a mist, but I finally manage to lift the fog and behind it is the man who is my lover but only he is not a man but a woman and well I think the woman is you and I wake up when I see that and I'm ashamed and scared, promising myself never to have that dream again and yet I know it's there, in the pillows, in the sheets, waiting for me to come to bed and dream it once again.

WILMA. (*Laughing.*) What do you expect. We've been in this no man's land for days, waiting and waiting. Just waiting. I'm so horny I have wet dreams even when I'm awake!

PAULETTE. But with a woman . . . ?? I'm not like that!

WILMA. It's only a dream. You don't have to be afraid. It's only a dream. You know what . . . sometimes I think . . . about . . . that too. Well why not? We've been used, hurt, and abandoned by our men. Is it so wrong to look for an alternative to pain even if it's only in our subconscious?

PAULETTE. What are we going to do? What are we going to do?

WILMA. (*Putting her arms around* PAULETTE.) Right now we're gonna have these babies. And do what we have to. And one day, I hope that we won't have to be afraid of our own dreams.

SCENE 10

PASHA'S *boudoir.* PARKER *is lying down, feverish.* PASHA *is wiping his brow.*

PARKER (*Suddenly jumping up.*) I'm on . . . it's time for me to go on the bandstand!

(PASHA *struggles with him, trying to make him lie down, but he breaks free of her.*)

PASHA. Lie down, you are feverish.
PARKER. GET OUT OF MY WAY. I'm on. It's time for me to go on the bandstand.

(*Music: "Cherokee" plays softly underneath.*)

CHARLIE CHAN. (*Stepping out of the corner.*) Good evening, ladies and gentlemen, and welcome to the world-famous Birdland. . . . Here's Charlie Parker and "Cherokee."

(PASHA *begins to dance and sway and snap her fingers to the music.*)

PARKER. Hear that, *my* music. You know what *they* call it? "Bebop." Yeah, that's right, "be-bop be-bop be-bop!" How can anyone take music that's called "be-bop" seriously?
CHARLIE CHAN. Good evening, ladies and gentlemen, and

welcome to the world-famous Birdland. . . . Here's Charlie
Parker and "Cherokee."

PARKER.

When I go on that Bandstand
I want folks to hear me as I am
Low-down and funky
Hear me without tears
Without pity
Let them wish they could cook like me
When I go on that Bandstand
I want folks to see me as I am
Shouting and happy
See me wild
See me free
Got to go now. . . . It's time for my solo!

CHARLIE CHAN. Good evening, ladies and gentlemen . . .
and welcome to the world-famous Birdland. Here's
Charlie Parker and "Cherokee"!

PARKER.

Nobody lives for a lifetime
I'm even wanting to go
I'm not worried about my body
I've used it, it's finished, I'm glad
All I ever waited for was the music
All the beauty there has ever been
A dog's bark, a child's cry
The voice the wind had in Africa
The intention of trees
And memories
Waiting . . . and suffering
Looking at the sky
It's right here . . . inside the music.

SCENE 11

Hide-A-Wee living room. ALL FIVE GIRLS *are sitting and
waiting.* CHAN *adjusts the clock, which begins to tick ominously.*

MATTIE *gets up and puts a shawl on her shoulder and
takes a necklace from her pocket, primping as if she were
going out for a stroll.*

MATTIE. (*Looks straight at audience.*) I got this false I.D. card that says I'm eighteen. Had it made up on 42nd Street in one of those stores. And when I put on my makeup and shit I know I can pass maybe even for twenty-one. Wish I could use it now and go down to Birdland and listen to some music and have a beer or something. . . . That place of Momma's . . . not secret enough to keep their eyes and hot man smell offa me. You got to hide under the wallpaper to get safe. Were you there? I couldn't see who it was . . . they just pinned me down and tore off my panties . . . but fuck it . . . I got something for you mothers. (*She whips an ice pick from her bosom.*) Meet Foo-Foo, my best friend. Foo-Foo used to be the name of my doll I used to sleep with. . . . Now I sleep with this here Foo-Foo . . . anybody come near me . . . WHOOOSH! (*She stabs an invisible assailant.*) I don't want a son-of-a-bitch to even look like he gone ask me for some pussy much less *take* it. . . . I . . .

CONSUELO. Okay, sugar . . . take off my shawl . . . and give me that.

PAULETTE. You better put that away before you hurt yourself. Aw, baby . . . not my necklace . . . didn't I tell you to stay out of my suitcase?

MATTIE. Are you referring to these old things. . . . My boyfriends gave 'em to me, nice, huh? (*Then suddenly angry, throwing things at them.*) Here, take your shit. . . . Here, you take your shit too.

CONSUELO. Ohh, Mattie . . . the ice pick . . . give us the ice pick.

PAULETTE. (*Holding out the necklace to* MATTIE.) You can have it . . . if you let me have the ice pick. Here, girl, wear them . . . they are yours . . . I was only kidding.

MATTIE. (*Backing away from them.*) No . . . no, don't touch. . . . Don't give me anything.

(PAULETTE *and* CONSUELO *go to* MATTIE *and hug her.* MATTIE *drops the ice pick to the floor.*)

I mean, what would I do with a gift . . . anyhow?

SCENE 12

HIDE-A-WEE *and* PASHA's *boudoir. All characters are on-stage. The structure of this scene is nearest to a spontaneous jazz piece. Free-form saxophone music dominates and is played steadily throughout, sometimes underneath, sometimes up front, but always there. The entire drama bursts into music and voices. The characters repeat the following dialogue over and over, weaving in and out of, on top and below each other, accelerating in pace, volume and intensity.* CHAN *opens the scene by fixing the clock. As the scene grows,* CHAN *jerks and twists in agony, his frantic body movements almost in time to the music as if he has internalized everybody's pain.*

NURSE JACOBS. (*Watching* CHAN *fix clock.*) It's time!
PAULETTE. No . . . It is not time . . . already . . . it couldn't be.

(*The saxophone plays a refrain over and over.*)

WILMA. (*Hugging her stomach and rocking.*) It's only in the head of a musician that I begin to understand. Only a musician can make sense for me. Only a musician knows how to connect shoes with cardboard to cover holes to P.S 184 on 116th Street and Lenox Avenue to the red taste of watermelon and mocking white smiles to Anthony's smile and smell of Florida Water to late night loneliness and . . . this . . .
NURSE JACOBS. You have all made a mistake and now is the time to correct it.
CONSUELO. He's not coming, is he? Tell my mother he's not coming.
MIDGE. This place is the only place
NURSE JACOBS. And of your own free will
MATTIE. Why do I have to have a baby?
WILMA. Oooweeeeee the pain . . . it hurts
MIDGE. This place is the only place
PAULETTE. DADDY!
CONSUELO. Mother . . . he's not coming, he's not here
PARKER. Breakingintobreakingintobreakingintobreaking-

intothesongthesongthesongbreakintothesongsongsong-
songsong

PASHA. Once . . . I had a thousand nipples

NURSE JACOBS. Relinquish your child foreverrelinquish-
yourchildforever

WILMA. I'm pushing! It's coming! I need you! need, need,
need.

PARKER. You hear it? the songthesongsongsongsong-
youhearitthesongthesongsongsong?

MATTIE. (*To audience.*) Listen, you think I could come
and cook for you sometime? I could make hot dogs and
chili and you can be my boyfriend. Please, huh? Not
now. I mean later . . . after . . .

NURSE JACOBS. Who is keeping her baby and who is giving
it away?

PAULETTE. There is no way of preparing for this. You
know it's coming and you think about it all the time but
there is no way of getting ready.

NURSE JACOBS. (*Raising her hand as if swearing an oath.*)
I voluntarily and of my own free will relinquish my child
. . . forever.

CONSUELO. No! Some of us have got to get out of here
right now.

MIDGE. Impossible! There's no way for us to be anywhere
else, anyplace but where we are right now.

MATTIE. I never even had a boyfriend. Why do I have to
have a baby when I never even had a boyfriend?

NURSE JACOBS. I voluntarily

PARKER. You hear it? You hear it? You hear it? Finally
escaping. Can you hear the song I'm breaking into,
breaking into, breakingintobreakinginto

WILMA. O god! Ahhhhh my baby's coming
Uhhhhhhhhhhhhhhhhh!

PASHA. I suckled a thousand men

WILMA. Ooooooooweee . . . the pain . . . it hurts . . .
unnnnnnAh

NURSE JACOBS. Call my daughter my niece forever

CONSUELO. Mother . . . tell my mother he's not here . . .

WILMA.   OhhhhhhhahhhhAHHHHHHHHHOHHHH-
WEEuhhhhhhhhhhhhhhhh!

PARKER. youhearityouhearityouhearityouhearityouhearit?

WILMA. Ogod the PAIN it huRTS! Uhhhhahhhhhhh-
hhhooooooOOOOOOOOOUhhhhhhhhhhhhhhhhhssss-
sssssssss I WISH I COULD SING!

(WILMA *screams an unearthly sound, half song, half animal pain all mixed up in one long note at the exact instant a note is blown on the saxophone, and both sounds fade away as* PARKER *dies. Darkness.*)

CHARLIE CHAN'S VOICE
   While Unfinished Women Cry in No Man's Land
   The Bird Dies in a Gilded Cage
   Could a Baby's cry
   Be Bird's musical notes
   That hang in the air . . . forever?

   CURTAIN

Ntozake Shange

spell #7

Powerful. Gripping. Eloquent. Moving. Intense. Bitter. Shattering. These are only some of the adjectives used to describe the play that propelled Ntozake Shange into theatrical fame, *For colored girls who have considered suicide when the rainbow is enuf*. Born out of the women's collectives on the West Coast in the early 1970s, the play candidly explored the emotional lives of young black women, exposing their vulnerability to the men they love. A series of "choreopoems," the play introduced a new theatrical form to the stage.

The play was controversial in black communities because it exposed some negative images of black men in a society all too ready to exploit them. Shange was hailed as a champion of women's issues by many, but was reviled as a man-hater by others who were angered that the play was often considered to be typical and representative of all black women's experiences.

Because *For colored girls* . . . addressed the choices made and forced upon young black women, it seemed that Shange's primary and only target was black men rather than the society that creates the pressure cooker of racism and sexism. In *spell #7* Shange uses a giant minstrel mask onstage under which the actors perform to dramatize the oppressive character of society's roles for both women and men. In discussing her choice of this theatrical device, Shange noted that "taking risks in a performance is virtually prohibited in this country. . . . It was risky for us to do the minstrel dance in *spell #7*, but I insisted on it because I thought the actors in my play were coming from pieces they didn't want to be in but pieces that helped them pay their bills. . . . I had the minstrel dance because that's what happens to black people in the arts no matter how famous we become. . . . Black Theater is not moving forward the way people like to think it is. We're not free of our paint yet!"[1]

To extend the minstrel theme, the play features a magician who guides the audience from the grotesque minstrel opening into the warmth and reality of the characters' play-acting. The contradictory limitations and potential of black life are emphasized in the three wishes he offers: "scarlet ribbons for yr hair/ a farm in mississippi/ someone to love you madly/ all things are possible but ain't no colored magician in his right mind gonna make you white." He sets the bittersweet tone of the work by claiming that he is "fixing you up good & colored & you gonna be colored all yr life & you gonna love it/ being colored/ all yr life/ colored & love it love it/ bein colored."

When the actors remove their minstrel masks, they are still, ironically, actors gathering in a favorite bar to socialize and catch up on personal news. The actors move fluidly in and out of improvised scenes that emphasize the gap between the roles they are expected to play in the theatre (that microcosm of American society) and the reality of their lives. Although the men are present and involved in the action, the bulk of the scenes (and the most memorable ones) are focused on the women. The "universally unloved black woman" is the theme of one very powerful scene, which parodies the efforts of men throughout the world to take advantage of the black woman's low status. Because the men gleefully play the sexist male roles, they provide a comment on the behavior of their colleagues. In this and other scenes, the men take an active role in helping to tell or portray the women's stories, thus uniting the two sexes in understanding and presenting their common oppression.

White feminists who fell in love with *For colored girls* . . . may have some difficulty with Shange's attack on the cherished image of the white woman. When one of the black actresses assumes the role of a "white girl," nothing is left sacred: "what's the first thing white girls think in the morning/ do they get up being glad they aint niggahs/ do they remember mama/ or worry abt getting to work/ do they work? do they play isadora & wrap themselves in sheets & go tip toeing to the kitchen to make maxwell house coffee/ oh i know/ the first thing a white girl does in the morning is fling her hair." Relentlessly, Shange's character satirizes the studied innocence, the willful ignorance and voluntary uselessness of the white female image, showing the audience the extent of the minstrel mask's power.

An intense and powerful drama that demands the complete concentration of performers as well as audience, *spell #7* was received well by critics, but was not praised as highly as Shange's first play. Upon its opening at the Public Theatre in New York City on July 15, 1979, Richard Eder of the *New York Times* called it "a most lovely and powerful work. . . ." Clive Barnes, writing for the *New York Post*, praised Shange's poetic ear and sensibility. Although *Variety* (July 25, 1979) believed that it lacked the passion and emotional impact of *For colored girls . . .* , the critic "confirmed [Shange's] standing as one of the most gifted of the younger legit writers."

Although Shange is critical of the artistic constraints imposed by the professional theatre on black writers and performers, she continues to write for the medium because of "the adventure that's available in that little, three-dimensional stage." Shange has directed many of her plays and acted in all of them; these works include: *A Photograph: A Study of Lovers in Motion* and *A Photograph: A Still Life with Shadows/A Photograph: A Study of Cruelty*, both produced in 1977; *Boogie Woogie Landscapes* (1979), and an adaptation of Bertolt Brecht's *Mother Courage* in 1980. Her published works include *Nappy Edges*, a book of poems, *Sassafras: A Novella*, and *Three Pieces*, a collection of three plays. Currently, Ms. Shange, who received a B.A. from Barnard College in 1970 and an M.A. in English literature from the University of California at Los Angeles, teaches in the Theatre Department at the University of Houston.

NOTES

1. "Ntozake Shange" in Claudia Tate, *Black Women Writers at Work*, New York: Continuum, 1983, p. 173.

spell #7:
geechee jibara quik magic trance manual for technologically stressed third world people

A Theater Piece

by
Ntozake Shange

spell #7 was originally produced by Joseph Papp's New York Shakespeare Festival in New York City, 1979, with the following personnel; Oz Scott, Director. Dianne McIntyre, Choreographer. Original Music by David Murray and Butch Morris. Scenery by Robert Yodice. Costumes by Grace Williams. Lighting by Victor En Yu Tan. With: Mary Alice, Avery Brooks, Laurie Carlos, Dyane Harvey, Larry Marshall, Reyno, La Tanya Richardson, Beth Shorter, and Ellis Wiliams. Jay Fernandez, Samuel L. Jackson, and Jack Landron also appeared during the run. Many thanks to Production Stage Manager, Jacqueline Yancey.

CAST
(in order of appearance)

LOU	a practicing magician
ALEC	a frustrated, angry actor's actor
DAHLIA	young gypsy (singer/dancer)
ELI	a bartender who is also a poet
BETTINA	dahlia's co-worker in a chorus
LILY	an unemployed actress working as a barmaid
NATALIE	a not too successful performer
ROSS	guitarist-singer with natalie
MAXINE	an experienced actress

this show is dedicated to my great aunt marie, aunt lizzie, aunt jane and my grandma, viola benzena, and her buddy, aunt effie, and the lunar year.

ACT ONE

there is a huge black-face mask hanging from the ceilling of the theater as the audience enters. in a way the show has already begun, for the members of the audience must integrate this grotesque, larger-than-life misrepresentation of life into their preshow chatter. slowly the house lights fade, but the mask looms even larger in the darkness.

   once the mask is all that can be seen, LOU, *the magician, enters. he is dressed in the traditional costume of Mr. Interlocutor: tuxedo, bow tie, top hat festooned with all kinds of whatnots that are obviously meant for good luck, he does a few catchy "soft-shoe" steps & begins singing a traditional version of a black play song*

LOU. (*singing.*)
     10 lil picaninnies all in bed
     one fell out and the other nine said:
     i sees yr hiney
     all black & shiny
     i see yr hiney
     all black & shiny/ shiny

(*as a greeting.*)

     yes/ yes/ yes   isnt life wonderful

(*confidentially.*)

     my father is a retired magician
     which accounts for my irregular behavior
     everything comes outta magic hats
     or bottles wit no bottoms & parakeets
       are as easy to get as a couple a rabbits
     or 3 fifty-cent pieces/ 1958
     my daddy retired from magic & took
     up another trade cuz this friend of mine

from the 3rd grade/ asked to be made white
on the spot

what cd any self-respectin colored american magician
do wit such an outlandish request/ cept
put all them razzamatazz hocus pocus zippity-doo-dah
thingamajigs away   cuz
colored chirren believin in magic
waz becomin politically dangerous for the race
& waznt nobody gonna be made white
on the spot just
from a clap of my daddy's hands
& the reason i'm so peculiar's
cuz i been studyin up on my daddy's technique
& everything i do is magic these days
& it's very colored/ very now you see it/ now you
dont mess wit me

(boastfully.)

                          i come from a family of retired
sorcerers/ active houngans & pennyante fortune tell-
   ers
wit 41 million spirits/ critturs & celestial bodies
on our side
               i'll listen to yr problems
               help wit yr career/ yr lover/ yr wanderin
                  spouse
               make yr grandma's stay in heaven more
               gratifyin
               ease yr mother thru menopause & show yr
                  son
               how to clean his room

(while LOU *has been easing the audience into acceptance of
his appearance & the mask [his father, the ancestors, our
magic], the rest of the company enters in tattered fieldhand
garb, blackface, and the countenance of stepan fetchit when
he waz frightened. their presence belies the magician's promise
that "you'll be colored n love it," just as the minstrel shows
were lies, but* LOU *continues.)*

       YES YES YES 3 wishes is all you get
            scarlet ribbons for yr hair

> a farm in mississippi
> someone to love you madly
all things are possible
but aint no colored magician in his right mind
gonna make you   white
i mean
> this is blk magic
you lookin at
& i'm fixin you up good/ fixin you up good & colored
& you gonna be colored all yr life
& you gonna love it/ bein colored/ all yr life/ colored
  & love it
love it/ bein colored. SPELL #7!

(LOU claps his hands, & the company which had been absolutely still til this moment/ jumps up. with a rhythm set on a washboard carried by one of them/ they begin a series of steps that identify every period of afro-american entertainment: from acrobats, comedians, tap-dancers, calindy dancers, cotton club choruses, apollo theatre du-wop groups, til they reach a frenzy in the midst of "hambone, hambone where ya been"/ & then take a bow à la bert williams/ the lights bump up abruptly.

the magician, LOU, walks thru the black-faced figures in their kneeling poses, arms outstretched as if they were going to sing "mammy." he speaks now [as a companion of the mask] to the same audience who fell so easily into his hands & who were so aroused by the way the black-faced figures "sang n danced.")

LOU.

why don't you go on & integrate a german-american school in st. louis mo./ 1955/ better yet why dont ya go on & be a red niggah in a blk school in 1954/ i got it/ try & make one friend at camp in the ozarks in 1957/ crawl thru one a jesse james' caves wit a class of white kids waitin outside to see the whites of yr eyes/ why dontcha invade a clique of working class italians trying to be protestant in a jewish community/ & come up a spade/ be a lil too dark/ lips a lil too full/ hair entirely too nappy/ to be beautiful/ be a smart child trying to be dumb/ you go meet somebody who wants/ always/ a lil

less/ be cool when yr body says hot/ & more/ be a mistake
in racial integrity/ an error in white folks' most absurd
fantasies/ be a blk kid in 1954/ who's not blk enuf to
lovingly ignore/ not beautiful enuf to leave alone/ not
smart enuf to move outta the way/ not bitter enuf to die
at an early age/ why dontchu c'mon & live my life for
me/ since the dreams aint enuf/ go on & live my life for
me/ i didnt want certain moments at all/ i'd give em to
anybody . . . awright. alec.

(the black-faced ALEC *gives his minstrel mask to* LOU *when
he hears his name/* ALEC *rises. the rest of the company is
intimidated by this figure daring to talk without the protection of black-face. they move away from him/ or move in
place as if in mourning.)*

ALEC.
   st. louis/ such a colored town/ a whiskey black space of
history & neighborhood/ forever ours to lawrenceville/
where the only road open to me waz cleared by colonial
slaves/ whose children never moved/ never seems like
mended the torments of the Depression or the stains of
demented spittle/ dropped from the lips of crystal women/
still makin independence flags/
   st. louis/ on a halloween's eve to the veiled prophet/
usurpin the mystery of mardi gras/ i made it mine tho
the queen waz always fair/ that parade of pagan floats
& tambourines/ commemorates me/ unlike the lonely
walks wit liberal trick or treaters/ back to my front door/
bag half empty/
   my face enuf to scare anyone i passed/ gee/ a colored
kid/ whatta gas. here/ a tree/ wanderin the horizon/ dipped
in blues/ untended bones/ usedta hugs drawls rhythm &
decency here a tree/ waitin to be hanged
   sumner high school/ squat & pale on the corner/ like
our vision waz to be vague/ our memory of the war/ that
made us free/ to be forgotten/ becomin paler/ linear
movement from sous' carolina to missouri/ freedmen/
landin in jackie wilson's yelp/ daughters of the manu-
mitted swimmin in tina turner's grinds/ this is chuck
berry's town disavowin miscega-nation/ in any situation/
& they let us be/ electric blues & bo didley/ the rockin
pneumonia & boogie-woogie flu/ the slop & short fried
heads/ runnin always to the river chambersburg/ lil italy/

i passed everyday at the sweet shoppe/ & waz afraid/
the cops raided truants/ regularly/ & after dark i wd not
be seen wit any other colored/ sane & lovin my life

*(shouts n cries that are those of a white mob are heard, very
loud . . . the still black-faced figures try to move away from
the menacing voices & memories.)*

VOICES.
   hey niggah/ over here
ALEC.
   behind the truck lay five hands claspin chains
VOICES.
   hey niggah/ over here
ALEC.
   round the trees/ 4 more sucklin steel
VOICES.
   hey niggah/ over here
ALEC.
   this is the borderline
VOICE.
   hey niggah/ over here
ALEC.
   a territorial dispute
VOICES.
   hey niggah/ over here
ALEC.*(crouched on floor.)*
      cars loaded with families/ fellas from the factory/
      one or two practical nurses/ become our trenches/
      some dig into cement wit elbows/ under engines/
      do not be seen in yr hometown
      after sunset/ we suck up our shadows

*(finally moved to tear off their "shadows," all but two of
the company leave with their true faces bared to the audience. DAHLIA has, as if by some magical cause, shed not
only her mask, but also her hideous overalls & picaninny-
buckwheat wig, to reveal a finely laced unitard/ the body
of a modern dancer. she throws her mask to ALEC, who
tosses it away. DAHLIA begins a lyrical but pained solo as
ALEC speaks for them.)*

ALEC.
   we will stand here

our shoulders embrace an enormous spirit
my dreams waddle in my lap
run round to miz bertha's
where lil richard gets his process
run backward to the rosebushes
& a drunk man lyin
down the block to the nuns
in pink habits/ prayin in a pink chapel
my dreams run to meet aunt marie
my dreams haunt me like the little geechee river
our dreams draw blood from old sores
this is our space
we are not movin

(DAHLIA *finishes her movement*/ ALEC *is seen reaching for her*/ *lights out. in the blackout they exit as* LOU *enters. lights come up on* LOU *who repeats bitterly his challenge to the audience.*)

LOU.

why dontchu go on & live my life for me
i didnt want certain moments at all
i'd give them to anybody

(LOU *waves his hand commanding the minstrel mask to disappear, which it does. he signals to his left & again by magic, the lights come up higher revealing the interior of a lower manhattan bar & its bartender,* ELI, *setting up for the night.* ELI *greets* LOU *as he continues to set up tables, chairs, candles, etc., for the night's activities.* LOU *goes over to the jukebox, & plays "we are family" by sister sledge.* LOU *starts to tell us exactly where we are, but* ELI *takes over as characters are liable to do. throughout* ELI's *poem, the other members of the company enter the bar in their street clothes, & doing steps reminiscent of their solos during the minstrel sequence. as each enters, the audience is made aware that these ordinary people are the minstrels. the company continues to dance individually as* ELI *speaks.*)

this is . . .

ELI.

MY kingdom
there shall be no trespassers/ no marauders
no tourists in my land

you nurture these gardens   or   be shot on sight
carelessness & other priorities
are not permitted within these walls
i am mantling an array of strength & beauty
no one shall interfere with this
the construction of myself
my city   my theater
my bar   come to my poems
but understand we speak english carefully
& perfect antillean french
our toilets are disinfected
the plants here sing to me each morning
come to my kitchen my parlor even my bed
i sleep on satin   surrounded by hand made
infants who bring me good luck & warmth
come even to my door
the burglar alarm/ armed guards vault from the east
     side
if i am in danger   a siren shouts
you are welcome
to my kingdom   my city   my self
but yr presence must not disturb these inhabitants
leave nothing out of place/ push no dust under my
     rugs
leave not a crack in my wine glasses
no finger prints
clean up after yrself in the bathroom
there are no maids here   no days off
for healing   no insurance policies
for dislocation of the psyche
aliens/ foreigners/ are granted resident status
we give them a little green card
as they prove themselves non-injurious
to the joy of my nation
i sustain no intrusions/ no double-entendre romance
no soliciting of sadness   in my life
are those who love me well
the rest are denied their visas . . .
is everyone ready to boogie

(finally, when ELI *calls for a boogie, the company does a
dance that indicates these people have worked & played
together a long time. as dance ends, the company sits &
chats at the tables & at the bar. this is now a safe haven for*

these "minstrels" off from work. here they are free to be
themselves, to reveal secrets, fantasies, nightmares, or hope.
it is safe because it is segregated & magic reigns.

LILI, *the waitress, is continually moving abt the bar, taking*
orders for drinks & generally staying on top of things.)

ALEC.
   gimme a triple bourbon/ & a glass of angel dust these
   thursday nite audiences are abt to kill me

(ELI *goes behind bar to get drinks.*)

DAHLIA.
   why do i drink so much?
BETTINA, LILY, NATALIE. (*in unison.*)
   who cares?
DAHLIA.
   but i'm an actress. i have to ask myself these questions
LILY.
   that's a good reason to drink
DAHLIA.
   no/ i mean the character/ alec, you're a director/ give
   me some motivation
ALEC.
   motivation/ if you didn't drink you wd remember that
   you're not workin
LILY.
   i wish i cd get just one decent part
LOU.
   say as lady macbeth or mother courage
ELI.
   how the hell is she gonna play lady macbeth and macbeth's a white dude?
LILY.
   ross & natalie/ why are you countin pennies like that?
NATALIE.
   we had to wait on our money again
ROSS.
   and then we didnt get it
BETTINA.
   maybe they think we still accept beads & ribbons
NATALIE.
   i had to go around wit my tambourine just to get subway
   fare

ELI.
   dont worry abt it/ have one on me
NATALIE.
   thank you eli
BETTINA. (*falling out of her chair.*)
   oh . . .
ALEC.
   cut her off eli/ dont give her no more
LILY.
   what's the matter bettina/ is yr show closin?
BETTINA. (*gets up, resets chair.*)
   no/ my show is not closin/ but if that director asks me
   to play it any blacker/ i'm gonna have to do it in a
   mammy dress
LOU.
   you know/ countin pennies/ looking for parts/ breakin
   tambourines/ we must be outta our minds for doin this
BETTINA. no we're not outta our minds/ we're just sorta
   outta our minds
LILY.
   no/ we're not outta our minds/ we've been doing this
   shit a long time . . . ross/ captain theophilis conneau/ in
   a slaver's logbook/ says that "youths of both sexes wear
   rings in the nose and lower lip and stick porcupine quills
   thru the cartilage of the ear." ross/ when ringlin' bros.
   comes to madison square garden/ dontcha know the white
   people just go
ROSS.
   in their cb radios
DAHLIA.
   in their mcdonald's hats
ELI.
   with their save america t-shirts & those chirren who
   score higher on IQ tests for the white chirren who speak
   english
ALEC.
   when the hockey games absorb all america's attention
   in winter/ they go with their fists clenched & their tongues
   battering their women who dont know a puck from a 3-
   yr-old harness racer
BETTINA.
   they go & sweat in fierce anger

ROSS.
  these factories
NATATLIE.
  these middle management positions
ROSS.
  make madison square garden
BETTINA.
  the temple of the primal scream

(LILY *gets money from cash register & heads toward juke-*
box.)

LILY.
  oh how they love blood
NATALIE.
  & how they dont even dress for the occasion/ all incon-
  spicuous & pink
ELI.
  now if willie colon come there
BETTINA.
  if/ we say/ the fania all stars gonna be there in that nasty
  fantasy of the city council
ROSS.
  where the hot dogs are not even hebrew national
LILY.
  and the bread is stale
ROSS.
  even in such a place where dance is an obscure notion
BETTINA.
  where one's joy is good cause for a boring chat with the
  pinkerton guard
DAHLIA.
  where the halls lead nowhere
ELI.
  & "back to yr seat/ folks"
LILY.
  when all one's budget for cruisin
LOU.
  one's budget for that special dinner with you know who
LILY.
  the one you wd like to love you
BETTINA.
  when yr whole reasonable allowance for leisure activity/
  buys you a seat where what's goin on dont matter

DAHLIA.
    cuz you so high up/ you might be in seattle
LILY.
    even in such a tawdry space
ELI.
    where vorster & his pals wd spit & expect black folks
    to lick it up
ROSS. (*stands on chair.*)
    in such a place i've seen miracles
ALL.
    oh yeah/ aw/ ross
ROSS.
    the miracles

(*"music for the love of it," by butch morris, comes up on
the jukebox/ this is a catchy uptempo rhythm & blues post
WW II. as they speak the company does a dance that high-
lights their ease with one another & their familiarity with
"all the new dance steps."*)

LILY.
    the commodores
DAHLIA.
    muhammad ali
NATALIE.
    bob marley
ALEC.
    & these folks who upset alla 7th avenue with their glow/
    how the gold in their braids is new in this world of hard
    hats & men with the grace of wounded buffalo/ how
    these folks in silk & satin/ in bodies reekin of good love
    comin/ these pretty muthafuckahs
DAHLIA.
    make this barn
LILY.
    this insult to good taste
BETTINA.
    a foray into paradise
DAHLIA, LILY, ALEC, NATALIE, & ROSS. (*in unison.*)
    we dress up
BETTINA, ELI, & LOU. (*in unison.*)
    we dress up
DAHLIA.
    cuz we got good manners

ROSS.
    cd you really ask dr. funkenstein to come all that way
    & greet him in the clothes you sweep yr kitchen in?

ALL.
    NO!

BETTINA.
    cd you say to muhammad ali/ well/ i just didnt have a
    chance to change/ you see i have a job/ & then i went
    jogging & well, you know its just madison square garden

LOU.
    my dear/ you know that wont do

NATALIE.
    we honor our guests/ if it costs us all we got

DAHLIA.
    when stevie wonder sings/ he don't want us lookin like
    we ain't got no common sense/ he wants us to be as
    lovely as we really are/ so we strut & reggae

ELI.
    i seen some doing the jump up/ i myself just got happy/
    but i'm tellin you one thing for sure

LILY.
    we fill up where we at

BETTINA.
    no police

NATALIE.
    no cheap beer

DAHLIA.
    no nasty smellin bano

ROSS.
    no hallways fulla derelicts & hustlers

NATALIE.
    gonna interfere wit alla this beauty

ALEC.
    if it wasnt for us/ in our latino chic/ our rasta-fare our
    outer space funk suits & all the rest i have never seen

BETTINA.
    tho my daddy cd tell you bout them fox furs & stacked
    heels/ the diamonds & marie antoinette wigs

ELI.
    it's not cuz we got money

NATALIE.
    it's not cuz if we had money we wd spend it on luxury

LILY.

it's just when you gotta audience with the pope/ you
look yr best

BETTINA.

when you gonna see the queen of england/ you polish
yr nails

NATALIE.

when you gonna see one of them/ & you know who i mean

ALEC.

they gotta really know

BETTINA.

we gotta make em feel

ELI.

we dont do this for any old body

LOU.

we're doin this for you

NATALIE.

we dress up

ALEC.

is our way of sayin/ you getting the very best

DAHLIA.

we cant do less/ we love too much to be stingy

ROSS.

they give us too much to be loved ordinary

LILY.

we simply have good manners

ROSS.

& an addiction to joy

FEMALE CAST MEMBERS. (*in unison.*)

WHEE . . .

DAHLIA.

we dress up

MALE CAST MEMBERS. (*in unison.*)

HEY . . .

BETTINA.

we gotta show the world/ we gotta corner on the color

ROSS.

happiness just jumped right outta us/ & we are lookin
good

(everyone in the bar is having so much fun/ that MAXINE
*takes on an exaggerated character as she enters/ in order to
bring them to attention. the company freezes, half in respect/
half in parody.)*

MAXINE.
  cognac!

*(the company relaxes, goes to tables or the bar. in the mean-
time,* ROSS *has remained in the spell of the character that*
MAXINE *had introduced when she came in. he goes over to*
MAXINE *who is having a drink/ & begins an improvisation.)*

ROSS.
  she left the front gate open/ not quite knowing she wanted
  someone to walk on thru the wrought iron fence/ scram-
  bled in whiskey bottles broken round old bike spokes/
  some nice brown man to wind up in her bed/ she really
  didnt know/ the sombrero that enveloped her face was
  a lil too much for an april nite on the bowery/ & the
  silver halter dug out from summer cookouts near riis
  beach/ didnt sparkle with the intensity of her promise
  to have one good time/ before the children came back
  from carolina. brooklyn cd be such a drag. every street
  cept flatbush & nostrand/ reminiscent of europe during
  the plague/ seems like nobody but sickness waz out walkin/
  drivels & hypes/ a few youngsters lookin for more than
  they cd handle/ & then there waz fay/

*(*MAXINE *rises, begins acting the story out.)*

  waitin for a cab. anyone of the cars inchin along the
  boulevard cd see fay waznt no whore/ just a good clean
  woman out for the nite/ & tho her left titty jumped out
  from under her silver halter/ she didnt notice cuz she
  waz lookin for a cab. the dank air fondled her long saggin
  bosom like a possible companion/ she felt good. she
  stuck her tin-ringed hand on her waist & watched her
  own ankles dance in the nite. she waz gonna have a good
  time tonight/ she waz awright/ a whole lotta woman/ wit
  that special brooklyn bottom strut. knowin she waznt
  comin in til dawn/ fay covered herself/ sorta/ wit a light
  kacky jacket that just kept her titties from rompin in the
  wind/ & she pulled it closer to her/ the winds waz
  comin/ from nowhere jabbin/ & there waznt no cabs/
  the winds waz beatin her behind/ whisperin/ gigglin/ you
  aint goin noplace/ you an ol bitch/ shd be at home wit
  ur kids. fay beat off the voices/ & an EBONY-TRUE-
  TO-YOU cab climbed the curb to get her. *(as cabdriver.)*

hope you aint plannin on stayin in brooklyn/ after 8:00 you dead in brooklyn. (*as narrator.*)

she let her titty shake like she thot her mouth oughtta bubble like/ wd she take off her panties/ i'd take her anywhere.

MAXINE. (*as in cab.*)

i'm into havin a good time/ yr arms/ veins burstin/ like you usedta lift tobacco onto trucks or cut cane/ i want you to be happy/ long as we dont haveta stay in brooklyn

ROSS

& she made like she waz gypsy rose lee/ or the hotsy totsy girls in the carnival round from waycross/ when it waz segregated

MAXINE.

what's yr name?

ROSS.

my name is raphael

MAXINE.

oh that's nice

ROSS.

& fay moved where i cd see her out the rear view mirror/ waz tellin me all bout her children & big eddie who waz away/ while we crossed the manhattan bridge/ i kept smilin. (*as cabdriver.*) where exactly you going?

MAXINE.

i dont really know. i just want to have a good time. take me where i can see famous people/ & act bizarre like sinatra at the kennedys/ maybe even go round & beat up folks like jim brown/ throw somebody offa balcony/ you know/ for a good time

ROSS.

the only place i knew/ i took her/ after i kisst the spaces she'd been layin open to me. fay had alla her $17 cuz i hadn't charged her nothin/ turned the meter off/ said it waz wonderful to pick up a lady like her on atlantic avenue/ i saw nobody but those goddamn whores/ & fay

(MAXINE *moves in to* ROSS & *gives him a very long kiss.*)

now fay waz a gd clean woman/ & waz burstin with pride & enthusiasm when she walked into the place where I swore/ all the actresses & actors hung out

(the company joins in ROSS's *story; responding to* MAXINE
as tho she waz entering their bar.)

oh yes/ there were actresses in braids & lipsticks/ wigs
& winged tip pumps/ fay assumed the posture of someone she'd always admired/ etta james/ the waitress asked
her to leave cuz she waz high/ & fay knew better than
that

MAXINE. *(responding to* LILY's *indication of throwing her
out.)*

i aint high/ i'm enthusiastic/ and i'm gonna have me a
gooooooood/ ol time

ROSS. she waz all dressed up/ she came all the way from
brooklyn/ she must look high cuz i/ the taxi-man/ well i
got her a lil excited/ that waz all/ but she waz gonna cool
out/ cuz she waz gonna meet her friends/ at this place/
yes. she knew that/ & she pushed a bunch of rhodo-
dendrum/ outta her way so she cd get over to that table/
& stood over the man with the biggest niggah eyes &
warmest smellin mouth

MAXINE.

please/ let me join you/ i come all the way from brooklyn/
to have a good time/ you dont think i'm high do ya/ cd
i please join ya/ i just wanna have a good ol time

ROSS. *(as* BETTINA *turns away.)*

the woman sipped chablis & looked out the window
hopin to see one of the bowery drunks fall down some-
where/ fay's voice hoverin/ flirtin wit hope

LOU.

(turning to face MAXINE.*)* why dont you go downstairs
& put yr titty in yr shirt/ you cant have no good time
lookin like that/ now go on down & then come up &
join us

*(*BETTINA & LOU *rise & move to another table.)*

ROSS.

fay tried to shove her flesh anywhere/ she took off her
hat/ bummed a kool/ swallowed somebody's cognac/ &
sat down/ waitin/ for a gd time

MAXINE. *(rises & hugs* ROSS.*)*

aw ross/ when am i gonna get a chance to feel somethin
like that/ i got into this business cuz i wanted to feel

things all the time/ & all they want me to do is put my
leg in my face/ smile/ &

LILY. you better knock on some wood/ maxine/ at least yr
workin

BETTINA.
& at least yr not playin a whore/ if some other woman
comes in here & tells me she's playin a whore/ i think i
might kill her

ELI.
you'd kill her so you cd say/ oh dahlia died & i know
all her lines

BETTINA.
aw hush up eli/ dnt you know what i mean?

ELI.
no miss/ i dont/ are you in the theater?

BETTINA.
mr. bartender/ poet sir/ i am theater

DAHLIA.
well miss theater/ that's a surprise/ especially since you
fell all over the damn stage in the middle of my solo

LILY.
she did

ELI.
miss theater herself fell down?

DAHLIA.
yeah/ she cant figure out how to get attention without
makin somebody else look bad

MAXINE.
now dahlia/ it waznt that bad/ i hardly noticed her

DAHLIA.
it waz my solo/ you werent sposed to notice her at all!

BETTINA.
you know dahlia/ i didnt do it on purpose/ i cda hurt
myself

DAHLIA.
that wd be unfortunate

BETTINA.
well miss thing with those big ass hips you got/ i dont
know why you think you do the ballet anyway

(the company breaks; they're expecting a fight.)

DAHLIA. *(crossing to* BETTINA.*)*
i got this

(demonstrates her leg extension.)

   & alla this

(DAHLIA turns her back to BETTINA/ & slaps her own backside. BETTINA grabs DAHLIA, turns her around & they begin a series of finger snaps that are a paraphrase of ailey choreography for very dangerous fights. ELI comes to break up the impending altercation.)

ELI.
   ladies ladies ladies

(ELI separates the two.)

ELI.
       people keep tellin me to put my feet on the ground
       i get mad & scream/ there is no ground
       only shit pieces from dogs horses & men who dont
         live
       anywhere/ they tell me think straight & make myself
       somethin/ i shout & sigh/ i am a poet/ i write poems
       i make words cartwheel & somersault down pages
       outta my mouth come visions distilled like bootleg
       whiskey/ i am like a radio but i am a channel of my
         own
       i keep sayin i write poems/ & people keep askin me
       what do i do/ what in the hell is going on?
       people keep tellin me these are hard times/ what are
       you gonna be doin ten years from now/
       what in the hell do you think/ i am gonna be writin
         poems
       i will have poems inchin up the walls of the lincoln
         tunnel/
       i am gonna feed my children poems on rye bread with
         horseradish/
       i am gonna send my mailman off with a poem for his
         wagon/
       give my doctor a poem for his heart/ i am a poet/
       i am not a part-time poet/ i am not a amateur poet/
       i dont even know what that person cd be/ whoever
         that is
       authorizing poetry as an avocation/ is a fraud/
       put yr own feet on the ground

BETTINA.
   i'm sorry eli/ i just dont want to be a gypsy all my life

(the bar returns to normal humming & sipping. the lights change to focus on LILY/ *who begins to say what's really been on her mind. the rest of the company is not aware of* LILY's *private thoughts. only* BETTINA *responds to* LILY, *but as a partner in fantasy, not as a voyeur.)*

LILY. *(illustrating her words with movement.)*
   i'm gonna simply brush my hair. rapunzel pull yr tresses back into the tower. & lady godiva give up horseback riding. i'm gonna alter my social & professional life dramatically. i will brush 100 strokes in the morning/ 100 strokes midday & 100 strokes before retiring. i will have a very busy schedule. between the local trains & the express/ i'm gonna brush. i brush between telephone calls. at the disco i'm gonna brush on the slow songs/ i dont slow dance with strangers. i'ma brush my hair before making love & after. i'll brush my hair in taxis. while windowshopping. when i have visitors over the kitchen table/ i'ma brush. i brush my hair while thinking abt anything. mostly i think abt how it will be when i get my full heada hair. like lifting my head in the morning will become a chore. i'll try to turn my cheek & my hair will weigh me down

*(*LILY *falls to the floor.* BETTINA *helps lift her to her knees, then begins to dance & mime as* LILY *speaks.)*

   i dream of chaka khan/ chocolate from graham central station with all seven wigs/ & medusa. i brush & brush. i use olive oil hair food/ & posner's vitamin E. but mostly i brush & brush. i may lose contact with most of my friends. i cd lose my job/ but i'm on unemployment & brush while waiting on line for my check. i'm sure i get good recommendations from my social worker: such a fastidious woman/ that lily/ always brushing her hair. nothing in my dreams suggests that hair brushing/ per se/ has anything to do with my particular heada hair. a therapist might say that the head fulla hair has to do with something else/ like: a symbol of lily's unconscious desires. but i have no therapist

(she takes imaginary pen from BETTINA, *who was pretending to be a therapist/ & sits down at table across from her.)*

& my dreams mean things to me/ like if you dreamed abt tobias/ then something has happened to tobias/ or he is gonna show up. if you dream abt yr grandma who's dead/ then you must be doing something she doesnt like/ or she wdnta gone to all the trouble to leave heaven like that. if you dream something red/ you shd stop. if you dream something green/ you shd keep doing it. if a blue person appears in yr dreams/ then that person is yr true friend

& that's how i see my dreams. & this head full hair i have in my dreams is lavender & nappy as a 3-yr-old's in a apple tree. i can fry an egg & see the white of the egg spreadin in the grease like my hair is gonna spread in the air/ but i'm not egg-yolk yellow/ i am brown & the egg white isnt white at all/ it is my actual hair/ & it wd go on & on forever/ irregular like a rasta-man's hair. irregular/ gargantuan & lavender. nestled on blue satin pillows/ pillows like the sky. & so i fry my eggs. i buy daisies dyed lavender & laced lavender tablemats & lavender nail polish. though i never admit it/ i really do believe in magic/ & can do strange things when something comes over me. soon everything around me will be lavender/ fluffy & consuming. i will know not a moment of bitterness/ through all the wrist aching & tennis elbow from brushing/ i'll smile. no regrets/ "je ne regrette rien" i'll sing like edith piaf. when my friends want me to go see tina turner or pacheco/ i'll croon "sorry/ i have to brush my hair."

i'll find ambrosia. my hair'll grow pomegranates & soil/ rich as round the aswan/ i wake in my bed to bananas/ avocados/ collard greens/ the tramps' latest disco hit/ fresh croissant/ pouilly fuissé/ ishmael reed's essays/ charlotte carter's stories/ all stream from my hair.

& with the bricks that plop from where a 9-year-old's top braid wd be/ i will brush myself a house with running water & a bidet. i'll have a closet full of clean bed linen & the lil girl from the castro convertible commercial will come & open the bed repeatedly & stay on as a helper to brush my hair. lily is the only person i know whose every word leaves a purple haze on the tip of yr tongue. when this happens i says clouds are forming/ & i has to close the windows. violet rain is hard to remove from blue satin pillows

(LOU, *the magician, gets up, he points to* LILY *sitting very still. he reminds us that it is only thru him that we are able to know these people without the "masks"/ the lies/ & he cautions that all their thoughts are not benign. they are not safe from what they remember or imagine.*)

LOU.
   you have t come with me/ to this place where magic is/ to hear my song/ some times i forget & leave my tune in the corner of the closet under all the dirty clothes/ in this place/ magic asks me where i've been/ how i've been singin/ lately i leave my self in all the wrong hands/ in this place where magic is involved in undoin our masks/ i am able to smile & answer that. in this place where magic always asks for me i discovered a lot of other people who talk without mouths who listen to what you say/ by watchin yr jewelry dance & in this place where magic stays you can let yrself in or out but when you leave yrself at home/ burglars & daylight thieves pounce on you & sell yr skin/ at cut-rates on tenth avenue

(ROSS *has been playing the acoustic guitar softly as* LOU *spoke.* ALEC *picks up on the train of* LOU's *thoughts & tells a story that in turn captures* NATALIE's *attention. slowly,* NATALIE *becomes the woman* ALEC *describes.*)

ALEC.
   she had always wanted a baby/ never a family/ never a man/ she had always wanted a baby/ who wd suckle & sleep a baby boy who wd wet/ & cry/ & smile suckle & sleep when she sat in bars/ on the stool/ near the door/ & cross from the juke box/ with her legs straddled & revealin red lace pants/ & lil hair smashed under the stockings/ she wd think how she wanted this baby & how she wd call the baby/ "myself" & as she thot/ bout this brown lil thing/ she ordered another bourbon/ double & tilted her head as if to cuddle some infant/ not present/ the men in the bar never imagined her as someone's mother/ she rarely tended her own self carefully/

(NATALIE *rises slowly, sits astride on the floor.*)

just enough to exude a languid sexuality that teased the
men off work/ & the bartender/ ray who waz her only
friend/ women didnt take to her/ so she spent her after-
noons with ray/ in the bar round the corner from her lil
house/ that shook winsomely in a hard wind/ surrounded
by three weepin willows

NATALIE.

my name is sue-jean & i grew here/ a ordinary colored
girl with no claims to any thing/ or anyone/ i drink now/
bourbon/ in harder times/ beer/ but i always wanted to
have a baby/ a lil boy/ named myself

ALEC.

one time/ she made it with ray

NATALIE.

& there waz nothin special there/ only a hot rough ban-
gin/ a brusque barrelin throwin of torso/ legs & sweat/
ray wanted to kiss me/ but i screamed/ cuz i didnt like
kissin/ only fuckin/ & we rolled round/ i waz a peculiar
sorta woman/ wantin no kisses/ no caresses/ just power/
heat & no eaziness of thrust/ ray pulled himself outa
me/ with no particular exclamation/ he smacked me on
my behind/ i waz grinnin/ & he took that as a indication
of his skill/ he believed he waz a good lover/ & a woman
like me/ didnt never want nothin but a hard dick/ &
everyone believed that/ tho no one in town really knew

ALEC.

so ray/ went on behind the bar cuz he had got his

NATALIE.

& i lay in the corner laughin/ with my drawers/ twisted
round my ankles & my hair standin every which way/ i
waz laughin/ knowin i wd have this child/ myself/ & no
one wd ever claim him/ cept me cuz i waz a low-down
thing/ layin in sawdust & whiskey stains/ i laughed &
had a good time masturbatin in the shadows.

ALEC.

sue-jean ate starch for good luck

NATALIE. like mama kareena/ tol me

ALEC.

& she planted five okras/ five collards/ & five tomatoes

NATALIE.

for good luck too/ i waz gonna have this baby/ i even
went over to the hospital to learn prenatal care/ & i kept
myself clean

ALEC.
sue-jean's lanky body got ta spreadin & her stomach waz taut & round high in her chest/ a high pregnancy is sure to be a boy/ & she smiled

NATALIE.
i stopped goin to the bar

ALEC.
started cannin food

NATALIE.
knittin lil booties

ALEC.
even goin to church wit the late nite radio evangelist

NATALIE.
i gotta prayer cloth for the boy/ myself waz gonna be safe from all that his mama/ waz prey to

ALEC.
sure/ sue-jean waz a scandal/ but that waz to be expected/ cuz she waz always a po criterish chile

NATALIE.
& wont no man bout step my way/ ever/ just cuz i hadda bad omen on me/ from the very womb/ i waz bewitched is what the ol women usedta say

ALEC.
sue-jean waz born on a full moon/ the year of the flood/ the night the river raised her skirts & sat over alla the towns & settlements for 30 miles in each direction/ the nite the river waz in labor/ gruntin & groanin/ splittin trees & families/ spillin cupboards over the ground/ waz the nite sue-jean waz born

NATALIE.
& my mother died/ drownin/ holdin me up over the mud crawlin in her mouth

ALEC.
somebody took her & she lived to be the town's no one/ now with the boy achin & dancin in her belly/ sue-jean waz a gay & gracious woman/ she made pies/ she baked cakes & left them on the stoop of the church she had never entered just cuz she wanted/ & she grew plants & swept her floors/ she waz someone she had never known/ she waz herself with child/ & she waz a wonderful bulbous thing

NATALIE.
the nite/ myself waz born/ ol mama kareena from the hills came down to see bout me/ i hollered & breathed/ i did exactly like mama kareena said/ & i pushed &

pushed & there waz a earthquake up in my womb/ i
wanted to sit up & pull the tons of logs trapped in my
crotch out/ so i cd sleep/ but it wdnt go way/ i pushed
& thot i saw 19 horses runnin in my pussy/ i waz sure
there waz a locomotive stalled up in there burnin coal
& steamin & pushin gainst a mountain

ALEC.
finally the child's head waz within reach & mama ka-
reena/ brought the boy into this world

NATALIE.
& he waz awright/ with alla his toes & his fingers/ his lil
dick & eyes/ elbows that bent/ & legs/ straight/ i wanted
a big glassa bourbon/& mama kareena brought it/ right
away/ we sat drinkin the bourbon/ & lookin at the child
whose name waz myself/ like i had wanted/ & the two
of us ate placenta stew . . . i waznt really
sure . . .

ALEC.
sue-jean you werent really sure you wanted myself to
wake up/ you always wanted him to sleep/ or at most to
nurse/ the nites yr dreams were disturbed by his cryin

NATALIE.
i had no one to help me

ALEC.
so you were always with him/ & you didnt mind/ you
knew this waz yr baby/ myself/ & you cuddled him/ carried him all over the house with you all day/ no matter
what

NATALIE.
everythin waz going awright til/ myself wanted to crawl

ALEC. (*moving closer to* NATALIE.)
& discover a world of his own/ then you became de-
spondent/ & yr tits began to dry & you lost the fullness
of yr womb/ where myself/ had lived

NATALIE.
i wanted that back

ALEC.
you wanted back the milk

NATALIE.
& the tight gourd of a stomach i had when myself waz
bein in me

ALEC.
so you slit his wrists

NATALIE.
  he waz sleepin
ALEC.
  sucked the blood back into yrself/ & waited/ myself shriveled up in his crib
NATALIE.
  a dank lil blk thing/ i never touched him again
ALEC.
  you were always holdin yr womb/ feelin him kick & sing to you bout love/ & you wd hold yr tit in yr hand
NATALIE.
  like i always did when i fed him
ALEC.
  & you waited & waited/ for a new myself. tho there were labor pains
NATALIE.
  & i screamed in my bed
ALEC.
  yr legs pinnin to the air
NATALIE.
  spinnin sometimes like a ferris wheel/ i cd get no child to fall from me
ALEC.
  & she forgot abt the child bein born/ & waz heavy & full all her life/ with "myself"
NATALIE.
  who'll be out/ any day now

(ELI *moves from behind the bar to help* NATALIE/ *or to clean tables. he doesnt really know. he stops suddenly.*)

ELI.
  aint that a goddamn shame/ aint that a way to come into the world sometimes i really cant write sometimes i cant even talk

(*the minstrel mask comes down very slowly. blackout, except for lights on the big minstrel mask which remains visible throughout intermission.*)

ACT TWO

all players onstage are frozen, except LOU, *who makes a motion for the big minstrel mask to disappear again. as the mask flies up,* LOU *begins.*

LOU.
    in this place where magic stays you can let yrself in or
    out

(he makes a magic motion. a samba is heard from the jukebox & activity is begun in the bar again. DAHLIA, NATALIE & LILY *enter, apparently from the ladies room.)*

NATALIE.
    i swear we went to that audition in good faith/ & that
    man asked us where we learned to speak english so well/
    i swear this foreigner/ asked us/ from the city of new
    york/ where we learned to speak english.
LILY.
    all i did was say "bom dia/ como vai"/ and the english-
    man got red in the face.
LOU. (*as the englishman.*)
    yr from the states/ aren't you?
LILY.
    "sim"/ i said/ in good portuguese
LOU.
    but you speak portuguese
LILY.
    "sim" i said/ in good portuguese
LOU.
    how did you pick that up?
LILY.
    i hadda answer so simple/ i cdnt say i learned it/ cuz
    niggahs cant learn & that wda been too hard on the man/
    so i said/ in good english: i held my ear to the ground
    & listened to the samba from bêlim

272

DAHLIA.
   you should have said: i make a lotta phone calls to cas-
   çais, portugao
BETTINA.
   i gotta bahiano boyfriend
NATALIE.
   how abt: i waz an angolan freedom fighter
MAXINE.
   no/ lily/ tell him: i'm a great admirer of zeza motto &
   leci brandao
LILY.
   when the japanese red army invaded san juan/ they poi-
   soned the papaya with portuguese. i eat a lotta papaya.
   last week/ i developed a strange schizophrenic condition/
   with 4 manifest personalities: one spoke english &
   understood nothing/ one spoke french & had access to
   the world/ one spoke spanish & voted against statehood
   for puerto rico/ one spoke portuguese. "eu naõ falo
   ingles entaõ y voce"/ i dont speak english anymore/ &
   you?

*(all the women in the company have been doing samba
steps as the others spoke/ now they all dance around a table
in their own ritual/ which stirs* ALEC & LOU *to interrupt this
female segregation. the women scatter to different tables,
leaving the two interlopers alone. so,* ALEC & LOU *begin
their conversation.)*

ALEC.
   not only waz she without a tan, but she held her purse
   close to her hip like a new yorker. someone who rode
   the paris métro or listened to mariachis in plaza santa
   cecilia. she waz not from here

(he sits at table.)

LOU. (*following suit.*)
   but from there
ALEC.
   some there where coloureds/ mulattoes/ negroes/ blacks
   cd make a living big enough to leave there to come here/
   where no one went there much any more for all sorts
   of reasons
LOU.
   the big reasons being immigration restrictions & un-

employment. nowadays, immigration restrictions of every kind apply to any non-european persons who want to go there from here

ALEC.

some who want to go there from here risk fetching trouble with the customs authority there

LOU.

or later with the police, who can tell who's not from there cuz the shoes are pointed & laced strange

ALEC.

the pants be for august & yet it's january

LOU.

the accent is patterned for pétionville, but working in crown heights

ALEC.

what makes a person comfortably ordinary here cd make him dangerously conspicuous there.

LOU.

so some go to london or amsterdam or paris/ where they are so abounding no one tries to tell who is from where

ALEC.

still the far right wing of every there prints lil pamphlets that say everyone from there shd leave & go back where they came from

LOU.

this is manifest legally thru immigration restrictions & personally thru unemployment

ALEC.

anyway the yng woman waz from there/ & she waz alone. that waz good. cuz if a person had no big brother in gronigen/ no aunt in rouen

LOU.

no sponsor in chicago

ALEC.

this brown woman from there might be a good idea. everybody in the world/ european & non-european alike/ everybody knows that rich white girls are hard to find. some of them joined the weather underground/ some the baader-meinhof gang.

LOU.

a whole bunch of them gave up men entirely

ALEC.

so the exotic lover in the sun routine becomes more difficult to swing/ if she wants to talk abt plastic explosives & the resistance of the black masses to socialism/ instead of giving head as the tide slips in or lending money

LOU.

just for the next few days

ALEC.

is hard to find a rich white girl who is so dumb/ too

LOU.

anyway. the whole world knows/ european & non-european alike/ the whole world knows that nobody loves the black woman like they love farrah fawcett-majors. the whole world dont turn out for a dead black woman like they did for marilyn monroe.

ALEC.

actually/ the demise of josephine baker waz an international event

LOU.

but she waz a war hero the worldwide un-beloved black woman is a good idea/ if she is from there & one is a young man with gd looks/ piercing eyes/ & knowledge of several romantic languages

(throughout this conversation, ALEC & LOU *will make attempts to seduce, cajole, & woo the women of the bar as their narrative indicates. the women play the roles as described, being so moved by romance.)*

ALEC.

the best dancing spots/ the hill where one can see the entire bay at twilight

LOU.

the beach where the seals & pelicans run free/ the hidden "local" restaurants

ALEC.

"aw babee/ you so pretty" begins often in the lobby of hotels where the bright handsome yng men wd be loiterers

LOU.

were they not needed to tend the needs of the black women from there

ALEC.

tourists are usually white people or asians who didnt come all this way to meet a black woman who isnt even foreign

LOU.

so hotel managers wink an eye at the yng men in the
lobby or by the bar who wd be loitering/ but are gonna
help her have a gd time

ALEC.

maybe help themselves too

LOU.

everybody in the world/ european & non-european alike/
everybody knows the black woman from there is not
treated as a princess/ as a jewel/ a cherished lover

ALEC.

that's not how sapphire got her reputation/ nor how mrs.
jefferson perceives the world

LOU.

you know/ babee/ you dont act like them. aw babee/
you so pretty

ALEC.

the yng man in the hotel watches the yng blk woman sit
& sit & sit/ while the european tourists dance with each
other/ & the dapper local fellas mambo frenetically with
secretaries from arizona/ in search of the missing rich
white girl. our girl sits &

FEMALE CAST MEMBERS. (*in unison.*)

sits & sits & sits

ALEC. (*to* DAHLIA & NATALIE, *who move to the music.*)

maybe she is courageous & taps her foot. maybe she is
bold & enjoys the music/ smiling/ shaking shoulders. let
her sit & let her know she is unwanted

LOU.

she is not white & she is not from here

ALEC.

let her know she is not pretty enuf to dance the next
merengue. then appear/ mysteriously/ in the corner of
the bar. stare at her. just stare. when stevie wonder's
song/ "isnt she lovely"/ blares thru the red-tinted light/
ask her to dance & hold her as tyrone power wda. hold
her & stare

(ROSS & ELI *sing the chorus to stevie wonder's "isn't she
lovely."*)

LOU.

dance yr ass off. she has been discovered by the non-
european fred astaire

ALEC.
let her know she is a surprise/ an event. by the look on
yr face you've never seen anyone like this black woman
from there. you say: "aw/ you not from here?"/ totally
astonished. she murmurs that she is from there. as if to
apologize for her unfortunate place of birth
LOU.
you say
ALEC.
aw babee/ you so pretty. & it's all over
LOU.
a night in a pension near the sorbonne. pick her up from
the mattress. throw her gainst the wall in a show of exotic
temper & passion: "maintenant/ tu es ma femme. nous
nous sommes mariés." unions of this sort are common
wherever the yng black women travel alone. a woman
traveling alone is an affront to the non-european man
who is known the world over/ to european & non-european alike/ for his way with women
ALEC.
his sense of romance/ how he can say:
LOU.
aw babee/ you so pretty . . . and even a beautiful woman
will believe no one else ever recognized her loveliness
ELI.
or else/ he comes to a cafe in willemstad in the height
of the sunset. an able-bodied/ sinewy yng man who wants
to buy one beer for the yng woman. after the first round/
he discovers he has run out of money/ so she must buy
the next round/ when he discovers/ what beautiful legs
you have/ how yr mouth is like the breath of tiger lilies.
we shall make love in the/ how you call it/ yes in the
earth/ in the dirt/ i will have you in my/ how you say/
where things grow/ aw/ yes/ i will have you in the soil.
probably under the stars & smelling of wire/ an unforgettable international affair can be consummated

(the company sings "tara's theme" as ELI *ends his speech.*
ELI & BETTINA *take a tango walk to the bar, while* MAXINE
*mimics a 1930s photographer, shooting them as they sail
off into the sunset.)*

MAXINE.
at 11:30 one evening i waz at the port authority/ new

york/ united states/ myself. now i waz there & i spoke
english & waz holding approximately $7 american cur-
rency/ when a yng man from there came up to me from
the front of the line of people waiting for the princeton
new jersey united states local bus. i mean to say/ he gave
up his chance for a good seat to come say to me:

ROSS.

i never saw a black woman reading nietzsche

MAXINE.

i waz demure enough/ i said i have to for a philosophy
class. but as the night went on i noticed this yng man
waz so much like the other yng men from here/ who use
their bodies as bait & their smiles as passport alterna-
tives. anyway the night did go on. we were snuggled
together in the rear of the bus going down the jersey
turnpike. he told me in english/ that he had spoken all
his life in st. louis/ where he waz raised:

ROSS.

i've wanted all my life to meet someone like you. i want
you to meet my family/ who haven't seen me in a long
time/ since i left missouri looking for opportunity . . .

(he is lost for words.)

LOU. (*stage whisper.*)

opportunity to sculpt

ROSS.

thank you/ opportunity to sculpt

MAXINE.

he had been everyplace/ he said

ROSS.

you arent like any black woman i've ever met anywhere

MAXINE.

here or there

ROSS.

i had to come back to new york cuz of immigration
restrictions & high unemployment among black american sculptors abroad

MAXINE.

just as we got to princeton/ he picked my face up from
his shoulder & said:

ROSS.

aw babee/ you so pretty

MAXINE.

> aw babee/ you so pretty. i believe that night i must have looked beautiful for a black woman from there/ though i cd be asked at any moment to tour the universe/ to climb a 6-story walkup with a brilliant & starving painter/ to share kadushi/ to meet mama/ to getta kiss each time the swing falls toward the willow branch/ to imagine where he say he from/ & more. i cd/ i cd have all of it/ but i cd not be taken/ long as i don't let a stranger be the first to say:

LOU.

> aw babee/ you so pretty

MAXINE. after all/ immigration restrictions & unemployment cd drive a man to drink or to lie

(she breaks away from ROSS.*)*

> so if you know yr beautiful & bright & cherishable awready/ when he say/ in whatever language:

ALEC. (*to* NATALIE.)

> aw babee/ you so pretty

MAXINE.

> you cd say:

NATALIE.

> i know. thank you

MAXINE.

> then he'll smile/ & you'll smile. he'll say:

ELI. (*stroking* BETTINA'*s thigh.*)

> what nice legs you have

MAXINE.

> you can say:

BETTINA. (*removing his hand.*)

> yes. they run in the family

MAXINE.

> oh! whatta universe of beautiful & well traveled women!

MALE CAST MEMBERS. (*in unison.*)

> aw babee/ i've never met anyone like you

FEMALE CAST MEMBERS. (*in unison, pulling away from men to stage edges.*)

> that's strange/ there are millions of us!

(men all cluster after unsuccessful attempts to persuade their women to talk. ALEC *gets the idea to serenade the women;* ROSS *takes the first verse, with men singing back-up. song is "ooh baby," by smokey robinson.)*

ROSS. (*singing.*)
    i did you wrong/ my heart went out to play/ but in the
      game
    i lost you/what a price to pay/ i'm cryin . . .
MALE PLAYERS. (*singing.*)
    oo oo oo/ baby baby. . . . oo oo oo/ baby baby

(*this brings no response from the women; the men elect* ELI
to lead the second verse.)

ELI.
    mistakes i know i've made a few/ but i'm only human
    you've made mistakes too/ i'm cryin . . .
    oo oo oo/ baby baby . . . oo oo oo/ baby baby

(*the women slowly forsake their staunch indignation/ returning to the arms of their partners. all that is except* LILY,
who walks abt the room of couples awkwardly)

MALE CAST MEMBERS & LILY. (*singing.*)
    i'm just about at the end of my rope
    but i can't stop trying/ i cant give up hope
    cause i/ i believe one day/ i'll hold you near
    whisper i love you/ until that day is here
    i'm cryin . . . oo oo oo/ baby baby

(LILY *begins as the company continues to sing.*)

LILY.
    unfortunately
    the most beautiful man in the world
    is unavailable
      that's what he told me
    i saw him wandering abt/ said well this is one of a kind
    & i might be able to help him out
    so alone & pretty in all this ganja & bodies melting
    he danced with me & i cd become that
    a certain way to be held that's considered in advance
    a way a thoughtful man wd kiss a woman who
    cd be offended easily/ but waznt cuz
    of course the most beautiful man in the world
      knows exactly what to do
    with someone who knows that's who he is/
    these dreads fallin thru my dress

so my nipples just stood up
these hands playin the guitar on my back
the lips somewhere between my neck
& my forehead
talking bout ocho rios & how i really must go
marcus garvey cda come in the door & we/
we wd still be dancin that dance
the motion that has more to do with kinetic energy
than shootin stars/ more to do with the impossibility
of all this/ & how it waz awready bein too much
our reason failed
we tried to go away & be just together
aside from the silence that weeped
with greed/ we didnt need/ anything/ but one another
for tonite
but he is the most beautiful man in the world
   says he's unavailable/
& this man whose eyes made me
half-naked & still & brazen/ was singin with me
since we cd not talk/ we sang

(MALE PLAYERS *end their chorus with a flourish.*)

LILY.
  we sang with bob marley
  this man/ surely the most beautiful man in the world/ &
  i
  sang/ "i wanna love you & treat you right/

(*the couples begin different kinds of reggae dances.*)

  i wanna love you every day & every nite"
THE COMPANY. (*dancing & singing.*)we'll be together with
    the roof right over our heads
    we'll share the shelter of my single bed
    we'll share the same room/ jah provide the bread
DAHLIA. (*stops dancing during conversation.*)
  i tell you it's not just the part that makes me love you
  so much
LOU.
  what is it/ wait/ i know/ you like my legs
DAHLIA.
  yes/ uh huh/ yr legs & yr arms/ & . . .

LOU.
   but that's just my body/ you started off saying you loved
   me & now i see it's just my body
DAHLIA.
   oh/ i didn't mean that/ it's just i dont know you/ except
   as the character i'm sposed to love/ & well i know rehearsal is over/ but i'm still in love with you

(they go to the bar to get drinks, then sit at a table.)

ROSS.
   but baby/ you have to go on the road. we need the money
NATALIE.
   i'm not going on the road so you can fuck all these
   aspiring actresses
ROSS.
   aw/ just some of them/ baby
NATALIE.
   that's why i'm not going
ROSS.
   if you dont go on the road i'll still be fuckin em/ but you
   & me/ we'll be in trouble/ you understand?
NATALIE. *(stops dancing.)*
   no i dont understand
ROSS.
   well let me break it down to you
NATALIE.
   please/ break it down to me
BETTINA. *(stops dancing.)*
   hey/ natalie/ why dont you make him go on the road/
   they always want us to be so goddamned conscientious
ALEC. *(stops dancing.)*
   dont you think you shd mind yr own bizness?
NATALIE.
   yeah bettina/ mind yr own bizness

(she pulls ROSS *to the table with her.)*

BETTINA. *(to* ALEC.)
   no/ i'm tired of having to take any & every old job to
   support us/ & you get to have artistic integrity & refuse
   parts that are beneath you
ALEC.
   thats right/ i'm not playing the fool or the black buck

pimp circus/ i'm an actor not a stereotype/ i've been trained. you know i'm a classically trained actor

BETTINA.

& just what do you think we are?

MAXINE.

well/ i got offered another whore part downtown

ELI.

you gonna take it?

MAXINE.

yeah

LILY.

if you dont/ i know someone who will

ALEC. (*to* BETTINA.)

i told you/ we arent gonna get anyplace/ by doin every bit part for a niggah that someone waves in fronta my face

BETTINA.

& we arent gonna live long on nothin/ either/ cuz i'm quittin my job

ALEC.

be in the real world for once & try to understand me

BETTINA.

you mean/ i shd understand that you are the great artist & i'm the trouper.

ALEC.

i'm not sayin that we cant be gigglin & laughin all the time dancin around/ but i cant stay in these "hate whitey" shows/ cuz they arent true

BETTINA.

a failure of imagination on yr part/ i take it

ALEC.

no/ an insult to my person

BETTINA.

oh i see/ you wanna give the people some more make-believe

ALEC.

i cd always black up again & do minstrel work/ wd that make you happy?

BETTINA.

there is nothin niggardly abt a decent job. work is honorable/ work!

ALEC.

well/ i got a problem. i got lots of problems/ but i got one i want you to fix & if you can fix it/ i'll do anything

you say. last spring this niggah from the midwest asked
for president carter to say he waz sorry for that for-
gettable phenomenon/ slavery/ which brought us all together. i never did get it/ none of us ever got no apology
from no white folks abt not bein considered human beings/
that makes me mad & tired. someone told me "roots"
was the way white folks worked out their guilt/ the success of "roots" is the way white folks assuaged their
consciences/ i dont know this/ this is what i waz told. i
dont get any pleasure from nobody watchin me trying
to be a slave i once waz/ who got away/ when we all
know they had an emancipation proclamation/ that the
civil war waz not fought over us. we all know that we/
actually dont exist unless we play football or basketball
or baseball or soccer/ pélé/ see they still import a strong
niggah to earn money. art here/ isnt like in the old coun-
try/ where we had some spare time & did what we liked
to do/ i dont know this either/ this is also something i've
been told. i just want to find out why no one has even
been able to sound a gong & all the reporters recite that
the gong is ringin/ while we watch all the white people/
immigrants & invaders/ conquistadors & relatives of london debtors from georgia/ kneel & apologize to us/ just
for three or four minutes. now/ this is not impossible/
& someone shd make a day where a few minutes of the
pain of our lives is acknowledged. i have never been
very interested in what white people did/ cuz i waz able/
like most of us/ to have very lil to do with them/ but if
i become a success that means i have to talk to white
folks more than in high school/ they are everywhere/ you
know how they talk abt a neighborhood changin/ we
suddenly become all over the place/ they are now all
over my life/ & i dont like it. i am not talkin abt poets
& painters/ not abt women & lovers of beauty/ i am
talkin abt that proverbial white person who is usually a
man who just/ turns yr body around/ looks at yr teeth
& yr ass/ who feels yr calves & back/ & agrees on a
price. we are/ you see/ now able to sell ourselves/ & i
am still a person who is tired/ a person who is not into
his demise/ just three minutes for our lives/ just three
minutes of silence & a gong in st. louis/ oakland/ in los
angeles . . .

(the entire company looks at him as if he's crazy/ he tries to leave the bar/ but BETTINA *stops him.)*

BETTINA.
  you're still outta yr mind. ain't no apologies keeping us alive.

LOU.
  what are you gonna do with white folks kneeling all over the country anyway/ man

*(*LOU *signals everyone to kneel.)*

LILY.
  they say i'm too light to work/ but when i asked him what he meant/ he said i didnt actually look black. but/ i said/ my mama knows i'm black & my daddy/ damn sure knows i'm black/ & he is the only one who has a problem thinkin i'm black/ i said so let me play a white girl/ i'm a classically trained actress & i need the work & i can do it/ he said that wdnt be very ethical of him. can you imagine that shit/ not ethical

NATALIE.
  as a red-blooded white woman/ i cant allow you all to go on like that

*(*NATALIE *starts jocularly.)*

  cuz today i'm gonna be a white girl/ i'll retroactively wake myself up/ ah low & behold/ a white girl in my bed/ but first i'll haveta call a white girl i know to have some more accurate information/ what's the first thing white girls think in the morning/ do they get up being glad they aint niggahs/ do they remember mama/ or worry abt gettin to work/ do they work?/ do they play isdora & wrap themselves in sheets & go tip toeing to the kitchen to make maxwell house coffee/ oh i know/ the first thing a white girl does in the morning is fling her hair/
  So now i'm done with that/ i'm gonna water my plants/ but am i a po white trash white girl with a old jellyjar/ or am i a sophisticated & protestant suburbanite with 2 valiums slugged awready & a porcelain water carrier leading me up the stairs strewn with heads of dolls & nasty smellin white husband person's underwear/ if i was

really protected from the niggahs/ i might go to early morning mass & pick up a tomato pie on the way home/ so i cd eat it during the young & the restless. in williams arizona as a white girl/ i cd push the navaho women outta my way in the supermarket & push my nose in the air so i wdnt haveta smell them. coming from bay ridge on the train i cd smile at all the black & puerto rican people/ & hope they cant tell i want them to go back where they came from/ or at least be invisible.

i'm still in my kitchen/ so i guess i'll just have to fling my hair again & sit down. i shd pinch my cheeks to bring the color back/ i wonder why the colored lady hasn't arrived to clean my house yet/ so i cd go to the beauty parlor & sit under a sunlamp to get some more color back/ it's terrible how god gave those colored women such clear complexions/ it take em years to develop wrinkles/ but beauty can be bought & flattered into the world.

as a white girl on the street/ i can assume since i am a white girl on the streets/ that everyone notices how beautiful i am/ especially lil black & caribbean boys/ they love to look at me/ i'm exotic/ no one in their families looks like me/ poor things. if i waz one of those white girls who loves one of those grown black fellas/ i cd say with my eyes wide open/ totally sincere/ oh i didnt know that/ i cd say i didt know/ i cant/ i dont know how/ cuz i'ma white girl & i dont have to do much of anything.

all of this is the fault of the white man's sexism/ oh how i loathe tight-assed thin-lipped pink white men/ even the football players lack a certain relaxed virility/ that's why my heroes are either just like my father/ who while he still cdnt speak english knew enough to tell me how the niggers shd go back where they came from/ or my heroes are psychotic faggots who are white/ or else they are/ oh/ you know/ colored men.

being a white girl by dint of my will/ is much more complicated than i thought it wd be/ but i wanted to try it cuz so many men like white girls/ white men/ black men/ latin men/ jewish men/ asians/ everybody. so i thought if i waz a white girl for a day i might understand this better/ after all gertrude stein wanted to know abt the black women/ alice adams wrote *thinking abt billie*/ joyce carol oates has three different black characters all with the same name/ i guess cuz we are underdeveloped individuals or cuz we are all the same/ at any rate i'm gonna call this thinkin abt white girls/ cuz helmut new-ton's awready gotta book called *white women*/ see what i mean/ that's a best seller/ one store i passed/ hadda sign said/

> ### WHITE WOMEN
> ### SOLD OUT

it's this kinda pressure that forces us white girls to be so absolutely pathological abt the other women in the world/ who now that they're not all servants or peasants want to be considered beautiful too. we simply krinkle our hair/ learn to dance the woogie dances/ slant our eyes with make-up or surgery/ learn spanish & claim argentinian background/ or as a real trump card/ show up looking like a real white girl. you know all western civilization depends on us/

i still havent left my house. i think i'll fling my hair once more/ but this time with a pout/ cuz i think i havent been fair to the sisterhood/ women's movement faction of white girls/ although/ they always ask what do you people really want. as if the colored woman of the world were a strange sort of neutered workhorse/ which isnt too far from reality/ since i'm still waiting for my cleaning lady & the lady who takes care of my children & the lady who caters my parties & the lady who accepts quar-ters at the bathroom in sardi's. those poor creatures shd be sterilized/ no one shd have to live such a life. cd you hand me a towel/ thank-you caroline. i've left all of maxime's last winter clothes in a pile for you by the back door. they have to be cleaned but i hope yr girls can make gd use of them.

oh/ i'm still not being fair/ all the white women in the world dont wake up being glad they aint niggahs/ only some of them/ the ones who dont/ wake up thinking how can i survive another day of this culturally condoned incompetence. i know i'll play a tenor horn & tell all the colored artists i meet/ that now i'm just like them/ i'm colored i'll say cuz i have a struggle too. or i cd punish this white beleagered body of mine with the advances of a thousand ebony bodies/ all built like franco harris or peter tosh/ a thousand of them may take me & do what they want/ cuz i'm so sorry/ yes i'm so sorry they were born niggahs. but then if i cant punish myself to death for being white/ i certainly cant in good conscience keep waiting for the cleaning lady/ & everytime i attempt even the smallest venture into the world someone comes to help me/ like if i do anything/ anything at all i'm extending myself as a white girl/ cuz part of being a white girl is being absent/ like those women who are just with a man but whose names the black people never remember/ they just say oh yeah his white girl waz with him/. or a white girl got beat & killed today/ why someone will say/ cuz some niggah told her to give him her money & she said no/ cuz she thought he realized that she waz a white girl/ & he did know but he didnt care/ so he killed her & took the money/ but the cops knew she waz a white girl & cdnt be killed by a niggah especially/ when she had awready said no. the niggah was sposed to hop round the corner backwards/ you dig/ so the cops/ found the culprit within 24 hours/ cuz just like emmett till/ niggahs do not kill white girls.

i'm still in my house/ having flung my hair-do for the last time/ what with having to take 20 valium a day/ to consider the ERA/ & all the men in the world/ & my ignorance of the world/ it is overwhelming. i'm so glad i'm colored. boy i cd wake up in the morning & think abt anything. i can remember emmett till & not haveta smile at anybody.

MAXINE. (*compelled to speak by* NATALIE'S *pain.*)
whenever these things happened to me/ & i waz young/ i wd eat a lot/ or buy new fancy underwear with rhinestones & lace/ or go to the movies/ maybe call a friend/ talk to made-up boyfriends till dawn. this waz when i waz under my parents' roof/ & trees that grew into my room had to be cut back once a year/ this waz when the birds sometimes flew thru the halls of the house as if the ceilings were sky & i/simply another winged creature. yet no one around me noticed me especially. no one around saw anything but a precocious brown girl with peculiar ideas. like during the polio epidemic/ i wanted to have a celebration/ which nobody cd understand since iron lungs & not going swimming waznt nothing to cel-

ebrate. but i explained that i waz celebrating the bounty of the lord/ which more people didnt understand/ til i went on to say that/ it waz obvious that god had protected the colored folks from polio/ nobody understood that. i did/ if god had made colored people susceptible to polio/ then we wd be on the pictures & the television with the white children. i knew only white folks cd get that particular disease/ & i celebrated. that's how come i always commemorated anything that affected me or the colored people. according to my history of the colored race/ not enough attention was paid to small victories or small personal defeats of the colored. i celebrated the colored trolley driver/ the colored basketball team/ the colored blues singer/ & the colored light heavy weight champion of the world. then too/ i had a baptist child's version of high mass for the slaves in new orleans whom i had read abt/ & i tried to grow watermelons & rice for the dead slaves from the east. as a child i took on the burden of easing the ghost-colored-folks' souls & trying hard to keep up with the affairs of my own colored world.

when i became a woman, my world got smaller. my grandma closed up the windows/ so the birds wdnt fly in the house any more. waz bad luck for a girl so yng & in my condition to have the shadows of flying creatures over my head. i didn't celebrate the trolley driver anymore/ cuz he might know i waz in this condition. i didnt celebrate the basketball team anymore/ cuz they were yng & handsome/ & yng & handsome cd mean trouble. but trouble waz when white kids called you names or beat you up cuz you had no older brother/ trouble waz when someone died/ or the tornado hit yr house/ now trouble meant something abt yng & handsome/ & white or colored. if he waz yng & handsome that meant trouble. seemed like every one who didnt have this condition/ so birds cdnt fly over yr head/ waz trouble. as i understood it/ my mama & my grandma were sending me out to be with trouble/ but not to get into trouble. the yng & handsome cd dance with me & call for sunday supper/ the yng & hndsome cd write my name on their notebooks/ cd carry my ribbons on the field for gd luck/ the uncles cd hug me & chat for hours abt my growing up/ so i counted all 492 times this condition wd make me victim to this trouble/ before i wd be immune to it/ the way colored folks were immune to polio.

i had discovered innumerable manifestations of trouble: jealousy/ fear/ indignation & recurring fits of vulnerability that lead me right back to the contradiction i had never understood/ even as child/ how half the world's population cd be bad news/ be yng & handsome/ & later/ eligible & interested/ & trouble.

plus/ according to my own version of the history of the colored people/ only white people hurt little colored girls or grown colored women/ my mama told me only white people had social disease & molested children/ and my grandma told me only white people committed unnatural acts. that's how come i knew only white folks got polio/ muscular dystrophy/ sclerosis/ & mental illness/ this waz all verified by the television. but i found out that the colored folks knew abt the same vicious & disease-ridden passions that the white folks knew.

the pain i succumbed to each time a colored person did something that i believed only white people did waz staggering. my entire life seems to be worthless/ if my own folks arent better than white folks/ then surely the sagas of slavery & the jim crow hadnt convinced anyone that we were better than them. i commenced to buying pieces of gold/ 14 carat/ 24 carat/ 18 carat gold/ every time some black person did something that waz beneath him as a black person & more like a white person. i bought gold cuz it came from the earth/ & more than likely it came from south africa/ where the black people are humiliated & oppressed like in slavery. i wear all these things at once/ to remind the black people that it cost a lot for us to be here/ our value/ can be known instinctively/ but since so many black people are having a hard time not being like white folks/ i wear these gold pieces to protest their ignorance/ their disconnect from history. i buy gold with a vengeance/ each time someone appropriates my space or my time without permission/ each time someone is discourteous or actually cruel to me/ if my mind is not respected/ my body toyed with/ i buy gold/ & weep. i weep as i fix the chains round my neck/ my wrists/ my ankles. i weep cuz all my childhood ceremonies for the ghost-slaves have been in vain. colored people can get polio & mental illness. slavery is not unfamiliar to me. no one on this planet knows/ what i know abt gold/ abt anything hard to get & beautiful/

anything lasting/ wrought from pain. no one understands that surviving the impossible is sposed to accentuate the positive aspects of a people.

(ALEC *is the only member of the company able to come immediately to* MAXINE. *when he reaches her,* LOU, *in his full magician's regalia, freezes the whole company*)

LOU.

      yes yes yes   3 wishes is all you get
        scarlet ribbons for yr hair
        a farm in mississippi
        someone to love you madly
      all things are possible
      but aint no colored magician in his right mind
      gonna make you white
      cuz this is blk magic you lookin at
      & i'm fixin you up good/ fixin you up good & colored
      & you gonna be colored all yr life
      & you gonna love it/ bein colored/ all yr life
      colored & love it/ love it/ bein colored

(lou beckons the others to join him in the chant, "colored & love it." it becomes a serious celebration, like church/ like home/ but then lou freezes them suddenly.)

LOU.

      crackers are born with the right to be
      alive/ i'm making ours up right here
      in yr face/ & we gonna be
      colored & love it

(the huge minstrel mask comes down as company continues to sing "colored & love it/ love it being colored." blackout/ but the minstrel mask remains visible. the company is singing "colored & love it being colored" as audience exits)

Kathleen Collins
THE BROTHERS

Like the 1960s playwrights who gave voice to the ghetto and street life, an aspect of black reality that had not been shown on stage before, Kathleen Collins gives fresh texture and definition to the black middle class. They are neither stereotyped nor glorified. They are simply humans who have sometimes made foolish choices and now live out the consequences.

Against the dramatic backdrop of the Ghandi and King assassinations (1948–1968), Collins displays the static, wasted lives of *The Brothers*, their wives, and sister. Although the men are never seen in this play, their presence is felt through the women who take care of them. It is these women whom the audience watches; they are like leaves that the unseen wind of maleness tosses about. The Edwards brothers are proud men who have spent all their lives trying to escape "the Negro void," the burden of being black. At the center of the play's action is Nelson, once an Olympic gold-medal winner who, with no new races to run, has retired to his bed at the age of twenty-seven. The sister and wives who once basked in his glory are now reduced to rushing about responding to his every childish demand, a dramatic display of their wasted potential and loss of self. As Nelson and his brothers find themselves caught in middle-aged lives with no new worlds to conquer, the "women's work" becomes increasingly futile. Their painful self-awareness reveals that they know, in varying degrees, the extent of their loss. These talented people are completely untouched by the momentous events evoked by people of color between 1948 and 1968 when Gandhi leads his people to an independent India and King leads black Americans to expanded civil rights. Although the wives comment wryly on the pointlessness of their personal choices in the face of world events, their words only emphasize their impotence. Just as the women are addenda to the men's lives, so the entire family lives on the periphery of the great movements that are changing the world. They cannot answer the disturbing questions about "the Negro's place in time, his reasons for being in the scheme of things." The overwhelming sense of futility is real, for there is more than mere surprise in the dramatic reaction of Nelson's wife to this quandary, and more than a passing irony in the play's final words: "All colored men do is die."

A departure from upbeat, affirming dramas of black life, *The Brothers* explores the "terrible brooding over what being colored really means." Collins is unapologetic for her subject matter; there is none of the reticence so prevalent among some writers in the 1960s, adopted for fear that such characters would be derided as "too white," or not black enough. Collins's characters may try to escape the burden of blackness, but their lives are nevertheless framed by the color of their skins and their consciousness of its influence.

Critical response to this play was encouraging. *New York Times* critic Frank Rich called her "a promising writer . . . capable of passions both tender and angry; she can be funny; she is also . . . fond of the sound of words" (April 6, 1982). In response to the play's initial reception, however, Collins revised the script, eliminating two male characters who appeared in the original production. The revised version is published in this volume.

The Brothers was Kathleen Collins's second play; it won for her a National Endowment for the Arts Playwriting grant and led to her nomination for the Susan Blackburn Prize for Playwriting, for which she emerged as one of ten finalists. *The Brothers* was also nominated by the Audelco Society as one of the best plays of 1982 and was selected for the Plays-In-Process series of the Theatre Communications Group as one of twelve outstanding plays of the 1982 season. *In the Midnight Hour*, an intimate study of a black middle-class family's relationships, was produced in 1982 by the Richard Allen Center for Culture and Art. Collins's most recent play, *Only the Sky Is Free*, is a fictional meditation on the life of Bessie Coleman, the first black aviatrix, which was produced off-Broadway in the spring of 1986 at the Richard Allen Center for Culture and Art. *Remembrance*, another recent work, was scheduled as part of the Women's Festival of One-Acts in December 1985, at the American Place Theatre.

Ms. Collins, who is an associate professor of film at the City College of New York, is also a filmmaker, writer, director, and coproducer with three films to her credit: *Gouldtown: A Mulatto Settlement*, *The Cruz Brothers and Miss Malloy*, and *Losing Ground*, a dramatic feature. *Losing Ground* won the prize for the First Feature at the Portuguese International Film Festival, was purchased by several European television stations, and invited to the Munich, Berlin and London film festivals. Ms. Collins has also received grants from the American Film Institute, New York State Council on the Arts, and the National Endowment for the Arts. She will direct her second feature film, *Summer Diary*, based on her original screenplay, in the summer of 1986.

The Brothers

Kathleen Collins

to The Conwell Family

The Brothers was first presented at the American Place Theatre on March 31, 1982. The play was directed by Billie Allen, with set by Christina Weppner, costumes by K.L. Fredericks, and lighting by Ann Wrightson. Music was composed by Michael Minard. The cast was as follows:

Danielle Edwards	Josephine Premice
Marietta Edwards	Trazana Beverley
Mr. Norrell	Duane Jones
Lillie Edwards	Janet League
Rosie Gould	Leila Danette
Letitia Edwards	Marie Thomas
Caroline Edwards	Seret Scott
The Doctor	Duane Jones
Voice of Newscaster	Duane Jones

The Brothers was also produced by the Kuntu Repertory Theatre in Pittsburgh from February 19 through March 12, 1982.

The present version of the play was revised by the author as of July 1982. In this revision the characters of Mr. Norrell and The Doctor were eliminated.

CHARACTERS

MARIETTA EDWARDS, the sister
LILLIE EDWARDS, a wife
ROSIE GOULD, Lillie's mother
DANIELLE EDWARDS, a wife
CAROLINE EDWARDS, a wife
LETITIA EDWARDS, a wife

All of the characters are Negro.

TIME
Act I—Sunday, February 1, 1948

Act II—A Sunday four months later
Act III—Friday, April 5, 1968

PLACE
The living room of Danielle Edwards' house; adjacent spaces
that exist in the minds and memories of the characters.

ACT ONE
Living room of Danielle Edwards' house,
Sunday, February 1, 1948.

In the center, a living room, furnished in middle-class taste. Prominent in the room a staircase that leads to an upstairs that is not visible. Characters disappear upstairs but can still be heard. Various noises—thumps, footsteps, even snatches of conversation drift down from up there. In fact, it might be fair to say that the real drama takes place in that Upper Room and what we witness below is its sheer reverberation.

Off from the living room should be other horizontal spaces fanning out in all directions. Spaces that can be almost anything—a kitchen, a garden, a memory, for these spaces exist more profoundly in the characters' minds than in actual fact.

When the play opens, LILLIE EDWARDS *is alone in the living room, pacing. A stunning woman around 30, she is fair enough to pass for white. Dressed in a simple silk, her manner polished and well-bred, she is an imposing figure with a shy, defensive sense of humor.*

A radio is on. We hear a NEWSCASTER *speaking.*

NEWSCASTER'S VOICE. . . . and President Truman expressed the hope that the assassination would not retard the peace of India and the world. Similar expressions of regret were voiced in London, where the King and the Queen and Prime Minister Attlee were among the many leaders to pay tribute to Mr. Gandhi and to deplore the violence that struck him down . . .

(A high-pitched female voice, that of MARIETTA EDWARDS, *screeches across the* NEWSCASTER's *voice.)*

MARIETTA. *(From upstairs.)* You don't mean to say he's thinking of never leaving his bed, he can't mean to do such a stubborn, morbid thing . . .

(Like a shrill burst, MARIETTA EDWARDS *comes bounding down the stairs. She is a well-dressed woman in her mid*

30's with an anxious, intense face. There is an old-maidish quality about her, an abruptness, an edgy dissatisfaction. She can be funny, is always sharply observant, but there is something profoundly off-center about her. She rushes over to LILLIE.)

MARIETTA. There's nothing wrong with him so the doctors say except a touch of asthma causing him to snort and groan, lose his breath every now and then . . .

LILLIE. Good, I can breathe again! I feel as if I'd been roped in at the waist!

MARIETTA. But he won't move! He's declared that he has no intention of ever leaving his bed!

LILLIE. Why, in God's name . . .

MARIETTA. (*Embarrassed.*) It's not easy to repeat . . .

LILLIE. Tell me . . . what reason he could possibly give . . .

MARIETTA. He says it's futile . . . that negro life is a void . . .

LILLIE. (*Almost laughing.*) Stop it, Marietta.

MARIETTA. His words exactly.

LILLIE. (*Without conviction.*) That's silly.

MARIETTA. Nelson, our baby . . .

LILLIE. And stubborn . . .

MARIETTA. What in God's name made him think of such a thing . . .

(The women are lost momentarily in their private thoughts.)

LILLIE. (Out of the blue.) Gandhi's dead.

MARIETTA. (*Confused.*) That refers to what?

LILLIE. (*Almost giggling.*) Chaos, both large and small.

*(*MARIETTA *gives* LILLIE *a long, disapproving look. Then footsteps are heard overhead and she is instantly distracted.)*

MARIETTA. That must be Franklin, about to ask the Lord's intervention . . .

(She rushes up the steps, colliding with DANIELLE EDWARDS *who is on her way down.* MARIETTA *rushes past without a word.)*

DANIELLE. (*To* LILLIE.) Aren't you going up, the ceremony's about to begin, the stars are gathering in the Upper Room.
LILLIE. I'm not dressed for the occasion . . .

(DANIELLE *continues down the steps, amused. She is around 27, stunning too but without* LILLIE's *polished grace. Earthy, easy-going with a deep, raspy voice from too much smoking, she is a woman whose dry sense of humour sets her apart. Unwilling to take life at more than face value, she approaches everything with good-natured mockery.*)

DANIELLE. (*To* LILLIE.) You want some coffee—though something sharper would cut the taste.
LILLIE. Coffee.

(DANIELLE *goes into the kitchen, returns with both coffee and a drink. She hands the coffee to* LILLIE, *who sits there shivering.*)

DANIELLE. Cold? I could turn up the heat . . .
LILLIE. Don't bother, I'm sure it's me. (*She sips her coffee.*) Marietta says he's not sick, not really . . .
DANIELLE. That's right, though he snorts and grunts like an old steam engine. The man's 31, his body's just as tight and trim as the last time he flew down that track, now you tell me where it comes from, all this maudlin despair . . . (*Restless, she lights a cigarette.*) Franklin can pray all he wants, Christ Himself could not get Nelson to rise from that bed.

(*Just then,* MARIETTA *appears on the steps.*)

MARIETTA. (*Breathless.*) He's calling for you, Danielle.
DANIELLE. (*Annoyed.*) He's not dying, Marietta, these are not his final words, he either wants to pee, or he's finally decided on breakfast. No doubt Franklin's prayers have released his appetite . . .

(*Reluctantly, she starts up the steps. Seconds later,* MARIETTA *comes down.* LILLIE *sits shivering, her hands wrapped around her coffee cup.*)

MARIETTA. (*Without feeling.*) You look cold.

LILLIE. It's 5° below outside, so the radio says. The idea
must influence me. (*She shivers.* MARIETTA *looks annoyed.*)

MARIETTA. You should have heard Franklin's prayer, a
splendid plea for God's speedy intervention . . . (*Eyeing* LILLIE *accusingly.*) . . . you didn't come up.

LILLIE. I said my own prayer, Marietta, a private chorus
to Franklin's strident notes . . .

MARIETTA. (*Baffled.*) That's such a literary turn of phrase,
I'm never sure I follow you . . . what did Lillie say,
I ask myself, what did Lillie really say. (*Annoyed,
upset,* NELSON's *announcement preys on her mind.*)
He *can't* mean it . . .

LILLIE. (*Deliberately obtuse.*) Mean what?

MARIETTA. This morbid decision not to leave his bed.

LILLIE. I've never heard of a more ridiculous thing. (*Suddenly giggling.*) . . . though it is restful. (MARIETTA
gives her a disapproving glance.)

MARIETTA. Has Lawrence arrived?

LILLIE. (*Still feeling silly.*) Not before my eyes.

MARIETTA. He'll pump some sense into him, it's Lawrence's cruel and heavy hand we need.

LILLIE. (*Suddenly impatient.*) Is he coming down soon?

MARIETTA. (*Deliberately obtuse.*) Who?

LILLIE. (*Defiantly.*) My Frankie Boy.

MARIETTA. (*It's her turn to giggle.*) There she goes again
with those *descriptive* phrases.

LILLIE. He'll stay up there too long, let Nelson bend his
ear with all that mournful talk. (*Getting more annoyed.*) Nelson's just spoiled, that's all, all of you let
him have his way too often and too long.

MARIETTA. (*Proudly.*) He's our baby . . . (*She goes over
to the mantelpiece, looks admiringly at several of his
trophies.*) . . . flew through the air two Olympics in a
row, glittered with medals, broke one world's record
after another . . . Nelson, our baby . . .

LILLIE. I'm going up. (*She runs into* DANIELLE, *who's on
her way down.*)

DANIELLE. (*With dry humor.*) I wouldn't go up right now,
they're having a heart-to-heart about Nelson's despair.

LILLIE. Franklin can't talk any sense into him, it'll wind
up in a fight . . . wait and see . . .

(They look at each other sympathetically. DANIELLE *goes into the kitchen. Irritated,* LILLIE *turns on* MARIETTA.*)*

LILLIE. . . . there's something in all of you that defies a happy ending.
MARIETTA. *(With placid meanness.)* This is no story, Lillie, we're not polished souls, smooth and prim. *(She makes an affected gesture, then is off on a new track.)* . . . where's Lawrence, where's my fast, determined brother who tolerates no confusion! Lawrence will get him out of that bed, if he were here now, Nelson would be standing once again on his own two feet . . .

(Suddenly upset, she begins to weep. DANIELLE *comes in, drink in one hand, cigarette in the other. She stops when she notices* MARIETTA.*)*

DANIELLE. What's the matter . . . what sudden Edwards flutter did I miss? *(*MARIETTA *looks disapprovingly at the drink.* DANIELLE *raises her glass defiantly.)* What about a little music, or is that an unholy thought?
MARIETTA. It's Sunday.
LILLIE. *(Mischievously.)* And Gandhi's dead . . .
MARIETTA. *(With sudden fury.)* What has *that* got to do with a thing!
DANIELLE. *(Giggling.)* Please, Marietta, save your fury for the Upper Room . . . *(She looks upstairs imagining the scene.)* I bet the old boy's down on his knees by now, weeping and gnashing, confessing his despair . . . *(She falls to her knees, begins a prayer-like intonation, mimicking* NELSON*'s whining voice.)*
Yea that the Negro athlete
Could forever wear his crown
Never stumble
Never falter
Never end his race victorious
In that somber Negro void . . .
MARIETTA. *(Rising.)* That's blasphemous!
LILLIE. *(Amused.)* They call it poetic license, Marietta, truth in the form of free-fallen verse . . . *(She and* DAN- IELLE *exchange amused glances.* MARIETTA *moves indignantly towards the steps.)*
MARIETTA. It's no easy thing for a man to fall from grace.
DANIELLE. *(Rising.)* He didn't fall, Marietta, he took off

his track shoes, grew mortal and flat-footed like the rest
of us . . .

MARIETTA. (*To both of them.*) I don't know which I find
more distasteful, your queasy way of putting things, or
Lillie's overblown prose . . .

(*Just then there is a loud scuffling noise from upstairs, the
sound of male voices raised in anger.*)

MARIETTA. (*Instantly hysterical.*) My boys, my boys, what's
going on with my boys? (*She flies up the stairs.* DAN-
IELLE *almost follows, then stops.*)

DANIELLE. I will *not* go up.

LILLIE. (*Backing away.*) They're fighting . . .

DANIELLE. (*Dryly.*) . . . or we could pretend they're choir-
boys struggling to reach high C . . .

LILLIE. It always finishes in a fight . . .

MARIETTA. (*From upstairs.*) Stop this silly, childish skir-
mishing, what provoked you boys to rage . . .

LILLIE. (*Angry.*) All this high-pitched fury, time and time
again! (*There is the sound of further scuffling.*)

MARIETTA. (*From upstairs.*) Stop it, I say! Give your poor
sister a chance to intervene!

LILLIE. (*Inside her own fury.*) Screeching and screaming
like black crows in heat!

MARIETTA. (*From upstairs.*) Look what you've done!
Driven Franklin to distraction, caused him to strike
out against your nasty old spells, you deserve a whip-
ping . . . (*Furiously clapping her hands.*) . . . one two
three, I'd have you up in a minute . . . it's not fitting
for an Edwards to languish in despair! (*She begins to
cry.*)

LILLIE. (*Outraged.*) And it always ends with the damn
weeping! (DANIELLE *comes over to calm her down.*)

DANIELLE. Why don't you go up, try and persuade Franklin to take time-out from the ring. (LILLIE *hesitates.*)
Go on . . .

LILLIE. I'll do my best . . .

(*She disappears upstairs.* DANIELLE *goes into the kitchen,
returns with a fresh drink, then raises the volume on the
radio. We come in on the end of another newscast.*)

NEWSCASTER'S VOICE. . . . elsewhere, Orville Wright who
   with his brother, the late Wilbur Wright, invented the
   airplane, died last night at Miami Valley Hospital at
   the age of 76 . . .

(Late 40's cool jazz [early Monk or Miles] blares out as
DANIELLE *switches the station, then begins puttering around*
the room.)

DANIELLE. (*To herself.*) . . . before despair there was the
   glitter and the glamour! London, Germany, the New
   York track scene when it was all the way with Nelson!
   He was cruising! Legs flying . . . light years ahead of
   whoever took second! Caught his trophies from princes
   and queens! (*She begins to preen.*) . . . I powdered
   my nose, rouged my cheeks, slipped in and out of
   silks, we were flying! Jet-settin' it negro-style across
   the Continent . . . breakfast at the Carleton at two in
   the afternoon, lavish old parties we dropped in on at
   dawn. We had a flair for the hot-steppin' life . . . (*She*
   looks upstairs.) . . . didn't we . . . (*Suddenly outraged.*)
   Now you tell me why you're up there crying in your
   pillow when there are midnight bars across the continent to make life a slow, *easy* kind of thing! (*She*
   grows sullen.) . . . places we could stroll, drift along
   on a little whiskey and gin . . . (*She drifts into a song.*)
   . . . I took a trip on a train and I thought about you
   . . . two or three stars caught under the sky . . . a
   winding road . . . (*She gets even more moody.*) . . .
   I'm hanging loose on the vine, while he's up there
   playing the Buddha! Turning himself into the Negro
   Job . . . (*Amused by her own humor.*) And God said:
   "Let there be Despair!" And Nelson *dropped* from
   the sky . . . oh boy oh boy . . . (*She giggles to herself,*
   when MARIETTA's *voice interrupts.*)
MARIETTA. (*From upstairs.*) Danielle! (*Startled,* DANIELLE
   turns around. MARIETTA *is standing on the steps.*) He
   wants his Ralston . . .
DANIELLE. (*Quick on the trigger.*) Piping hot, with raisins
   and brown sugar . . .
MARIETTA. (*Taken aback.*) He did put it that way,
   yes . . .
DANIELLE. Tell him I couldn't get any Ralston, only Whea-

tena, but I can fix it the same, he won't even know
the difference . . .

MARIETTA. I'll tell him that, yes . . .

(She disappears upstairs. DANIELLE *goes into the kitchen.
We hear her clattering about, among the pots and pans,
making an awful racket.)*

DANIELLE. *(From the kitchen.)* . . . is this the Big Time,
is this what Nelson meant by the Big Time . . .

*(*MARIETTA *appears on the steps, leans over the railing, and
yells into the kitchen.)*

MARIETTA. He insists that it's not the same . . .

*(*DANIELLE *comes to the doorway, looks up at her.)*

MARIETTA. *(Proudly.)* He has fond memories of Momma
fixing only Ralston in the morning.
DANIELLE. *(Biting her tongue.)* Tell him it will be crunchy,
and creamy sweet just like Ralston . . .

*(*MARIETTA *hesitates, gives off suspicious airs.)*

DANIELLE. *(Moving in for the kill.)* With all her teeth out,
and her hair falling into the bowl, your *Mother* could
have eaten it . . .

(Shocked, MARIETTA *retreats up the steps. Satisfied,* DAN-
IELLE *goes back into the kitchen.)*

DANIELLE. *(Mumbling.)* Let's see now . . . I got my tray,
a dainty napkin for his Highness, the raisins and brown
sugar, a little fresh cream . . . *(She emerges carrying
her tray, crosses the room and starts upstairs.)* . . .
now I ask you, is this the life for a woman of my
quality . . . have I fallen, have I fallen . . . *(She
disappears upstairs. We hear her talking to* NELSON.*)*
. . . you keep telling yourself it's Ralston, it's got
raisins and brown sugar, it's crunchy and creamy sweet,
just like Ralston . . . eat the cereal, Nelson . . .
(Getting louder.) Taste it, for God's sake . . . *(And
louder.)* Taste it! You . . . baby! *(*LILLIE *emerges, slips*

down the stairs.) . . . did anyone ever tell you you're a baby baby baby!!!

(LILLIE *crosses the room. Sudden pain makes her double up, almost lose her balance. She sits down in the nearest chair.*)

LILLIE. (*To herself.*) I can't stand it, not one more minute of it . . .

(*She closes her eyes. Lights dim. Fade-up on* ROSIE GOULD, *standing in her doorway wrapped in a shawl. She is a woman in her 60's with silver hair, skin as fair as* LILLIE'S. *She has a charming manner, gracious, yet not without a sharp, rather aloof edge.* LILLIE *comes rushing up the steps in a fur coat and hat, shivering intensely. There is a feeling of wind, bitter cold in the air.*)

LILLIE. (*Breathless.*) I brought the children, Momma. Nelson's sick, we might have to be there all day, do you mind?

ROSIE. Where's Franklin?

LILLIE. In the car . . . is it alright, Momma, it's not any fun for them at Nelson's . . .

ROSIE. It's cold, child, go bring them in, I know they're in a mood for hot chocolate and cake . . .

LILLIE. (*Relieved.*) Thank you, Momma . . . when I told them they might be coming to you, Rowena squealed, "We're going to Rosie's, our Rosie's, our Rosie's," she shouted . . . (*Laughing oddly.*) . . . where it's sweet-smelling and clear and the odor of death is nowhere about.

ROSIE. (*Stiffening.*) Those are no child's words.

LILLIE. (*Ashamed.*) I'm sorry, Momma . . . I'm not well, I feel like I'm coming apart. The house is too small, there's no room to breathe. I have to stay by the phone and record who's died. Franklin depends on me to keep track of all the details, when the funeral will be, what flowers will go on the grave, what size casket they need. I could almost embalm them, Momma, I've grown so familiar with the rituals of death.

ROSIE. (*Distancing herself.*) Stop, child, stop whining as if life were no more than a morbid dream! (*A car horn honks briskly.*)

LILLIE. That's my Frankie Boy . . . I'll feel better, Momma
. . . soon Franklin will have his degree and this catering
to death will be over. (*The horn honks again.*) He's
bound to succeed, a man that impatient is bound to
succeed. All the Edwards ride a proud, hungry edge.
(*She rushes down the steps.*)

ROSIE. (*Under her breath.*) So do race horses and fools.

(*We hear the car door open and* LILLIE *speaking to the
children.*)

LILLIE. (*Out of sight.*) See Rosie, our sweet Rosie . . .
(MARIETTA's *voice cuts across.*)

MARIETTA. (*Out of the dark.*) Lillie . . .

(*Lights go out on* ROSIE, *come up on* MARIETTA *tiptoeing
down the steps.*)

Lillie . . . (*No answer. She looks around, the room
remains mostly in shadow.*) I'll bet you anything she's
gone for a walk, that's just like her to tiptoe away,
come rushing back all a-flutter about her Frankie boy.
(*She mimicks* LILLIE's *genteel tone.*) ". . . oh Frankie
Boy, don't get yourself so worked up, oh Frankie Boy
. . ." (*Annoyed.*) . . . while Franklin looks at her with
moony eyes. He's too stern for such foolishness . . .
it's not often he laughs, except with me . . . there are
things between us that make us fall out in a fit . . .
secret things that go back to childhood, to heavy rooms,
Pop's stern forbidding ways . . .

(*Lights change as she drifts into the past and relives a conversation with* FRANKLIN. *Her voice changes to whispered
fright.*)

Pop's in a fury, Franklin. Lawrence failed the Post
Office exam . . . you should hear him. Lawrence came
within inches of getting the thrashing of his life. (*She
mimicks her father's violent, stentorian tone.*) ". . . I
expected one of my boys to put in a good show down
there . . . you keep out of this, Margaret, I know what
each and every one of these boys better turn out to
be. I may be too skin deep, locked forever behind
this stone wall but I will not tolerate from my boys

any *scrawny colored lives!*" (*Nervous and excited.*) Oh Franklin, he pitched a fit! You know how he gets . . . his glasses fall off and he has to squint . . . he can't see two feet in front of him but he keeps *roaring* away! (*They laugh.*) I guess Lawrence couldn't find a way to cheat . . . he would have and you know it. I don't care what you say, he's a schemer, he can think of more devious things . . . that's because you refuse to see bad in anything, you're too . . . (*She searches for the right word.*) . . . *upstanding* . . . the righteous one in the clan. Lawrence will knock people over to get where he wants to go . . . not you, you'll work hard, be truthful, persevere . . . of course you'll make it, you'll be First Colored at something just the way Pop dreams. (*They laugh.*) . . . you met who . . . when did this happen . . . oh Franklin, tell me everything . . . who is she . . . a Gould! Why they're queer, eccentric, the haughtiest Negroes around! Live off by themselves on their own private acres, never mingle nor mix with any other souls . . . how did you meet her . . . oh I know she's beautiful, they're a handsome tribe, take great pride in their land and their color, breed themselves as white as any negro stock can be. (*That provokes a chuckle.*) Do the boys know? Lawrence will be jealous, I can tell you that much . . . not Jeremy, he's always good-natured. (*She mimicks Jeremy's stuttering.*) . . . th . . . th . . . that's j . . . j . . . jus . . . st gr . . . gr . . . and, Fr . . . Fr . . . Franklin . . . I . . . 'm s . . . so ha . . . ha . . . ppy f . . . f . . . for y . . . ou . . . Dear dear Jeremy . . . and of course Nelson will think it's wonderful, he thinks the world of you . . . me? Why ask such a thing. I'm sure I'll like her, I can't see why not, unless she's flighty or silly . . . or doesn't like me . . . well I might be too plain for her taste . . . there's nothing fancy about me . . . I'm not subtle or delicate as I suspect her to be. (*Suddenly feeling self-conscious.*) She's not been raised around four boys all her life . . . pushing and pulling and tugging at me . . . till sometimes I feel like an abrupt male thing. (*Growing even more self-conscious.*) . . . who am I anyway . . . am I just you boys' shadow that no one will ever see? (LILLIE's voice interrupts.)

LILLIE. (*Out of the dark.*) Marietta . . .

(Lights go out quickly. Come up on LILLIE *still sitting in the chair where she's fallen asleep.)*

Marietta . . . I thought I heard her speak . . . where is everyone? *(She goes towards the steps when* MARIETTA *appears startling her.)* I thought I heard you . . .

MARIETTA. I was in the kitchen fixing myself some tea.

LILLIE. I fell asleep.

MARIETTA. I thought you'd gone for a walk.

LILLIE. *(Shivering.)* Too cold.

MARIETTA. *(Oddly.)* I said to myself, Lillie's walking around . . .

LILLIE. *(Amused.)* You talk about me like I'm not here. Is there more tea?

MARIETTA. I made a fresh pot. *(*LILLIE *starts towards the kitchen,* MARIETTA *blocks her path.)* Don't move, don't move. *(She goes quickly into the kitchen, returns almost as quickly with tea and things on a tray.)* Bring that coffee table over here. *(*LILLIE *does as she's told,* MARIETTA *puts down the tray.)* Sit down. *(Again,* LILLIE *obeys.* MARIETTA *begins ceremoniously to serve tea.)* Those are sweets. Danielle baked them, so I'm sure they're no good. *(She mimicks* LAWRENCE's *acid tongue.)* ". . . it should be clear to all of us by now that Danielle has no flair for the domestic sciences . . ." *(Giggling.)* . . . that's how Lawrence puts it.

LILLIE. *(Gently.)* . . . though her humour is often better than a good meal. *(Silence reigns. After a while.)* Tell me what it is *I* do wrong in your eyes.

MARIETTA. *(Annoyed.)* Now how am I supposed to answer that, by taking you apart?

LILLIE. You think I'm too flat, too low-keyed for someone with Franklin's temperament.

MARIETTA. *(Growing testy.)* And what does that mean . . . flat, low-keyed, as if you were a piece of music, you have this irritating way of speaking in tongues, alluding to things, as if nothing had a proper name.

LILLIE. *(Bluntly.)* You think I'm weak.

MARIETTA. *(Backing off.)* Slow . . . for the Edwards speed.

LILLIE. Haughty.

MARIETTA. Too refined.

LILLIE. *(Bizarrely.)* A clinging vine.

MARIETTA. *(Getting nasty.)* All sweetness and light.

LILLIE. (*Bluntly.*) You don't like me.

MARIETTA. (*Spitefully.*) What has *that* got to do with a thing! (*Silence.*)

DANIELLE. (*From upstairs.*) . . . that's exactly right, that's the least he can do.

(*She comes stomping down the steps.* MARIETTA, *uneasy, gets up and starts towards the steps.*)

Where are my cigarettes? (MARIETTA *brushes past her and goes upstairs.*)

LILLIE. How is it up there?

DANIELLE. There's an effort underway to get him to use the bathroom. (*She grabs a cigarette.*) Depression is one thing, urinary warfare is quite another.

LILLIE. (*Angry.*) What's the point?

DANIELLE. Of never getting out of bed? (*They look at each other. The absurdity of the thing hits them and they break out laughing.*) He thinks he has a right to his despair.

LILLIE. Because he's colored. (*They can't stop laughing.*)

DANIELLE. (*Giggling.*) You should hear him up there pontificating . . . (*She begins to mimick* NELSON's *dry, whining drawl.*) ". . . now Franklin, you and I both know that the Negro athlete, once he falls from grace has nowhere to run . . . the track and field were his last defense, once that falls, he returns to the void, negro life is a void, Franklin, you and I both know that." (*She giggles.*) Then Franklin starts in on him. (*Assuming* FRANKLIN's *crisper, sterner tone.*) ". . . It does none of us any good to hear you talk like that, Nelson . . . what would we do if the whole race went back to bed." (*They can't stop laughing.*)

LILLIE. (*Giggling.*) Can't you see it . . . armies of Negroes taking to their beds . . .

DANIELLE. (*Giggling.*) Declaring Nelson King of the Void . . . (*The laughter subsides.*) . . . which makes me what . . . Queen of the Bed Pans . . . (*She can't help wincing.*) . . . that's kind of hard to get dressed up for. (*Suddenly frightened.*) I could lose my bearings, Lillie. I'm only built for speed.

(*Just then there is a loud scream from upstairs.*)

MARIETTA. (*Upstairs.*) Don't do that! Stop it, Nelson. Franklin, stop him, he could suffocate. Take it from him . . . he's mad, completely mad, abuses all our kindness, oh God, I can't stand to see him treat himself this way! (*She comes rushing down the steps.*) He just tried to bury himself under his pillow! (*The doorbell rings.*) . . . it's Lawrence, thank God! Our charger's on the scene! (*She starts towards the door. Lights go out.*)

END OF ACT ONE

ACT TWO

SCENE 1
DANIELLE EDWARDS' LIVING ROOM, ROSIE GOULD'S GARDEN.
A SUNDAY FOUR MONTHS LATER.

Lights fade up on DANIELLE'*s living room. We hear her upstairs talking to* NELSON.

DANIELLE. (*From upstairs.*) I'm applying all my culinary skills to this meal, the least you could do is make it to the table. I'm asking you to walk a few hundred feet, crawl, if you have to, I don't give a damn how you get there . . . speak up, god damnit, or else write me one of your notes . . . what's no use? What are you always crying about . . . (*She comes to the steps, shouts back at him.*) . . . you think you're the Prophet, Nelson the Negro Prophet leading his people through the Valley of Tears! (*She stomps down the steps.*) Just get up and go to work! We could have a few drinks, a few kids, *then* you can die. Honest to God, Nelson, I'm gonna get old, how much longer you want to play this Job scenario . . . the whole damn race is Job, what makes you so special . . . (*She sits down at the bottom of the steps.*) This could get bleak . . . me, a bottle of gin and a looney-tune colored man. (*That makes her laugh in spite of herself.*) Colored or not, I'm not built for despair . . . must be a high yaller impulse to keep things light. I'm descended from too long a line of sallow women who taught me to look stylish and shut my mouth . . . wear my skin like it was a precious jewel . . . wait for choice negro offerings to line up at my door. I was supposed to have myself a doctor, or a lawyer, why I chose Nelson is more than I can explain. (*She laughs at herself.*) It must have been those quick-moving limbs, that sly

315

baby-face grin, the old boy looked like he was good for many years in the fast lane. Together I thought we'd ride above the storms, turn negro life into a stardust melody . . . no bleak strolls into despair, no questions asked at all. (*She yells loud enough for him to hear.*) It was not my intention to think life through! Wind up with answers that lead nowhere but down! (*The phone rings throwing her off-balance. She takes her time answering.*) Hello . . . yes, Franklin . . . is Lillie any better? . . . I'm sorry, Franklin, tell her I'll try to come see her next week but it's hard for me to get away . . . no he hasn't moved . . . I told him you were all coming to dinner but I think that made things worse . . . I can't say, it's rare nowadays that he uses the spoken word . . . he prefers to write notes . . . (*Just then there is a loud thump overhead.*) . . . and when that fails, he pounds on the floor like a damn inmate . . . hold on a second. (*She goes over to the steps, furious.*) What's the matter with you, I'm talking to Franklin. (*Now the doorbell rings, followed by another loud thump or two from upstairs.* DANIELLE *is beside herself.*) And I'm supposed to *manage* this act. (*She goes to the door.* MARIETTA *comes in, just as* NELSON *thump-thumps again.* MARIETTA *looks puzzled.*) He started that yesterday, will you go upstairs and shut him up, Franklin's on the phone. (MARIETTA *rushes upstairs.* DANIELLE *goes back to the phone.*) I'm sorry, Franklin, maybe it would be better if you all didn't come, the idea seems to have set him off, he swears there's some kind of conspiracy to get him to go to work. (*The thumping starts again.*)

MARIETTA. (*From upstairs. Urgent.*) Danielle.

DANIELLE. (*Quickly.*) I gotta go, if you can't reach Lawrence, then please come, I can't handle the charger by myself . . . all right. (*She hangs up, starts immediately up the steps.*) . . . I'm coming, though I wish to hell they'd put me in a strait-jacket, and cart me off. (*She disappears upstairs, talking to* NELSON.) His Highness rang.

(*The doorbell rings. No one seems to hear it. It rings again. Finally, the door opens, and* CAROLINE EDWARDS *steps in. She is a woman in her mid 30's, exquisitely dressed in an expensive fur coat that fits her to perfection. A sense of style, clothes-wise, and an instinct to flaunt it, should strike one immediately. There is, in general, a defiant quality about her, a gruff way of speaking and behaving that lacks refinement. She crosses the stairway, talking to herself.)*

CAROLINE. Where's everybody . . . probably gathered already in the Upper Room. (*She starts to go up, changes her mind.*) . . . I'll wait for Lawrence . . . though the minute he hits that door he'll fly right by me. (*Amused by that, she mimicks his brusque manner to perfection.*) ". . . gotta check on Nelson, gotta check on Nelson, fix me a drink, fix me a drink . . ." Then he'll *charge* up the steps, and the fireworks will begin. Maybe I should warn them that he's on his way . . . give them a chance to cool Nelson down. (*She acts out the idea with amusement.*) Greetings everybody, Lawrence sent me on ahead. He's hot on the trail of some fast-moving real estate deal, suggested I play advance man for his act. (*That truly amuses her.*) . . . that'll set things off. Marietta will have to pee, the thought of Lawrence always sends her racing to the bathroom. Danielle will sneak three quickies before he gets through the door. Nelson will bury himself under his pillows, while Franklin tries in vain to raise him from the dead. Poor Lillie will miss all the fun and explosions, I guess too many sparks have flown in her eye. (*Again she starts to go up, but changes her mind.*) I need the charger. (*Restless, she goes to a mirror to check her appearance. She is taking off her coat, when* MARIETTA *appears on the steps, sees her, rushes down quickly.*)

MARIETTA. When did you come in, where's Lawrence?

CAROLINE. He'll be late. How's Nelson?

MARIETTA. I think he's gone to the moon, or some other planet where depressed souls go. He's propped up in bed, and if you ask him anything, he writes you a note. I said to him, wouldn't you like to come downstairs for dinner . . . he thought about it awhile, then wrote: (*Reciting the note.*) "He who lives in silence defies Negro pain." Now what has that got to do with coming down to dinner? He won't let Danielle out of his sight, has a fit whenever she tries to leave the room . . . which reminds me, she sent me down here to check the roast.

(She goes quickly into the kitchen. CAROLINE *goes to the window, looking for* LAWRENCE. *When* MARIETTA *comes back in, she picks up* CAROLINE's *fur coat.)*

Is that new?

CAROLINE. Sort of.

MARIETTA. (*Coolly.*) There are tangible benefits to Lawrence's brutal deals. (*She drops the coat, plops down in a chair.*) I'm tired, I spent the morning with Lillie who looks appropriately languid as only Lillie can look.

CAROLINE. But she's sick, really sick, according to Lawrence, they say there's something wrong with her spine.

MARIETTA. Well, she's staying with Rosie who I'm sure will pamper her back to health.

(She closes her eyes. CAROLINE *remains by the window. Neither of them speaks for the longest time. Intruding on their silence is* DANIELLE's *laughter.)*

DANIELLE. (*From upstairs.*) That's very good, but I can't think of any words that rhyme with Negro . . . how about gigolo? (*She laughs even harder, as if in response to something* NELSON *says.*) . . . that's better yet, you have the makings of a real bard. (DANIELLE's *laughter subsides.*)

MARIETTA. (*Touched.*) Nelson, our baby.

*(*CAROLINE *looks at her oddly but her eyes are closed. The silence continues until* CAROLINE, *feeling restless, lights a cigarette. The sharp striking of the match startles* MARIETTA, *who jumps awake.)*

I thought I heard Lawrence, it's just like him to surprise me with his presence.

CAROLINE. (*Amused.*) The charger never rings nor announces his arrival.

MARIETTA. (*Agreeing.*) All of a sudden, he's here . . . it's the same with you. You carry around his atmosphere.

CAROLINE. (*Distant.*) I've heard you say that we look alike.

MARIETT. (*Agreeing.*) That Lawrence would find his match has always surprised me, he was such a separate child, we had to remind ourselves that he was our brother. But the moment you entered the house, I thought to myself—Lawrence went off and found his twin. (*Amused.*) Two sleekly polished souls have we, two sleekly polished souls.

CAROLINE. I don't know whether to be flattered or not.

MARIETTA. (MARIETTA *laughingly repeats the same refrain.*) Two sleekly polished souls . . .

(*Over this refrain, "cool" music drifts in, disembodied like a memory.* CAROLINE *moves forward responding to it.*)

CAROLINE. (*Remembering.*) I'm standing on a cool balcony on a hot summer night. Alone. In a new floral gown. It's hot. The dance floor's crowded. I refuse to go down and sweat with the crowd. I look too good. I will not get all souped-up for some silly young thing . . . all of a sudden, Lawrence walks in. I watch him glide across the floor with his shiny black hair. He looks up, sees me . . . (*Mimicking* LAWRENCE's *gruff, raspy voice.*) "What you doin', what you doin' up there?" (*As herself.*) I don't want to sweat, it's nice and cool up here. (*As* LAWRENCE.) "I'll keep it the same down here." And he holds out his hand, his eyes leaping at me. (*She shivers.*) Down I go . . . wrapped in those cool arms before I know what hit me . . . that was the beginning.

(*She moves as if dancing. Cross-fade to* MARIETTA *who, too, has drifted back into the past and is once again talking with* FRANKLIN.)

MARIETTA. Who? Lawrence and that sleek little Fieldsboro thing? That story's as clear as a bell, those two will most certainly marry, they have the same greedy high-pitched dreams . . . who else was there . . . old Bus? With a girl? (*Slightly embarrassed.*) . . . oh I guess I was hoping he'd ask me . . . never mind. Did you meet Rosie . . . I could have told you that, they don't like anyone who's brown. Tell me what Lillie was wearing . . . that sounds exactly like her with her "Frankie Boy" this and her "Frankie Boy" that, really, Franklin, that's a truly embarrassing name, only Lillie would think of such a thing out of her wide-ranging memory for the coy, romantic touch she calls you her Frankie Boy. (*She shakes her head disapprovingly.*)

. . . I do like her, she's kind, even funny in a sweet, poetic way . . . and she certainly loves you . . . I don't know, that's her idea of romance, a singular adoration fixed forever on one chosen soul . . . I don't know if love everlasting fits the hard Edwards mold for dreams. (*Suddenly uptight.*) I'm not jealous and I won't be teased like already I'm some spinster fool . . . who . . . oh . . . Bus . . . don't call him that, Franklin, he's nice and he has a good job with the railroad, too . . . you mock anyone who comes near my door . . . (*Mimicking him.*) "He's not good enough for you, Marietta, not that scrawny negro fool." (*They laugh.*) . . . you're as bad as Pop . . . will he be among the first of the first of the coloreds, he'd say . . . (*They begin to giggle.*) . . . poor Bus, I bet you scared him away . . . well, he is a little slow . . . and he's got big feet . . . (*They are really giggling by now.*) And as Pop would say, he's a bit too colored for me. (*Laughter explodes out of her.*) . . . oh Franklin, there's nobody but nobody I ever laugh with like you. (*She leans over conspiratorially.*) Tell me again about old Slade Wilson, it's not true, Franklin, that he almost got himself embalmed. (*She giggles, listening, when a loud cry from* DANIELLE *cuts across.*)

DANIELLE. (*From upstairs. Hysterical.*) Marietta!

(*Lights go out quickly on* MARIETTA, *come up on* DANIELLE *standing on the steps as* MARIETTA *rushes in to see what's wrong.*)

I can't wake him . . . he's not breathing, or am I seeing things . . . call someone quick, my God, I better not leave him. (*Starts back up the steps, as* MARIETTA *rushes to dial the phone.*) . . . he's faking, that is just like him to fool me, he's good at holding his breath for as long as he wants. (*She disappears upstairs.*)

MARIETTA. (*On the phone.*) Dr. Wilkins, please . . . and quickly . . . it's my brother, Nelson Edwards, he's not breathing at all . . .

DANIELLE. (*From upstairs. Hysterical.*) Marietta!

(*Just then the doorbell rings with quick, insistent strokes.* MARIETTA *drops the phone.*)

MARIETTA. . . . oh thank God, it's the charger . . . he'll wake him up alright, pump some sense into that playful spirit, always scaring us with his games. (*As she rushes to answer the door,* LILLIE's *voice cuts across.*)

LILLIE. (*Out of the dark.*) Momma!

(*Lights black out on* MARIETTA, *a dim light fades up on* LILLIE's *face. Her eyes are closed, she moves restlessly, as if talking in her sleep.*)

What happened then . . . oh Frankie boy, he's not dead, no one ever dies . . . they sleep, they dream, nothing is as it seems . . .

ROSIE. (*Out of the dark.*) Lillie . . .

(*Lights come up. We're in* ROSIE's *garden.* LILLIE *is stretched out on a chaise lounge, an afghan thrown across her. She wakes up in confusion, while* ROSIE *stands there holding a tray.*)

LILLIE. I fell asleep. Marietta always wears me out. I was dreaming about Nelson, he was trying to strangle himself with his pillow. I thought it was funny but Franklin thought he was dead. I was sure he wasn't, I kept saying, you can't strangle yourself with a pillow, no one can strangle themselves with a pillow but he wouldn't listen and started to cry . . . (*She looks at* ROSIE *who gives her back an aloof gaze.*) I suppose you'd call that a morbid dream.

ROSIE. It has no bright overtones, no : . . (*She sets down her tray.*) I brought you some tea, a slice of lemon pound cake and some strawberries, the first from my garden.

LILLIE. They look lovely, Momma, plump and cheerful like you'd like me to be. (*She smiles at her mother.*) I've seen everything come into bloom, watched your forsythia spread along that fence, followed your magnolia and dogwood as they burst open, now your roses have come and almost gone. Do they watch me, I wonder, laugh and shake their heads at this dying old vine . . . (*She grows nervous.*) . . . where are the children?

ROSIE. Rowena's in the kitchen learning to make floating island, I just put the baby down for a nap.

LILLIE. They tiptoe around me like they knew I needed silence to keep me alive. (ROSIE *stiffens.*) I don't get better, do I, Momma, and it's me not the illness that's wasting away.

ROSIE. Don't talk like that, child. (*She serves her some tea.*)

LILLIE. I'll brighten up, I'll be just like those peonies, haughty and proud as you raised me to be. (*Suddenly anxious.*) Did Franklin call?

ROSIE. Not since this morning.

LILLIE. (*Upset.*) You should have wakened me, Momma, it upsets him to feel cut off from me. He has a funeral today, his classes this evening, then he'll try to run by Nelson's before he goes to work. He won't call if he thinks it's too late.

ROSIE. I should go in, I promised to teach Rowena how to separate eggs. (LILLIE *tries to get up.*)

LILLIE. (*In pain.*) Help me up, Momma. (ROSIE *goes to help her. Together they manage to get her on her feet, which pleases* LILLIE *greatly.*) Now, what can I do . . . if I were home, I could answer the phone for my Frankie Boy, tell him who died, it's always a proud moment when I rush down the stairs. Frankie Boy, someone's dead, we can pay our bills, go out to dinner, have a night on the town, we're rich, Frankie Boy, look at the pleasures death will loan us for an hour! (*She holds tight to* ROSIE.) Let's walk a bit, Momma, it's the least I can do. (*They begin to walk. She falters, grabs hold of* ROSIE, *crying out in pain.*) I can't even do that, my back's too broken to carry me to the gate . . . it's funny to watch this body splinter itself to bits. (ROSIE *leads her back.*)

ROSIE. (*Matter-of-factly.*) It's the sun that's too hot, we'll wait till it's cool and there's a breeze to carry us.

LILLIE. That's just like you, Momma, keep things clear and simple, like tea and flowers were the only real things. (*She mocks her mother in nursery rhyme prose.*)
My Rosie lives outside of race
She never lets it reach her gate
She grows her flowers
Bakes her sweets
Race is a stranger she never meets.

ROSIE. (*Furious.*) Stop it! I won't be made fun of! I said to you what any Mother would have said. It was the best advice I could offer, don't mock me because it's true. (*She tries to soften her anger.*) I shouldn't leave the children this long . . . try to sleep and dream for once of all the *bright* things that surround you. (*She leaves.* LILLIE, *on the verge of crying, tries to get up but can't.*)

LILLIE. (*Sad and upset.*) Oh Momma, you don't know my Frankie Boy when he's at his best . . .

(*She begins to cry, drifts fretfully into sleep. The scenes that follow are her dreams: 40's music, the cool early jazz of Miles Davis, drifts across. Lights fade up on what must feel like a dance hall.* LILLIE *drifts in as if dancing with someone. She is vibrant and bright in a silk gown and responds to her partner as if engaged in conversation.*)

. . . I came with my cousin, Winston Gould. (*Responding.*) . . . I agree, it's a dark, morbid name but it fits him, he's (*Drifting into rhyme.*)
Always stiff
Always sad
Never does anything
Good or bad
(*Responding.*) I always do that, I learn who people are by putting them in verse. (*Responding.*) I don't know you well enough. Tell me at least three things about you. Mortuary science, you mean corpses, embalming, that kind of thing . . . that's morbid, going to school to learn about death! . . . then what are you really studying . . . I see you better as that, you'll make a wonderful teacher, eager, upstanding, stern to a fault . . . (*She stops dancing.*) . . . I don't know. You don't smile—that's a sign of sternness and there's a crease in your forehead . . . right there . . . it's frowning at me even though you're trying to smile. You're too serious! (*She giggles, suddenly excited.*) Momma!

(*Lights come up on* ROSIE, *sitting in a rocking chair crocheting.* LILLIE *rushes in, breathless and excited.*)

It was a lovely dance! I danced every dance with Franklin Edwards from Riverview, a handsome man who will be magnificent one day . . . not now, he's

only a mortician, a watchman at night to make ends
meet. But he's in school, an education major like
myself, he'll be a teacher one day, then a principal,
he's determined to succeed, it's written all over his
face. (*Hesitant.*) . . . he's brown, Momma, not very,
but a little browner than any of us. (*She waits for an
answer.* ROSIE *doesn't say a thing.* LILLIE *bursts out
laughing.*) I call him my Frankie Boy. (*She drifts into
rhyme.*)
Last night at a dance
I fell into a trance
A silly old spell
Perhaps no one could tell
Except the stranger
I met and married at a glance
It's he, of course
Who put me in a trance.
(*She kneels beside her mother.*) Tell me why you don't
like my Frankie Boy.

ROSIE. (*Distant.*) You already know the answer . . . every
bit of the answer.

LILLIE. You think I'm weak.

ROSIE. To ask for trouble, brooding Negro trouble is a
weakness, yes.

LILLIE. But there must be room for love, Momma.

ROSIE. A slippery platform, child, don't plant your feet on
such a slippery platform.

(*Lights go out. In the dark: somber organ music. We come
up slowly on* LILLIE *sitting by an open window writing.*)

LILLIE. From my window I can see
Death arrive, it follows me
In and out my door it goes,
Caskets, flowers, tales of woe
No one smiles
No one rejoices
Somber faces, somber choices . . .

(*Footsteps are heard. She gets up, puts her writing aside.*)

Is that you, Frankie Boy? (*Responding.*)
No . . . no calls,
No deaths

No one sees fit
To take their rest
(*Amused.*) I've been sitting at the window all morning
making up verses. Come hold me, I don't mind anything when you hold me. (*She moves towards him
when a sudden pain grips her.*) . . . I don't know, ever
since Rowena it comes and goes as if something came
apart at her birth. Don't frown, it's only plumbing, a
loose valve, you're back, now it will dissolve. (*She
reaches out to touch him but he doesn't respond.*) Don't
brood, it's only the warehouse. It's our prison, it keeps
us apart in the still of the night, makes mornings come
in slow and somber . . . (*Refusing depression.*) . . .
but it won't last forever! Soon you'll have those degrees . . . oh Frankie Boy, don't brood, every second
of life's not dangerous and sad . . . hold me, please,
hold me.

(ROSIE'*s voice cuts across the scene. Lights go out quickly.*)

ROSIE. (*Out of the dark.*) Lillie . . .

(*Come up on* ROSIE, *like a shadow. She hovers a moment
over* LILLIE *eclipsing her from our sight.*)

Wake up, child . . .

(LILLIE *wakes up in confusion as though she were a small
child again.*)

LILLIE. (*Defensively.*) Don't blame me for my dreams,
Momma, I tried hard to make them bright and harm-
less.
ROSIE. Franklin just called, he'll be here shortly after his
classes, he has the night off from the midnight shift.
I'll bring you your dinner.

(*Excited,* LILLIE *starts to get up.*)

LILLIE. I can get up, Momma, I'd like to eat with the
children, my Frankie Boy's coming, I think I'll even
change.

(She pulls herself up violently. The effort sends her sprawling, knocking over the table and chair beside her lounge.)

I'm a joke, Momma. (ROSIE *tries to lift her but can't.*)

ROSIE. I'll need help to lift you, child, just lay still for a moment. (*She rushes away.* LILLIE *lays there growing increasingly delirious.*)

LILLIE. Frankie Boy, here lies your Lillie, a crumpled heap . . . (*She cries out in pain.*) Oh God, what a mess dying is. I don't want him to find me all disordered like this. (*She tries to move but the pain defeats her.*) Rosie will fix me, she'll make me look lovely, I can see myself stretched out under her gaze . . . surrounded by flowers . . . lilies of the valley, white roses, delphiniums, I'll be decked out like a queen . . . Queen of the Bed Pans. (*She giggles. By now she is completely delirious.*) . . . oh Danielle . . . don't let their pride defeat you, it's a sickness, they're all too angry to breathe . . . (*With sudden defiance.*) I will *not* live off of anger, dead bodies, defeated dreams! Watch my Frankie Boy brood on all the unfair negro things . . . no, the drab passages are too much for me! (*Collapsing with shame.*) What a mess I've made of things. (*Weeping.*) Frankie Boy, my Frankie Boy . . . (*Something begins to change inside her body.*) My strength's coming back, my body feels so light and free just as if it were leaving me. (*She screams out in panic.*) Momma! I don't want to die just yet, tell my children they don't have to remember me. (*A violent movement rocks her body.*) . . . flowers *burst* into bloom, Momma, all of a sudden they thrust themselves free!

(She dies. Lights fade slowly. After awhile, they come up on ROSIE *sitting in her rocking chair in a darkened corner.)*

ROSIE. A dead daughter, that's a fine thing to talk about, I never speak of a dead daughter. There are letters, of course, photographs taken up to the age of 30, a little child who screams from the top of the stairs . . . where's my Mommie. (*Retreating into haughtiness.*) How many times do I have to tell you, child, your Mother has gone to Heaven, where all dead

Mothers go . . . to Heaven where it is fragrant, sweet-smelling, and white lilacs are in bloom the year round.

(*She claps her hands feverishly. Lights go out.*)

ACT TWO

Scene 2
Danielle Edwards' living room, a few days later.

A dim light surrounds DANIELLE, *who is standing on the steps, dressed in black.*

DANIELLE. He's asleep, worn out like a baby . . . looks just as peaceful, too, all the brooding gone from his face, you'd never imagine he was the least bit unhappy.

(*As she starts down the steps, lights fade up, and we see* MARIETTA, *also dressed in black standing at the bottom of the steps.*)

MARIETTA. The car will be here shortly.

(CAROLINE *comes in from the kitchen. She is not dressed in black, wears instead a handsome beige outfit, with her hair pulled back severely.*)

CAROLINE. I boiled water for coffee or tea, which would you prefer?
DANIELLE. (*Coming down.*) Neither.
MARIETTA. You're not going to drink before Lillie's wake! (DANIELLE *glances at her.* MARIETTA *goes all mournful.*) Dear Lillie, dead Lillie, why did she go so fast . . . (*She moves away, upset.*) Already, Franklin is not the same, has shut himself up, closed the door on me . . .
DANIELLE. He's in shock, Marietta, all of us are. (*She looks upstairs.*) . . . he liked Lillie so, she used to

scold him with her rhymes, try to tease him out of bed . . . (*Gently mimicking* LILLIE.)
Nelson Nelson
Isn't it a shame
For you to stay in bed like this
As if you were lame!
Pretending to be sick
With the negro blues
When all you really want
Is to take a snooze . . .
(*Fondly amused.*) There are verses like that, sent to him from Rosie's, when she was too sick to move . . . he'd write back, send her his own brand of wit, and poetic humour. (*Taking on* NELSON'S *dry, whining drawl.*)
Dear Lillie
Isn't it silly
That we're both in bed
Playing dead
While the world goes on around us . . .

(*She grows sad, uneasy, can't help looking upstairs.*)

MARIETTA. (*Like a refrain.*) Dear Lillie, dead Lillie, why did she go so fast . . . ? (*She shifts into indignation.*) I can hear Rosie's people now, they'll swear Lillie didn't die a natural death, that it had to do with Franklin being too dark, too poor, and not yet finished with school . . . in their hearts they'll blame Franklin . . . and Franklin will blame himself, that's the worst of the story. (*This upsets her.* DANIELLE *goes to comfort her, when the phone rings.* CAROLINE *answers it.*)
CAROLINE. Hello . . . No, they're waiting for the car . . . I'm staying with Nelson until she gets back . . . he can't . . . stop foaming, I'll be here about two hours, then I'll meet you at the wake . . .
MARIETTA. Is that Lawrence? (CAROLINE *nods.*) May I speak to him? (CAROLINE *coolly yields the phone.*) Lawrence . . . tell me first about Jeremy and when he's due to arrive . . . someone has to meet him . . . don't talk that way . . . stop it, Lawrence, that's too unkind, it's as if he were an orphan, or step-child in the clan . . . (*Adamant.*) It's not fair that he come so far without a welcome, if you won't do it, I'll ask Mr.

Norrell to send a car . . . alright . . . really? That's just like them, no pomp and circumstance, if it were up to Rosie there'd be no funeral at all . . . who . . . the cousins? Aren't they a *sight* . . . all washed out and anemic looking with those faded blue eyes . . . (*She mimicks their light Southern twang.*) ". . . Rosie's child had no business takin' up with no undertaker. . . why she spent her last days playin' secretary to the dead . . ." (*Growing more upset.*) They will blame it all on Franklin. (*She goes to pieces.* CAROLINE *takes the phone.*)

CAROLINE. I'll come as soon as they get back . . . how much . . . I don't know, you could get burned in a deal like that . . .

MARIETTA. (*Eavesdropping.*) He can't be wheeling and dealing behind Lillie's grave!

CAROLINE. (*Uneasy.*) I better go . . . I wouldn't move too fast on that. (*She hangs up.*)

MARIETTA. (*Pouncing.*) All of us grieving, while he hustles some nasty deal!

CAROLINE. There's no need to take it personally, Marietta.

MARIETTA. (*Indignant.*) His own brother left unattended!

CAROLINE. (*With growing irritation.*) He said he'd pick him up.

MARIETTA. (*Consumed with indignation.*) Poor Jeremy will look for a welcome, and where will Lawrence be . . . around the corner shaking some greasy palm. (*Now she turns on* CAROLINE.) And *you* in sleek disdain, won't even dress for mourning!

CAROLINE. (*Defiant.*) What I put on my back has no place in this exchange. (*She moves aggressively close.* MARIETTA *retreats slightly.*)

MARIETTA. Dear Lillie, dead Lillie, why did she go so fast . . . (CAROLINE *turns to* DANIELLE.)

CAROLINE. Will he wake up for lunch?

DANIELLE. I couldn't say, he's got no predictable habits. I gave him his medicine. I hope that'll make him sleep until I get back. But he's very good at faking. (*She looks upstairs.*) . . . it's possible he's not asleep at all. (*The door bell rings.*)

MARIETTA. (*Abruptly.*) That will be the car. (*She opens the door, disappears quickly down the steps.*)

DANIELLE. (*To* CAROLINE.) I guess I better follow suit . . .

(She bows with mock graciousness, then exits. CAROLINE *goes to the window.)*

CAROLINE. *(Watching* MARIETTA.*)* Look at her, she can't even get in the car without giving instructions to the driver . . . that woman . . . *(We hear the car drive away. Still irritated,* CAROLINE *moves away from the window.)* . . . the charger will straighten her out, one of his fast verbal punches, and she'll keel over quick . . . *(She jabs the air playfully, like a boxer.)* . . . I'd like a good match with her myself. None of this hit-and-run stuff either . . . always playing the lady when it gets too hot. *(Almost unconsciously she slips on her fur coat, seeks out the nearest mirror for reassurance.)* . . . the sleeves are too short, he's right about that, though he only says it to get my goat. *(There is a sudden thumping overhead.)* No, he didn't . . . go and wake up the second she's gone.

(She goes to the steps and waits. The thumping is repeated. She yells up.)

Danielle's gone, Nelson, she went to Lillie's wake. *(A loud, angry thump in response, followed by intermittent sobs.)* Oh God, he's crying . . . he must be having one of his fits . . . I wish the charger were here . . . *(She disappears upstairs.)* What's the matter . . . are you upset about Lillie . . . we all feel pretty bad . . . you want some lunch, Danielle left you some soup and there's chicken for a sandwich . . . what . . . a piece of paper . . . and a pen . . . all right . . . *(We hear her moving around.)* . . . there you go . . . *(Reading his note.)* . . . she ran away . . . who . . . Lillie? No, she died, Nelson, Lillie died, she didn't run away . . . *(Reading more.)* . . . she ran away into death . . . oh, that's a bit morbid, Nelson, she just got sick, that's all and died . . . let me fix you some lunch . . . no? What about a cup of tea . . . nothing? You're sure? Well, thump . . . I mean call if you need anything, all right?

(She emerges hugging her coat. Once downstairs, she lets out a sigh.)

The man's a basket case . . . he makes Lawrence seem almost sane.

(Uneasy and restless, she walks over to the mantelpiece and looks at photographs of the brothers.)

. . . though none of them are too with it. *(She looks at each one of them in turn. Lights dim on* CAROLINE, *while the photographs begin to loom large in the light.)* . . . there's Franklin, the Righteous One presiding as usual over all family disputes . . . look at Nelson, pampered and spoiled in the days of his athletic glory . . . and Jeremy . . . what's there to say about Jeremy except that he had the good sense to put distance between himself and the clan, moved to Chicago where he slaughters sheep and stutters to his heart's content . . . and Lawrence, my Lawrence, the mad stallion of the clan . . . riding herd over all of them with his lies and maneuvers . . . for a colored man Lawrence takes up a *tremendous* amount of space . . .

(She chuckles. We hear the sudden, brutal slamming of a door. CAROLINE *moves forward clutching her coat. We hear footsteps, the sound of someone entering the room.* CAROLINE *slips eerily into* LAWRENCE'*s voice.)*

"What you doin', what you doin' " . . . *(As herself.)* I'm watching you, that's all, you don't enter a room like normal people, you charge in, the door *flies* open and there you are. *(As* LAWRENCE.*)* "Nothin' special about me . . ." *(We hear footsteps pacing, the sound of furniture being moved.)* " . . . genuine Chippendale chair. I like that chair . . . man's comin' next week with two genuine Persian rugs, I'm gonna put one in the dining room, put one right here . . . what you think, what you think . . ." *(As herself.)* You have a fine eye for things, it's an Edwards trait, you should've all been born white, you spend your lives trying to jump out of your skin . . . *(That amuses her but makes* LAWRENCE *turn mean.)* "Listen to the maid . . . got five cents' worth of education and she's tryin' out *ideas* . . ." *(As herself.)* Stop saying that! That's how you got through all those schools! *(As* LAWRENCE.*)* "That's right, I thank Caroline the maid." *(Screaming at him.)*

Cut it out! I scrubbed floors all right, while you *cheated* your way through school! I thought we were pretty evenly matched . . . tit for tat, tit for tat! (*As* LAWRENCE.) "Get dressed for the theatre . . . and look sleek, look sleek, I don't want to be seen with you unless you look sleek." (*As herself, hesitant.*) Well, I won't be looking sleek for much longer. (*As* LAWRENCE, *pacing.*) "What's that supposed to mean . . . huh, what's that supposed to mean?" (*As herself, almost girlish.*) . . . that even in your quick, hurried fashion, something must've took . . . (*As* LAWRENCE.) "What you tryin' to say . . . ?" (*As herself.*) I'm having a baby! The charger *raced* through me and look what he left behind! (*As* LAWRENCE.) ". . . That's pretty funny, pretty funny . . ." (*As herself.*) If it's a boy, I know he'll fly through my womb in Edwards style! (*As* LAWRENCE.) " . . . could be a girl, some fussy thing with your instincts to serve." (*She winces, deeply wounded.*) Don't keep turning things nasty, I want this child to breathe something new between us.

(*There is a sudden rapid thumping from upstairs. Disoriented,* CAROLINE *spins around.*)

What . . .

(*Lights come up as she moves towards the steps. The thumping is relentless, harsh, angry. It puts* CAROLINE *in a fury.*)

What's the matter with you . . . what's the matter with *all* of you! You think we're a bunch of bleeding stagehands! (*She stomps up the steps and disappears. Lights go out.*)

END OF ACT TWO

ACT THREE

Lights fade up on LETITIA EDWARDS, *alone in the living room. She stands rather stiffly by the window. She is a woman in her late '50s with hair that is neatly composed, a prim, overly polite manner that disguises many bitter edges. When she speaks, there is a sing-song quality about her voice that conveys a kind of false elegance.*

After a while, MARIETTA *appears on the steps. Always nervous,* MARIETTA *has grown more hysterical with the years, approaching life now with constant suspicion, as if treachery and bad tidings lay in wait at every turn. Her voice, never melodic, is now even more astringent, and masculine in intensity. She leans over the balcony addressing Letitia.*

MARIETTA. No word from Lawrence?

LETITIA. No, Marietta. (MARIETTA *slips down the steps, looking back several times.*)

MARIETTA. I shouldn't leave her alone . . .

LETITIA. Does she have anything to make her sleep?

MARIETTA. (*Scornfully.*) There are Nelson's left-over drugs, if she wants something like that.

LETITIA. I was thinking of something milder.

MARIETTA. (*Switching gears.*) Has Franklin called?

LETITIA. Not yet, Marietta.

MARIETTA. He promised to call from Mr. Norrell's.

LETITIA. He can only just have arrived, Marietta.

MARIETTA. (*Switching again.*) It's to be a midnight service with the casket closed. No eulogy. He's asked that no words be spoken on his behalf. It's not right that no one should speak! He was an athlete of great stature who went down in defeat!

LETITIA. (*Matter-of-factly.*) He died of asthma, Marietta, he simply couldn't breathe.

MARIETTA. (*Ignoring that.*) And the tombstone's to read: He who labors in a colored vineyard labors in vain! Where did he come up with such a morbid saying . . . oh God, I can't stand it . . . Nelson, our baby . . . (*She grows more upset.*)

LETITIA. Don't get yourself all worked up, Marietta.

MARIETTA. (*Looking around.*) Every Sunday for twenty years we have gathered in this house . . . gone up those steps to greet Nelson in his tomb . . . that's what it was, you know, that bed was really his tomb! All of us coaxed and prayed over him, did everything we could to bring him back to life! If I had a nickel for every prayer Franklin offered in his behalf . . . and Lawrence with that nasty temper of his tried to whip him out of bed more times than I care to remember . . . (*With more gentleness.*) I'd just sit with him . . . Sometimes I'd get him to walk with me as far as the window . . . look at Old Man Hawkins, I'd say, sitting under the trees enjoying the sunshine! Take a walk with me, Nelson, look at life from outside where it's sunny and bright! (*She takes on Nelson's moroseness.*) "Nobody can see me, Marietta . . . it's too dark inside my skin." (*Snapping herself out of it.*) Oh, Nelson . . . why take it to heart! Life goes on anyway! (*Pulled under again.*) "Well it can go on without me . . ." and he'd start back to his bed. (*Outraged.*) He was young! He once flew around that track like a bird on wings! There was *haughty* negro blood in his veins! (*She is beside herself.*)

LETITIA. Try not to upset yourself, Marietta. Can I fix you some coffee or tea, which would you prefer? (MARIETTA *shivers violently.*) Are you all right, Marietta?

MARIETTA. (*Uneasy.*) For a second I thought I heard Lillie speak . . . Gandhi's dead, she said . . . clear as a bell . . . (*She shivers again.*)

LETITIA. Let me make you some tea, Marietta.

(*Letitia goes into the kitchen. Intuitively, as if drawn to it, Marietta turns on the radio. We hear a* NEWSCASTER *speaking.*)

NEWSCASTER'S VOICE. . . . of the AFL-CIO urged Vice
President Humphrey to enter the race . . . the National
Guard has been called out in Memphis where just last
night the Reverend Martin Luther King was fatally
shot by a gunman as he stood on the balcony of his
motel. President Johnson postponed his scheduled trip
to Hawaii to confer with his military strategists about
Vietnam. Instead, he telephoned Mrs. King in Atlanta
and made a brief television appeal for calm and non-
violence to prevail . . .

*(She shuts it off abruptly. When she turns around, she is
startled to find* LETITIA *standing there with her tea. She
jumps back.)*

LETITIA. I didn't mean to startle you . . .
MARIETTA. King's dead.
LETITIA. I heard.
MARIETTA. I bet Lillie's laughing at me . . . (LETITIA *looks
at her strangely. Lost in her thoughts,* MARIETTA *wan-
ders over to the window.)* There'll probably be Ne-
groes rioting . . .
LETITIA. It could happen, though the irony is that he de-
plored such things.
MARIETTA. Who?
LETITIA. Martin Luther King.
MARIETTA. If Lillie were here I'd apologize for that.
LETITIA. (*Confused.*) I'm not following you, Marietta.
MARIETTA. King's dead, I'd say, that's the same as Gandhi
any day . . . (*She begins to cry uncontrollably.*)
LETITIA. Don't get yourself all worked up, Marietta.
MARIETTA. (*Weeping.*) Maybe Nelson was right to have
slept through it all. (*She stands staring out the window.*
LETITIA *picks up her knitting and sits down.)*
LETITIA. They'll want Franklin to speak about him in the
Assembly . . . (MARIETTA *doesn't seem to hear.*) . . .
he'll say something gracious, though he'll be mad as
can be. I can hear him now . . . (*Speaking like* FRANK-
LIN.) "Just because I'm the only . . . (*She has a hard
time saying the word.*) . . . Black, they'll expect me
to speak . . . like I was the spokesman for Negro
grief." (*She sighs.*) He hates the race stuff politics
locks him into.

(MARIETTA *doesn't respond. She seems to have drifted inside her own grief. After awhile, she moves almost hyp-
notically towards the steps.*)

MARIETTA. (*Thinking of* NELSON.) He choked on his own
    saliva.
LETITIA. It could not have been a pleasant death, Marietta.
MARIETTA. When Danielle came in, she found him buried
    under his pillow.
LETITIA. As I recall, Marietta, that was one of his favorite
    tricks.
MARIETTA. He must have been crying. Recently, he cried
    almost all the time.
LETITIA. (*With some bite.*) He made no effort to hide his
    despair. (MARIETTA *grows increasingly sad, almost
    morbid.*)
MARIETTA. Jeremy's sick . . . he won't even be able to
    make the funeral . . .
LETITIA. I'm sure he feels badly about that, Marietta . . .
    he's loyal to the family in his own way.
MARIETTA. He's so far away, we never see him . . . with
    Nelson gone that leaves just us three.
LETITIA. (*Ironic.*) Well, together you keep up a pretty
    lively chorus, Marietta.
MARIETTA. (*Increasingly morbid.*) Franklin could go in a
    flash . . . and Lawrence . . . both of them move at
    breathtaking speed.
LETITIA. It's an Edwards trait . . . you go at a pretty fast
    clip yourself, Marietta.
MARIETTA. (*Snapping.*) Don't "Marietta" me this and
    "Marietta" me that. (LETITIA *visibly draws in her breath
    as if accustomed to* MARIETTA'S *rude outbursts.*)
LETITIA. I was obliging you with polite conversation, Mar-
    ietta.
MARIETTA. (*Malicious.*) That's all you *can* do with your
    dry understanding. (*She grows violently impatient, starts
    to pace.*) Franklin should have called by now. I should
    make a list of who's to be notified . . . what food we'll
    need prepared . . .

(*She disappears into the kitchen in a few rapid strides.* LETI-
TIA *sits aggressively knitting, her needles making a loud,
clicking sound.*)

LETITIA. (*To herself.*) . . . I suppose she expects that to roll off my back as if I were so thick-skinned nothing got through. (*She grunts.*) Hmph . . . to all of them I'm the Rock, the Buddha, the Immovable Object between Franklin and dead Lillie. (*Pained.*) . . . they have never recovered from my intrusion on the scene. When I was first introduced as the replacement for dead Lillie, mouths fell, heads turned as if Franklin had dragged me up from the bottom of the sea. All of them flared and snorted like race horses at the gate. Lawrence had the awful dramatic gall to call me a negro nun. (*Wounded.*) . . . the scenes I have witnessed in this room . . . (*Returning to the present.*) . . . I should try and reach the girls. Lillian will be quite upset, he was her favorite uncle though I never understood why. Rowena will go to pieces but for no good reason, she found Nelson's behavior embarrassing in the extreme but in the end she'll give in to hysteria . . . she has the Edwards need for dramatic release. (*Her needles click hard.*) . . . I suppose that's what they hold against me, that I have no performance value . . . (*Grunting.*) . . . and as they are all fine performers, they expect us in-laws to measure up. (*Reviewing the scene.*) . . . Danielle holds her own with a kind of dry repartee . . . the quick draw, I call it, Danielle is the mistress of the quick draw . . . Lawrence certainly found his match in Caroline, they are forever at each other violent tit for tat . . . Nobody speaks of Aurora but then nobody speaks of Jeremy who dare not speak for himself because he stutters too badly. Aurora and Jeremy are the poor relations in the clan . . . I suppose Marietta never found anyone brave enough to match wits with her brothers, she is herself a *hard* act to follow . . . (MARIETTA, *at that very moment, comes bustling in.*)

MARIETTA. (*Brusquely.*) I thought I heard voices.

LETITIA. . . . just my knitting needles, Marietta, they make a loud sound.

(*The phone rings. Instantly,* MARIETTA *grabs for it.*)

MARIETTA. Hello . . . oh Franklin . . . have you spoken to Lawrence . . . no, we haven't heard a word, I can't imagine where he can be . . . have you seen his body

. . . poor baby . . . I know it's too hard to believe
. . . oh Franklin, don't you start to grieve, I won't be
able to stand it. (*She grows more upset.* LETITIA, *worried, gets up.*) . . . no, Franklin, we did everything we
could . . . he just wouldn't budge. I just never expected
he'd go like this . . . just shrivel up and die . . . (*Both
she and* FRANKLIN *are crying by now.*) I'd like to sit
with him, Franklin . . . just you and me for a while
. . . alright . . . (*She starts to hang up,* LETITIA *signals
her to hold the line.*) . . . Franklin . . . (*No answer.
Coldly.*) He's upset about Nelson . . .

LETITIA. That's no reason why we couldn't speak. (*They
stare at each other.* DANIELLE's *voice startles them.*)

DANIELLE. They'll be asking for a suit . . .

(*They look up. She stands at the top of the stairs. A great
deal older, she wears the years well as if that mocking sense
of humour had held her in good stead. There is, however,
a nervousness in the way she moves, a slight trembling
around the face and neck, the result of too much booze.
As she comes down the steps, it should be clear that she's
already a bit drunk.*)

How's everybody holding up . . . where's Franklin
and Lawrence?

MARIETTA. Franklin's over at Mr. Norrell's, no one's heard
from the charger since we told him the news.

DANIELLE. He'll be along . . . blow in like a drill sergeant
and ruffle everybody's feathers . . . it's an Edwards
trait to make their women jump . . . (*She chuckles
inwardly.*) . . . here we sit in the eye of the storm
. . . blown around like they were the wind. (*She looks
around, badly in need of another drink.*) Now, what
was I about to do . . . ?

MARIETTA. You said we have to choose a suit.

DANIELLE. (*Mechanically.*) . . . a final statement for Nelson to wear.

MARIETTA. (*Brusquely.*) And you should have something
to eat, some coffee, too . . .

DANIELLE. (*Mechanically.*) . . . whatever it takes to dry
the old girl out . . .

MARIETTA. (*Brusquely.*) There are things to be done, cards
to be sent out, people to call . . .

DANIELLE. (*Mechanically.*) . . . all the details of death the dead leave behind . . .

MARIETTA. (*Snapping.*) Stop this weary repetition and get a grip on yourself! (DANIELLE *stares at her.*) Would you like me to go up and look for a suit?

DANIELLE. (*Quietly.*) You do that, Marietta, you go up there and rummage around among the ruins.

(*They look at each other.* MARIETTA *moves quickly past her and up the steps.*)

That oughta keep her pants on for a while . . . (*She becomes aware of* LETITIA *sitting in a corner knitting.*) You gotta watch out for the steam roller or she'll mow you down. (*She chuckles loudly.* LETITIA *gives her a wan smile. Shrugging it off,* DANIELLE *disappears into the kitchen.*) . . . all my sterling good humour is lost on that one . . . (*Mocking* LETITIA.) . . . you need a sense of humour, Letitia, you cannot gather ye among the clan without a sense of humour! (*We hear her opening and closing cupboards.*) Damnit, there must be one somewhere that I hid from myself.

(*Smarting from* DANIELLE's *remark,* LETITIA *starts to retreat to her chair but catches herself in the mirror and can't help a moment's awkward preening.*)

LETITIA. (*Flustered.*) . . . in his crueler moments Franklin has been known to remark that I'm one of those women whose dresses are always getting caught between their buttocks. (*Embarrassed, she tugs at herself.*) . . . I see myself still in the early days of our marriage struggling in and out of silks and gabardines only to provoke again and again the sharp rebuke that my dress had slipped somewhere between my buttocks. (*She turns away, no longer willing to look at herself.*) . . . there is reason to still ask why he married me. He needed a mother for his children and he needed one quick before Rosie went to court to keep them. I think I came along in the nick of time. Franklin moved with his usual swiftness and snatched me up. I was 38 . . . there were no long lines blocking his way. (*Any minute, one gets the feeling, she might run and hide.*) . . . I was most certainly untouched . . . no man had

ever laid a finger on me . . . when it came Franklin's
turn, I lay exceedingly still . . . he was very handsome
with his light eyes, his fine crinkly hair, I think I was
flattered, that his speed and daring overwhelmed me.
(*Trying to recover her balance.*) . . . why else would
a woman almost forty marry a man with two daughters! Rowena had just turned six, Lillian was less than
two . . . a shy child who fastened herself to me, became
my shadow. (*A sense of maternal pride touches her,
then shifts.*) Not so Rowena, she was too full of memory, it was dead Lillie this and dead Lillie that and
where oh where could dead Lillie be now! There was
no end to her whining and stomping about. Franklin
would come home, the child would start to flail and
scream he'd swear I'd been beating her, come after
me, fists raised, eyes burning . . . (*With sudden indignation.*) . . . he has the *worst*, the very worst temper
I've ever witnessed in my life! I'm told his father was
the same . . . a terrifying kind of anger that comes at
you in violent doses! All of them have it. Marietta
goes shrill the moment she enters a room. Lawrence
would kill if he could just go unpunished. Nelson turned
his inwards and beat himself to death . . . poor Jeremy
hides his behind a stutter and a twitch. Mad souls
every one of them! I landed smack dab in the lion's
den!

(*From the kitchen there is a sudden loud crash of broken
dishes falling to the floor. We hear* DANIELLE *muttering
and cursing.*)

DANIELLE. (*From the kitchen.*) Don't tell me I'm left high
    and dry without a nickel's worth of gin! (LETITIA *shud-
    ders, retreats to her chair.*)
LETITIA. . . . I did not leave . . . I think that is my great
    accomplishment, that I did not leave.

(DANIELLE *wanders in looking for a drink. She seems not
to be at all aware of* LETITIA. *She looks everywhere, finally
gets down on her knees and begins peeking under the couch.
She pulls something out.*)

DANIELLE. (*Triumphant.*) I knew there was one some-
    where. (*She holds up a bottle.*) . . . if I didn't know

better, I'd swear I must have hid it myself . . . but why would I do such a dumb thing when I'm the only one who drinks . . . couldn't have been Nelson, he hasn't been down those steps in twenty years, except today . . . when they wheeled him away . . . (*She stares at the steps as if seeing* NELSON *carried down them, goes to pour herself a drink*.) I bet you a fat man Marietta hid that bottle, the way she sneaks around whenever my back is turned. (*As she starts to drink, she notices* LETITIA.) . . . it's hard to remember you're around.

LETITIA. (*Carefully*.) Without a sense of humour I'm hard to see.

DANIELLE. (*Chuckling*.) Touché, touché . . . (*There is a moment of sympathy*.) Where's the steam roller?

LETITIA. Upstairs, looking for a suit.

DANIELLE. Right . . . I should tell her to pick out one of his ditty bop numbers from the jazz days . . . the old boy might like to go out in style.

LETITIA. Would you like me to fix you something to eat?

DANIELLE. (*With mock daintiness*.) No tea or toast, thank you.

LETITIA. (*Embarrassed*.) I was just trying to . . . (DAN-IELLE *stops her with a wave of her bottle which she holds out proudly*.)

DANIELLE. This must have been a present from one of Nelson's track buddies. They always came back to check on the old boy. He's read them his usual Sermon on the Void and when they'd had enough of that, they'd come down and chew the fat with me, polish off a taste or two, reminisce, until the room was full of smoke and booze just like the old days . . . do you mind a little music?

LETITIA. No.

(*She goes and puts on Carmen McCrae or Anita O'Day singing "Isn't This a Lovely Day" and begins to dance in a clumsy way*.)

DANIELLE. . . . they'd get me on my feet . . . (*As if talking to* NELSON's *cronies*.) The old girl can still hop about . . . I'm fading fast in the ring but I still got my hand in . . . (*Sadness overwhelms her*.) But the sallow beauty's cracking under the strain . . . I've been living too long in the Land of Oz and all the glitter's gone. (*She almost breaks down.*)

LETITIA. (*Trying to save her.*) You're still light on your feet. (*For some reason that makes* DANIELLE *chuckle.*)

DANIELLE. I was built for speed . . .

(MARIETTA'*s voice cuts across. She's standing at the top of the steps holding a suit.*)

MARIETTA. Does this look fitting . . . ? He'll look handsome in gray, don't you think? I must remember to tell Mr. Norrell to part his hair in the middle and smoothe it back away from his face, that's how he wore it in the old days with a mustache . . . his light eyes . . .

DANIELLE. (*Angry but fighting tears.*) . . . the baby-faced prince working his act . . .

MARIETTA. What kind of tie, something a little splashy or should we keep it simple?

DANIELLE. Suit yourself, Marietta . . . do what you can to resurrect his charm.

(*She turns away, pained.* MARIETTA *feels it, too.*)

MARIETTA. He's the first of my boys to go . . . one by one they'll leave me, I'll be the last to go.

(*She retreats into a conversation with* FRANKLIN. *The light changes so that she is spotlighted while the women below become shadows.*)

. . . She's not dead, Franklin, she can't be. I saw her this afternoon . . . she looked a little tired but nowhere near dead . . . we just put Pop in the ground, it seems like just the other day . . . dead . . . not Lillie . . . she was too snappy and fresh for death. I'm so sorry, Franklin. How could such a thing be . . . (*Suddenly seeing.*) There's something morbid about us, isn't there, Franklin? . . . something in how fast we breathe . . . all steamed-up and running the hard course that Pop set. We'll never be happy, will we . . . (*Frightened by what she sees.*) Look at Nelson . . . he's going to take it to an extreme . . . this terrible brooding in us over what being colored really means.

(She seems to drift away. Lights come up on DANIELLE *taking a huge swig from the bottle.)*

DANIELLE. . . . they'll be crowding in here soon, I should straighten things up a bit . . . these rooms are all my living, I should put them on good display . . . *(She makes an effort to straighten things when the doorbell rings with a sharp insistence.* DANIELLE *stops dead in her tracks.)* There he is . . . the North Wind himself.

LETITIA. *(Unnerved herself.)* Lawrence . . .

DANIELLE. . . . he'll come in here and blow us to bits . . .

(The bell rings again, more insistently. DANIELLE *doesn't move. It's* LETITIA *who gets up finally to open the door.* CAROLINE *stands on the threshold.)*

CAROLINE. *(Defiantly.)* Where is he?

(She steps into the room wearing as always an expensive fur coat. With the years her face has grown severe and she wears too much make-up. Her voice, never pleasant, is now a good deal harsher, and there is something a bit disheveled about her appearance as if the coat was thrown over the first outfit she grabbed.)

LETITIA. Was he on his way here?

CAROLINE. He's been gone all night, he's gone a lot of nights. I expected Nelson's death would bring him home for a change . . .

LETITIA. We haven't seen him.

DANIELLE. *(Mischievously.)* Maybe he went up in smoke . . . he does everything so fast he could blow himself up.

(A childish giggle escapes. Fast on its heels is a faint chuckle from LETITIA *that she cannot quite repress.* CAROLINE *looks from one to the other.)*

CAROLINE. I don't get the joke.

LETITIA. Could I get you some coffee, I bet Lawrence will be along any second now.

(CAROLINE *waves aside the idea of coffee, begins to pace
with increasing agitation.*)

CAROLINE. Where is he? It'll be the same old story . . . a
sudden real estate deal, legal tie-ups that lasted through
the night. (*She shakes her head disbelieving.*) There's
only one thing that keeps him out through the night.
DANIELLE. (*Opening that line wide.*) . . . the charger lets
it *rip* . . . pummels his way up San Juan Hill . . . (*She
breaks out in raucous laughter.*) . . . SEX with the
Brothers! (*Subsiding to a giggle.*) . . . not exactly your
all-time bawdy romp in the hay . . .

(*At this point* DANIELLE *and* CAROLINE *should be separated
by isolated pools of light as if revealing their intimate feelings
only to themselves.*)

CAROLINE. (*To herself.*) . . . I tell myself that if he's out
there looking, it can only be for a shot in the dark,
he wouldn't linger long enough to call anybody's name.
(*Feeling lost.*) . . . it's Laura's death that sends him
out there . . . the house is too silent, it was her childish
cries that made it feel like a home.
DANIELLE. (*To herself.*) . . . Even with him laying up there
flat on his back, it was rare that the old boy *rose* to
the occasion. (*She mimicks his whining drawl.*) " . . .
Colored people can't have true intimate relations
. . . we are too exposed in this world for any further
undressing . . ." (*Numb.*) . . . ain't *that* the cat's meow.

(*Silence. Then the sharp jangle of the phone.* CAROLINE
grabs for it aggressively.)

CAROLINE. Hello . . . where are you . . . where are you
and where have you been . . . don't give me that,
honest to God, I don't want to hear it again . . . no,
they're all here . . . I don't know . . . (*To* LETITIA.)
Where's Franklin?
LETITIA. He's at Mr. Norrell's.
CAROLINE. (*To* LAWRENCE.) . . . at Mr. Norrell's . . . are
you coming here . . . what do you want me to do
. . . I'm not dressed to go to the Funeral Home. (*She
becomes more aware of her disheveled look.*) . . . could

you pick me up . . . I'd like it if you picked me up
. . . that's not the point . . . I'd just like it, that's all
. . . (*Getting crazy.*) . . . Would you pick me up,
please. You want me to bow and scrape . . . (*Going
out of control.*) . . . I've already done that, remember,
that's how it began with me down on my knees . . .
Lawrence . . . (*There is no answer. She screams as if
it were wrenched from the center of her.*) Lawrence!!!!

(*The room grows quiet, the women having withdrawn into
their own silence. Only* DANIELLE *continues to move about
in an uneasy, drunken way. After a while, she even begins
to sing, softly, snatches of melodies.*)

DANIELLE. (*Singing.*) . . . I took a trip on a train and I
thought about you . . . two or three stars caught under
the sky . . . a winding road . . . (*She starts talking to*
NELSON *as if she were standing by his bed.*) They're
gonna serve the Edwards Requiem on you soon, old
boy . . . milk that final act for all it's worth. (*As if
fluffing his pillows.*) How are your pillows . . . you
should let me change the sheets, those are getting bed-
ridden . . . get up Nelson and let me make the bed
. . . Go take a bath and shave . . . you can't be . . .
how can you be tired when you never move! (*The
absurdity of it hits her.*) Get up . . . long enough for
me to change the sheets . . . you can sit in that chair
if you won't bathe . . . (*She begins changing the sheets.*)
. . . what do you mean . . . because I was too lazy, I
guess to lift myself up . . . go somewhere, anywhere
. . . even across the street . . . (*She smoothes the
sheets.*) . . . instead I sat around with you . . . let time
go backwards on me . . . let your grieving get into my
bones, like damp chill . . . (*She shivers.*) Are you cold
. . . come on, you can lay back down . . . then I drifted
inside your shadow the way women can do . . . (*She
fluffs his pillows again.*) . . . drift and drift like they
got no place to go . . . (*A terrible weariness seeps in.*)
. . . next thing I know I've been sitting here for years
. . . soaked clean through on the thin excuses you
exchanged for a life . . . (*Numb with anger.*) . . . I'm
fixing your pillows, changing your sheets, carrying
Ralston up and down the steps like the joke was still
funny . . . you're waking me up in the middle of the

night, full of questions about the Negro's place in time, his reasons for being in the scheme of things . . . (*She relives a conversation.*) . . . I don't know why, Nelson, why they think we're dumb or different or inhuman . . . I can't answer those questions for you . . . it's late, Nelson, try to go back to sleep, don't torment yourself like this . . . and don't start to cry, oh God, Nelson, please, don't weep . . . (*Panic seeps in.*) Stop it, Nelson . . . you'll have a convulsion if you go on like this . . . shut off the tears before the damn flood gates burst! You're spilling all over the place, your sheets and pillows are drenched with tears . . . (*Going out of control.*) Stop it, stop acting like a baby! I'll have to leave the planet if you don't cut out this act! (*Then with real violence, she acts it out.*) Stop it, I say, or I'll drown you my own self, hold this pillow over you till you're blue in the face . . .

(*Which she does, pressing it down harder and harder until death stops his tears and her own can start.* DANIELLE *begins to sob uncontrollably. In the heat of the wreckage,* MARIETTA*'s voice drifts across carrying its own private excitement that is oblivious to the scene below.*)

MARIETTA. Look what I found . . . (*She comes to the top of the steps.*) . . . one of Lillie's poems . . . hidden under Nelson's pillow . . . (*She giggles.*) . . . I bet it's some silly thing . . . (*She starts to read it quite frivolously.*)
Gandhi's dead
so I said
She only turned and stared
Nelson's in bed
so she said
I only laughed and glared
Gandhi's dead
I said again
What's that to me, she replied
Nelson's in bed
Again she said
All colored men do is die.

(*Hold. For a long time. Then let the lights come down.*)

END

Elaine Jackson
PAPER DOLLS

In *Paper Dolls*, Elaine Jackson takes on a fundamental issue that is both personal and political for black women—beauty. *Paper Dolls* attacks the standards of beauty that dominate American films and television. Using a minstrel show format, the play satirizes women's preoccupation with the "right look," an attitude that makes them easy objects of exploitation.

Two aging black beauty queens, Miss Emancipation of 1930 and her first runner-up, return to judge an international beauty contest fifty years after their victory. While these wizened, feisty women wait for the contest to begin, they play scenes from their past like vaudevillian actors (with the help of several extras), moving freely between the real and imagined, the past and the present. Truly anything can happen in this setting as Margaret-Elizabeth, the more flamboyant of the two, decides to write new endings to the old, embarrassing incidents from her history as a model and actress in the hope that her godson's generation will learn to revere the natural beauty of black women. Jackson spares nothing in this delightful, fresh satire: the lecherous film director who tells a young Margaret-Elizabeth to learn how to tap dance if she wants a film career; the "coveted prizes" for the beauty queen—a gift certificate from Marianne's Steak and Chop House, a full-throated, singing canary from Lacey's Pet Shop, a wall-sized replica of the American flag, a brass ring from Avery's Five and Dime . . . and so on.

Throughout the play, the beauty of black women is stamped, pressed, pushed, and crushed into anything other than its natural self, transformed into the stereotypes demanded by the entertainment industry. Then, in one telling scene, Margaret-Elizabeth, utterly fed up with a white woman who paints the "real" black female as an Aunt Jemima, "rewrites" the ending of the scene by giving the painter a much-needed lesson in art. In a blistering speech, she tongue-lashes the painter for missing the rhythm, vitality, and color intensity of the black model, for failing to give the black woman's legs and hips their artistic due. "You see, the color *black* has within itself many colors. It is a very complex color and at the same time simple and delicate. It can be made to appear formidable and mysterious in a dark, unlit cave, or can appear as bright and inviting as the twinkling eyes of a child." Finally, she dismisses the painter as primitive and unenlightened. The finale—the presentation of the beauty contest finalists—erupts into a spectacular, full-fledged minstrel show that exorcises those "demons of beauty" in a grotesque parody.

The destruction of innocence in the world of black girls and women is a recurring theme in Jackson's work. Her first published play, *Toe Jam*, was featured in Woodie King's *Black Drama Anthology* and received wide distribution. Published in 1971, it was one of very few plays at the time that explored the realities of black girlhood. This theme, unusual in the rush of plays about male identity and social confrontation, made it a popular choice in community theatres and colleges and universities during the early 1970s. At one time, several theatres in the San Francisco area produced the play during the same season. Jackson's *Cockfight* was produced by the American Place Theatre in 1978. She is currently working on *Afterbirth*, a drama which she is turning into a musical.

A graduate of Wayne State University, Jackson won the Rockefeller Award for Playwriting in 1978–79, the Langston Hughes Playwriting Award in 1979, and earned a National Endowment for the Arts Award for playwriting in 1983.

Paper Dolls

by
Elaine Jackson

Paper Dolls was first presented as a staged reading at the American Place Theatre in New York City in November 1982. It was subsequently produced by the Richard Allen Center for Culture and Art (New York City) in January of 1983. The late Hazel Bryant was the producer. Duane Jones was the coordinating director of the production. *Paper Dolls* was completed in 1979. This script is the fourth draft of the play.

CAST OF CHARACTERS

MARGARET-ELIZABETH (black)
LIZZIE (black)
WOMAN ONE (black)
WOMAN TWO (white)
MAN ONE (black)
MAN TWO (white)

ACT ONE

SCENE 1

PLACE: *Canadian Border (Windsor, Ontario)*
TIME: *1980—spring*
SCENE: *Morning. Two women (MARGARET-ELIZABETH and LIZZIE) are seated uncomfortably Downstage Left on one of several long benches. Above them, a sign reads "Canadian Customs Detaining Area."* MARGARET-ELIZABETH *is wearing a large, wide-brimmed, picture-frame hat and a low-cut, many-layered, flamboyantly flowered, chiffon whirly-gig of a dress.* LIZZIE *is sedately dressed in a matronly, rayon print dress with Peter Pan collar and a veiled, pillbox-type hat. Both women are wearing high-heeled shoes and white gloves. They are surrounded by lots of luggage on the floor and on the adjacent benches. Some of the luggage is opened and askew.*

LIZZIE. (*Quiet anger.*) If he so much as dares to put his infested, fat, red fingers in my personal, private belongings—I'm gonna just . . . I'm gonna just . . . *fling* everything in his puffed-up face!

MARGARET-ELIZABETH. (*Quiet control.*) Shut up, Lizzie. I think we're in enough trouble because of you, without me having to sit here and listen to you pretend. When that man comes back in here all you're gonna do is burst into a flood of tears. You're not gonna do anything! You never do anything—except *cry*. That's your solution for everything—*tears*. Occasionally, but very rarely—you LAUGH!—a nerve-racking, hysterical, nervous laugh (*Dramatically imitates laughter*), Aaahaahahaa, Aaahaahahahaaa, Uuhahuhaaaa! . . . but, most of the time . . .

LIZZIE. (*Teary.*) I am upset . . .

353

M-E. You're upset? I happen to be just an innocent traveling companion . . . I had no idea . . .

LIZZIE. . . . I am angry . . . and I'm just about to get *mad*. You know how crazy I can be when I get mad . . .

M-E. (*Sarcastically.*) Yes, I do.

LIZZIE. It's not so much that I mind that they rummaged through my clothes—that's their job . . . but the *insult* . . . I'm gonna walk right up to him . . . you know how I walk when I get mad . . .

M-E. (*Sarcastically.*) Yes, I do.

LIZZIE. . . . the pure-dee *insult* . . .

M-E. Da punckety, punckety, punck . . . da punckety, punckety, punck . . . da punckety, punckety, punck . . .

LIZZIE. What's that? What're you mumbling?

M-E. That's how you walk. Da punckety, punckety, punck . . . an' it don't matter whether you mad or not . . , That's how you walk. Da punckety, punckety, punck . . .

LIZZIE. Margaret, look at me. Do I look like . . .

M-E. I hope you don't think I'm delighted by this whole thing.

LIZZIE. Look! Look at me! Do I look like . . .

M-E. I'm sitting here like some kind of desperado because of you!

LIZZIE. (*Loudly.*) Do I look like . . . a criminal?

M-E. Stop making so much fuss! (*Whispering.*) Right now we both look like criminals. It was in *your* bag. They found it in *your* bag. I'm just trying to catch my breath over the whole thing . . . (*Suddenly facing Lizzie almost nose to nose.*) *And* I'm looking at you! I'm looking right at you . . . for the first time in all the . . . "ho hum" years I've known you, I just don't recognize you!

LIZZIE. (*Drily.*) Fifty years.

M-E. Yes? Yes? What're you saying?

LIZZIE. Fifty years! We've known each other for fifty years . . . or, at least you *told* me you were seventeen when I met you. There's been quite a bit of debate on that through the years as you know.

M-E. Don't you start that with me now. I'm not playing with you.

LIZZIE. Well what am I supposed to think? Joan of Arc was supposed to be seventeen . . . and you were *sup-*

posed to be seventeen! To this day, no one has explained to *me* why you never played the role of Joan of Arc!

(LIZZIE *has obviously shaken* M-E. M-E *sits for some time in an emotional reverie. She begins a soft laughter that attempts to mask her vulnerability.*)

M-E. Them people from Hollywood sure had us fooled when they told us they were going to put us in the movies! Had the nerve to tell all the people in Boley that we was playin' the leading roles! . . . and, Oh, my God! . . . (*Laughing*) first part! . . . they tied my head up and blackened my face . . . we went shoppin' in downtown Boley . . . 'member?

WOMAN ONE. (*Playing a youthful* MARGARET-ELIZABETH; *Southern accent.*) Had me goin' shoppin' wid' you talkin' 'bout what color dress you was going to wear for your first appearance . . .

M-E. We go into all the dress shops in Boley . . . and nobody had a dress to suit me. And everytime we leave a store—we start singing that song . . . that song . . . 'bout . . . ?

LIZZIE. (*Drily.*) Millie Biggers.

M-E. That's it! Millie Biggers! I'd try on every dress they had; and you'd say . . .

WOMAN ONE. "Margaret? What color you lookin' for?"

M-E. . . . And I'd say, "Ask Millie Biggers!" So we go skipping to the next store—askin' Millie Biggers: (*Chanting.*) "Oh, will you wear red, Millie Biggers?" (*To Lizzie.*) G'won! Say your part! (*No response from Lizzie.*) Oh, you done forgot that, huh? (*Continuing.*) *And* then we leave another store and you say . . .

WOMAN ONE. "What color you lookin' for, Margaret?"

M-E. . . . An' I say, "Ask Millie Biggers!" (*Chanting.*) "Oh, will you wear blue, Millie Biggers?" (*Pause.*) Don't remember nothin' 'bout it, do you, Maggie?

WOMAN ONE. (*Drily beginning the chant.*)
"You sholy would wear gray?
You sholy would wear gray?
You sholy would wear gray, Millie Biggers?"
(*Looks to* M-E *for response. No response from* M-E.)
"Well, will you wear white?
Well, will you wear white?

Well, will you wear white, Millie Biggers?"

M-E. (*Slowly and softly.*)

"I won't wear white,
I'd get dirty long 'fore night.
I'll wear me a cotton dress,
Dyed wid copperse and oak-bark."

WOMAN ONE. Oh! Well . . .

"Now will you wear black?
Now will you wear black?
Now will you wear black, Millie Biggers?"

M-E. (*Beginning softly, ending dramatically.*)

"I might wear black,
Cause it's the color o' my back;
An' it looks lak my cotton dress,
Dyed wid copperse an' oak bark."

(*Laughing.*) Oooh! Ha' mercy! Little did I know!
. . . that . . . *that* was *exactly* what I was gon' end up
wearin'—a ol' dinky, dyed-up, cotton dress! *Every*
role I played—I had the same dress on! Girl! I was
one foolish somebody then!

LIZZIE. . . . come to the studio wearin' a fur coat . . .

M-E. . . . over my apron . . .

(*They laugh—a bittersweet laugh.*)

Did you forget about those times, Lizzie?

LIZZIE. (*Quietly.*) I didn't forget, Margaret. I just don't
have any reason to keep remembering.

(WOMAN ONE *exits.*)

M-E. At least my foolishness was under the guise of youth!

LIZZIE. That's debatable! You certainly never looked seventeen to me.

M-E. Don't let me start telling you how old you are, Lizzie!
The last time someone told you you were sixty-seven
years old—you collapsed! Your legs just folded up
right under you and you fell flat on your face. So you
just shut up!

LIZZIE. You didn't hear what I told the bus driver?

M-E. What bus driver?

LIZZIE. (*Shouting.*) The bus driver! . . . that brings you
over this bridge!

M-E. (*Quietly.*) No. What did you tell the bus driver, Lizzie?

LIZZIE. I told him I was fifty-five years old and he nearly fell out of his seat.

M-E. No wonder! He was in shock. You're sixty-nine!

LIZZIE. That's it! That's *it*! I'm not saying another word to you! I'm not going to talk to you anymore, Margaret. (*Long, angry silence as they both stare straight ahead. Finally.*) If I happen to speak to you again, it's because you're the only somebody in here that I know.

M-E. (*Incredulously.*) *What* am I doing sitting here talking to you like this? *Seven* customs agents surrounded us the moment we crossed this border . . . and I'm still trying to coax my heart to come up outta' my knees. . . !

LIZZIE. Oh, Margaret! Don't be so dramatic. *Three!* There were only three agents.

M-E. That's easy for you to say—you don't wear glasses.

LIZZIE. An' you don't wear them like you're supposed to. Your vanity is obnoxious, Margaret.

M-E. Don't argue with me! Not now, please! I can't figure out why in the *hell* you brought that stuff with you in the first goddamn place!

LIZZIE. There's no need to get nasty, Margaret. Especially since you *know* I always travel with it. Did I *ever* visit you and didn't have it with me? I never travel without baking soda—never. I don't know why you actin' like this is the first time you've ever seen me with it.

M-E. (*Loudly.*) Why do you need so much of the goddamn stuff?

LIZZIE. (*Hurt. Teary.*) And I don't know why you shouting at me, Margaret. (*Shouting back.*) Now you just stop it!

M-E. (*Quietly, between clenched teeth.*) Why do you need so much of the goddamn stuff?

LIZZIE. Margaret, *soda* is *very* pure . . . *very* natural! (*Rising intensity.*) Smell my feet! (*Reaches down as if to remove a shoe.*)

M-E. Lizzie! Lizzie!

LIZZIE. You can't smell 'em! Every day I sprinkle that stuff between my toes . . . *you cannot smell my feet!*

M-E. Lizzie! Lizzie!

LIZZIE. TEETH! (*Proudly baring teeth.*) SEE! SEE! (*Manic.*) UNDER MY ARMS!

M-E. (*Commanding.*) Lizzie!

LIZZIE. CLEAN THE HOUSE WITH IT!

M-E. Lizzie, for Christ's sake!

LIZZIE. I EAT IT!

M-E. Don't you dare sit here and tell these customs agents (*Raising voice.*) this bizarre baking soda story . . . 'cause if you do they gonna . . . YOU *EAT* IT? (*Disgust.*)

LIZZIE. (*Standing up, writhing in anger, shaking with fury, shouting to the empty rooms.*) I WILL! I'LL TELL THEM EXACTLY WHAT I THINK ABOUT THEIR LOW INSULTS . . .

M-E. (*Pulling Lizzie back into her seat.*) SHUT UP! They can see us! (*Sitting rigidly as her eyes search the room.*) They are looking at us *right now!*

LIZZIE. (*Furtively looking around.*) Looking at us? How?

M-E. Through a two-way . . . two-way mirror of course. Act normal. They're watching everything we do to see if we're trying to hide and cover up anything.

LIZZIE. (*Looking, trying to discover the two-way mirror.*) Really?

(*They both sit silently and rigidly self-conscious for some time. When* MARGARET-ELIZABETH *speaks, she speaks from the side of her mouth, so as not to be observed by the officials.*)

M-E. One thing is very clear—they don't know who we are.

LIZZIE. That's true, Margaret.

M-E. I think we ought to tell them who we are.

LIZZIE. Absolutely. (*Pause.*) But . . . Margaret? . . . who are we? (MARGARET-ELIZABETH *gives her an impossibly bitter stare.*) I mean . . . are we somebody . . . (*Groping for words and shrinking under Margaret-Elizabeth's stare.*) that . . . they're gonna . . . treat . . . nicely . . . ?

M-E. My dear girl, *always* let people know how important you are. Don't tell me you've forgotten who you are?

LIZZIE. (*Too embarrassed to admit it.*) NOooo! (*Giggling.*) I haven't forgotten, Margaret.

M-E. Good. Because there's more than one way to tell people who you are.

LIZZIE. (*A great mystery.*) Really?

M-E. (*Staring straight ahead and feigning decorum. Loud whisper.*) Lizzie. Lizzie! Follow me. Do everything that I do but do it quietly and unobtrusively. Are you listening to me? Okay, follow me.

(*They delicately, in unison, remove their gloves. They cautiously rummage through their luggage with one hand as they stare straight ahead. After a short search, M-E removes a packet of papers.*)

(*Holding up papers.*) Take out your judge's notebook. (*She waits impatiently as* LIZZIE *continues to search.*)

LIZZIE. (*Finally, after searching for some time.*) What judge's notebook?

M-E. (*Impatiently forgetting decorum. Waving the folder.*) There! In big, bold, letters! "Official Judge—MISS INTERNATIONAL SEPIA—1980"! Christ!

LIZZIE. Margaret, if you're not going to be nice to me— don't talk to me!

M-E. (*Looking as though she is counting to ten before she speaks.*) Okay. Okay. (*Breathing deeply.*) I'm sorry. Okay? I'm sorry. (*Holding folder in her lap like a schoolteacher. Calm restraint.*) Judge's notebook.

LIZZIE. (*Removing papers.*) They call this a judge's notebook? I didn't know that.

M-E. It . . . really doesn't matter what we call it, Lizzie . . . just take it out. Quietly. Quietly, Lizzie. Try not to overreact. Now open it up. (*Pause, as* LIZZIE *rummages through papers. Still staring straight ahead.*) Tell me what you see.

LIZZIE. (*Reading papers.*) Tally sheet for scores . . .

M-E. Umh, humm . . .

LIZZIE. List of finalists . . .

M-E. Quietly. Quietly, Lizzie . . .

(*They both begin leafing through the folders.*)

LIZZIE. . . . program notes . . . special events . . . contest rules . . .

M-E. (*Dramatically.*) Look, Lizzie. Our banners.

(*She pulls out a colorful, ribboned beauty contest banner that reads, "Miss International Sepia—1980."*)

LIZZIE. Oooh, oooh . . . oooh . . . with a special blue
   ribbon that says, "Judge"—Awww . . . doesn't that
   make you feel important?

(M-E *stands and slips the banner on. She defiantly removes
the blue "Judge" sticker.*)

M-E. Miss International Sepia—1980!
LIZZIE. (*Shocked.*) Oh, Margaret! Stop it!
M-E. Everything with a flourish, Lizzie. *Now* I feel im-
   portant.
LIZZIE. (*Intrigued. Beginning to smile a little.*) Margaret,
   how can you?
M-E. Just like we did fifty years ago!
LIZZIE. (*Delightedly shocked.*) Oh, Margaret! How can
   you?
M-E. Like this.

(*She takes* LIZZIE *by the shoulders and delicately gets her
to stand up.* M-E *slips the remaining banner on* LIZZIE *as*
LIZZIE *excitedly looks around to see who's watching.*)

LIZZIE. (*Giggling like a schoolgirl.*) Oh, Margaret!

(M-E *leans over and removes the "Judge" sticker from* LIZ-
ZIE'S *banner.*)

   You're sensational!

(*They sit demurely back down wearing their beauty queen
banners.*)

M-E. We have been in Canada for about . . . (*Looking at
   wristwatch*) twenty-five minutes, and already they're
   whispering about . . . "those two front-runners for
   some international smuggling organization."
LIZZIE. Who? Who, Margaret? Who is that?
M-E. Oh, Lizzie, you make me so tired! US! They're whispering about *US*.
LIZZIE. (*Giggling.*) Isn't it exciting! (*Looking around defiantly for the hidden mirrors. As if talking to the customs agents or the walls. Politely.*) Thank you. Thank
   you very much. I never expected a few simple bags
   of bicarbonate of soda would gain me such notoriety.

M-E. No, Lizzie. Not a few simple bags of bicarbonate of
soda. PLASTIC BAGS! You had it in PLASTIC
BAGS! *Ten*, balloon-size, plastic bags full of baking
soda! Stuffed in your goddamn luggage! (*Shouting.*)
I could kill you, woman!

(*At this point, four* CUSTOMS AGENTS [MAN ONE *and* TWO
and WOMAN ONE *and* TWO] *enter detaining area carrying
the six large plastic bags filled with white powder.*)

MAN TWO. (*Dangling one bag in front of Lizzie.*) We found
this in your luggage.
LIZZIE. (*Quietly defiant.*) That's right.

(*There is a long pause as everyone seems to be holding their
breath.*)

MAN TWO. (*Clearing his throat.*) Our analysis shows that
this is . . . uh . . .
MAN ONE, WOMAN ONE AND TWO. . . . bicarbonate of
soda . . .
MAN TWO. Yes. Uh . . . bicarbonate of soda . . . and
. . . uh . . . we are . . .
MAN ONE, WOMAN ONE AND TWO. . . . we are sorry for
the inconvenience . . .
MAN TWO. Yes. We are sorry for the uh . . . inconvenience.

(*The* CUSTOMS AGENTS *deliver all the plastic bags to* M-E
and LIZZIE. *The two women line them up on the bench.*)

LIZZIE. Is that all? Is that all they're gonna say to us?
M-E. (*Seething.*) I'm angry.
LIZZIE. I'm mad.

(*The* CUSTOMS AGENTS, *clustered Upstage, watch the two
women, who are Downstage.*)

I'm mad. Margaret, I'm mad. I just don't want to
walk out of here like this. Feel me! Feel my forehead!
(*Takes* M-E's *hand and presses it to her forehead.*) I'm
flushed hot! (*Breathing heavily.*) My whole back is
burning with shame and anger.
M-E. I don't want it to end like this.

LIZZIE. If I walk out of here like this—my whole trip is
    gonna be in shambles.

M-E. I don't want it to end like *this*!

LIZZIE. Well, what do you want to do, Margaret?

M-E. Something. Something . . . Do you remember? . . .
    What was that movie? It was . . . Myra and . . . Myra
    and . . . they were on the train . . .

LIZZIE. AH! Wait! Wait! Don't tell me! . . . Myra and
    Porter . . . Porter Campbell . . . And they were on
    the train . . .

*(First MINISCENE: Throughout the script, the two women
re-create scenes from the movies they have been in. These
scenes are identified as MINISCENES.)*

M-E. *(Becoming Myra.)* And Myra says, *(English accent)*
    "I won't take it! I won't take it! from anyone! And
    you know how devastating I can be when I get mad!"
    (Pause as she waits for LIZZIE to join in. To LIZZIE.)
    G'won! Say your part.

LIZZIE. I don't want to do that part. I wanna do Myra.

M-E. Oh, come on, Liz. I'm just trying to remember the
    words.

LIZZIE. I remember her part. "I won't! I won't take it from
    anyone. Nobody speaks to me that way! Nobody!
    Eggghuggh! I'm mad! And you know how I am when
    I get mad!" *(To M-E.)* You do the other part.

M-E. Lizzie, I'm just trying to . . .

LIZZIE. You always try to play the best parts.

M-E. *(Firmly.)* Lizzie, just say your part, please.

LIZZIE. *(Butterfly McQueen.)* "Miss Myra! Miss Myra! Don't
    hit *me*! I didn't do it!"

M-E. *(As Myra.)* "Well, *somebody* did it! And by the saints—
    I'll make 'em pay!" *(She begins to toss clothing from
    the open luggage around the room.)*

LIZZIE. *(In character.)* "Miss Myra! I didn't do it! Don't
    hit me! *(Watching items sail across the room.)* Them's
    yo' good clothes! Oh, Lordy! Woe is me! Woe is me!"

*(The two women are flushed with laughter and excitement
as they finish the scene.)*

M-E. *(Laughing.)* Why the hell you need so much of this
    goddamn stuff?

LIZZIE. I just didn't want to run out . . .

M-E. (*Instigating.*) He put his fat, red, rusty fingers in it.

LIZZIE. He did? He did, didn't he?

M-E. It ain't pure no more.

LIZZIE. He sure did, didn't he?

M-E. I don't want it to end like this, Lizzie.

LIZZIE. Me neither.

(*They look at one another as they each pick up one of the filled plastic bags.*)

M-E. Ready! Aim!

M-E AND LIZZIE. FIRE!

(*They throw the plastic bags at the* AGENTS. *The bags burst open as they make contact. White powder begins to fly everywhere.*)

LIZZIE. (*Jumping with glee.*) I got his feet! It smashed all up against his shoes! Haaahahaahaaa!

M-E. I think I hit his head!

(*They scream with glee as they begin a rapid-fire attack. They throw the remaining plastic bags with abandon.*)

(*Throwing another bag.*) Oooh, my God! I hit the ceiling! Eeehahahaaaha!

(*White dust showers the room. The two women embrace and almost dance with excitement.*)

LIZZIE. (*Taking aim.*) I wanna hit that little short one!

M-E. I wanna hit the one with the shit-grin!

LIZZIE. Which one is that?

M-E. The one on the end.

LIZZIE. I see him! I see him! Let's get him, girl! Get him!

(*They throw the last bags.*)

M-E. (*Shaking hands and formally congratulating Lizzie.*) I'm very proud of you, Lizzie. This is clearly one of the finest things you've ever done.

LIZZIE. (*Blushing.*) Thank you.

M-E. You did good, Lizzie.

LIZZIE. (*Proudly.*) I did, didn't I?

M-E. Really good. (*Embraces* LIZZIE.)

(*They put on their white gloves, dust themselves off, adjust their beauty queen banners, and begin to gather up their luggage.*)

"An' then Myra walked off the train onto the beach . . ."

LIZZIE. " . . . an' Porter stood on the boardwalk . . . his eyes misted over . . . and he waved to Myra . . . (*Throws her hand up in a broad gesture of waving*) and . . . and . . . (*Begins to cough from the soda dust that Margaret is pounding from her luggage.*) AND . . . (*Waving dust from her vision*) when the dust cleared . . ."

M-E. No, no, no! " . . . and Myra took off her shoes and left her footprints in the . . ."

(*They both pause and look dramatically around the room.*)

M-E AND LIZZIE. BAKING SODA!

(*They laughingly pick up their luggage and begin to walk off as the lights dim.*)

END OF SCENE 1

ACT ONE

SCENE 2

TIME: *Late afternoon—next day*
PLACE: *Luxury hotel, Windsor, Ontario*
SCENE: *A wide ramp, resembling a city freeway, bridges the entire upstage area from Stage Right to Stage Left. At the center of the ramp, which arches several feet from the floor, is the first-floor balcony of a luxurious, lake-front hotel in Windsor, Ontario. A large banner that reads, "Welcome—Miss International Sepia" is located at the Center of the ramp. Glass doors open out onto a European-style balcony overlooking a courtyard. Arching over the Downstage Left entrance to the ramp is a latticework trellis entwined with plastic flowers and vines.*

(MAN ONE *and* MAN TWO, *now dressed in black-and-white waiter's jackets, begin to set up small café tables and chairs Downstage. There is the heightened sound of many birds as* M-E *enters the hotel balcony wearing a satin dressing gown.*)

M-E. Shoo! Scat! Get away! (*Scattering birds from the breakfast dishes.*) Off! Off! (*Turns, calls back into the room.*) Lizzie! Look at this! Birds everywhere!

(M-E *brusquely begins to remove the breakfast trays. She spies a newspaper on the table. She picks it up and reads it.*)

It's Sunday. The only way I can ever tell it's Sunday anymore is by reading the newspapers. Seems like there was a time when you could *smell* a Sunday or *hear* a Sunday, but now you have to read about it.

365

(*Calling in to* LIZZIE.) This is a marvelous hotel! Look at that lake! (PAUSE.) We paid for this room—not the birds. So stop inviting them to dine with us.

LIZZIE. (*From inside.*) I forgot.

M-E. (*She stands, musing. Then, still talking loudly to* LIZZIE, *who remains inside.*) You know who would have liked this hotel? William. First time I ever stayed at any hotel was with William. Did I tell you . . . ? William called me? After all these years. After all these years. And do you know what he wanted? He wanted for us to get back together! I didn't laugh in his face . . . but you know what I told him? I told him. I said, "If you can match me possession for possession—bank account for bank account—I'll consider it." Which I knew he couldn't do—'cause . . . he was nothing but a wastrel . . . *but* that's what I told him . . . (*Pause.*) I think this is the best hotel I've ever stayed in. Is that possible? (*Gives a small, startled scream as she discovers a bird is still on the balcony.*) Shoo, bird! Shoo! Get away from here! (*Calling in to* LIZZIE *again.*) It is the natural proclivity of birds to eat the food left unattended on the balcony.

LIZZIE. (*From inside.*) I forgot.

M-E. (*Sharing big secret with audience.*) She's afraid of birds. (*Laughs.*) She won't even come out here if I tell her they're still here . . . (*To* LIZZIE.) If you want them to start living here with us . . .

LIZZIE. (*From inside.*) I forgot!

M-E. (*Imitating* LIZZIE.) "I forgot, I forgot, I forgot." (*Spanks her hand as if reprimanding* LIZZIE.) Naughty. Naughty.

(*Below, the two waiters,* MAN ONE *and* MAN TWO, *prepare small café tables for cocktails in the Downstage dining area.*)

(M-E, *in a childlike prank, tiptoes to the balcony doors, slowly opens them, and then shouts to* LIZZIE.)

M-E. (*Mockingly.*) There's birds out here, Lizzie!

LIZZIE. (*In the process of dressing for cocktails.*) Oh, God, no! I'm afraid of birds! (*She gingerly steps out on the balcony to see if the birds have disappeared.*) Are they all gone? I like to watch them from a distance—'cause they look like all the beautiful poetry that's ever been written about them—but, up close, I can't stand to be near them . . . they frighten me. It's their fluttering . . . so erratic . . . like a desperation . . . (*She returns inside.*)

M-E. Did you notice when we came through the lobby? Everyone staring at us? Well, you know what they think . . .

LIZZIE. (*Appearing at balcony doorway.*) And MOTHS! Birds and Moths! (*Starts to exit back into the hotel, suddenly returns.*) And CHICKENS! Chickens are like that too, you know . . . all fluttery. It seems as if they're too . . . vulnerable . . . too easily devoured by everything else. Their lives seem so tenuous. From the moment they exist they must lead desperate lives— afraid of the future because each *hour* becomes the future. (*Exits back into the hotel.*)

M-E. They think we're the contestants. I'm serious. Beauty *lives*! It's not something you can put on in the morning and take off at night—even after fifty years.

LIZZIE. (*Still dressing as she enters the balcony.*) . . . and BUTTERFLIES! Oooh, I must not forget butter-flies—I *hate* them! (*She returns to hotel room.*)

M-E. I still wear the same size dress I did then. We are still pretty fancy after all these years.

LIZZIE. (*Entering balcony.*) Get dressed, Margaret! Please don't embarrass me by being late to everything! (*Exits back into hotel.*)

M-E. Very fancy. We've finally gone international. Been trying to get to the end of this story for fifty years. Fifty years is a long time. (*Disappears briefly into hotel room. Returns with a strapless, satin cocktail dress. A sinister pronouncement.*) I hate butterflies. (*Calling in to* LIZZIE.) Lizzie! Did I ever tell you about how I hate butterflies? I tried to kill one once. Let's see . . . I was still living on the farm . . . so I must have been around . . . four years old. And this butterfly—this beautiful butterfly—beautiful from a distance, but up close it was ugly . . . I tried to kill it. I picked up this wooden plank that was lying on the ground—it had a rusty nail sticking out of one end . . . I chased the butterfly all over the yard—stabbing him with that rusty nail. I remember ripping its wings a few times, but it kept flying. It kept flying like it was . . . crazy. And then it seemed to fly right at me—like it wanted to dash itself in my face—like it had the *nerve* to fight back. A little measly butterfly . . . attacking me. Boy, I threw that plank down and started running from that butterfly—screaming. (*Calling in to* LIZZIE.) Nobody respects you if you're normal, Lizzie! Only the crazy things survive. (*She has begun to dress throughout this speech.*) I have an awful lot of respect for butterflies. (*Pause.*) Well . . . I don't have to worry about the important things in my life anymore. (*Pause.*) My second husband . . . (*Reflects, as if counting*) *third* husband! I'm sorry . . . my third husband! . . . always called me Lizzie . . . can I tell you something? I actually *married* a man who called me Lizzie. Now that was my third husband . . . and I gotta tell you something else . . . my second husband called me Liza. But that wasn't as bad as my first husband. He called me Maggie! That was my first husband and my first mistake. And I done had *five* . . . (*Pauses to count*) mistakes since then. You tell me! I would *never* marry a man who calls me Maggie—and, for that matter, I ain't gon' marry nobody who calls me Lizzie no more either. And who was it that had the nerve to call me *Meg*?

LIZZIE. (*Entering balcony.*) Sam! I wish you would stop dawdling and get dressed! You make me so nervous! (*Exits back into hotel.*)

M-E. (*Still dressing.*) I believe that *was* Sam—I think so . . . yeah! Sam. Had to be Sam—let's see . . . (*Recalling*) William, Arthur . . . No! William . . . *Charlie* . . . Arthur, Sam . . . Well, anyway, it was my third husband, Arthur, who called me Lizzie. He thought he was very smart, you know. He called himself a big-time adventurer. Said he didn't like nothing commonplace—that's why he married me. Everytime I do something . . . the first thing he'd say was . . . "Lizzie, surprise me! Give me a shock! Make me gasp—once, because you've done something that I didn't already know you were going to do."

LIZZIE. (*Almost completely dressed in her neat little suit, hat, and gloves.*) I wasn't going to tell you because I didn't want to hear your tongue clicking and clacking in my ear! . . . but now, I'm going to tell you—and I beg you . . . PLEASE be silent! (*Defiant pronouncement.*) I gave up the house. I no longer live in the city and I do not live alone. (*Silence.*) Well, what do you have to say?

M-E. You . . . you . . . what can I say?

LIZZIE. Okay. There. That's it. (*She straightens her attire and approaches the ramp.*) The only thing that this *marvelous* hotel is missing is an elevator! Hurry up, Margaret. I'll meet you downstairs.

(LIZZIE *goes down and is seated at a table. Lights dim briefly and back up as* M-E *emerges through the glass doors completely dressed in extravagant attire: a strapless cocktail dress. She slips the beauty contest ribbon on over her dress and finally places a rhinestone tiara on her head.*)

M-E. (*From balcony, as if to herself.*) I'll tell you what! I don't ever intend to wear anymore of them dinky, gray-dyed, cotton, scrubwoman, tattered, faded—RAGS! Anymore!

(*She descends the ramp as if she were the beauty contestant—flashing a brilliant smile, rhinestone tiara glittering, "Miss International Sepia" banner emblazoned across her satin dress.*)

LIZZIE. (*As* M-E *approaches.*) You're late!

(MAN TWO [WAITER] *gives* M-E *a menu.*)

What if I were dying and you were late?

M-E. (*Studying menu.*) Lizzie, must you be so gruesome?

LIZZIE. I don't think reality is gruesome. You do plan to die one day don't you? Or are you above that? Face it. Death could happen . . . within . . . the next ten minutes.

M-E. Well . . . in that case . . . I'd better hurry up and order.

LIZZIE. I've already ordered—the usual.

M-E. Pink Ladies? (*Loudly.*) Pink ladies be damned!

(LIZZIE *self-consciously stoops near the table as if she is looking for something.*)

(*To* LIZZIE.) What *are* you *doing*? Pretending you don't know me?

LIZZIE. Yes.

M-E. Get up. Get up, Lizzie. I'm thinking. You know what
I think, Lizzie? I think . . . I don't know . . . I think
we can afford to be . . .

LIZZIE. Intelligent, Margaret! Act intelligent . . . PLEASE!

M-E. We could very easily be standing at the pinnacle of
a new epoch in our lives. Think about it. Does it seem
fitting to celebrate such a potentially auspicious time
with something as creatively lacking as Pink Ladies?
No. No. Lizzie, while we're here for what may be an
unparalleled occasion—let's do everything with a great
flourish! And the first thing I say is—Pink ladies be
damned!

LIZZIE. Well it took you a long time to say it, Margaret.
What do you have in mind?

M-E. (*To* WAITER.) An Irish coffee! (*Looking excitedly at*
LIZZIE *with a gleefully devilish glint.*) Don't you remember?

(MINISCENE.)

(*Butterfly McQueen–type charaterization.*) "Someone's at the door. Why don't you answer it, Beulah?"

LIZZIE. Oh! Uhm . . . uhm . . . (*In half surprise, she begins
to recognize the moment and assumes a similar char-
acterization.*) Uhm . . . "I cain't. I'se scared!"

(*They laugh.*)

Was that it? Was that it? What was it . . .? Something
about . . . ?

M-E. She was standing drenched and shivering in the
rain . . .

LIZZIE. (*Laughing.*) Oh, yes. And he lifted her in his
arms . . .

M-E. Pale and near death . . .

LIZZIE. . . . and he carried her into the drawing room and
placed her crumpled form on the couch in front of
the fireplace . . . and then he served her . . .

M-E AND LIZZIE (*Together.*) IRISH COFFEE!

LIZZIE. Of course!

M-E. (*To* WAITER.) That's it! That's what I want. I want
an Irish coffee!

LIZZIE. Margaret, you're such a genius. That sounds so delightful! Do I dare?

M-E. (*Lowering her voice as if divulging a big secret.*) You know what you could try, Lizzie? A hot toddy! (*Suppressing her glee with a knowing look at* LIZZIE) It was Miss Flora. Remember? (*Prodding.*) Miss Flora?

LIZZIE. Oooh . . . you're right!

(MINISCENE.)

"Miss Flora, sweet chile. Massa Tim say it too early fo' you to get out of bed wid' yo' sick self."

M-E. (*As Miss Flora.*) "Master Tim doesn't run my life. I must get up—Courtney is waiting for me. Courtney . . . Courtney . . . Ooooh . . ."

LIZZIE. "Miss Flora has fainted! Massa Tim! Massa Tim! Miss Flora has fainted!"

M-E. And then . . . he fixed her . . .

M-E and LIZZIE (*Together.*) A HOT TODDY!

LIZZIE. (*To* WAITER.) A hot toddy, please! Thank you, Margaret, thank you! I'm so glad we're making the most of this occasion.

(WAITER *exits.*)

The hotel is sensational! The people have been gorgeous! Something here makes me feel like I used to feel when Charlie and I built our first house. (*Pause.*) Was it Charlie?

M-E. Arthur. It was Arthur.

LIZZIE. Something here reminds me of it. I know what it is. It's spring! It's Sunday and it's spring! You can't beat that combination. I tell you, I'm always surprised to find anyone alive after the winter is over.

M-E. Lizzie? Is there any subject you can discuss that doesn't involve the "Grim Reaper"? Hmmm? If there is—I wish you would find it. (*Pause.*) Did you see the two in the lobby when we passed through?

LIZZIE. Two who?

M-E. The two *ladies*.

LIZZIE. There were two ladies? Watching us? (*Pause.*) What are you talking about?

M-E. Lizzie! For Christ's sake, what are we here for? The two ladies in the lobby!

LIZZIE. Give me a clue. Help me. What's the subject?

M-E. Oh, my God! The first thing I'm going to do in the morning is practice increasing my lung capacity. I need more air in my lungs in order to have the strength to explain things to you. The beauty contestants in the lobby! I know . . . I know . . . (*Mocking.*) "What beauty contestants?" Gasping for more air, I reply, "The beauty contestants that we're here to judge." "Oh, *those* beauty contestants." You didn't see them?

(LIZZIE *just stares blankly.*)

Are you with me? I'm telling you I saw two of the contestants in the lobby.

LIZZIE. I thought . . . we were still talking about . . . you know . . .

M-E. From now on I'll label the subjects so you won't get lost. Guess who's trying to win it again this year? (*Pause.*) Bridget and Gidget!

LIZZIE. (Shocked.) NOooo! NOooo!

M-E. Yesss! Yesss!

LIZZIE. Nooo!

M-E. Yes! (*Pause.*) It's gonna be a doozie of a choosy this year. (*Pause.*) This is a nice hotel, isn't it? It's very nearly the finest one I've been in. Of course I'm giving it a few extra stars for all the cute waiters. Have you noticed? (*Coyly.*) *And* have you noticed how they've been staring at us?

LIZZIE. Margaret!

M-E. Lizzie, do you live behind a blank wall? You haven't noticed they've been staring at us? (*Adjusts the beauty contest banner across her dress.*) We could do it again, Lizzie.

LIZZIE. Hmmmm . . . what could we be talking about now?

M-E. I went to little Arthur's birthday party last week. (*Pause.*) My godson . . . little Arthur? He was fourteen years old last week. *And* . . . I was given the . . . privileged honor . . . of actually being invited into his room—(*Proudly*) a privilege usually reserved only for those under fifteen years old. I walked into his room—neat as a pin! And the walls—the walls were covered . . . *plastered* with posters of women. And there was not-one-picture-of-us, Lizzie—not *one*.

THERE! Do you see? Do you see why we must do
it again?

LIZZIE. (*Completely lost.*) What's the subject?

M-E. US! US, Lizzie! We have to get some new posters
for little Arthur's room!

LIZZIE. Oh, dear.

M-E. We have to do it again, Lizzie. We have to go back
and set the record straight. We have to do it right.
it's as simple as that. My darling Lizzie! Beauty is
alive! . . . and doing quite well, thank you. I don't
think it is unfounded vanity to state that after having
won the official titled distinction of being the world's
first . . . (*Clearing her throat as if making an announcement*) "After having won the official titled distinction of being the world's first ebony-hued beauty—
Miss Emancipation of 1930—I can still do it again!
And *you*, my pretty handmaiden—first runner-up to
the queen . . . you could still do it again too!

LIZZIE. You got a lot of nerve! If I did it again it certainly
wouldn't be as runner-up to *you*! I guarantee you that!
You think you always supposed to be the queen!

M-E. We have to change history, Lizzie. We did it wrong
the first time. We let everyone down.

LIZZIE. I don't want to do it again, Margaret. I just wanna
be two old lad . . . no! Not *old* . . . two . . . *mature*
ladies here on a visit as honorary judges.

M-E. Think of all the time we put into it. Fifty years! Do
you know how many of those years I pinched my nose?

LIZZIE. (*Tired.*) What's the subject?

M-E. It's the same subject, Lizzie. Everytime I washed my
face I would leave lots of soap on my nose and let it
dry while I pinched my nose—and, voila!—my nose
would stand up straight.

LIZZIE. Margaret, you didn't.

M-E. Yeah. I did.

LIZZIE. Well . . . I pinched my mouth. My mother taught
me how to do it. You can make your lips smaller if
you tighten them over your teeth like this. (*Demonstrates.*) See. (*Talks with tightened lips.*) Do you see
what that does to your lips?

M-E. We both used to tuck our fannies.

LIZZIE. That's right! "Tighten your fannies!"

M-E. . . . and straighten your hair . . .

LIZZIE. . . . had to use bleaching cream every night . . .

M-E. We were classics. I will not turn the title over to anyone who doesn't even have the bare standards. I'm a classic!

LIZZIE. Maybe we're antiques.

M-E. Oh, come on, Lizzie. There have to be standards.

LIZZIE. I agree . . . wide-set eyes, long bones . . .

M-E. We're gonna do it right this time, Lizzie.

LIZZIE. (*Exhilarated.*) YES! YES! OOOHH, YES! (*Suddenly.*) Have you ever thought that . . . this might be . . . the last time?

M-E. This is the beginning, Lizzie! We're gonna put new endings on old stories!

LIZZIE. No, no. I mean . . . the last time . . . for us. (*Trying to find a way to say it delicately.*) Ten years from now we'll be seventy-seven years old—or (*Giggles nervously*) . . . whatever.

M-E. So?

LIZZIE. They only ask us to come every ten years.

M-E. Oh. I see. You're sounding the death knoll again.

LIZZIE. Well, you must admit that the great majority of people that were with us at the beginning are those who have passed on.

M-E. There must be something masochistic in my character that makes me want to be with you. You are so morbid.

LIZZIE. You can pretend to be perennial if you want to.

M-E. Lizzie. Lizzie. It must be fearful. *Thinking* about it all the time. I'm not afraid of dying; but *thinking* about it all the time seems far more horrible than the actual event.

LIZZIE. (*Defending herself.*) I am not afraid of dying! I look forward to it. I embrace it. It'll be a great experience! I am totally prepared. The first thing I did when Sam died . . . I joined a memorial society. I wouldn't have come to this trip if I hadn't finished paying for the cemetery plot!

M-E. The what!

LIZZIE. The vault and the plot alone cost me fifteen hundred dollars! I promised Sam on the day we got married that I would be buried next to him.

M-E. Was that what you discussed on your honeymoon?

LIZZIE. (*Angry.*) Laugh, Margaret! Big joke! Ahhhaha-haaa!

M-E. (*Patronizingly.*) Aahh . . . Lizzie is upset. What-is-it-Lizzie? What-are-you-upset-a-bout?

(*Silence.*)

My God, Lizzie. You're serious!

(*Silence.*)

My God, Lizzie! Are you serious?

LIZZIE. (*Teary.*) It is a rather serious matter; and it happens to be all I have to be serious about. I am not going to stick my head in the sand and deny that it exists.

M-E. Are you telling me that you've spent . . . all these years preparing . . . to die?

LIZZIE. (*Near tears.*) You see! You see how you try to make it sound stupid! Do you think you can just keel over and die without preparing for it? (*Shouting.*) HAVE YOU PAID FOR YOUR EMBALMING? Huhmmm? Two hundred dollars to be embalmed! Make me look stupid! The casket! THE CASKET? *Seven thousand dollars!* You're not prepared. A hearse! Oh! Oh, now! What about the flower car, the mortician's fee, the limousines, the . . . (*Crying.*)

M-E. (*Stopping her, calming her.*) Oooh, poor baby. Oh, sweetheart. I'm sorry. I didn't know.

LIZZIE. You must start thinking about it, Margaret.

M-E. I will, dear. I will.

LIZZIE. This contest is a very brief moment in your life. When the contest is over you have to return to reality.

M-E. Yes, Lizzie. I'll start thinking about . . . (*Unable to say the word*) it.

LIZZIE. I'm sorry if I'm spoiling your trip . . .

(WAITER *enters with drinks.*)

M-E. Don't stare. But notice how the waiter looks at us.

(*They sit silently as the* WAITER *serves their drinks. They suppress smiles as they covertly check to see if he is looking at them.* WAITER *exits. They raise their glasses in a toast.*)

"To the new 'Miss International Sepia'—may she carry
on the tradition!"

LIZZIE. Hear! Hear!

(They sip.)

M-E. Hmmm! Oh, this is gorgeous! The topping tastes like
ice cream! I wonder if Barbie's in it this year?

LIZZIE. *(Returning her drink to the table with a sour gri-
mace.)* Ugh! This tastes like water warmed over in
rusty pipes. I don't like my drink.

M-E. Really? Here. Taste this. *(Slides her drink to Lizzie.)*

LIZZIE. *(Sipping M-E's drink.)* Yes. This is nice. You always manage to get the best. I don't like mine.

M-E. Let me see. *(Sips LIZZIE's drink.)* That is a peculiar
drink. It tastes like hot water . . .

LIZZIE. . . . warmed over in rusty pipes.

M-E. Yes. It does, sorta. Like . . . the beginning of tea
. . . without the teabag. *(Laughing.)* With a little tea
and sugar in it—it might work.

LIZZIE. Well, I don't know if I'm going to be able to drink
this. I wish I had ordered your drink.

M-E. Why, Lizzie?

LIZZIE. Why? Why . . . ? Because I don't like this drink.
That's why.

M-E. *(Scooping all the whipped cream off her drink. Eating
it like ice cream.)* No. No. I mean—*why* did you get
rid of your house?

LIZZIE. Oh. Oh, that. It was the stairs, Margaret. Just too
many stairs.

M-E. Hmmm. The whipped cream is so good. *(Pushes the
sugar in front of LIZZIE.)* Here. Sweeten it with a little
sugar. See if that helps.

LIZZIE. That's a good idea. *(Spoons sugar into her drink.
Tastes it.)*

M-E. Well?

LIZZIE. No. I think it's worse.

(They sip silently for a while.)

M-E. Well, I enjoyed the whipped cream, but the drink is
not so tasty anymore.

LIZZIE. Makes you realize, doesn't it? All those movies

. . . they made those drinks seem like the pure-dee lifeblood of goodness, didn't they?

M-E. You know what might work? Lemon! Ask the waiter for a slice of lemon. That ought to help it.

LIZZIE. *Some*thing! It definitely needs help! (*Signals for* WAITER.) Please. May I have a slice of lemon? (WAITER *exits. To* MARGARET-ELIZABETH.) What are you doing?

M-E. I'm putting a *little* sugar in my drink. (*Tastes it.*) Well . . . it's not exactly . . . delightful. Here, try it.

LIZZIE. (*Tasting Margaret-Elizabeth's drink.*) Uhm, hum. It's better—but, you know . . . ? Cinnamon!

M-E. Ooh!

LIZZIE. Yes. When the waiter comes back ask him if he'll bring you a cinnamon stick.

(WAITER *appears carrying a small dish with lemon slices.*)

M-E. Waiter! Could you bring me a cinnamon stick? Yes. You know. A cinnamon stick.

(*He exits.* LIZZIE *squeezes lemon into her drink.*)

LIZZIE. (*Tasting.*) Oh! Oh! I'm *on* to something *now*! Taste this.

M-E. (*Tasting Lizzie's drink.*) Needs . . . (*Suspense, as she tastes it again*) Mint!

LIZZIE. You're right! You are right, my dear Margaret! Why didn't I think of that? Oh, that's perfect! (CALLS.) Waiter!

(WAITER *is entering with a cinnamon stick on a little dish.*)

Waiter. Could I have a little sprig of mint?

WAITER. (*As he places the cinnamon on the table.*) Mint?

LIZZIE. Yes. Just a little sprig.

(*They give flirting glances to the* WAITER. WAITER *exits.*)

M-E. (*Grinning contentedly.*) You do realize that we're still very fancy after all of these years, don't you, Lizzie?

LIZZIE. Now, what you do is . . . you stir the coffee with the cinnamon stick.

M-E. I know that, Lizzie. (*Stirs and tastes.*) It's devilish!

LIZZIE. (*Grabbing a sip of* MARGARET-ELIZABETH's *drink.*)
    Huhmmm! It is!
M-E. It's downright devilish! (*Pronouncement.*) You can
    change *anything* until it suits your taste, Lizzie!

(*They raise their glasses in a toast.*)

LIZZIE. "To *Class!*" We had that, didn't we, Margaret?
    CLASS!
M-E. Ooh . . . we fairly reeked of it. It simply oozed from
    our pores!
LIZZIE. (*Seriously.*) The *first* and *primary* criteria that I
    shall *demand* from every contestant . . . is CLASS!
    Margaret. How many hours did we spend? Every hair
    . . . carefully and immaculately in place . . .
M-E. Well, the wind-blown look was becoming quite pop-
    ular.
LIZZIE. For you, Margaret, not for me. I don't know how
    you could let people see you with your hair standing
    all over your head.
M-E. But it was a carefully planned wind-blown look—
    every curl left askew—carefully—for effect.
LIZZIE. And . . . white gloves! Margaret, do you remember
    we washed our gloves out every night before we went
    to bed.

(WAITER *returns with mint sprig on little dish.*)

M-E. I think he's bashful. It's hard to find bashful men
    anymore.
LIZZIE. It's hard to find bashful people anymore. Every-
    one's so brazen.

(*They sit demurely as* WAITER *places dish on table.*)

LIZZIE. Thank you. Uuh . . . (*To* WAITER) could you bring
    me one of those cinnamon sticks too . . . (*Naughty
    giggle. To* MARGARET-ELIZABETH.) In case the mint
    doesn't quite do it.

(WAITER *exits trying to contain himself.* LIZZIE *bruises the
mint sprig into her drink.*)

(*Who has been looking through her contest papers.*)
Well, damn-it-to-hell! They don't even list it in here!
CLASS! They don't have it on here! Look! (*Reading.*)
"Poise, charm, talent, intelligence . . ." But no class!

M-E. Well, that's the stuff that class is made of, Lizzie.
That all adds up to class. How's your drink?

LIZZIE. (*Sips.*) Cold.

M-E. (Sips her drink.) So's mine.

LIZZIE. I wish I'd a' ordered a pink lady.

END OF SCENE 2

ACT ONE

Scene 3

SCENE: *As the lights fade up,* MAN ONE, *dressed in representative black tie and tails, approaches the top of the ramp and proceeds to reverse the date section on the "Welcome" banner. He flips the dates, like a calendar, over the original 1980. The year now reads 1930.* MARGARET-ELIZABETH, *in a dressing gown, rushes out through the glass doors of the hotel balcony.*

M-E. Oh, God no! What are you trying to do to me?

(MAN ONE *flips the date to 1940.*)

(*Shudders.*) Oøougggh. . . . No.

(MAN ONE *flips the date to 1950.* MARGARET-ELIZABETH *stands stauch and sullen.* MAN ONE, *showing a slight impatience, flips the date to 1960.*)

Well . . . (*Smiles*) ye—ss. Yes. YES! Good year! That was definitely a good year! (*She exits.*)

(MAN ONE *begins to descend the ramp, Stage Left.*)

MAN ONE. (*Calling offstage.*) We're ready! (*He exits.*)

(*The amplified voice of* MAN ONE *is heard on the loudspeaker. He now becomes the Master of Ceremonies.*)

(*Offstage.*) Ladies and Gentlemen! It is with great pleasure that I announce the new "Miss Emancipation of 1960!"

(MAN ONE, *still dressed in tie and tails and carrying a hand-held microphone, enters the stage to the sound of loud cheering from audience.* WOMAN TWO *dramatically enters through the glass doors. She is wearing a one-piece bathing suit over black leotards with a banner across the front that reads, "The Queen." She stands on the balcony waving and blowing kisses until* WOMAN ONE *enters the balcony. She is dressed identically, but her banner is blank.* MARGARET-ELIZABETH *dramatically enters the balcony through the glass doors and stands between the two women.* M-E *is wearing a one-piece bathing suit with a banner across the front that reads, "Miss Oklahoma." Her bosom is an enormously exaggerated, padded affair that practically overflows her bathing suit. Her hair is tied up in a bouncy ponytail with a big, bright ribbon on top.* MAN ONE *gestures, and she begins her descent down the ramp, Stage Left. She smiles the huge, flashing, brilliant smile of a beauty contestant. She does not stop smiling until the pageant is over. Her speech and manner revert to a childlike coyness.* M-E *smiles and walks regally down the ramp Stage Left as a great burst of carnival music accompanies her. Simultaneously,* WOMAN ONE *and* TWO *descend the ramp, Stage Right. Their hair and manner are an imitation of* M-E's. MAN TWO *enters. He pulls a child's red wagon [slowly, almost in slow motion] in front of the Stage Left entrance to the ramp. The wagon is covered with artificial flowers like a float. As* M-E *passes under the flower-covered archway,* WOMAN ONE *and* TWO *flank her on either side. They all stand under the arched trellis until* MAN TWO *places a bouquet of red roses in* M-E's *arms and a rhinestone tiara on her head. The music changes dramatically to "Caldonia" as* MAN TWO *helps* M-E *sit in the wagon. Once seated, she strikes a coy pose. He begins to pull the wagon around the stage in what seems to be almost suspended motion.* MAN ONE *begins to sing "Mammy" [in half time] over the microphone while* M-E *waves, smiles, and blows kisses to the audience.*

LIZZIE *enters through the glass doors and leans over the balcony. She is wearing a one-piece swimsuit over black leotards. Her banner is blank. As she speaks, the motions of the others continue, but all sound stops temporarily, as if the needle had been removed from a record.*)

LIZZIE. (*Calling down to* M-E.) I'm going to tell the judges about your TITS!

(Sound resumes.)

MAN ONE. And now—the prizes! (*His voices changes into a calm, modulated, emotionless drone—as if he were a guide on a sight-seeing tour of the city. Reading.*) "From Sarah's Sweet Shop—a special cake with the winner's name and title on it."

(Cheers from the audience.)

"From The Lyons Bootery—one pair of shoes of the winner's choice."

(Cheers from the audience.)

"From The Johnson's Jewelry Shop—a wristwatch."

(Cheers from the audience. His voice continues to announce the "prizes" over the loudspeaker throughout the remainder of the scene while he continues to interact, returning to his old "barker" style personality.)

Boley is blessed! Do you hear me, ladies and gentlemen? Boley is blessed! There she is—our new and magnificent queen!

(He sings a few more lines from "Mammy" as white lights flash intermittently and silhouette the images on the stage as if photos are being taken.)

May I take this time to introduce our surprise judge for this year's event—all the way from Holly-Wood, California!—MR. G. W. CASTLE!

(There is cheering from the audience as he motions for LIZZIE to come forward. She stands staunch and resentful on the balcony.)

(*Again.*) MR. G. W. CASTLE!

(Sound stops.)

WOMAN ONE. Where is he, Margaret?
LIZZIE. I'm certainly not going to do it, Margaret!

WOMAN TWO. (*Sarcastically.*) Who's going to crown the queen?

(MAN TWO *disappears.*)

M-E. (*Jumping out of the wagon—no longer the beauty contestant.*) You've been crying all these years because you were runner-up! Now I'm offering you a major part! What the hell do you want?

WOMAN ONE, TWO. I'm not going to do it, Margaret!

M-E. (*Fuming.*) You promised. You *said* you wanted to do this. *Every*body's waiting. What do you want . . . ? Do you want me to beg? Okay, I'll beg. "Please . . . please . . . DO IT!"

LIZZIE. You've changed everything. That's not my part.

M-E. I told you . . . it's gonna be different. Who knows . . . you could . . . end up . . . the queen. Help me. After all these years I would think you would be happy to finish it once and for all.

WOMAN TWO. You're not doing it right!

WOMAN ONE. You've got the whole thing wrong!

LIZZIE. You've got the wrong year . . . you've changed the entire . . .

M-E. (*Laughing.*) Oh, come on, Lizzie! 1930! I wouldn't be caught dead in those ugly bathing suits! A little vanity! Vanity never hurt anybody. Truthfully! How do you think I got where I am? Telling the straight of things?

LIZZIE. Truthfully? You don't want anyone to know how long ago it was. (*Shouting.*) MARGARET! It's not just the year that you've randomly plucked out of a hat . . . !

M-E. It's my story and I can tell it any way I want to! I have kept this body in excellent condition and I intend to show it off! Now you can either cooperate—or get out of it!

LIZZIE, WOMAN ONE, TWO. (*Laughing.*) You're so funny, Margaret . . . Ahaaa, ha, ha, haaa . . .

M-E. There are ever so many ways to tell a story, Lizzie. You can write people in or write 'em out—you're only a small part of this story. The most important thing is how it all ends.

WOMAN ONE. What about the beginning?

M-E. (*Impatient.*) I'm here to find new endings for old

stories. It's too late for new beginnings! Now anyone who doesn't want to do what we agreed . . . Make up your mind! (*Under her breath, as if to the audience.*) I can't believe this! I'm begging her to do this part!

LIZZIE. You just want someone to play runner-up to you again!

WOMAN ONE. You've got the wrong date . . .

WOMAN TWO. You've got the wrong title . . .

M-E. I know that. I started it all, Lizzie. Don't your forget that! *I* was the beginning!

WOMAN TWO. (*Laughing uproariously.*) *I* was the beginning!

LIZZIE. Every time you want to be queen!

M-E. That's not true. That's not true. I want it to come to an *end*. A satisfactory ending. A good ending. A decent ending. One that I can . . . *rest* with! Now I know what I want. 1960 . . . was a good year for beauty.

WOMAN TWO. Well, if it's that flexible . . . I'll be queen!

WOMAN ONE. ME!

LIZZIE. ME!

M-E. (*Mortified.*) You were the runner-up! I was "Miss Emancipation" and you were "Miss Emancipation Proclamation." All good things in due time, Lizzie. Each time I come I see . . . changes.

WOMAN TWO. The only thing that's changed is the title . . .

WOMAN ONE. And the bathing suits . . .

WOMAN TWO. And the people . . .

WOMAN ONE. And the time . . .

M-E. Thank God for that! (*Changing her approach.*) I need you, Lizzie. I need you very badly. It's a good part. I promise.

WOMAN ONE, TWO, LIZZIE. The runner-up . . .

M-E. Now, you see. You thought you were gonna be the runner-up. I wouldn't ask you to do that part. You've done that. I want to give you a challenge. I need you to do the most important part of all.

LIZZIE, WOMAN ONE, TWO. The queen?

M-E. (*Sweetly.*) Nooo . . . (*Carefully.*) Mr. Castle.

LIZZIE, WOMAN ONE, TWO. MR. CASTLE! (*They all laugh hysterically.*)

LIZZIE. (*Still laughing until she bursts into tears.*) I-WON'T-DO-IT!

M-E. You get to decide my fate.

LIZZIE. (*Tearfully.*) I'm the runner-up! Now you want to take that away from me! You . . . you . . . you . . .

LIZZIE, WOMAN ONE, TWO. (*Deliberately.*) . . . *black cow*!

M-E. (*Reproachfully.*) Uh . . . Lizzie! There is no need for you to sink to such low superlatives! (*Pause.*) Don't you understand who Mr. Castle is?

LIZZIE. Yes. He's a *man*. Do I look like a *man* to you? (*Crying.*) You always want to make me look like the horse's hiney.

M-E. Without him there is no story, Lizzie. I have to call on you for the best part. Think about that. It's the best part in the whole story. Trust me. (*She looks at Lizzie for a few beats then nods to the announcer to continue.*)

(*Sound resumes.* WOMAN ONE *and* WOMAN TWO *begin waving, smiling, and posing under the archway.*)

MAN ONE. (*Embarrassed recovery.*) Uh . . . Ladies and gentlemen . . . Mr. Castle is a talent scout from the fabled land of Hollywood! He . . . has the power to . . . make a star. The . . .

(*Sound stops.*)

LIZZIE. I'm not going to do it, Margaret.

M-E. Okay, you don't want to be Mr. Castle? Then I don't want you in it! You made me waste an entire trip!

LIZZIE. (*Pointing to* WOMAN ONE *and* TWO.) What about Maggie. Make her do it. She was there. And Ginger! She knows the part! I don't wanna do it, Margaret.

WOMAN ONE. I'm not going to do it.

WOMAN TWO. I'm not going to do it, either.

M-E. FINE!

LIZZIE. (*Crying.*) I'm the runner-up! *Not* Mr. Castle!

M-E. Okay! (*Holding back a smile at having won.*) You can *be* the runner-up! I'll get someone else to play his part.

LIZZIE, WOMAN ONE, TWO. You always get to play the best part!

(*Sound resumes.* M-E *again becomes the beauty contestant.* LIZZIE, WOMAN ONE, AND WOMAN TWO *stand under the vine-covered trellis waving, smiling, and tossing plastic flowers to the audience.)*

MAN ONE. Ladies and gentlemen! There she is! The Queen of Boley! Miss Emancipation, 1960! And *now*—the man that can crown her Queen of the Stars. I give you—MR. G. W. CASTLE!

(MAN TWO snaps on an oversized necktie and proceeds with stiff dignity down the ramp.)

MAN TWO (MR. CASTLE). *(He speaks humbly and sincerely into the microphone.)* Citizens of Boley. The circumstances that brought me here to your beautiful little town are not as important as what I have discovered here today. I came here under the auspices of a major motion picture company to inaugurate an unprecedented event—the premiere of a major motion picture—HERE! in the all-black township of Boley, Oklahoma.

LOUDSPEAKER. *(Prize announcement.)* "From the Metropolitan Movie House—two free tickets to the movie of the winner's choice."

MAN TWO (MR. CASTLE). I did not expect to be a judge today, but after witnessing and participating in today's event, I am overwhelmed by the talent that exists here.

(Cheering from the audience.)

(Breaking in and quieting the cheers.) SO . . . So overwhelmed that I am taking the liberty to offer a special prize to the winner—a SCREENTEST! . . .

(Cheers from the audience.)

(Calming the audience.) . . . for . . . FOR a new film that our studios are very excited about. A film about the life of a great saint—JOAN OF ARC! I can't help but feel that your new queen . . . the new "Miss Emancipation" . . . would make an outstanding Joan of Arc. *(He smiles benignly at MARGARET-ELIZABETH who is now standing under the archway between the two women. To audience.)* Our studios have gone out

on a limb to dare to make a film that shows colored people as . . . as . . . PEOPLE! (*Preaching.*) Too long have you stood in the wake of sour images! That is why we were *certain* that this was the *only* place to premiere our new film. I urge you all to place your vote for humanity and the eradication of racism by attending this film. I feel that Fate brought me here for many reasons, not the least of which was to end my search for Joan of Arc.

(*The audience cheers, and he motions for* MARGARET-ELIZ-ABETH *to come forward to the microphone. She joins him.*)

(*To* MARGARET-ELIZABETH.) I have been to almost every major city in America and *never* have I seen such beauty and talent as you have displayed here today. I have just one question to ask of such a talented young lady as yourself. (*To audience.*) Where did you get such pretty legs?

LOUDSPEAKER. "From Marianne's Steak and Chop House— a gift certificate for an evening's free dining."

(*Cheers from the audience.*)

M-E. (*Giggling.*) My mama gave 'em to me.
MAN ONE (ANNOUNCER). (*Resuming microphone.*) WHAT A NIGHT! Ladies and gentlemen—our queen! Take a long, long look, for it may be the last time you get to see her in person until you see her on the SILVER SCREEN! What a night! TONIGHT! Tonight is the big night, ladies and gentlemen . . . the PREMIERE of the newly released film entitled . . . entitled . . . ? (*He looks at Mr. Castle who leans over and whispers something in his ear.*) Uh . . . Yes! Our own special premiere of the newly released film, *BLACK, WHITE, AND IN TROUBLE!* LADIES AND GENTLE-MEN—Don't miss it! *Black, White, and in Trouble!*
LOUDSPEAKER. "From Ronald's Novelty Shop—a wall-sized replica of the American flag."

(*Cheering from the audience.* MR. CASTLE *leans forward with a patronly smile and whispers something else into his ear.*)

MAN ONE (ANNOUNCER). LADIES AND GENTLEMEN!
I have just been told of another new development to
highlight this Night of Nights. Our queen . . . OUR
QUEEN will ride through the main street of Boley
on a special studio-made float tonight to officially open
the world premiere of this new film. And . . . AND
. . . to the first twenty-five people to attend—FREE
ADMISSION! What a night! What a night! I urge you
all not to miss this exciting film.
LOUDSPEAKER. "From Lacey's Pet Shop—one full-throated
singing canary."

(A floodlight washes across the stage. MARGARET-ELIZ-
ABETH *returns to the wagon.* MAN ONE *now pulls her slowly
around the stage as she waves, smiles, and tosses flowers.
They are trailed by* WOMAN ONE *and* WOMAN TWO, *who
do the same. The blinding lights of photos being snapped
continues intermittently.* MR. CASTLE *begins to ascend the
Stage Left ramp entrance.* MARGARET-ELIZABETH *jumps
from the wagon and pursues him. The* WOMEN *return to
the archway.)*

M-E. *(Calling after him.)* Mr. Castle! Mr. Castle! *(Giggles.)*
The . . . the . . . premiere was nice . . . uhm . . .
thank you for the honor of . . .
MAN TWO (MR. CASTLE). Aah! You're the little girlie from
the beauty contest.
M-E. Yes. *(Giggles.)*
MAN TWO (MR. CASTLE). What did you say your name
was?
M-E. Gidget. Like in *Gidget Goes to the Beach.*
MAN TWO (MR. CASTLE). Yes. Well you're very attractive.
And you look a lot like Gidget . . . with your, uh
. . . pony tail . . . the . . . uh . . . well . . . How'd
you like it sweetheart?
M-E. *(Gushing.)* Oh, it was really exciting. All those flowers . . . my friends couldn't believe . . . that I was
sitting there . . . on this float—riding through the
center of town. . . .
MAN TWO (MR. CASTLE). No, no. The film. How'd you
like the film, girlie?
M-E. Well . . . I liked the part where the Black Monster
starts coming up from the sewers and . . . grabbing
all the people . . . I started screaming when he started

ripping all the clothes off the women . . . I just wanted
to leave. (*Giggles.*)

WOMAN ONE. You're so phony, Maggie! SMUT! Tell him
it was the absolute height of smut!

WOMAN TWO. Pure SMUT!

M-E. . . . but I liked it. (*Giggles.*)

MAN TWO (MR. CASTLE). Good. Good. That's what we
want. Excitement. Well, girlie, what can I do for you?

M-E. Uh . . . well you said . . . uh
. . . the screentest . . . for Joan of Arc.

MAN TWO (MR. CASTLE). Screentest. Uhhh . . . let me see
your legs, sweeetheart.

M-E. For Joan of Arc?

MAN TWO (MR. CASTLE). Well, now, come, come, dearie.
You see, you have to understand that there's a lot of
sexual implication in the fact that Joan of Arc posed
as a man.

(MARGARET-ELIZABETH *coyly displays her legs.* LIZZIE,
WOMAN ONE AND TWO *do the same.*)

MAN ONE. (*Standing on wagon.*) Oooh, Mama! Where'd
you get those fine legs?

MAN TWO (MR. CASTLE). Hey, girlie, who gave you those
fine legs?

M-E. (*Giggling.*) I don't know. I was just born this way.

WOMAN ONE AND TWO AND LIZZIE. (*Giggling.*) My mama
gave 'em to me!

MAN TWO (MR. CASTLE). Perfect. You were born perfect.
Listen, how old are you, sweetheart?

(WOMAN ONE AND TWO *laugh uproariously.*)

WOMAN ONE. 25!

WOMEN TWO. 28!

M-E. Eighteen.

MAN TWO (MR. CASTLE). Fuck. Fuck. Well, that's that.
Joan of Arc was only seventeen.

LOUDSPEAKER. "From the Wilson Memorial Park Association—a free pass to the Greatest Show On Earth—
The Circus."

M-E, WOMAN ONE AND TWO. Oh.

MAN TWO (MR. CASTLE). That's a goddamn shame. You
would have been perfect. Tell me something. Do you

have a lot of fire and passion? A thought just occurred
to me.

M-E. Passion?

(WOMAN ONE AND TWO *begin to breathe passionately*.)

MAN TWO (MR. CASTLE). Yeah. Our studio's been sitting
on this hot story . . . love story. The lead in the movie
has to have a lot of passion. The role was originally
written for a male transvestite . . . but I think I can
work something out. C'mere girlie, show me if you're
passionate. (*He begins to embrace her*.)

M-E. Well, I don't know . . . I thought I was going to have
a screentest.

MAN TWO (MR. CASTLE). You are! You are, sweetheart!
It's happening right before your very eyes. Hey, look,
honey. That camera is like a big, hot cock. It comes
right in and fucks you. There's no fakin' it. Now that's
the fuckin' truth. C'mon, sweetie, give me some passion. (*He kisses her*.) What's the matter, don't you
like to be kissed?

M-E, WOMAN ONE AND TWO. NO! (*Struggling*.)

M-E. I mean . . . well . . . (*He kisses her again*.) Stop it!

MAN TWO (MR. CASTLE). Well, look . . . (*Backing off*),
uh . . . as it stands now, I'm only here for a one-day
promotional tour.

MAN ONE, MAN TWO (MR. CASTLE), WOMAN ONE AND
TWO. I'LL BE BACK NEXT YEAR!

MAN TWO (MR. CASTLE). We'll see what we can work out
then.

M-E. Next year? But you said . . . you announced to everyone . . .

MAN TWO (MR. CASTLE). What can I say? Joan of Arc was
only seventeen . . . now that's the fuckin' truth. Look,
uh . . . what did you say your name was?

(MARGARET-ELIZABETH *quickly fluffs her ponytail into an
instant "tousled" hairdo and assumes a "girlie" pose. The*
WOMEN *do the same*.)

M-E. Bridget. Like in . . .

WOMAN TWO. *Bridget Goes to Bed*.

MAN TWO (MR. CASTLE). Oh yeah. Of course. Dead ringer.
Perfect. With your . . . tousled hair and the . . . pouty

lips, and the . . . uhm, uh . . . you're very beautiful!

M-E. Thank you.

MAN TWO (MR. CASTLE), MAN ONE, WOMAN ONE AND
   TWO. . . . TELL YOU WHAT I'M GONNA DO . . .

(MAN ONE *exits*.)

MAN TWO (MR. CASTLE). I'm gonna change your image.
   Something . . . different. I think . . . we'll start with
   your name. Stand where you are and just let me look
   at you. (*Sizing her up.*) Uhm, uhm . . . I have the
   power to make you the most beautiful woman in the
   world. Do you believe me?

M-E. Yes.

MAN TWO (MR. CASTLE). Good. Now! What's your name?

M-E. Barbie. Like in . . . *Barbie Goes to Hawaii*.

MAN TWO (MR. CASTLE). Let's see . . . Ebony . . . Jet
   . . . Raven . . . No, no, no. Hmmm . . . Jet . . .

M-E. Tammy. Like in . . . *Tammy Rides the Surf*.

MAN TWO (MR. CASTLE). JETA! JETA! . . . Johnson! You
   see . . . how easy it is. Already we're onto something.
   We've conjured up an entire new image just by changing your name. Already you're a novelty. Someone
   no one has ever heard of before. Jeta Johnson! Now!
   The next step is promotion. How shall we promote
   you? Something different. Let . . . me . . . see. Hmmm.
   Uh huh! Uh huh! (*Studying her.*) Hmmm. Did anyone
   ever tell you that you look a little bit Polynesian? Well
   you do! In profile. You look a little bit Polynesian.
   Uh huh. The high cheekbones . . . American Indian!
   Nobody could argue with that. Okay, what have we
   got? Polynesian. American Indian . . . and . . . something . . . something . . . Brazilian! Yes! The forehead.
   Definitely a Brazilian flair to the forehead. And damn
   it! if your eyes don't look Turkish . . . Well, girlie, I
   think we're getting someplace. What d'ya think?

M-E. Oh, my God!

(WOMAN ONE AND TWO *begin speaking gibberish*.)

MAN TWO (MR. CASTLE). HEY! Just for the fun of it . . .
   we'll throw in a little Irish. Listen, sweetheart, I've
   handled the best of them. I made them all what they
   are. What'd you think of that?

M-E. Well! We-lll . . . I got a little problem. I don't speak
    any of those languages.
MAN TWO (MR. CASTLE). No, no, no! What the hell, sweet-
    heart! The trick is . . . silence. Don't speak. If you
    have to talk, use one or two syllable words.

(MINISCENE: MARGARET-ELIZABETH *and* LIZZIE *change into
Butterfly McQueen types.*)

M-E. Who dat?
LIZZIE. Who dat?
WOMAN ONE, TWO, LIZZIE. Who dat what say "Who dat"
    when I say who dat?
MAN TWO (MR. CASTLE). Whenever you're in doubt about
    what to say—just smile. Got it? (MARGARET-ELI-
    ZABETH *smiles broadly.*) You're gonna be a winner,
    kid. You're gonna be imitated from coast to coast.
    Damn it, you're cute!

(*They have reached the Center of the ramp.* MR. CASTLE
rushes on ahead as M-E *remains at the Center of the ramp.*)

MAN TWO (MR. CASTLE). (*Calling back.*) And listen, gal
    . . . uh, what did we decide to call you?
M-E. Jet. Like in . . . jet black.
MAN TWO (MR. CASTLE). Right. Listen, Jeta, you got a
    year to work on it. Learn to tap dance! Smile! And
    don't lose your southern accent. See you next year!
    (*Exits.*)

(M-E *stands at the Center of the ramp looking after* MR.
CASTLE. *Lights dim.* LIZZIE, WOMAN ONE, *and* WOMAN
TWO, *quietly enter stage and look at* M-E *in great disap-
pointment.* M-E *stomps her foot angrily. She repeats the
angry stamping a few times until there is the hint of a rhythm.*
LIZZIE *gradually joins her and they begin a shuffling tap
rhythm.* WOMAN ONE *and* TWO *slowly join the "stamp dance"
until they are all angrily stomping out a tap rhythm that
ends on a furious note.*)

END OF ACT ONE

ACT TWO

SCENE 1

Hotel balcony. Morning of the following day. MARGARET-ELIZABETH *is standing on the balcony. She is wearing a long, flowing nightgown.*

M-E. I ought to be sitting here getting some of this sun. (*Pulls chair to the side of the table. Sits. Props her legs up on table.*) Let the sun shine on those legs, my dear! (*Leans backs.*) Oh! Oh, no, no! I can't! My back! This hurts my back! Oh, for heaven's sake! (*Gently, to herself.*) Okay. Okay. Sit up. Slowly. Slowly. Oooaaaww . . . Old! You're gonna convince me that you're old! It *does* hurt. I know pain when I feel it. Charlie had to . . . was it Charlie? Sam! Sam had to rub my back every night. (*Firmly.*) There is nothing wrong with this back that regular exercise wouldn't cure. This is the back cure! (*Rolls over on the floor into a modified headstand. Remains there.*)

LIZZIE. (*Casually entering balcony from hotel room.*) You look nasty!

M-E. (*Coming out of the position.*) Everything looks nasty to you.

LIZZIE. (*Looking out over the balcony railing.*) Margaret! People are looking up here! I bet they could see your tail!

M-E. Really! (*Momentarily embarrassed.*) Well, damned if I care! I paid good money to be here and if they keep looking long enough, they'll get to see everything! I plan to be myself on this trip. Before this trip is over, I plan to *free* myself—and, if that includes showing my tail—then so be it! Anybody wanna look at this well-kept, sixty-seven-year-old body, can damn well help themselves. I'd consider it a great compliment to all the years I've struggled to keep this form fit.

It's like showing off your good china. I did not come here to be old! These legs . . . (*Showing her legs*) these are the legs that won the crown, Lizzie! The very same legs. They haven't changed a bit. I made sure of it.

LIZZIE. You did it again! You might as well strip butt-naked out here! I didn't know you were cuckoo! I'm going inside. (*Exits into hotel.*)

M-E. Ain't nobody looking up here! (*Flounces back and forth across the front of the balcony, holding her gown apart to reveal her legs.*) What good did it do you . . . saving your legs all them years? Only made *one* picture where they let my legs show . . . can't remember her name. I played . . . a native girl . . . what was her name? Uhm, uhm, uhm. Sure did, didn't I? Goodness knows, I'd almost forgotten that. (*Calling in to* LIZZIE.) Darn it, Lizzie! I'd almost forgotten that movie. "Bugga Wanna, Bugga Wanna, Bugga Wanna Wanna Na."

(LIZZIE *steps curiously out on balcony.*)

Those were my lines. Those were the lines I had to say when they brought me back to my tribe. "Bugga Wanna, Bugga Wanna, Bugga Wanna Wanna Na."

LIZZIE. It's too bad you remembered them, Margaret. It sorta makes you want to throw up.

M-E. Listen, dear, you are not going to make me feel guilty about what I did. The times predicted what I had to do—but the times have changed.

LIZZIE. Margaret. Let's be honest. The odds are very much against your being available to judge the next contest.

M-E. They got you, Lizzie. They really sucked you in. I am truly angry about it!

LIZZIE. I know! You've told me a thousand times! Please don't start . . .

M-E. I'M ANGRY ABOUT THE WHOLE THING!

LIZZIE. Yes, yes! Plee-ase . . . (*Pause.*) What whole thing? What are you . . . ? Okay, Margaret, what's the subject? You've gone and changed the subject on me. I can tell.

M-E. I'm angry about how they made the whole process so mysterious.

LIZZIE. What! What! What's so mysterious? Am I supposed to guess or are you supposed to remain floating around on your lofty incoherence?

M-E. The life process, for God's sake! They took all the natural things of life and made a mess out of them! Do you realize that we spent our entire lives traumatizing over things that had been carefully worked out? Someone decided everything was too simple . . . the Grand Design just wasn't complex enough . . . so they threw a monkey wrench into the whole goddamn works. Life! Growing up! Growing old! . . . And most of all—Beauty! . . . *but*, finally, Death! Simple, natural acts . . . were just turned into . . . they took a simple little hole in the ground and dug a tunnel that leads right back to the hole. Now that's unnatural!

LIZZIE. The only unnatural thing I've done recently is to come here with you.

M-E. Oh, poo poo! When I was thirteen years old, my mother went around telling everyone I was nine. When I was sixteen, she told people I was twelve. I've lived my whole life never experiencing my true age. I wore ribbons in my hair until I was thirty-five years old! Mother said, "When you're young, people allow you to make mistakes. They forgive you."

LIZZIE. Well . . . we all did that, Margaret.

M-E. That's just what I'm talking about! If we hadn't spent so much time in awe of the natural rules of nature, we could have devoted more time to . . . to . . . putting gold trim on the overcoat!

LIZZIE. (*Suspicious.*) Putting . . . gold trim . . . on-the-overcoat, Margaret? (*Sighs.*) Oh, dear! What's the subject?

M-E. Lizzie, you make me so tired when I talk to you— putting gold trim on the overcoat instead of always having to worry about the underwear!

LIZZIE. Hmmmm . . .

M-E. As it is . . . it's just a plain old overcoat because I've been so preoccupied with the underwear.

LIZZIE. Hmmmm . . .

M-E. I should have been about certain things—automatically . . . with my left hand, so to speak . . . and saved my right hand for more ornate things. I mean, there's nothing wrong with being thirteen years old, for Christ's

sake! (*Shouting, as if to the world.*) WELL, I'M SIXTY-
SEVEN YEARS OLD, GODDAMIT!

LIZZIE. And you're more foolish now than you ever could
have been at thirteen! Good God, woman!

(*The* TWO MEN *are seen preparing the stage. They set up
a large artist's canvas and place a chaise lounge near Stage
Right.*)

M-E. (*Continuing to shout.*) I'm sixty-seven years old and
I'm tired of pretending I'm fifty! (*To* LIZZIE.) Just
because I'm not a predictable, withered, white-haired,
crippled . . .

LIZZIE. You dye your hair, Margaret.

M-E. My mother had coal-black hair until her last
day . . .

LIZZIE. You dye your hair, Margaret.

M-E. I have to tell you something right now, Lizzie. I've
bitten my tongue about it for years, but I think there's
no better time than now to help you explore some of
your shortcomings. I don't know of any polite way to
say it, so I'm just going to be blunt . . . you're a tired,
weak, snivelling, old . . . *Old* . . . 'fraidy cat! You
don't have the nerve to be anything else. You're scared!
You're scared because my hair is naturally black; you're
scared of my flamboyance and style . . . you've always
been scared of me . . . long before I won the beauty
contest. Now why do you hang around? . . . in the
expectation that someday I'll rub off on you!

LIZZIE. Okay, Margaret. I'm not going to argue with you.
I have to learn to stop arguing with you. I get a little
pain right here (*Points to her heart.*). I'd hate to be
arguing with you and suddenly drop over with foam
running out of my mouth. I'm not young enough to
spend this much energy arguing over something that
don't have any meaning—not now. And besides, you
didn't win the beauty contest because you were beautiful.

M-E. Of course not! I carry beauty around with me! Beauty
is in the eye of the beholder! I walk beautiful. I think
beautiful. Therefore people perceive me as beautiful.
You are as upset now as ever you were because people
still think I'm only fifty years old. Admit it. You can't
handle it.

LIZZIE. I'm not going to talk to you anymore. You've lost your senses.

M-E. Well, since we're here to have things turn out the way we want them to—you can be any age you want. Why don't you pass for forty-five. See if you can pull it off.

LIZZIE. I'm not going to talk to you anymore. (*Silence.*) If I speak to you again, it's because you happen to be all I have left to be interested in . . . so I might have to speak to you. (*Timidly.*) Margaret . . . now don't get upset. I'm not trying to spoil the trip . . . honest. I just want to . . .

M-E. Here we go! You're gonna be depressing. You're gonna ring the ole bell again, aren't you? Tell me something, Lizzie? When did you die? You must have died one day when I wasn't looking. I had no idea I would be traveling with a dead person.

LIZZIE. Margaret! I'm not talking about that! I'm thinking. I'm thinking . . . Have you ever thought . . . that a . . . rest home wouldn't be such a bad idea. (*Pause.*) At least we would have a lot in common with the other people there. You know, the same interests.

M-E. Same interests, hah! A bunch of people dying together! Before I die I'm going to demand an understanding of why I've been living!

LIZZIE. Ask me where I've living now.

M-E. (*Annoyed.*) I don't have to ask you, Lizzie. I could take one of about . . . three guesses!

LIZZIE. You're wrong, Margaret. I am now a full-time resident of the Memorial Society Rest Home. (*Silence.*) It's no sin to be living in a rest home, Margaret!

M-E. Did I say that?

LIZZIE. It's a very comfortable life. I eat—watch television—and, if I want to, I can even prepare my own meals.

M-E. That sounds nice.

LIZZIE. I don't have to stand here and defend myself to you, Margaret!

M-E. (*Gently.*) Of course not, Lizzie. You're a sweet girl. I'm sure it took a lot of nerve to commit yourself. Well, I'm going across the finish line—my way. Growing old . . . older . . . growing older is as natural as having a regular bowel movement. I'm tired of passing.

LIZZIE. (*Drily.*) I can assure you that you've made a wise decision because you would have found it progressively more difficult. (*Pause.*) The eye of the beholder! Look at yourself! (*Using her hand, she mimes a mirror and presses it in front of Margaret's face.*) Your eyes have grown dim, my dear. (*Pointing into the mirror.*) You see those little things. They're called lines. Some people call them wrinkles. Frankly, after you pass the age of sixty, who's going to quibble with you over a few years one way or the other.

M-E. (*Stares into the mirror, smiles, then laughs.*) That's what they did to me.

LIZZIE. What? Who?

M-E. Not who—*What!* My lines! The lines on my face. (*Speaking in the mirror to her lines.*) Such a shame! They had me spend half my life trying to get rid of these two lines. Think of it, Lizzie. All the pain and time and creams and massages, and *glue* we spent trying to erase these two big lines—and all they were there for was to help us have the proper space to laugh with. They just turned everything around. They just made a tragedy out of everything. Everyone wants to forget that we have to cross the finish line. Well, they're not going to rob me of that experience. I am going to finish with honesty.

LIZZIE. . . . the rest home. It's very nice.

M-E. That's terribly dishonest, Lizzie. I shall remain on the battlefield. I refuse to cloister myself away like a nun.

LIZZIE. (*Sighing.*) Let's get on with it.

M-E. Naturally. (*Suddenly looking off into the distance.*) Ooh, look! The sailboat! Can you see it? Ooh, it's so beautiful! It doesn't look real. It looks like a painting! (*Pause.*) Everything here looks like a painting.

(*The* TWO MEN *stand under the balcony and wave. They have completed setting the stage.*)

LIZZIE. That's the cue, Margaret. Get ready.

(MARGARET-ELIZABETH *rushes into the room through the glass doors.*)

(*Shouting to* M-E.) Why can't I tell this story?

M-E. (*Dressing as she sticks her head out of the door.*) Because you have the same solution for everything— TEARS! Don't you dare end up crying anymore, Lizzie.

LIZZIE. (*Pouting.*) You always get to play the best part.

M-E. (*Entering the balcony, laughing as she dresses.*) The best acting you ever did, Lizzie—you was crying. Do you remember that? It was Miss Rose's wedding. (*Acting.*) "I'm sorry I got to go and die on you now, Miss Rose. This s'posed to be the happiest day of your life. Now I got to go an' spoil yo' trip to the altar. I prayed to the Good Lord to just let me live one mo' day—I wanted to see my baby smilin' . . ."

LIZZIE. That's not it! You not doing it right. Here you go. (*Crying.*) "I'm sorry I got to go an' die on you now, Miss Rose. This s'posed to be the happiest day of your life. Now look what I done done. I had to go an' die on yo' weddin' day. I prayed to the Good Lord to just let me live long enough to see my baby smilin' as she marched to the altar. Oh, Miss Rose, forgive me."

M-E. Lordy, Chile! You can do that moaning and crying! I never could get that stuff straight.

LIZZIE. That's why you ain't made no more movies to this day.

M-E. It didn't exactly further your career either.

LIZZIE. I retired.

M-E. Retired! Retired! OoohAaahahaaa . . . Well, we ain't gon' end up crying this time, Lizzie. This time we're going to get it right.

LIZZIE. I want to tell it!

M-E. (*Exiting into the hotel room.*) You don't know what to do with a story. You never get to the end. Tears! That's why we have to keep doing it over.

LIZZIE. (*Loudly.*) You better hope that I don't die before we get to the end.

(WOMAN ONE *emerges dressed as a high-fashion model. She appears to be in her early twenties.* M-E *follows* WOMAN ONE *out onto the balcony dressed in identical garb.*)

M-E. (*Angrily entering.*) You'd like that, wouldn't you, Lizzie? That way we'd never have to finish the story. Well I don't want any dead people in my story.

LIZZIE. Naturally.

M-E. Naturally.

WOMAN ONE. Naturally.

(WOMAN TWO, *dressed in an artist's smock, approaches the easel, Downstage. She sets up her supplies and is trying to paint on the canvas that is facing Upstage. The* THREE WOMEN *on the balcony step out onto the Center ramp.*)

M-E. What strange pictures we've been given.

LIZZIE. Pictures that don't work.

WOMAN ONE. I wonder if they ever worked?

LIZZIE. They must have been real once—how else could anyone have ever thought of them?

M-E. Yes. Someone painted a pastoral scene once.

WOMAN ONE. It was painted by an artist who never saw the scene.

LIZZIE. He painted it from a description given to him by a traveler . . .

WOMAN ONE. . . . who had heard of it from a farmer . . .

LIZZIE. . . . who had it handed down to him as a legend by his great-great-great-grandfather . . .

WOMAN ONE. . . . who got it from the Bible . . .

M-E. . . . who got it from a vision . . .

LIZZIE. . . . that came from God . . .

M-E. . . . WHO was the only one who ever really saw it.

LIZZIE. And we keep running through the grass and flowers that the artist painted . . .

WOMAN ONE. . . . only to discover that it's really mud.

M-E. We ought to bring those pictures up to date.

END OF ACT TWO, SCENE 1

ACT TWO

SCENE 2

M-E *descends the ramp, Stage Left. The other* TWO WOMEN *line up behind her and follow her down the ramp. As they reach the bottom of the ramp, a doorbell chimes.* M-E *and* LIZZIE *disappear.* WOMAN ONE *crosses toward* WOMAN TWO (THE ARTIST.) *She speaks with the breathless affectation of a "glamour girl."*

WOMAN ONE. Hi. I'm answering your ad for an . . . artist's model?

(WOMAN TWO [THE ARTIST] *stands unanswering, staring at her.*)

(*Nervous.*) Your ad in the paper? (*Yanks out newspaper and hurriedly scrambles to page.*) Uh . . . (*Reads.*) "Wanted: Black female artist's model. Should be between the ages of twenty and fifty. Reasonable pay."
ARTIST. Oh yes! Oh! I'm . . . I'm surprised! You're not at all what I had in mind.
WOMAN ONE. (*Gushing.*) Well . . . I've done some modeling before . . . most of it was . . . back home. I used to model a lot for . . . the Smutterbugs? I mean, they weren't artists . . . well, I mean they *were* artists, but not . . . you know, uh . . . painters. They did . . . photography and I used to . . . uh, you ever hear of them?
ARTIST. Yes. Yes. Uh, NO! No. Listen, I . . . I-don't-know, you . . . uhm . . . let me look at you.

(WOMAN ONE *stands pivoting and turning like a model. She begins to strike classic poses.*)

ARTIST. My God, you're thin!

WOMAN ONE. (*Proudly.*) Yes. 34-24-35. One hundred and
fifteen pounds!

ARTIST. How did you let yourself get that thin? FLESH!
I need FLESH! You should never have allowed yourself to get like that. Well, look, I don't know how,
but I'm going to give it a try. (*Dramatically.*) When
an artist is overcome with this . . . *feeling*—this . . .
brilliance—any delay in the execution of it can be a
death blow. I'm anxious to start. Too anxious. Take
off your shoes.

WOMAN ONE. (*Squealing.*) Oooh! Oooh, no! Oh, God.
You're not going to believe this! I had no idea you
were going to ask me to go barefoot! I didn't polish
my toenails!

ARTIST. (*Studying her.*) Hmm . . . hmm . . . hmm, hmm,
hmm, *hmm*. (*Takes off her apron and hands it to*
WOMAN ONE.) Here. Tie this around you.

(WOMAN ONE *ties on apron.* ARTIST *stands back looking
at her.*)

Nope. Nope. That's not going to work. I thought I
could work it out with you . . . I . . . I don't
know . . .

WOMAN ONE. (*Anxious.*) What do you want me to do?
I'm rather flexible. I can pose any way you want. You
want to try something lying down. (*Strikes a reclining
pose on the sofa.*) How's this? I mean, it's whatever
you want.

ARTIST. What I want? What I want? I know exactly what
I want but *you*, through no fault of you own, do not
happen to be it! Now I'm trying, dear—I'm trying to
fit you in. What I want to do is to paint a composite
impression of The Female. More specifically, the Black
Female. I want to show the myriad spectrum of the
sum of her parts: The mysterious, erotic, exotic, the
Earth Mother (*Afterthought*), the Mother. Yes, and
even the negative parts: the whore, the slave, the
. . . the . . .

WOMAN ONE. . . . the woman?

ARTIST. Yes, the woman. The concept is brilliant. The
execution of it will be brilliant. But you—you, my
dear, are more than I had in mind—or is it less? You've

given me a problem. At the height of my creative surge, you've presented a problem. Why have you done this to me? *But*, I accept the challenge—and, hopefully, with my help, we will find our way there, no matter the obstacles. So! Cool your little toesies, while I think! I'm going to apologize because I know that I've lost my temper. I'm apologizing up front because I'm probably going to get worse. Please be patient enough to understand that it's not directed at you personally—even though I shall probably scream, shout, and cuss in your direction. You see, here I am at the pinnacle of freeing my creative energies to work on this inspiration and everyone knows it—and everyone wants to fuck over me! Well, you say, "Well I don't know you. I just came here in answer to your ad." Right! But *HE* knows me! AND he knows that I am at the beginning of this *moment*—so what does he do? Today of all days? He wants to fuck! Oh, God, he's such an asshole!

(Uncomfortable silence. Finally WOMAN ONE *decides to speak.)*

WOMAN ONE. Uh . . . who?

ARTIST. Sweetheart, it's not your problem . . . but, do you see what I'm talking about? As an artist, you learn to foretell the weather. It's either fair or foul. Now, in fair weather, the gods are with you. Why, you have but to smile, and their gifts come pouring down on you. They share their genius with you so freely that you begin to question whether or not you're the prime mover of this exciting moment. Well, when the weather is foul, and believe me, it can conspire against you in the most unbelievable manner—your impulse is to abandon the whole thing. Allow me to bore you, please! because I have to say this out loud! You came in on my problem. You added to my problem. So therefore you have to listen to my problem. Ohhh, I'm wasting all of this time and I need to be working . . . let me look at you . . . *(She stares at her for a while.)* You know what I see? Primary colors! That's it! While we were talking?—I suddenly got a microscopic view of you and I picked up—primary colors! I know it's right. I can feel it's right! *(She stares at her again, but this time she pinches her face into a tight scowl as she throws her head back.*) Oooh! Ooooh! I just got the whole thing! Red! RED! I was standing here, talking, and I blurred my vision. I do that sometimes. I deliberately squint my eyes and view everything through my eyelashes and it gives me this blurred vision—and I saw RED! Stay right where you are. Don't move!

(WOMAN TWO [THE ARTIST] *looks around distractedly as if looking for something she's not quite sure of.* M-E *enters carrying a long piece of red fabric with white polka dots on it. She hands it to* WOMAN TWO. *She exits.*)

This is getting exciting! (*Tosses* WOMAN ONE *the fabric.*) Here. Try this one.

(WOMAN ONE *casually drapes it across her shoulders.*)

Anyway, I keep telling this guy, "Look, so okay, I'm freaky. I'm an artist—what do you expect." I knew a guy once that could do it just by rubbing my shoulders. Uhmm . . . uhm! I mean, there's an art to the thing! So that's where we had our big blowout, you know. So, I'm thinking—I hate to see the thing end without having communicated properly. So I write him this letter . . . (*Observes* MARGARET-ELIZABETH) No, no, no, no! . . . the scarf goes on your head! (*Continuing.*) So I wrote him this letter and I . . .

(WOMAN ONE *has draped the fabric very elegantly across her hair.*)

(*Looking up at her.*) Noooo, sweetheart. No. No. Like this, honey. (*Takes the scarf and ties it, Aunt Jemima—style, around* WOMAN ONE'S *head.*) Yes! Yes. That's it. See, I'm going to concentrate on the *red*—framing your face. (*Studying her again.*) Umm hmm. (*Pause.*) Uh, unh. I need something else. Something's wrong. Some-thing's . . . wrong. Excuse me. Just ignore me. I'm blurring my vision again. (*Tosses her head back and squints her eyes, squeezing her face into a tight frown.*) Okay. Take off your makeup! You've got red tones in your makeup.

WOMAN ONE. Well . . . probably . . .

ARTIST. That's what is it—and your lipstick—too much.
  Wipe it off.
WOMAN ONE. Uh . . . my makeup?
ARTIST. EVERYTHING! I'm going to create . . . and I
  don't want any suggestions! I don't want to be sub-
  consciously influenced.

*(M-E enters with a jar of cold cream and tissues. She hands
them to* THE ARTIST *and gives* WOMAN ONE *a look of dis-
appointment.)*

M-E. *(Whispering to* WOMAN ONE.*)* When are you gonna
  change this?
WOMAN ONE. *(Annoyed. Whispering to* M-E.*)* Soon. Soon.
  Get out of here!

(M-E exits. WOMAN TWO [THE ARTIST] *smears cold cream
all over* WOMAN ONE's *face and begins to wipe it off.)*

ARTIST. So, this letter . . . this letter I wrote him . . . I
  wanted him to be able to see my bare-assed psyche—
  you know? Well, it's no little trick to open your psyche
  up to someone. So I asked myself, "What's happening
  to you *right now*! I mean, what's really going on at
  this very minute?" *(Finishing the removal of the
  makeup.)* There. Much better. Oh, dear, I just caught
  sight of something. I don't like it.
WOMAN ONE. The . . . the . . . scarf? The . . . ?
ARTIST. The dress. *(Laughs.)* You look like a fashion model.
  Uh. Uh. Uh. Hold it! Do I have a bag of tricks today!

*(M-E and LIZZIE enter carrying a bright calico blouse [yel-
low with large red flowers] and a large, many-colored, many-
tiered, calico skirt. They hand the blouse to* WOMAN ONE
and remain standing nearby holding the skirt.)

  Here you are. *(Passes blouse to* WOMAN ONE.*)* This
  is going to work. *(Watches as she puts it on.)* Perfect!
  Now! Now we're getting someplace. Oh, wait! You're
  not going to believe what I just thought of.
LIZZIE. *(With disgust.)* A banjo?

(WOMAN TWO motions, and M-E and LIZZIE hand her the skirt. They remain standing side by side holding onto a small box.)

ARTIST. Da, da, da, dum, de, dum! Here, dear. Slip this on under your apron. *(Watches her.)* Yikes! I *like* it! Ummuh! Oh. Oh. And some jewelry! Uh, uh . . . *(Looking around.)*

M-E. *(Gaily.)* Gold hoop earrings?

ARTIST. *(As if WOMAN ONE had spoken.)* Hey! You're feeling it too. I know I'm on the right track when we can pick up the same feeling. Oh, damn! Earrings! Earrings!

(M-E extends the small box to THE ARTIST. She rummages through it.)

Oooh, you bet your sweet life! Look-a-here! Took down the stupid drapes last week . . . *(Dramatically.)* I needed *Light!* to see by! . . . I am so brilliant today, I must have somebody working with me—Rembrandt, or Picasso, or . . . What'd I tell you! *(Holds up brass rings.)* Brass rings! Brass drapery rings! *(Rushes over to WOMAN ONE and snaps the oversized earrings on her. She stands back admiringly.)* Uh! Uh! *(Southern accent.)* DE-VINE! CHILD! YOU LOOK DE-VINE! *(Returns to easel, begins to work.)* When I was little, the first school I ever went to was an all-girls' Catholic school—and everything in there was black and white. Black and white. Can you imagine. *(Suddenly.)* Oh, crap!

WOMAN ONE. What happened?

ARTIST. I just squinted at you again.

WOMAN ONE. What?

ARTIST. I just blurred my vision. You got some red tones in your skin. It wasn't your makeup. There's some red mixed in your skin color. How did that happen?

M-E. Turkish!

LIZZIE. Polynesian!

M-E. Brazilian!

LIZZIE. American Indian!

WOMAN ONE. A little Irish . . . I think there's a little Irish on my father's side.

ARTIST. Don't worry. Ginger-to-the-rescue. *(Dips her fin-*

gers into her color palate.) By the way, I didn't get your name. I'm Ginger. (*Approaches her*.) You too?

WOMAN ONE. Me too what?

ARTIST. Your name Ginger too?

WOMAN ONE. Elizabeth.

ARTIST. Yes?

WOMAN ONE. That's my name—Elizabeth. Margaret-Elizabeth.

ARTIST. Oh, like . . . (*Regally*.) Elizabeth-the-queen! (*She begins to smear black paint onto* WOMAN ONE'S *face*.)

WOMAN ONE. How did you know! That's it exactly! I'm Elizabeth. My sister was Victoria and my brother was James. Mother was very big on King James because of the Bible, but Daddy said the King James Version was a pile of rubbish because ole King James made up that version to suit his own perversions—which, of course, made Daddy have a little aversion to brother James . . .

ARTIST. (*Finishing* WOMAN ONE'S *face*.) Liza, honey! The gods are with us today! You look great! (*Admiring her handiwork*.) Uhm! Uhm! C'est si bon! We're on our way. Now what I want you to do is . . . just your eyes . . . not the rest of your body . . . look up.

(WOMAN ONE *rolls her eyes up*. M-E *and* LIZZIE *hide their faces in shame*.)

Got it! Don't move! (*Resumes painting at canvas*.) Now, as I was saying . . . uh, what was I telling you about?

WOMAN ONE. Black and white.

ARTIST. What?

WOMAN ONE. The black-and-white colors at the girls' Catholic school.

ARTIST. No, no, before that. Ooh, about this guy—anyway, I wrote him this letter, and I asked myself, "Now what am I doing at this very moment." Well, for one thing, I was ovulating. And I thought, "Well, what does that have to do with anything?" Now you have to understand, I wanted to be very honest with myself. I'm one of those few women who can really tell when I'm ovulating—and it does all kinds of hairy things to me. So, in all honesty, I had to admit that ovulating had *everything* to do with what I was into at that very moment. I was freakin' hungry for the man! So, I did what every honest, healthy girl oughta do . . . I smeared ovulation juice all over the letter I sent to him—and POW! he came running to me like a mad dog! Listen, I have a lot of philosophies, but my through-line philosophy is that you shouldn't have any hang-ups in this world. I mean, it's like you gotta be fuckin' crazy! (*Suddenly.*) Goddamnit!

WOMAN ONE. What's the matter?

ARTIST. It's not working.

WOMAN ONE. What's not working?

ARTIST. The whole thing—it's not working. No, no, it's not you. The concept is off. There's something wrong with the concept. You look too *pretty*. It's not your fault. (*Changing her voice for humorous effect.*) Goddamnit, girl, you're just too pretty! You see, what I had in mind was . . . Ohhh! Ooohhh!

(M-E *and* LIZZIE *exit.*)

WOMAN ONE. What'd you do?—blur your vision again?

ARTIST. Yes! Take off those clothes!

WOMAN ONE. Everything?

ARTIST. Yes. I just became a genius. I know exactly what I want.

(*She motions excitedly as* M-E *and* LIZZIE *enter carrying a number of articles of clothing.* THE ARTIST *examines them, tossing some away and excitedly exclaiming over others.* M-E *exits.* WOMAN ONE, *still dressed in her "Aunt Jemima" outfit, wanders Upstage to look at the painting.* LIZZIE *angrily follows her Upstage and, using her hand as a mirror, whirls* WOMAN ONE *around to stare at her reflection.*)

WOMAN ONE. (*Seeing her reflection.*) Eeek! Ginger! You black crow!

WOMAN TWO. (*No longer* THE ARTIST.) What the hell's wrong with you?

WOMAN ONE. (*Storming over to* WOMAN TWO.) Is that what you've done to me? Look at my face! Is that what you put on my . . . (*Rubs her hands across her face.*) Uunnggh! (*In great fury she pushes* WOMAN TWO.) You stop it! Stop it right now! This is *my* story! (*She begins to cry loudly.*)

WOMAN TWO. I'm *doing* your story! This is the way it happened! What do you want me to do? . . . change history to suit you . . . and King James!

M-E. If you're not going to do *my* story *my* way—then I might as well pack up and gome home!

WOMAN TWO. Jesus! Get the stuff straight!

M-E. Look at this mess!

LIZZIE. Black Devil!

WOMAN TWO. Black Gold!

LIZZIE. Black Sambo!

WOMAN TWO. Black Jewel!

LIZZIE. Black Sheep!

WOMAN TWO. Black Rose!

LIZZIE. Snow White and Rose Red! . . . and Black Tar Baby . . . and Black Dog!

M-E. Black Beauty!

LIZZIE. (*Erupting into laughter.*) A horse! A horse! (*Changing suddenly into tears.*) A horse! A horse!

(M-E *and* WOMAN TWO *go over to comfort* LIZZIE.)

M-E. Lizzie, calm down!

WOMAN TWO. Calm down, honey.

M-E. You want to change the ending? Well, we have to do it the way it happened in order to get to a new ending. Now would you just calm down?

WOMAN TWO. (*To* WOMAN ONE.) Put on the new clothes . . .

M-E. I promise you . . . the unexpected—a new ending! Trust me.

(LIZZIE *calms with resistance.* M-E *and* WOMAN TWO *begin to put the clothes on* LIZZIE. *They have an entire suit of men's clothing including shirt, suit jacket, pants, shoes, necktie, wig, and hat.* LIZZIE *is still challenging* M-E *as they help her dress.* WOMAN ONE, *dressed as "Aunt Jemima" stands by, arms folded in disgust and distrust—watching.*)

LIZZIE. (*To* M-E.) You always want to play the best parts.

WOMAN TWO. Listen, now . . . tell the truth . . . I haven't changed anything, *really*? Right?

LIZZIE. You certainly weren't supposed to blacken my face.

M-E. It was the same thing! Just be patient, I'm getting to
   the point.
LIZZIE. I know you're gonna have me end up foolish.
M-E. What could be more foolish than crying? Every time
   we do this story, you end it by crying—and you're
   never satisfied. We're not going to do it that way
   anymore. We're gonna make it end right. Trust me.
   You're gonna be the hero . . .
WOMAN ONE. Heroine.
M-E. I mean, heroine.
LIZZIE. Huhmmm . . .

(LIZZIE *has now changed into the entire suit of men's clothes,
with the exception of the short male wig.*)

WOMAN TWO. (*Playing the* ARTIST *again; lifting the male
   wig high in the air in grandiose style.*) And now, my
   friend, I do crown you . . . Elizabeth-the-queen!

(LIZZIE *and* WOMAN ONE *eye* M-E *suspiciously.*)

M-E. Trust me.
ARTIST. (*She motions for* LIZZIE *and* WOMAN ONE *to strike
   a pose as she returns to the canvas to paint.*) It won't
   be long now, my dear.

(*Lights dim. All* FOUR WOMEN *merge into a Buddha-like
oneness, a three-dimensional form, with arms, legs, and
torsos overlapping. It could be as simple as a "stadium
effect" with* M-E *in the forefront,* LIZZIE *standing* [sitting]
behind her, WOMAN ONE *standing* [sitting] *behind her,*
WOMAN TWO *etc.—all overlapping body parts. It could be
as abstract as an acrobatic stance, with arms, legs, and torsos
askew in varying shapes. As the lights come back up,* WOMAN
TWO [playing the ARTIST again] *is seen arranging, touching,
putting finishing touches on the* THREE WOMEN.)

ARTIST. Well, Queenie—how do you feel being party to
   a historic moment?

(M-E *extracts herself from the other* TWO WOMEN *and casually saunters around the remaining form. She studiously
evaluates herself and the other* TWO WOMEN, *who remain
locked in oneness throughout* M-E's *evaluation.* WOMAN

ONE *is staring cruelly at* M-E. LIZZIE *stares at* M-E *nearly in tears.*)

M-E. (*Finally. Smiling triumphantly at* WOMAN ONE *and* LIZZIE. *She begins to swagger.*) Personally, I don't think it's very original. I mean, it's been done before.

ARTIST. You're only a model, my dear. Your vision is not to be trusted.

M-E. (*Still assessing the form, sometimes reentering the form to make a point.*) It is apparent to me that you should have spent more time studying your subject in order to render it more believable. For instance, you should have employed more care in the depiction of your subject's legs and hips. The legs and hips are crucial in determining the self-image that your subject projects. Where's the rhythm and vitality and color intensity? Where's the elegance and intelligence of your subject? My main concern centers around your lack of the use of a more subtle brushwork on the face. You see, the color *black* has within itself many colors. It is a very complex color and at the same time simple and delicate. It can be made to appear formidable and mysterious, as in a dark, unlit cave, or can appear as bright and inviting as the twinkling eyes of a child. Since black is your foreground color, you should have used the full range of its potential in its color spectrum. Your primitive application of the primary colors shows a refusal or inability to employ enlightened artistic techniques—also known as intuition. In essence, you have failed to capture your subject's *BEAUTY*!

(WOMAN ONE *and* LIZZIE *smile in victorious aniticipation.*)

    (*Delighted at her own success.*) Heeey, *Now!*

LIZZIE. (*Rallying.*) Bring it on down front, Margaret!

WOMAN ONE. Talk, Margaret! Talk!

LIZZIE. Go 'head, Margaret!

WOMAN ONE. Finish this mess, girl!

(WOMAN TWO, *jolted out of* ARTIST *role, reacts with stunned silence, folding her arms in contemptuous, stubborn anger.*)

WOMAN TWO. If you want to tell the entire story by yourself, go ahead.

(There is a long silence as M-E *stands trying to bluff her way through her confusion.)*

LIZZIE. Well?
WOMAN ONE. Well?
M-E. *(Floundering.)* . . . well, now . . . uh, don't move, don't move . . . I'm getting there . . .
LIZZIE. Finish it, Margaret. Finish it.
M-E. Yes . . . uh . . . you have failed to . . . to . . . uh . . . capture . . .
WOMAN ONE. Margaret? What's the matter?
M-E. Nothing. Nothing. Just . . . hold on. Don't be so impatient.
LIZZIE. Fifty years is a long time to be patient. *(Pause.)* Margaret . . . ?
M-E. Yes?
LIZZIE. You don't have an ending, do you?
M-E. Of course I do. I'm just . . .
WOMAN ONE. This is the same ending, Margaret.
M-E. Will you shut up! I'm . . . I'm working on it . . .

(A buzzer sounds and MAN ONE *and* TWO *rush onstage.)*

MAN ONE AND TWO. Time! Time!

(The TWO MEN *busily begin to remove everything from Center Stage.* LIZZIE *and* WOMAN ONE, *in the throes of the gloomy reality, begin to extract themselves from their "one-ness."* WOMAN ONE *sadly begins to remove parts of her garment. They dejectedly begin to pack up.* WOMAN TWO *stands impatiently waiting to see if they are going to resume the action.)*

WOMAN ONE. This is the same ending, Margaret. *(She begins to walk slowly toward the ramp.)*
LIZZIE. This is the last time, Margaret. We're not going to do it again. *(Looking down at her clothes.)* LOOK AT ME! You did it again! *(Beginning to cry.)* You turned me into a flop! A pure-dee horse's hiney, FLOP! *(She bursts into a loud wailing as she runs up the ramp.)*
WOMAN TWO. *(Angrily removing her artist's smock and tossing it to the floor in disgust.)* That's it! That's the last time! *(She removes some of her supplies and stalks off Stage Right.)*

LIZZIE. (*Like an angry child as she runs up the ramp.*) You *said* you were going to make me the *hero*! You did it! (*Screaming from the top of the ramp.*) You did it— you black dog!

(M-E *rushes up the ramp after the* TWO WOMEN, *trying to console them.*)

M-E. (*Mounting the ramp.*) You didn't give me a chance!

WOMAN ONE. Give you a chance! You had every chance in the world!

M-E. There was one more thing!

WOMAN ONE. What?

LIZZIE. What?

M-E. (*In petulant anger to mask her uncertainty.*) You didn't give me a chance!

LIZZIE. What?

WOMAN ONE. What could it have possibly have been, for God's sake!

LIZZIE. Nothing! She didn't have a thing! She's lying! Ooh, I know you, Margaret! Pretending all the time!

M-E. I did too!

WOMAN ONE. What?

M-E. You'll never know. I'm not going to tell you. You'll never know! That's the ending you picked, that's the one you'll live with.

LIZZIE. (*Giving in.*) Okay, Margaret. What were we supposed to do?

M-E. Say! What were you supposed to say!

WOMAN ONE. Okay, Margaret. I hate to indulge you with this . . . but what were we supposed to say?

M-E. Fuck you! Those were going to be my last words . . . Fuck you!

WOMAN ONE. And then . . . ?

LIZZIE. And then . . . ?

M-E. (*Caught.*) "Only if you're ovulating." Then you were supposed to say, "Only if you're ovulating." (*She stands back suspiciously eyeing her effect.*)

(*There is a long silence as* WOMAN ONE *and* LIZZIE *stare in questioning disbelief.*)

WOMAN ONE. (*Shaking her head in disgust.*) Have you ever
    considered, Margaret . . . that you might be in the
    last stages of senility?
LIZZIE. (*Quietly, fighting back tears, holding onto* M-E *as
    if she were a child.*) Just say you didn't have an ending,
    Margaret. It's okay. Let's stop fighting now. Come on
    to the rest home. It's not bad . . . really.

END OF ACT TWO, SCENE 2

ACT TWO

SCENE 3

LIZZIE, *still dressed as a man, is leaning over the hotel balcony.* MARGARET-ELIZABETH, *dressed as the beauty queen with the exaggerated bosom, begins a slow, uncertain, soft-shoe tap routine.*

LOUDSPEAKER. "From Avery's Gift Shop—a fountain pen with the winner's name engraved in gold!"

(She struggles with the dancing until it improves. Downstage Right is a door frame that leads to a small room. The room contains a large chest of drawers with a huge mirror. The chest of drawers, with the exception of the mirror, has a long, wide strip of white fabric draped around it.)

LIZZIE (MR. CASTLE). *(Calling to* M-E.) Jeta! Little Miss Jeta! Learn to tap dance! Smile! And don't lose your southern accent. See you next year! *(Lights fade to dim on* LIZZIE.)

*(*M-E *begins to sing softly.)*

M-E. *(Singing and dancing.)*
Jet-a,
Jet-a,
Jet-a, Jeta, Jing, Jing, Jing.

(She continues singing and dancing until she is rather confidently and loudly performing.)

LIZZIE. *(Sighs.)* All I want to do is pick a new queen, go back home to my little room, eat, watch television . . .

(M-E *has entered the small room and is staring in the mirror atop the chest as she performs.*)

LOUDSPEAKER. "And now, ladies and gentlemen! Our five
     finalists!

(*The sound of festive music.* WOMAN ONE *and* TWO *enter dressed in identical men's suits.*)

LIZZIE. (*Excited.*) Margaret! They're starting! Hurry up!
     (*Calling.*) Margaret! We have to choose the new queen!

(*The* THREE WOMEN [JUDGES] *put on top hats and stand Downstage, looking up at the ramp, throughout the contest.*)

LOUDSPEAKER. Contestant Number One!

(MAN ONE, *dressed in black, slowly and regally ascends the ramp from Stage Right. He is wearing high-heeled shoes and carrying a large, oversized painted poster. The poster is the kind used in carnivals, fairs, or amusement parks, with a cutout opening for the head and arms.* MARGARET-ELIZABETH *is still staring in the mirror. When* MAN ONE *reaches the Center of the ramp, he faces the audience and pokes his head and arms through the cutout. Smiling, he poses and assumes the character of the cutout. The cutout is an exaggeration of Gidget.*)

LIZZIE. Margaret! It's Gidget!
WOMAN TWO. Gidget?
WOMAN ONE. Gidget's in it?
WOMAN TWO. 96! I'm giving her 96 points! I want her to
     win, don't you?
WOMAN ONE, TWO, AND LIZZIE. (*As if bidding at an auction.*) 96!

(MARGARET-ELIZABETH *snaps open the top of her bathing suit. The stuffing flies, flips, and bounces all over the floor. The stuffing consists of wads of toilet tissue, foam rubber, hankies, and stockings.* MAN ONE *exits to loud applause.*)

LOUDSPEAKER. CONTESTANT NUMBER TWO!

(MAN TWO *enters Stage Right. He is dressed the same as* MAN ONE *and carries a large poster cutout. When he reaches the Center of the ramp, he poses and assumes the character of his poster. The cutout is an exaggeration of Tammy.*)

LIZZIE. Margaret! It's Tammy!
WOMAN TWO. Do you believe that? Tammy's in it!
WOMAN ONE. Tammy?
WOMAN TWO. This is going to be a hard one.
WOMAN ONE. Okay. 97! There! I gave her a 97.
LIZZIE. What did you give her, Margaret?
WOMAN ONE, TWO, AND LIZZIE. 97!

(MARGARET-ELIZABETH *goes to the Upstage end of the white cloth that drapes the chest of drawers and wraps it around her bosom. She pirouettes Downstage, letting the cloth completely engulf her breasts. She then tucks the ends of the cloth neatly in place. She opens a drawer in the chest and removes a pair of shoulder pads like the ones used by football players. She straps them on. She begins to remove her makeup.*)

LOUDSPEAKER. CONTESTANT NUMBER THREE!

(MAN ONE *returns carrying a large poster cutout. He reaches the center of the ramp and poses as he assumes the character of his poster. The cutout is a bosomy exaggeration of Brigitte Bardot. He continues to pose and strut across the center of the ramp.*)

WOMAN ONE, TWO, AND LIZZIE. (*Squealing.*) Bridget!

(*The* THREE WOMEN [JUDGES] *nearly swoon like the teenage fans of a rock idol.*)

WOMAN ONE. EEEeekk!
WOMAN TWO. Yee-OWWw!
LIZZIE. Oooh! OH! OH! OH! Oh, Margaret! What are we gonna do! It's Bridget! 98! I'm giving her 98!
WOMAN ONE, TWO, AND LIZZIE. 98!

(MARGARET-ELIZABETH *opens up another drawer and puts on a man's shirt front with tie attached. She removes a pair of men's jockey shorts and puts them on over her bathing suit.)*

LIZZIE. (*Calling.*) Margaret! (*Throwing her arms up in victorious excitement.*) We finally got a contest with CLASS!

(MARGARET-ELIZABETH *begins to pick up the stuffing from the floor and pack it into the center of her jockey shorts. There should be a pocket sewn on the inside to allow her to stuff everything into it. The music continues.*)

LOUDSPEAKER. CONTESTANT NUMBER FOUR!

(MAN TWO *ascends the ramp with his poster and assumes his character. The poster is an exaggeration of Barbie.*)

WOMAN TWO. Barbie!
LIZZIE. Barbie!
WOMAN ONE. Barbie! (*To others.*) What d'ya say? I say 99!
WOMAN TWO. 99!
LIZZIE. 99!
WOMAN ONE, TWO, AND LIZZIE. 99!

(MARGARET-ELIZABETH *opens up another drawer and removes a man's suit. She puts it on. She now looks like the other women.* MAN TWO *exits.*)

WOMAN TWO. They're all winners!
WOMAN ONE. I'm going crazy! It's not fair.
LIZZIE. We've got to stop calling it a contest—it's a pageant. A pageant.

(MARGARET-ELIZABETH *now removes a short-cropped man's wig and puts it on. As her final gesture, she picks up a top hat, places it on her head, comes through the door frame, and joins the* WOMEN.)

   (*To* M-E.) Who did you vote for? It took you long enough! Did you see them? Who did you vote for?
M-E. Okay, let's go. We're gonna do the finale.
LIZZIE. Not now! The last contestant is about to appear.
M-E. Now.

WOMAN ONE, TWO, AND LIZZIE. Margaret!
M-E. Now.
WOMAN ONE AND TWO. Now?
M-E. Only the crazy things survive.

(The WOMEN *stand in sullen disbelief as* M-E *begins a slow, rhythmic, shuffling tap dance. They are about to do the stand-up comedy routines that were popular in the early minstrel shows. After* M-E *establishes a beat, she begins to sing the opening strains of "Swanee River.")*

    (Dancing.) "Way down upon the Swanee River . . ."

(The WOMEN *stand stiff and resisting.)*

    C'mon. You gotta get down on your knees, dearie.
WOMAN ONE. This is incredible.
LIZZIE. Who's gonna crown the queen?
M-E. We are. All in due time, Lizzie. Let's go.

*(*WOMAN ONE *and* TWO *reluctantly get on their knees.* LIZZIE *continues to stand.)*

    (Singing and dancing.) "Way down upon the . . ."
    (Commanding.) C'mon, Lizzie. Get down on your knees!

*(*LIZZIE *gets on her knees, and the* THREE WOMEN *pick up the rhythm in a swaying motion.* MINISCENE: M-E *becomes* BUBBA, *a stand-up comic, and* LIZZIE *becomes* POO-KEY, *her straight man, in a comic minstrel routine.)*

M-E (BUBBA). *(Now the complete minstrel man.)* Hey, Poo-key! What 'cha doin' on yer knees? You cain't dance on yer knees.
LIZZIE (POO-KEY). Oh, yeah I can. In fact, this what they paid me to do.
M-E (BUBBA). Is that a fact?
LIZZIE (POO-KEY). That's a fact. *(Pause.)* But I ain't jes' dancing on my knees.
M-E (BUBBA). No?
LIZZIE (POO-KEY). No. I'm dancin' on a dime.
M-E (BUBBA). A dime? A dime, you say?

LIZZIE (POO-KEY). That's right. A dime. That's all they payin' me fo' this show.

M-E (BUBBA). No kiddin'? What kinda money is that?

WOMAN ONE, TWO, AND LIZZIE. SHORTCHANGE!

ALL. Aaahhahaaa!

(The THREE WOMEN *stand. Everyone continues dancing and singing.)*

> "Way down upon the Swanee River,
> Far, far away . . ."

LIZZIE (POO-KEY). Hey, Bubba! You know, I just looked at you—and, you ugly!

M-E (BUBBA). Ugly? Ugly, you say!

LIZZIE (POO-KEY). Ugly, man, ugly! You got a monopoly on UGLY!

M-E (BUBBA). How you fix yo' mouth to say that, man?

LIZZIE (POO-KEY). My eyes said it first and then my mouth jes' followed!

ALL. Aaahhahaaa!

WOMAN ONE AND TWO. *(Chanting.)*
> Aww, kick it!
> Aww, kick it!
> Aww, get down wid' it!

ALL. *(Singing and dancing.)* "Way down upon the Swanee River . . ."

M-E (BUBBA). Hey, Poo-key! Only a ugly can recognize another ugly.

LIZZIE (POO-KEY). Well, you got plenty of ugly around you, man. Yo' wife ugly . . .

M-E (BUBBA). Yeah, my wife sho' is ugly.

WOMAN TWO. Her feets is bigger dan yo' banjo.

M-E (BUBBA). Yeah, she gots mighty big feets.

WOMAN ONE. Her head is bigger dan Caldonia's.

M-E (BUBBA). Yeah, she got a mighty big head.

LIZZIE (POO-KEY). Her hair so tight that even water cain't get through it.

M-E (BUBBA). Aw, yeah. She got some nappy hair!

WOMAN ONE AND TWO. An' her lips!

LIZZIE (POO-KEY). Her lips so big she have trouble breathin'.

M-E (BUBBA). Now that's a fact!

LIZZIE (POO-KEY). So you see—you surrounded by ugly.

M-E (BUBBA). Yeah, but, my wife is yo' sister!

WOMAN ONE, TWO, AND LIZZIE. Oh, Sweet Georgia Brown!

ALL. (*Singing and dancing.*) "Way down upon the Swanee River . . ."

WOMAN TWO. Hey, Bubba! How come you didn't tell nobody you had a condition?

M-E (BUBBA). Condition? What condition?

WOMAN ONE, TWO, AND LIZZIE. A LIVING CONDITION!

ALL. (*Singing.*)
Caldonia!
Caldonia!
What makes yo' big head so hard! BOOM!
(*Singing.*) "Way down upon the Swanee River . . ."

M-E (BUBBA). Hey, Poo-Key! You know something, man? You one *dark* Negro! You blacker dan coal.

WOMAN ONE AND TWO. Dan coal?

LIZZIE (POO-KEY). Watch yo'self now, Bubba—'cause me an' you the same color—an' you blacker dan de dead of night!

WOMAN ONE AND TWO. De dead of night?

M-E (BUBBA). Aw, naw! We ain't the same color 'cause you blacker dan Tar Baby.

WOMAN ONE AND TWO. Tar Baby!

LIZZIE (POO-KEY). You blacker dan chimney smoke!

WOMAN ONE AND TWO. Chimney smoke!

M-E (BUBBA). You blacker dan a patent leather shoe!

WOMAN ONE AND TWO. A patent leather shoe!

LIZZIE (POO-KEY). Aww, now you tryin' to hurt me—but, I'll tell you one thing—you blacker dan de devil!

WOMAN ONE AND TWO. (*Mock horror.*) DE DEVIL!

M-E (BUBBA). Man, you so black, it's hard to tell that you exist.

LIZZIE (POO-KEY). I sho' am glad ole Thomas Edison threw some light on you, man, 'cause you damn-near invisible yo'self.

M-E (BUBBA). Well, I want you to know—that even if the lights go out—it's one somebody always know I exist.

LIZZIE (POO-KEY). Who dat?

WOMAN ONE AND TWO. WH-OOOooo DAT!

LIZZIE (POO-KEY). Who dat what say "who dat" when I say "who dat"?

M-E (BUBBA). Dat God! God knows he put me here.

LIZZIE (POO-KEY). Say who?

M-E (BUBBA). I tell you what. I'ma prove dat I'm here. You see dis here mirror here?

(All the WOMEN *hold the palms of their hands toward their faces in mime gesture.)*

Dere me! (*Primps.*) Now tell me what you see.

(No longer the minstrel men, M-E *and* LIZZIE *revert back to character.)*

LIZZIE. Black Topsy.
M-E. Black Beulah.
LIZZIE. Black Mama.
M-E Black Whore.
BOTH. Black Man!

(All the WOMEN *resume the minstrel men character.)*

ALL. (*Singing and dancing.*)
     Way down upon the Swanee River,
     Far, far away . . .
LOUDSPEAKER. CONTESTANT NUMBER FIVE!

*(*WOMAN ONE, TWO, *and* LIZZIE *exit.* M-E *moves to the Stage Left entrance of the ramp. The lights fade on Downstage Center.* M-E *ascends the ramp smiling and with great poise. When she reaches the Center of the ramp, she begins to pose in all the masculine poses used in the Mr. America Contest. She takes her time and assumes each pose carefully and defiantly. She assumes all the classic poses and delights in hyping the audience with her show of form.)*

LOUDSPEAKER. Ladies and gentlemen! The moment we've all been waiting for! THE NEW MISS INTERNATIONAL SEPIA!

(The music blares up. The TWO MEN *rush onstage and place the "Miss International Sepia" banner on* M-E. *They place a bouquet of plastic roses in her arms and a string of tiny Christmas tree lights around her top hat. The lights flash on and off as she poses, waves, smiles, blows kisses, and struts across the ramp.)*

LOUDSPEAKER. And may we take this time to introduce the first runner-up to the Queen—Miss America!

(LIZZIE *enters Stage Right. She walks unenthusiastically across the ramp and stands beside* M-E. *She is carrying a large poster cutout. The poster is a composite image. On one half of the head, we see the red and white bandanna. On the other half of the head is a man's hat. A gold hoop earring hangs from one ear. The chest is a large, fat, busty affair, with the yellow-and-red flowered calico blouse on. One arm contains many gaudy bracelets, and the other is the sleeve of a man's suit. One leg is covered by a short miniskirted, figure-hugging, satin skirt and a shapely leg fitted into a stiletto-heeled, ankle-strapped shoe. The other leg is covered by the many-tiered, calico skirt and ends with a pair of men's pants sticking out from under the skirt and a man's shoe.* LIZZIE *sticks her head and arms through the cutouts, but she shows no excitement for the moment.*)

LOUDSPEAKER. And now! The prizes! "From Mom's Eatery—One Homemade Apple Pie!"

M-E. (*To* LIZZIE, *as she continues to wave and smile to the audience.*) Lizzie! Smile! We did it! Aren't you happy?

LIZZIE. (*Horrified.*) Look at you!

M-E. (*Marveling.*) Look at you!

LIZZIE. *Look* at me!

M-E Yes? WE WON! My darling Lizzie! WE WON!

LOUDSPEAKER. "From Avery's Five and Dime—A Brass Ring!"

LIZZIE. You always get to play the best part!

(*The lights fade with* MARGARET-ELIZABETH *flowing down the ramp, smiling, waving, and tossing flowers into the audience Downstage.*)

END

P. J. Gibson

BROWN SILK AND MAGENTA SUNSETS

During the turbulent 1960s, P. J. Gibson began to write seriously. But not until she saw a production of *To Be Young, Gifted and Black*, a drama based on the life of Lorraine Hansberry, did she turn to playwriting: "My friends and I sat in the audience after the show was over and cried." Then she went home to write a series of monologues, *The Black Woman*, which told the story of black women from slavery to 1969.

Gibson had heard the anguish of black men in the 1960s, whose literary voices had been relegated to bars and barbershops for too many years. But those voices, as important as they were, represented only one aspect of the reality of black life, according to this playwright. Remembering the advice of her early mentor, J. P. Miller (*Days of Wine and Roses*), to "write what you know," Gibson set out to bring to the stage the great variety of black women that she had observed during the years when she lived in Pennsylvania, New Jersey, and Washington, D.C. As she watched and listened to these women, she noticed the differences in what they said when the men were around and when they were not. She found these women fascinating, especially those who had lived a dual life-style: they had grown up poor, then through education, marriage, or some trick of fate or fortune had slipped into the middle class.[1]

Brown Silk and Magenta Sunsets is one of her newest works and among her boldest in its exploration of passionate and obsessive love. Lena Larsen Salvinoni is one of thousands of teenagers whose life was permanently changed by an affair with an older man and early motherhood. But in Gibson's hands, Lena becomes a fascinating woman. Seduced by the sensuousness of Roland's music, the adolescent Lena in turn seduces the man (who is sev-

eral years her senior) and spends the rest of her life trying
to relive the ecstasy of that ideal union. Now the reclusive
widow of a wealthy Italian, Lena is a voluntary prisoner
in her posh apartment, desperately pursuing affairs with
young men in order to recover the magic of her legendary
Roland. She lives in an alcoholic haze with bittersweet
memories ever-present in the three portraits of intimates
whom her obsessive love destroyed. Her psyche is turned
inside out as the portraits come to life and propel her back
and forth from present to past. Gibson makes little attempt
to explain Lena (a *tour de force* for any actress), nor to
counter stereotypes of the "loose woman," but rather presents her, resplendent in all her human contradictions.

"If I live to be 150, I still won't have enough time to
write about all the black women inside of me," says Gibson.[2] A prolific writer, she has completed twenty-three
plays, fifteen of which have been produced in various parts
of the United States, Europe, and Africa. *Long Time Since
Yesterday*, in which a group of college women have a re-
union after the suicide of one of their circle, was presented
by the New Federal Theatre in New York City in two
separate runs (January and October 1985) and won five
AUDELCO Awards, among them, Best Dramatic Production and 1985 Playwright of the Year. *Void Passage,
Konvergence*, and *My Mark, My Name* (a historical work)
were commissioned by the Rites and Reason Theatre of
Brown University; *The Unveiling of Abigail* was performed
at the 1981 Arts Festival in Torino, Italy. Among her writing awards are a Shubert Fellowship to study dramatic
writing at Brandeis University, where she received an
M.F.A. in theatre arts, and a National Endowment for the
Arts grant for playwriting.

NOTES

1. Unpublished interview of P. J. Gibson by Margaret B. Wilkerson, Berkeley: September, 1985.
2. *Ibid.*

Brown Silk
and
Magenta Sunsets

by
P. J. Gibson

Brown Silk and Magenta Sunsets was first presented as a staged reading by the Julian Theatre (San Francisco) in September, 1985. It is scheduled for production by the Women in Theatre Festival in Spring, 1987, Boston, Massachusetts.

CHARACTERS

LENA LARSEN SALVINONI	Attractive woman of forty-seven. She has a strong liking for cheap Scotch. She is the mother of FENDI and the past lover of ROLAND.
LENA LARSEN SALVINONI	(Younger LENA.) The eleven-, sixteen- and seventeen-year-old LENA of flashbacks.
VEEDA RICHARDS WATTS	Attractive woman of thirty-two. Past friend and mentor of LENA. Widow of ROLAND.
ROLAND WATTS	Handsome man of thirty-five. A jazz saxophonist. Past lover of LENA. Once married to VEEDA. Father of FENDI.
FENDI LARSEN WATTS SALVINONI	Attractive but shy woman of twenty-three. She is the natural daughter of LENA and ROLAND.
ABLE McKITCHEN	Handsome young man of nineteen. A delivery man, artist.

ACT ONE

SCENE 1

Interior of LENA LARSEN SALVINONI's *penthouse apartment. It is a wide, tall, spacious apartment decorated in fine acquisitions from the Orient and Africa.*

Three large paintings and one full window dominate the stage. The paintings are of individuals in LENA's *life. The paintings are life-sized, and the subjects of the paintings will be those of actors, frozen in time until brought to life in the mind and world of* LENA. *Each painting has a specific setting, atmosphere and mood. Arranged from Stage Right to Left the paintings are as follows:*

FENDI LARSEN WATTS SALVINONI, *attractive woman of twenty-three. She is seated in a deep dark gray comfort chair. She wears a bright red, strapless party dress. It has a full skirt, which is artistically draped over the edge of the chair.* FENDI *holds a single-stem blue rose in her hand.*

ROLAND WATTS, *handsome man of thirty-five, seated on fire escape with a saxophone resting between his thighs. He wears a sky blue short-sleeve shirt unbuttoned down to his waist and faded blue jeans. A magenta light, from the western sky's sunset, falls on his body.*

VEEDA RICHARDS WATTS, *attractive woman of thirty-two, sits at night club table with a cup of tea and teapot at her fingertips. A microphone and long cord rest on the table. She wears a yellow tank top, which she has cut wide across the neck. This allows the top to hang loose and low just above her braless breasts. She wears cutoff jeans, which are cut in a jagged Peter Pan fashion. Her long shapely legs are accentuated by high-heel slide-in pumps.*

431

*Above the three paintings is a second level. It runs the length
of the stage and serves as skylights, but its function is that
of a scrim. This is used for projections of the younger*
LENA, ROLAND *and* VEEDA *scenes.*

NOTE: *The younger* LENA *should be able to move from the
second level down the fire escape stairs and into the painting of* ROLAND.

SOUND: *Low seductive music of a saxophone.*

Lights slowly rise on the paintings.

Enter LENA LARSEN SALVINONI, *attractive woman of forty-
seven. She wears a Chinese-type dress that wraps closed
in the front. It is form-fitted and has slits high up both
thighs exposing stockingless legs. She wears slide-in back-
less, strapless high-heel pumps. She carries an empty
beautifully hand-crafted liqueur decanter and sherry glass.
She gestures her glass in toast towards the paintings and
then drains the contents.*

SOUND: *The phone rings.* LENA *stops, stares and then crosses
to the phone, reaches to retrieve the receiver and then
stops. The phone continues to ring.* LENA *picks up the
phone.*

NOTE: *The voice on the other end of the phone is that of
the young* FENDI LARSON WATTS. *It may be amplified
for effect. The audience should, however, be aware that
the* FENDI *in the portrait is the voice over the phone.*

FENDI. (*Voice-over.*) Momma. . . . Momma. . . . Talk to
me, Momma.

LENA *slams down the phone. Silence.* LENA *crosses to the
liqueur decanter; it is empty. She then crosses to the bar,
where she retrieves a cheap bottle of liquor. She quickly
drinks from the bottle. She then pours its contents into the
crystal decanter and then pours the liquor into the sherry
glass. She quickly drinks down the contents and then refills
the glass once more.*

SOUND: *The abrasive interruption of the door buzzer.*

LENA *composes herself as she crosses to the door. She looks through the peephole.*

Enter ABLE MCKITCHEN, *a young handsome man of nineteen. He carries a painting easel, a canvas frame and a large canvas bag full of his artist supplies.*

LENA. (*Elated.*) Able. . . . Come in. Come in. How is my Van DerZee of the paintbrush and canvas?

ABLE. Fine, excited . . . ready to start.

LENA. Yes, I . . . see . . . (*She refers to his supplies.*)

ABLE. I'm sorry to come so early but this is the only time Paul could drop me off. . . .

LENA. Paul? . . .

ABLE. He's one of the guys down at the studio, the only one with a van.

LENA. You could have taken a taxi and charged it to me.

ABLE. Can you imagine trying to get this . . . (*Indicates his supplies*) in a taxi?

LENA. Well, we could have rented a van.

ABLE. Paul didn't mind. In fact, he asked if you had a twin sister.

LENA. (*Thinks.*) A twin? . . . (*She finally understands the statement. She laughs.*) Oh, yes . . . I'm sure he would, um . . . he's also an artist?

ABLE. Yeah, but he's a sculptor, so if you ever decide to have a bust done, he's your man.

LENA. I'll keep that in mind.

(LENA *stares sensuously at* ABLE. ABLE *becomes a bit uneasy.*)

ABLE. Ah . . . Miss Lena . . .

LENA. Now Able, how many times have I told you. . . . It's not "Miss Lena" nor "Mrs. Salvinoni," it's Lena. Lena. Okay?

ABLE. Yes Miss Lena.

LENA. Able! . . .

(LENA *crosses to* ABLE. *She playfully takes his chin and lips in hand.*)

LENA. Lena. Can you say it for me?

ABLE. Lena.

LENA. Very good. (*She smiles a sensuous smile.*)

ABLE. (*Nervous and uneasy.*) Ah . . . Where should I put these? (*He refers to his supplies.*)

LENA. Any place that's convenient for you.

ABLE. (*Trying to keep things professional.*) Well . . . (*He scans the environment.*) I'm going to have to spread a drop cloth.

LENA. No problem.

ABLE. And I need to have good lighting.

LENA. Again, no problem. If what I have isn't sufficient. . . . I'll just run my fingers through the Yellow Pages and . . . (*She claps her hands.*) Solved. So. . . . Make yourself comfortable.

(LENA *crosses to refresh her drink.*)

LENA. I'd offer you a drink, but you don't partake. . . . I believe I have some herbal tea. That is the new craze, isn't it?

ABLE. I guess, but no, thank you, I'm not thirsty. . . . Anyway, I ah . . . can't stay too long. I've got classes and I've got to get over to Madison's. . . .

LENA. Madison's. . . . You're not still delivering for Madison's, are you?

ABLE. No ma'am . . . I mean, no. Just picking up my last check.

LENA. You were wasting yourself delivering meals for Madison's restaurant.

ABLE. It helped pay the bills and the tuition.

LENA. A young man with your attributes . . . (*She stares at* ABLE.) should have found something more suitable. In any case, you'll make far more here than you would have made in a year with Madison. And it will all be a labor of love. . . . (*She smiles.*) Your painting, that is. (*She strokes* ABLE'*s face.*) An artist should do what he does best, his art. You now have the opportunity.

ABLE. I sure do appreciate it. (*He sights an area he wishes to work in.*) Would this be a good spot?

LENA. I'm leaving it all to your discretion. (*She crosses to a large artist's portfolio. She flips through the sketches and renderings.*) You know, I went through these again early this morning and your work is quite good.

ABLE. Thank you. . . . I mean . . . This last week has been
    hell, I mean sleeping. I . . . Well I keep trying to
    convince myself this is all true, I mean the commis-
    sion.

LENA. Rest your mind, it is true.

ABLE. I know, I mean . . . I deposited my first check and.
    . . . Well . . . It's like this is something that happens
    in the movies and struggling artists' dreams.

LENA. It is?

ABLE. Yeah. . . . I mean, I've been delivering your orders
    from Madison's for months and then . . . a week ago
    you ask me what I do, I tell you what I do, and the
    next thing I know is . . .

LENA. You're a commissioned artist.

ABLE. To do work comparable to . . . (*He indicates the
    paintings.*) It's all kind of hard to believe.

LENA. You did say you were good, yes?

ABLE. Yes but . . .

LENA. But. . . . But. . . . Things merely happened with
    the flow. You came with your delivery. I had nothing
    smaller than a hundred. I apologized, not able to ac-
    commodate your tip. You said . . .

(*The lights begin to change as* LENA *and* ABLE *replay the
action of a week ago.*)

ABLE. I don't deliver here for tips.

LENA. No?

ABLE. (*Shyly.*) No, ma'am.

LENA. Isn't that how you really make your money?

ABLE. Yes, ma'am, but . . .

LENA. Then, why may I ask, are you in the business of
    "delivering" meals from Madison's if you are not doing
    it for tips?

ABLE. (*Embarrassed.*) I ah . . . It's sort of embarrassing.

LENA. Embarrassing? . . . Would it be too much to ask
    for an explanation?

ABLE. I . . . I use you for a study.

LENA. A study? . . .

ABLE. Yes, ma'am.

LENA. Able! Stop that. I am old but not that old. Okay?
    Now, what kind of a study. You casing my joint for
    a holdup?

ABLE. (*Emphatic.*) No, ma'am! I mean, no Miss Lena.

LENA. (*Correcting.*) Lena.

ABLE. Lena.

LENA. Relax. I'm only kidding. If you haven't hit me in
  the six months you've been coming up here with my
  orders of blanquette de veau, trout amandine, veal
  scallopini and sauerbraten you're not likely to do it
  now. So relax. Now, how and why are you studying
  me?

ABLE. It's sort of embarrassing.

LENA. Jesus, with the "embarrassing" again. Why is it
  embarrassing? (*She sips on her sherry.*)

ABLE. Because . . . It's sort of like invading on your privacy.

LENA. Invading my privacy. . . . How are you invading
  my privacy? Just what do you do besides make deliv-
  eries for Madison?

ABLE. I paint and go to school.

LENA. Ahh. . . . (*She refills her sherry glass.*) Care for
  some? (*Indicates her glass.*)

ABLE. No thank you.

LENA. "No thank you". . . . You are so well mannered
  and polite. You don't have to be polite, you know.
  You may have a drink if you wish.

ABLE. I don't care for any.

LENA. So you're making a character study of Lena Larsen
  Salvinoni. . . . I'm flattered. Are you good?

(LENA *sits and crosses her legs. The slit in the dress exposes
her well-kept thighs.* ABLE *notices and quickly looks the
other way.*)

ABLE. I would hope so.

LENA. Your work, is it as good as these?

(LENA *refers to the paintings.* ABLE *stares at the works but
does not respond.*)

LENA. Go ahead, get yourself a closer look.

(ABLE *crosses to the paintings.*)

LENA. Are you as good?

ABLE. Someday I'd like to be better. What I'd like to be
  is . . . I'd like to capture with the brush what Van

DerZee did with his camera. (*He turns to* LENA.) You know, capture the grand moments of our people. (*Shyly.*) My artistic aspirations.

LENA. (*Smiles.*) I like you, Mr. Able, the Van DerZee of canvas and brush.

ABLE. (*Uneasy.*) I'd better be going. I don't want Mr. Madison thinking . . .

LENA. You've been kidnapped by the eccentric Lena Salvinoni.

(ABLE *crosses to exit. He stops and turns to* LENA.)

ABLE. Miss Lena . . .

LENA. Yes.

ABLE. I've got a question I've wanted to ask for months.

LENA. Shoot.

ABLE. Actually it's two.

LENA. Make it three and you'll have a trio. (*She smiles and sips on the sherry.*)

ABLE. You'll pardon me, but ah . . . He don't look like no man named Salvinoni.

(ABLE *refers to the portrait of* ROLAND WATTS.)

LENA. Quite perceptive. . . . He wasn't.

(LENA *crosses to a Chinese chest and retrieves a gold-leaf frame from its surface. It is a photograph of* DOMINICK SALVINONI *and her.*)

LENA. (*Extending photograph to* ABLE.) This is Dominick Salvinoni.

(ABLE *studies the photograph and then shifts his focus to the immortalized painting of* ROLAND. LENA *crosses to portrait of* ROLAND.)

LENA. And this is Roland, the love of my life. (*She smiles.*) Confusing, yes? (*She smiles again.*) My first and only love. Everybody ought to have a love like Roland. (*Studying the painting.*) Roland Watts. . . . You know my whole world opened up the day he moved into the upstairs fifth-floor apartment. I discovered music. Nine years old and I discovered music could . . . Music could do things for you a double-dip ice cream never could. Roland sang sweet notes out of that sax. You know what I'm talking about?

(ABLE *smiles.*)

You ever visit one of those galleries and see a work of art that sings to you, moves you?

ABLE. Yeah, sometimes.

LENA. Well imagine whatever you felt multiplied ten-, fifteen-, twentyfold. This man could play. . . . Every day, rain or shine, he'd play. He had a habit of coming out on the fire escape steps for his practice sessions. He'd sit out on those wooden steps, face that sun and open up the whole world. I saw a ladybug fly up on the bannister and sit for one of his rehearsal sessions.

ABLE. A ladybug?

LENA. As God is my witness. It flew up on the bannister and just sat there until he finished. When he packed up the sax it flew away. This painting was taken from a snapshot Bob Fraizer took of him one hot August afternoon. I remember it clearly. I damn near drove Bob crazy begging for a copy. Finally one day he just handed over the photo. I had an artist friend do the painting. (*Studies the painting.*) You should have heard him, known him in those days. . . . Roland Watts. . . .

(LENA *stops. She turns to* ABLE, *crosses to him and takes the photograph out of his hands.*)

LENA. And his hands . . . (*She touches* ABLE's *hands.*) He had the softest touch. . . . (*She looks at* ABLE.) Not so bad yourself. (*She replaces the photograph on the chest.*) Roland was my first love.

ABLE. Is he dead?

LENA. I . . . guess you could say so. . . . I mean, yes, but . . . Sometimes, sometimes when I see him sitting there, when I look at his hands on that sax and see those eyes and remember those lips, his voice. . . . He's still alive for me. (*She reminisces.*) They all are. (*She indicates the other portraits.*)

ABLE. They're all dead?

(LENA *turns to the paintings. There is a pause.*)

LENA. Ummmm . . . ummm hum.

ABLE. It doesn't bother you, having paintings like this, of dead people on your walls?

LENA. Why should it? They're blood, family. . . . (*She crosses to the painting of* FENDI.) This is my daughter, Fendi. She sat for this painting the day before she died. (*She turns to* ABLE.) This of course is Roland. . . . (*She savors* ROLAND'*s portrait and then crosses to* VEEDA *portrait.*) And this . . . This is Veeda. She taught me how to sing. She was the first woman I ever saw polish her toenails, wear high-heel shoes without back straps and wear those short-short cutoff pants. That used to be scandalous back in the fifties. (*She turns to painting of* VEEDA.) She was a lot like a mother but also my friend, my mentor and in the end . . . Ah . . . who wants to hear about raindrops on parades. . . . Anyway. . . . These are my people. (*She indicates the portraits. Silence.*) You said you had another question.

ABLE. It can wait until another time.

LENA. No please. . . . What else have I to do but entertain your questions? (*She refills her glass.*) You're sure you won't have some?

ABLE. No. . . . I mean, yes, I'm sure.

LENA. To each his own. (*She drinks.*) Your question. . . .

ABLE. I don't know quite how to put it.

LENA. Don't put it any special way, just ask.

ABLE. I hear them talk about you, down at Mr. Madison's. . . . They say you've inherited a lot of money from Mr. Salvinoni.

LENA. I did.

ABLE. Then why do you live like this? I mean, a penthouse is nice, but . . . Well . . . I've been coming here for months, delivering you your meals and . . . From what I see you never go out. It's like this is a prison or something.

LENA. Prison? . . . Well, let's see. . . . I don't go out, but I can. I hold the key to the door you see, but . . . I choose not, so I guess you could say it is somewhat a prison and then you could say I'm merely a recluse or an eccentric.

(ABLE *looks confused.*)

ABLE. I don't understand. . . . Was that a stipulation of
    Mr. Salvinoni's will?

(ABLE *turns to the painting of* ROLAND. *He tries to place
the pieces of the puzzle together.*)

LENA. No, but . . . if he had been a different type of man
    I'm sure he would, but . . . Dominick was not that
    type. He was . . . too decent, too loving, giving. . . .
    It takes a special kind of man to marry a woman he
    knows loves another, but he did.
ABLE. Then why don't you go out?
LENA. Because . . . You ever been in love, Able?

(*He does not respond.*)

    I mean *passionately* in love. There's a difference in
    being "in love" and being "passionately in love." And
    there are consequences in life for the actions we take
    and make. I chose passion and . . . this . . . (*She
    indicates her environment.*) this is my sentence for
    "crimes of the heart," "crimes of passion."

(ABLE *becomes tensed.* LENA *crosses to* ABLE.)

LENA. Relax, Able. I'm merely rattling off with the mouth,
    spurting out bits of clichés. This is, though, a nice
    prison cell, wouldn't you say? Thought I'd give myself
    luxury the Watergate clan got when they served out
    their sentences, only I forwent the tennis courts and
    golf courses. (*She smiles and then fingers* ABLE's *face.*)
    I am really quite sane, Able. (*She stops and stares at*
    ABLE.) You've got nice lines, a nice face. You're going
    to be a very handsome man.
ABLE. Thank you.
LENA. Oh! Able . . . Your politeness and manners . . .
    You're going to drive me . . . You make me feel
    . . . (*She inhales and exhales deeply.*) Tell me, Able.
    . . . Do you have a last name?
ABLE. McKitchen.
LENA. (*Laughs.*) McKitchen! . . . How'd you happen by
    that one?

ABLE. It was given to me.

LENA. (*Suddenly stunned and then humored.*) Given to you. . . . Yes, I guess we are all given them, names. . . . Well Able McKitchen, you have nothing to fear, Lena Larsen Salvinoni is wrapped together tightly and . . . I have a brilliant idea. I want to seduce you into . . . terminating your employment with Madison and begin to work for me.

ABLE. Work for you?

LENA. Yes.

ABLE. I don't understand. What kind of work could I do for you?

(LENA *bursts into a hearty laugh.*)

LENA. What kind of work? . . . I like you, Able McKitchen.

(ABLE *stands before her speechless and a bit confused.*)

LENA. Ah, that look of innocence, it's so precious.

(ABLE *does not respond.*)

LENA. You don't understand, do you?

ABLE. No, I don't think so.

(LENA *bursts into a hearty laugh again.*)

LENA. It's simple. I want to commission you.

ABLE. Commission . . . as in me painting?

LENA. Yes. . . . What did you think? Maybe I'd shove you off into my kitchen and turn you into my cook? (*She laughs.*) Can you cook?

ABLE. Baked beans and hot dogs.

LENA. We'll settle for your more crafted skills. . . .

ABLE. But you've never seen my work, you've never . . .

LENA. How long have you been painting?

ABLE. With instructors, five years. On my own . . . since I was nine.

LENA. Nine.

ABLE. I got little awards, certificates, grants to artist camps. . . .

LENA. What are you worth?

ABLE. I don't understand.

442	*Brown Silk and Magenta Sunsets*

LENA. Your art, work. . . . What's it worth, monetarily? Now don't sell yourself cheap.

ABLE. You mean if I were to sell a piece of my work?

LENA. No, I mean if you were to be commissioned as you are being commissioned now. What are you worth?

ABLE. If I were an established artist I'd say . . . a hundred thousand . . .

LENA. But . . .

ABLE. I'm not, so . . . Five thousand, which could probably be bargained down to five hundred.

LENA. (*Frustrated.*) Which are you worth, five thousand or five hundred?

ABLE. (*Quickly.*) Five thousand.

LENA. Never mention what you don't want. If you're worth five thousand, you're worth five thousand. Tomorrow, when you deliver my order I want you to bring me a sample of your work.

ABLE. Tomorrow?

LENA. Tomorrow. You weren't running a con on Lena for her money, were you?

ABLE. No.

LENA. Then I'd like to see some of your work. Then if you are as good as you say you are, the up-and-coming Van DerZee of the paint, brush and canvas, then . . . I'll have a contract drawn up to the effect of . . . five thousand dollars, for a painting, a portrait of me. How does that sit with you?

ABLE. (*Overwhelmed.*) Are you serious?

LENA. Jesus! . . . (*She turns to the paintings and delivers the line to them.*) The child's gonna drive me to drink. (*To* ABLE.) Can you paint, Able McKitchen?

ABLE. Yes.

LENA. Are you good?

ABLE. Yes.

LENA. Then Lena Larsen Salvinoni is quite serious, despite the fact I live like some mad woman shut away in her castle in the sky. You'll find I am a woman of my word, so . . . tomorrow. . . .

(*The lights change back to those of the present.*)

LENA. Well, Able. . . . That tomorrow is this today and . . . Here you are with the tools of your trade . . .

(*She first looks at* ABLE *and then at his artist's supplies.*) ready to get things under way.

(ABLE *is absorbed in his own thoughts. He is totally oblivious to* LENA's *implications.*)

ABLE. A commission. . . . *A commission.* . . . *I GOT A REAL COMMISSION!*

(ABLE *spins around elated with this outburst.* LENA *looks on amused.*)

ABLE. (*Collecting himself.*) I'm ah . . . Sorry 'bout that, but . . . You know, last night I had the strongest urge to walk midway across the Brooklyn Bridge and scream out . . . "I GOT A COMMISSION!" . . .

LENA. Feels good, doesn't it?

ABLE. Damn real. . . . (*Collecting himself.*) I mean . . . Yes.

LENA. Why do you do that?

ABLE. What?

LENA. Fight your natural feelings. I've noticed that about you. . . . It's like suppressing your passion, and one should never suppress their passion.

ABLE. I don't suppress my passions.

LENA. No?

ABLE. No, I was just taught . . . Well, there's such a thing as respect.

LENA. Oh, respect. So, tell me, did you do it?

ABLE. What?

LENA. Stand in the middle of the Brooklyn Bridge and boast your joy?

ABLE. No.

LENA. Why?

ABLE. I just didn't.

LENA. You suppressed your passion. (*She crosses to the bar and retrieves a bag of thin pretzels, opens it and empties the contents into an ornate Chinese bowl.*) I've got a thing for these skinny little pretzels. A holdover from the days Roland introduced me to pretzels, beer and a few other things. Have some.

ABLE. No, thank you.

LENA. (*Pushing the bowl on* ABLE.) Have one. I will permit you to refuse my drink, because too much drink can be hazardous to the health, but my pretzels . . . you must eat.

(ABLE *takes a pretzel.*)

LENA. I have a passion for many things. Good drink. . . . (*She hold up her glass.*) Music. . . . (*She crosses to the* ROLAND *painting.*) Fine men. . . . (*She stares at the painting.*) The sky. . . . (*She crosses to the window.*) On a bright clear day like today, the sky . . . It's like nature having spread the most wonderful of beds with the promise of ecstasy waiting just before the close of day. (*To* ABLE.) Do you like sunsets?

ABLE. They're nice.

LENA. There is nothing, nothing like a sunset, magenta sunsets, magenta lights swallowing up the sky, kissing and embracing the horizon . . . I have a passion for magenta sunsets. A noted reason why I had the sky-lights put in. (*She indicates the skylights.*) The window wasn't enough so . . . Each evening, when the sky warms up with its promise of euphoria . . . I'm ready. And that light, when it fills this room . . . (*She catches herself.*) I'm rattling again, aren't I? (*She crosses to* ABLE. *She takes his hand in hers.*) You're such a sweet boy. Putting up with the mild rage of an eccentric hideaway. (*She studies his hands.*) Nice. . . . Nice and soft, your hands. . . . I wonder if these are the pre-requisite of the artist. He had soft hands. . . . (*She crosses to* ROLAND's *painting.*) Soft and tender. . . . Funny how things like touch draw the mind to mem-ory. Smells do that to me as well. You know, some-times, when there's a light breeze in the air, I smell picnic hamburgers. Up here, I do. I don't know where it comes from, but . . . on those days, that smell, it takes me back to Pittsburgh, puts me in the mind of outings to Kennywood Park, picnics of fried chicken, potato salad, hot dogs and those great hamburgers. Funny how a smell can do that, conjure up yesterday. But you know, for a moment, I'm back in Pittsburgh, a little girl stuffing my mouth with hamburgers loaded with mustard and sweet relish. (*She takes* ABLE's *hand again.*) The mind is an amazing thing, wouldn't you say?

ABLE. I guess. . . .

LENA. (*Fingering* ABLE'*s hand.*) Such soft hands. . . .

ABLE. Miss Lena . . . I mean Lena . . . I don't want to seem disrespectful but . . . I've got a class and I've got to stop by Madison's and Paul ought to be coming back to pick me up 'round about now. . . .

LENA. Paul?

ABLE. Yeah, my ride, the one with the van.

LENA. He's coming here?

ABLE. No, I'm supposed to meet him downstairs.

LENA. No problem. . . . Relax. Jordon will ring the buzzer when he comes.

(ABLE *reluctantly sits.*)

LENA. So, tell me, do you have a girlfriend?

ABLE. Yes and no.

LENA. "Yes and no," that's a strange way to have a girlfriend.

ABLE. She moved to Mississippi.

LENA. Mississippi? . . . (*She refreshes her drink.*) Not so good for your passion.

ABLE. I don't have too much time for passion, I mean school, starting this painting. . . .

LENA. One must always have time for . . . (*Caressing* ABLE'*s face.*) You must make time for passion. It is not good for your . . . your mind to be consumed in all work and no play. . . .

ABLE. Miss Lena. . . .

LENA. (*Seductively.*) Yes.

ABLE. (*Moving away from* LENA. *Abrasively.*) Why did you hire me?

LENA. To paint.

ABLE. No, I mean, why did you really hire me?

LENA. To paint.

ABLE. Then why all this . . . What's with this passion thing? Look, it's true I'm an artist, I'm poor, I'm more than flattered about the commission, but I am not for sale.

LENA. I didn't think you were.

ABLE. I mean it, Miss Lena, I'm not for sale. I know a lotta guys who'd jump at this opportunity, but . . .

LENA. You're not for sale.

ABLE. Right. So, what's it gonna be? Do I get my things and hit the door?

LENA. No! (*Thinking.*) No. . . . Ugh, I sometimes rattle

off. . . . It comes from being alone. I really do want
the painting. . . . Ugh . . . I, I . . . I just get a little
bit excited. . . . That's it, it's the excitement of having
you here. You must believe, my intentions are hon-
orable. That is what I should say, isn't it?

ABLE. I don't want you to say anything to appease me,
just the truth. Look, this means a lot to me. It's an
opportunity of a lifetime, at least for me. . . . If you
could understand . . .

LENA. I do.

ABLE. I don't think you do. Art, it's not a hobby with me.
. . . It's like that music you play sometimes, that
saxophone music. It's round, full, filling. . . . I want
to paint you.

LENA. Then you'll paint me.

ABLE. But that's all I want to do.

LENA. I understand.

(ABLE *crosses to the exit.*)

LENA. I suppose we won't be starting the painting this
evening.

ABLE. No, I think it'll be better if we start tomorrow, give
us some space.

LENA. (*Meekly.*) Yes, perhaps so.

(SOUND. *The buzzer.*)

LENA. That should be your friend.

ABLE. Yeah.

(ABLE *crosses to the door.*)

LENA. (*Slightly desperate.*) You will come tomorrow?

(*Silence.* ABLE *scans the room and then turns to* LENA.)

ABLE. Yes.

(SOUND. *The buzzer.* LENA *crosses to the intercom.*)

LENA. (*Spirit lifted.*) Jordon, you can tell . . . (*She looks
to* ABLE.)

ABLE. Paul.

LENA. Tell Paul Able is on his way down. (*She moves away from the intercom. She crosses to* ABLE.) Thank you.

ABLE. (*Understandingly.*) We just needed to get things straight.

LENA. Yes.

(LENA *brings her hand up to touch* ABLE's *face. Uneasily and cautiously she withdraws it.*)

LENA. Thank you.

(ABLE *exits.* LENA *leans against the closed door. Lights dim.*)

ACT ONE

Scene 2

Lights rise.
LENA *crosses to the stereo. She turns on a saxophone solo recording. She crosses to the bar top, where she opens food delivery cartons. She finger-tastes them and then closes them. She crosses to the window. The lighting reflects it is late afternoon. The lighting should shift during the scene to reflect the spill of the sunset's magenta light flooding the room.*

LENA. (*To the paintings.*) We're going to have a beautiful sunset tonight. No clouds, no obstructions. . . . Except for that building over there. Why did they have to build that tower there, and why so high? I miss my panoramic view. Why couldn't they have put that thing up somewhere else? (*She drinks. To the painting of* VEEDA.) How are you today, Veeda? No need to answer, I can see. You're doing fine as ever, aren't you Veeda? You and Roland. Both of you, doing fine and frozen in time, and young. Young! Can you believe that? Young. The two of you, frozen there young and me . . . I remember the time when I was young and you two were . . . That's what I hate about death. It cheats the living and changes the order of things. Me older than you two! . . . Never! I'm putting things in their proper place. I'm cheating death. I'm putting you and you (*She indicates* VEEDA *and* ROLAND) in your proper places.

(LENA *crosses to the Chinese chest. She removes the objects from the top, opens it and begins to retrieve articles; scrapbooks, old photo albums, record albums, a blue silk Chinese dress and a pair of long dangling earrings.*
The phone rings. LENA *freezes. She stares at the ringing*

ACT TWO

SCENE 3
Three days later.

ABLE *sits at the easel. He adds the finishing strokes to today's work on the canvas. He moves back from the canvas to get a better view of his work. He is dressed in his painting attire. Pleased with his work, he takes his brushes and crosses to three jars of water, where he begins the process of washing and rinsing them. He then wipes them dry on a cloth before he begins to shape the brushes in a very sensual manner. He does this while studying the work he has accomplished on the painting.*

LENA *enters while* ABLE *works on his brushes. She quietly studies his actions. She is not noticed by* ABLE. LENA *carries with her a small tray which holds a sandwich and Coca-Cola.*

LENA. I can see you put a lot of love and care into your work and instruments. (*She indicates* ABLE's *brushes.*)

ABLE. Yeah, well . . . Good brushes cost a pretty penny. You've got to treat them properly if you want them to do a good job.

LENA. You know, the more I watch you the more you remind me of Roland. Like your handling of those brushes. . . . If you could have seen him polishing his sax. . . . There was such a sensual relationship between the two, like you with your brushes.

ABLE. Sensual?

LENA. You probably don't even notice what you're doing.

ABLE. Guess not.

LENA. Oh! (*Remembering the tray.*) Your sandwich.

ABLE. Thanks, I really appreciate it.

LENA. Just make sure you get yourself a decent meal later.

ABLE. This is a decent meal.

LENA. Sardines on rye with mustard is not a decent meal.
(*She watches* ABLE *eat.*) You won't believe this but
that was a favorite of Roland's.

ABLE. What?

LENA. Sardines. Except he loaded his with mustard, Louisiana hot sauce and great big slices of raw onions.

ABLE. That's some combination.

LENA. Yes, you could say so.

(LENA *crosses to the painting.*)

LENA. I like this. It's coming along quite well.

ABLE. Thanks. It would have been a lot better if you had
done a live sitting.

LENA. Live? Never! Freeze myself for eternity like this?

ABLE. What's wrong with you?

LENA. What's wrong? Well, I guess you had to have a view
of my yesterdays to understand.

ABLE. I do have a view of your yesterday. I'm painting
from it.

LENA. So you are.

ABLE. That was one of the reasons I jumped at the opportunity to paint you. For the last six, seven months
I've been studying your lines, your eyes. You've got
things going on deep behind your eyes.

(VEEDA's *interjections into the scene are heard only by* LENA.)

VEEDA. (*From the painting. To* LENA.) The boy's got perception.

(LENA *glares at the* VEEDA *painting.*)

ABLE. Like there's something more than the smiles or the
nervous chatter of being cooped up in here too long.

VEEDA. (*To* ABLE.) Call a spade a spade, boy. Go on and
hit the nail on the head.

ABLE. That's what I wanted to paint, the real you.

VEEDA. Dear God, not too real. The horror would be too
much for the eyes of man.

(LENA *quickly rises and crosses to the drawstring on the
drapery cord. As she pulls the cord the drapes close across*

*the entire length of the room, covering both the window
and the paintings.* ABLE *is stunned and set back by this
action.*)

LENA. (*To* ABLE, *explaining.*) Now I know this is a little
    strange.
ABLE. That's putting it mildly.
LENA. The sun. . . . It was getting in my eye and . . .

(ABLE *awaits an explanation regarding the drapery.*)

LENA. The drapes? . . .
ABLE. I gotta say, that's a new one on me.
LENA. It's quite simple. You see, a couple years ago I got
    a visit from Sal Giordano, he was a friend of Dom-
    inick's.

(ABLE *still awaits an explanation.*)

LENA. And . . . He's in the drapery business, and a little
    on the old side and . . . in need of a little business.
    He hadn't done as well as Dominick. And . . . I felt
    sorry for him. I mean, a five-foot-four-inch man in his
    . . . late sixties pays me a visit out of respect to an
    old friend and the old country and he's somewhat
    down on his luck and . . . I could afford to be generous,
    so . . . I gave him an order to redo my windows. Little
    did I know that he was also going a bit senile. I must
    say, I did think it a bit odd when the boys installed
    that rod the entire length of the room, but . . . And
    then, after the drapes went up . . . Well . . . I didn't
    have the heart to call Sal on it.
VEEDA. (*From behind the drapes.*) What a crock. . . . You
    lie like a devil, Lena.
LENA. And so . . . My curtains are about as eccentric as
    I am.

(LENA *gives a quick short laugh and then refills her sherry
glass.*)

LENA. Now if it bothers you. . . . I can open them again.
ABLE. No, whatever suits you.
VEEDA. (*From behind the curtain.*) Now aren't you happy
    for that response. Enjoy yourself, Lena. A few more

drinks and these drapes won't mean a thing. I'll be
right out there joining the two you in your tête-à-tête.

(LENA *quickly sets down her drink.*)

LENA. (*To* ABLE.) I've been meaning to ask you, how is
  your mother?
ABLE. Fine. She gets discharged tomorrow.
LENA. Diabetes can be an ugly disease. Oh, should you
  be drinking that?
ABLE. What?
LENA. The soda. You know, the sugar. Shouldn't you watch
  things like that?
ABLE. The truth is, I was adopted and if I worried about
  possible physical weaknesses *I'd* be a candidate for
  Bellevue's top floor.
LENA. You never mentioned anything about being adopted.
ABLE. It's not something you offer with first-meeting sal-
  utations.
LENA. I guess not.
ABLE. Don't get me wrong. I love my parents.
LENA. Yes, I'm sure.
ABLE. They're good people.
LENA. What about your real parents.
ABLE. They are my *real* parents.
LENA. I mean your . . . natural parents.
ABLE. Who knows? New York's a big city. Could have
  been any of the millions I see everyday. Then on the
  other hand, could be none of them, could be a woman
  from Boston, D.C., Philly, Kansas, Oklahoma, Cal-
  ifornia, anywhere. I gave up trying to figure that one
  out when I was about ten.
LENA. I see.

(ABLE *crosses to the painting he has been working on. He
studies his work.*)

ABLE. There's something in your eyes.

(LENA *crosses to* ABLE, *glass in hand. She sips en route.*)

LENA. Good, I hope.
ABLE. I can't decide what it is. Sometimes it's a warmth,
  other times it's . . .

VEEDA. (*From behind the drapery.*) It's her fire and ice.

ABLE. Cool. . . . Almost like a quiet anger, maybe hurt, pain.

LENA. Let's see. (LENA *studies the painting.*) Well . . . I'd just turned thirty. Does that help?

ABLE. Maybe. Women are supposed to go through a thing when they turn thirty.

VEEDA. (*From behind the drapery.*) Lena went through a thing long before thirty.

ABLE. Yeah, maybe that's it.

LENA. You got it, the melancholia of the thirties. Oh! I almost forgot. I've got a little something for you.

ABLE. Now Lena, you've got to stop with these presents.

LENA. Allow an old lady a bit of happiness.

ABLE. You are not an old lady.

LENA. No?

ABLE. No.

LENA. (*Stroking his face.*) How kind of you.

ABLE. I wasn't being kind. You're an attractive woman. If you didn't shut yourself up in here like you do, you might find you have a lot worth living for. You'd also end up with a better self-image.

LENA. I have a great self-image.

ABLE. Then prove it. Instead of standing here, gazing out that window day after day at the sunset, take a ride over to Riverside Drive and see the real thing in its natural glory.

LENA. No, I don't think so.

ABLE. Why?

LENA. Because. . . .

ABLE. Because why?

LENA. Because . . . There are muggers out there. I heard on the news the other evening how a couple, that is a *man* and a woman, while sitting on one of those benches watching the sunset . . . They got mugged.

ABLE. Lena, how many people get mugged while sitting on a bench on Riverside Drive?

VEEDA. (*From behind the drapes.*) She's not worried about being mugged on a bench on Riverside Drive. She's worried about the possibility of runnin' into me. Aren't you, Lena? Not sure I'm dead, are you? Just took it for granted, believed the rumors, but you're not sure, are you? You're afraid you might have to meet my eyes, see me face to face. That would be your death,

wouldn't it, Lena? Havin' me be livin' proof of just
how low you can go.

(LENA *makes a quick cross to the bar where she refills her
glass. She drinks down the contents quickly.*)

ABLE. I'm sorry. I didn't mean to get you nervous.
LENA. Nervous?
ABLE. I know there are some people who have phobias
     about going out.
LENA. Phobia?
ABLE. Riverside Drive.
LENA. Riverside Drive? . . . Oh, yes. . . . Well . . .
     Someday, maybe . . . Someday.
ABLE. You mean that?
LENA. Yes. Now. . . . I was . . . (*She thinks.*) Oh yes
     . . . I was about to get you . . .

(LENA *retrieves an envelope and a small box.*)

LENA. For you. (*She hands* ABLE *the envelope and box.*)
ABLE. Lena.
LENA. What? Open . . . Open. First the envelope.

(ABLE *begins with the envelope.*)

LENA. I've been, well . . . Keeping tabs on you at school.
     They tell me you're a fine student.
ABLE. I try.
LENA. Why didn't you tell me you were having an exhi-
     bition?
ABLE. I know you don't go out.
LENA. Is that a reason not to tell me?
ABLE. No, but . . .
LENA. Framing is costly, isn't it?
ABLE. It can be.
LENA. Your work should be displayed . . . exquisitely.

(ABLE *retrieves a gift certificate from the envelope.*)

LENA. It's a gift certificate. I've made arrangements with
     Sam Flax's. . . . That was a good choice, wasn't it?
ABLE. Yeah, Flax is good. . . .

LENA. Good. Well, I've made arrangements. I thought five hundred dollars per month should suffice.

ABLE. Five hundred? . . .

LENA. Yes, I'm told good supplies are quite expensive.

ABLE. Five hundred? I can't take this.

LENA. You can and you will. What am I going to do with it? I have no children, no family. Let me do this.

VEEDA. (*From behind the curtain.*) Please do, Able. Appease her guilt.

(LENA *downs the contents of her glass.*

As LENA *drinks,* VEEDA *steps from behind the drapes.* VEEDA *is not noticed by* ABLE.)

VEEDA. (*Crossing to* LENA.) I told you . . . Each swig gives me a little more room. Have another.

(LENA *quickly places the glass on the table. She avoids* VEEDA *by crossing to* ABLE.)

LENA. You will let me help you, won't you?

VEEDA. (*To* ABLE.) Oh, does she want to help you. (*To* LENA.) Can't wait to help him, can you, Lena? Look at those strong arms, those firm thighs, those knowledgeable hands. Can't wait to help him, can you?

LENA. (*To* ABLE.) You can use the certificate to help with your supplies and framing. Whatever you don't use goes back to you as cash.

ABLE. I don't know, Lena.

LENA. What don't you know? Do you think Michelangelo said, "I don't know"? He seized the opportunity and ran with the ball, which you should do. Okay? . . .

(ABLE *does not respond.*)

Okay? . . .

ABLE. (*Softly.*) Okay.

VEEDA. (*To* LENA.) Bravo! The boy's hooked. Now what you gonna do? Fry him or eat him raw?

LENA. (*Ignoring* VEEDA. *To* ABLE.) Open the box.

(ABLE *opens the box.*)

VEEDA. (*To* LENA.) Got to admit you really do know how
    to work your stuff.

LENA. (*Whispering to* VEEDA.) Get back in there!

ABLE. You said something?

LENA. Ah . . . The drapes. Maybe I should draw open the
    drapes so that you can see better.

(LENA *crosses to the draw cord. She opens the drapes,
exposing once again the window and paintings. She gestures
for* VEEDA *to get back into the painting.* VEEDA *stands over*
ABLE *to get a better view.*)

LENA. Do you like?

(ABLE *withdraws a beautiful gold pocket watch from the
box.*)

ABLE. It's . . . Lena, I can't accept this.

LENA. Yes, you can.

VEEDA. (*To* LENA.) Well go 'head, girl. You burnin' this
    candle at both ends. (*To* ABLE.) Child, you ain't got
    a fightin' chance.

LENA. (*To* ABLE.) Just think how chic you'll look. . . .
    Standing there in your jeans, opened shirt . . . your
    artistic demeanor. . . . Someone asks you the time
    and you so stylishly slip this . . . (*She refers to the
    watch*) from your pocket. It'll be . . .

ABLE. Ostentatious.

LENA. Ostentatious? Why?

ABLE. I don't have an artistic demeanor. I don't wear
    opened shirts. I wear tee shirts and pullovers and I
    already have a watch.

VEEDA. (*To* ABLE.) Get it, boy! Put her in her place.

LENA. (*To* ABLE.) You're angry.

VEEDA. (*To* LENA.) You're damn real he's angry.

ABLE. Yes. No. . . . Look, I'm flattered, but I already
    have a . . .

LENA. Please . . . I had gotten this for Roland, years ago.

VEEDA. Oh Jesus! Here we go. She's about to pull that
    dramatic charm.

(VEEDA *sits in chair and observes.*)

LENA. I never got a chance to give it to him. . . . It's been packed away in that chest for years. Look at it. It's a Waltham. Waltham watches have been out of business for years. And it's new, just like the day I bought it. You can see for yourself. No trick.

ABLE. I believe you.

LENA. Maybe I came on a little strong with the dramatic description, but I thought . . . It seems to me each artist needs his own thing. You know, like an eccentricity.

VEEDA. Well, hey now. . . . "Eccentricity" . . . Life with Dominick must not have been all that bad. You got yourself a upper-class vocabulary. You sure as hell ain't learn that one back in Pittsburgh.

LENA. Seems to me it could have been part of your style.

ABLE. Yeah, I understand.

LENA. I don't want you to understand. I want you to accept it. Look, what am I going to do with a man's pocket watch? It'll just sit in that chest until my demise and then my attorney accompanied by a tax agent will fight over who keeps what before dealing with the legal handling of my estate. I'd rather you have it than one of them. Say you'll keep it.

ABLE. Why can't I stay mad with you?

LENA. Because I'm so lovable. (*She kisses* ABLE *on the forehead.*)

VEEDA. (*To* ABLE.) Watch out, baby. She's closing in for the kill. (*To* LENA.) Ain't you, Lena?

(LENA *stares into* ABLE'*s eyes. Suddenly she crosses away.*)

ABLE. You okay?

LENA. Fine.

(LENA *refills her glass.*)

ABLE. Do you have to do that?

LENA. What?

ABLE. Drink . . . so much.

LENA. It's only a little sherry.

VEEDA. Sherry my ass. Rotgut.

ABLE. You know I care about you, Lena, and . . .

VEEDA. (*To* ABLE.) Wrong! Wrong. You should have never said that.

ABLE. That can't be good for you. (*He indicates her drinking.*)

LENA. I know, but . . . I've got everything under control.

VEEDA. (*To* LENA.) You wish.

ABLE. You think so?

LENA. Yes, I do.

ABLE. Remember the first night I started on the painting? You were . . .

VEEDA. (*To* ABLE.) Ossified right out of her mind.

ABLE. Well beyond control.

LENA. I explained. I was going through a bad time. You know, memories . . . thinking about my baby. . . . (*She indicates the* FENDI *painting.*)

VEEDA. (*To* LENA.) Oh, bullshit. (*To* FENDI.) For that lie, Fendi, you ought to come on out and take up roost.

(LENA *quickly turns to the* FENDI *painting.* LENA *stares at the painting, daring* FENDI *to move.*)

ABLE. That drinking can't be good for your headaches.

LENA. To the contrary, it helps.

VEEDA. (*To* LENA.) Not the way you'd like. (*Crossing to* LENA.) You'd like it to knock you out, black you out so you'd hear no voices, see no faces, have no memories. But it don't always work that way, do it, Lena?

ABLE. You believe that?

LENA. What?

ABLE. Believe it helps?

LENA. Sure.

ABLE. I don't.

LENA. That's because you don't understand.

VEEDA. (*To* LENA.) Got that right. If the boy understood he'd be 'bout six thousand and eighty-four million miles away from here.

ABLE. You know, I have an uncle who has a drinking problem. I know a lot about the excuses.

LENA. I do not have a drinking problem. I sip sherry.

VEEDA. (*To* LENA.) You guzzle cheap Scotch.

LENA. Sometimes I use it for medicinal purposes.

VEEDA. (*To* ABLE.) To get drunk outta her skull.

ABLE. Okay. Whatever you say. Look . . . I think I've done all the painting I'm going to do today.

LENA. You're leaving?

ABLE. Yeah. I've got to study for midterms and . . .

LENA. Midterms? Oh, yes, school.

ABLE. I . . . I don't know how to thank you for these. (*He indicates his presents.*)

VEEDA. (*To* ABLE.) Don't worry, you will.

LENA. Just enjoy. . . .

(ABLE *crosses to the door.* LENA *accompanies him.*)

ABLE. You take care of yourself, okay?

LENA. I'll be fine. I might even treat myself to a glass of water. (*She laughs.*)

ABLE. Okay, see you tomorrow.

(ABLE *exits. Silence.*)

VEEDA. Well, well, well. . . . I got me a ringside seat to watch the hussy at work. You sure do run a mean game, Lena.

LENA. Shut up, Veeda.

VEEDA. You 'bout to work that boy's last nerve.

LENA. I said shut up.

VEEDA. He is a cutie, and really does put you in the mind of Roland. You know I get a better view of him from out here.

LENA. Why don't you get back up on your perch?

VEEDA. 'Cause I like it out here. Tell me, Lena, when you gonna bed down with the boy?

(LENA *takes a strong cross to* VEEDA. *She stands over* VEEDA *and points to the painting.*)

LENA. Get in there.

VEEDA. No. Now what you gonna do? Where's that cute little six-shooter Dominick gave you? You gonna threaten me with that again?

LENA. Why don't you leave me alone?!

VEEDA. Because I want you to pay!

LENA. For what?!!! What did I do to you?! What did I do to you?! You married him. If anybody ought to be paying, it ought to be you. He married you. I bore his children and he married you. Ain't that enough a price to pay?

VEEDA. No. (*She crosses to* LENA.) No. You let him die.

LENA. He was your husband. The vows say, "For better

or worse, sickness or health." You took the vows.

VEEDA. He needed help. He needed money. He came to you and you spit in his face. And you talk about love. . . . You did the same thing with Fendi.

LENA. Shut up, Veeda.

VEEDA. All that poor child's life you spit in her face.

LENA. I said, shut up.

VEEDA. Sendin' her to the best private schools, the best summer camps. . . . you got her out of your face 'cause you couldn't stand her. Your own baby, by the man you said you loved, you couldn't stand her.

LENA. Veeda. . . . Shut . . . up!

VEEDA. Right. You'd like us all to shut up like Fendi did. Wouldn't you? Wouldn't you, Lena?

(LENA crosses to the bar. She opens a new bottle of liquor.)

VEEDA. That's right, Lena, drink up, drink up and drink fast. Maybe you can pass out before memory conquers.

(LENA guzzles the Scotch.)

VEEDA. But I don't think the drunk will come soon enough. Can't you see her? Can't you hear her? (*She refers to* FENDI.) She's stirring. . . .

(Lights rise on FENDI as she moves out of the painting.)

Hurry, Lena. Drink up before . . .

(The lighting changes.)

Awwww, Lena. . . . You didn't drink up fast enough.

(VEEDA crosses to a seat and sits.)

FENDI. I don't want to wear this dress, Momma.

LENA. You're wearing this dress, Fendi. It's bright, it's cheery, it's not gray and Dominick likes it.

FENDI. You mean you like it. Why don't you wear it?

LENA. Listen, young lady. . . .

FENDI. I'm not a young lady. I'm twenty-three.

LENA. Then act like it.

FENDI. I am. I'm not wearing this dress.

LENA. You will wear this dress. You get my drift? You will wear this very dress. You will sit in that chair and you will put on your best smile and look your best because Dominick desires a portrait of his daughter and you will give him that honor.

FENDI. I am not his daughter.

LENA. You are legally his daughter and you will do this for his birthday. You got that? Are you listening to me, Fendi?

FENDI. Why do you hate me, Momma?

LENA. Jesus, Fendi! Enough of this!

FENDI. Why, Momma?

LENA. Fendi!!!

FENDI. Why?

(LENA *does not respond. She moves away from* FENDI. FENDI *pursues her.*)

FENDI. Why?

(LENA *moves again.* FENDI *continues her pursuit.*)

FENDI. Why?

LENA. Because you were born! You were born! Isn't that what you want to hear?

FENDI. Yes.

LENA. Yes. You ruined everything. A sperm and an egg. Who could have thought something so small . . . a sperm and an egg . . . You just had to come.

FENDI. Why didn't you abort?

LENA. The Larsen women don't do abortions.

FENDI. I wonder what they call it when you abort a child after it's born. What you call that, Momma? (*No response.*) I'm going to keep on this dress. I'm going to sit in that chair. I'm going to pose and smile . . . for Dominick. Seems to me he must be going through hell too. You sure do know how to make people want and love you . . . I'm going to do this for Dominick. I'm going to let you fool life and your friends into believing I'm that happy and contented daughter sitting there in that chair, but . . . when it's finished, Momma. When that last stroke's made . . . I'm going to be finished with you. I'm going to be finished with want-

ing and needing you. I'm going to be finished with
you.

(The lighting changes. FENDI *steps back into the painting
and assumes her original position.)*

VEEDA. Boy, was she finished with you. And did she give
    you red? . . . Blood red pouring out of her wrists,
    down her hands, between her fingers . . .
LENA. *(Crying.)* Awwwww God, Veeda . . . Please . . .
    Please . . . Please, just get back in there.
VEEDA. I want you to hurt. Hurt the way I hurt. *(Crossing
    to the* ROLAND *painting.)* You should have seen his
    face, his body. . . . You know what happens to the
    body when the liver goes bad?
LENA. Please. . . .
VEEDA. You should have seen. . . .
LENA. Please. . . .

*(*LENA *passes out. Lights dim to black.)*

ACT TWO

Lights rise on LENA *as she enters in a very attractive and sensuous red Oriental dress with high slits. She has taken an extra step in the application of makeup and her hairstyle. LENA crosses to the bar, where she rotates a bottle of champagne in an ice bucket. She then inspects two long-stemmed champagne glasses for spots by holding them up to the light.*

LENA crosses to a beautiful arrangement of exotic flowers. She reforms the bouquet.

VEEDA watches LENA's actions from the painting.

VEEDA. (*From the painting.*) Well, well. . . . Look at Miss Hot En Tot this evening. Haven't seen you in that little number in a long time. (*She refers to* LENA's *dress.*) What was that man's name . . . Winston, Westly, Webster? . . . You remember his name, Lena?

LENA. I'm ignoring you, Veeda. I don't have time for you today.

VEEDA. No?

LENA. No. This is a special day for Able. He sold one of his paintings.

VEEDA. Plannin' on gettin' you a piece this evenin', ain't you?

LENA. You're vulgar, Veeda.

VEEDA. Vulgar? You callin' me vulgar after the things I seen you do and the sounds I heard comin' outta that bedroom? You got the nerve. You plannin' on drinkin' that? (*She refers to the champagne.*)

LENA. Mind your business.

VEEDA. I heard tell you can do somethin' awful to yourself

switchin' from cheap stuff to the good stuff. I remember a man back on Frankstown Road was hooked on
one of the cheap plucks and one day Miss Willis gave
him a bottle of good vintage for cleanin' the leaves
outta her yard and the man when straight into the
DT's.

LENA. Shut up, Veeda.

VEEDA. Wonder what that'll look like, you spinnin' around
on the floor goin' through the DT's in front of that
child.

(LENA *continues her actions of meticulously checking that
everything is just so and in place.*)

LENA. Notice, I'm ignoring you, Veeda.

VEEDA. That what you call it?

(LENA *picks up a sherry glass and downs the contents.*)

VEEDA. You sure you want to mix that champagne with
that rot gut?

LENA. (*Turning to* VEEDA.) Shut up!

VEEDA. Well, excuse me.

(VEEDA *steps from the frame. She crosses to the bottle of
champagne. She reads the label.*)

VEEDA. Good stuff. Musta cost a pretty penny.

(LENA *ignores* VEEDA.)

VEEDA. I saw a bottle of this once. We did a gig for this
rich couple somewhere down in Connecticut.

LENA. Connecticut is up from New York.

VEEDA. But it's down from Pittsburgh.

LENA. No, it's northeast of Pittsburgh.

VEEDA. I thought you was ignorin' me.

LENA. I am, watch me.

(LENA *crosses to the bar. She picks up the decanter to refill
her glass. She hesitates, looks over at* VEEDA, *at the bottle
of champagne and then pours the liquor into her glass.*

VEEDA *crosses to the painting* ABLE *has been working on.*)

VEEDA. The boy's got talent.

LENA. Stop callin' him a boy.

VEEDA. That's what the child is, a boy.

LENA. Then they must not grow boys like they used to.

VEEDA. Watch out! Lena's on the prowl. Goin' after her some young stuff. Got on her sexy number, done done her hair, her nails, her face and . . . She's about to sink them fangs into some sweet young meat.

(VEEDA crosses to LENA and sniffs her perfume.)

VEEDA. Smells good, too. *(To LENA.)* That's a lot better than that stuff you used to wear. What was it? Evenin' in Paradise? And what were those awful Avon numbers you used to wear? Wishin' and Charisma. This is truly a move up in class. So is the boy, for that matter.

LENA. I told you, stop calling him a boy.

(VEEDA crosses to the ROLAND painting. She studies the painting.)

VEEDA. And he really does put you in the mind of Roland. Got a lot of Roland's looks and talent. . . . Not the same kind, but the child's really got what it takes.

(VEEDA crosses back to the painting ABLE is working on.)

VEEDA. I might also add the boy's been very kind to you.

(LENA crosses to VEEDA, she stares at the painting.)

LENA. What you mean, he's been kind to me?

VEEDA. Paintin' you like that.

LENA. He paints what he sees.

VEEDA. Then the boy can't see too good, 'cause them eyes . . . *(She refers to the painting of LENA)* and these eyes . . . *(She refers to LENA's actual eyes)* ain't the same.

LENA. You're just jealous, Veeda.

VEEDA. A you? . . .

(LENA crosses to her glass. She daintily sips from the sherry glass.)

VEEDA. Awwww, girl, won't you just pour that stuff in a water glass and gulp it down like the street hussy you is?

LENA. Again, I am ignoring you.

(LENA *crosses away.* VEEDA *crosses to the* ROLAND *painting.*)

VEEDA. What you got planned for the boy, Lena? You gonna introduce him to your brown silk? How old is the boy anyway, nineteen? (*No response.*) You gonna burn in hell for doin' what you 'bout to do. Messin' 'round with a boy young enough to be your son. (*She stares at the* ROLAND *painting.*) Fact, lookin' like he do, that Able boy . . . and lookin' at Roland. The child coulda been Roland's.

LENA. Get back in the painting, Veeda.

VEEDA. Don't tell me I done struck up on somethin' you done thought of. (*She studies* ROLAND.) Yeah, circumstances bein' what they are, Able bein' adopted and all . . . He could be your . . .

LENA. He ain't.

VEEDA. Could be.

LENA. You know how many adopted children live in New York?

VEEDA. No, how many?

LENA. Enough that he could be anybody's.

VEEDA. And he could be yours and Roland's.

LENA. Well he ain't.

VEEDA. (*Studying* ROLAND.) Look at the resemblance between that child and Roland.

LENA. Look at how many people look like me, or you, or anybody for that matter. Get on back in there and mind your business.

VEEDA. Be just like fate and God to stick it to you right here on earth, give you your hell right here. Yeah, be just like fate to have your son . . .

LENA. He ain't my son.

VEEDA. He look like your son.

LENA. He looks like Roland.

VEEDA. Do he, now? Like I said, he look like your son.

LENA. He ain't my son. I ain't never see my son.

VEEDA. Then how you know he ain't yours?

LENA. 'Cause he ain't.

VEEDA. Wishful thinkin'.

(LENA *crosses to refill her glass. She drinks.*)

VEEDA. What you gonna do, Lena? You gonna open up that Pandora's box of yours and blow that child's mind. That's what happened in that Greek story, ain't it? Remember that story you read me when you was in Westinghouse High School? 'Member that story 'bout the mother who slept with her . . .

LENA. Shut up, Veeda.

VEEDA. And you so hot, ain't you, Lena? How long's it been since you had a man? How long's it been since you had a man like Roland? And Able looks so much like Roland, don't he? Can't you just taste his mouth on them big hairy legs of yours?

LENA. Shut up!

VEEDA. Ooooo, I know you're hot. I know you when you get hot. You get that look you got in your eyes and that passion box of yours . . . It's just snappin' and wishin' and waitin' for him to come through that door. Ain't it waitin' on Able?

(LENA *does not respond.* VEEDA *crosses to* LENA.)

VEEDA. Awwwww, poor Lena's in a fix. She got the hots for her own son.

LENA. He ain't my son.

VEEDA. You ain't got to convince me. Convince . . . (*She crosses to the* ROLAND *painting*) Roland. Nah . . . Ain't got to do that. He never knew 'bout no son. Why not try and convince Fendi? (*She crosses to the* FENDI *painting.*) Think she'll care? She'd expect it of you, bein' the type of mother you were.

LENA. Why don't you just. . . . Can't you just sit still?

VEEDA. Sure I can, but why should I? (*She crosses to* LENA.) What you gonna do, Lena? Screw him or leave him?

LENA. None of your business.

VEEDA. I'm makin' everything my business. What you gonna do? What you gonna do?

(ROLAND and FENDI step from the paintings. They cross to LENA in what appears slow motion. Simultaneously the two deliver a slow haunting chant of the question.)

ROLAND. What you gonna do? What you gonna do? What you gonna do? What you gonna do? What you gonna do? What you gonna do? What you gonna do?

FENDI. What you gonna do? What you gonna do? What you gonna do? What you gonna do? What you gonna do? What you gonna do? What you gonna do?

(Their voices underwrite VEEDA's dialogue.)

VEEDA. What you gonna do, Lena? Wrap them legs around that boy's body? Put them hot wet lips on his mouth.

(ROLAND kisses LENA passionately on the mouth.

FENDI *slowly circles LENA softly continuing the chant.)*

VEEDA. You gonna let him run his hands up between your thighs?

(ROLAND runs his hands up between LENA's thighs. She is in ecstasy.)

You gonna pull his head down to your breasts?

(LENA pulls ROLAND's head down to her breasts.)

Can you feel it, Lena?
LENA. *(Enjoyingly.)* Yes.
VEEDA. Can you feel it, Lena?
LENA. Yes.

(ROLAND caresses Lena's body with both his hands ˙nd lips.)

VEEDA. Don't it just make you feel . . .
LENA. Good. . . . Yes!

(The lights begin a slow pulse-beat strobe of the three, giving the illusion of several still shots or frames. As the intensity

of VEEDA's *and* LENA's *lines build, the speed of the light builds.*

NOTE: *It is the intention of the author to simulate the act of making love, but in a tactful and tasteful manner.*

VEEDA *retrieves the bottle of champagne and the two glasses from the bar during these movements and while delivering the lines.*

ABLE *substitutes positions with* ROLAND *during the course of the movements.*

*There should be a moment there it is obvious that all three characters—*VEEDA, ROLAND *and* FENDI—*are standing around* LENA *and* ABLE *before they retreat back into the paintings.*

VEEDA. His sweet lips . . .
LENA. Yes.
VEEDA. His knowing hands . . .
LENA. Yes. Yes.
VEEDA. And he feels good.
LENA. Yes. Yes. He's so good. He's so . . . He's so . . .
   He's so . . .

(The strobe begins to speed up in pace.)

VEEDA. Say it, Lena.
LENA. He's so . . .
VEEDA. Say it, Lena.
LENA. (*To* ABLE.) YOU'RE SO GOOD!

(The strobe stops. VEEDA, ROLAND *and* FENDI *stand around* LENA *and* ABLE.

Blackness.

The strobe starts a slow wind-down rhythm.)

LENA. (*To* ABLE.) YOU'RE SO GOOD! Oh baby. . . .
   My baby. . . . My sweet, sweet baby. . . .

*(*LENA *pulls* ABLE's *head down to her breasts.*

Blackness.

The strobe once again starts a slow wind-down rhythm. The normal lighting should creep in.

VEEDA, ROLAND *and* FENDI *return to their positions in the paintings.)*

LENA. *(Softly to* ABLE.*)* You're so good.
VEEDA. *(From painting, to* LENA.*)* Passion. Caution goes to the wind when Lena's passion comes to roost. Ain't that right, Lena?

*(*LENA *tries to collect herself. She groggily studies* ABLE'*s face.*

ABLE *tenderly kisses* LENA. LENA *scans the room. She focuses on the opened champagne bottle and the two used glasses.*

LENA *turns to the* VEEDA *painting.)*

VEEDA. *(To* LENA.*)* Look what you done, Lena.
FENDI. *(To* LENA.*)* Look what you done, Momma.
ROLAND. *(To* LENA.*)* What you do, Lena?

*(*LENA *jumps up.* ABLE *is startled and confused by her actions.)*

ABLE. What's wrong?
LENA. *(To* ABLE.*)* Wrong? Wrong? *(Trying to collect her thoughts.)* Wrong? Yes, my headache. . . . It came back. The . . . *(She spots the champagne bottle.)* champagne. . . . It must have . . . given me . . . Oh, God. . . .
ABLE. What can I do?
LENA. Do?
ABLE. *(Crossing to* LENA.*)* I can massage it.

*(*ABLE *attempts to touch* LENA, *who jumps away.)*

LENA. No! . . . I mean . . . What I need is . . . *(She searches for an out.)* Rest. I've got to rest.
ABLE. Let me help you.

LENA. No. No. I'm fine. I'm fine.

ABLE. You're angry.

LENA. (*Sincerely*.) No.

ABLE. Then why won't you let me touch you?

LENA. It's my head . . . the pain. . . .

ABLE. Then let's call a doctor.

LENA. What I need is rest. I'll be fine. You go, I'll rest and everything will be fine. . . .

ABLE. I did something wrong, didn't I?

(LENA *crosses to* ABLE. *She caresses his face.*)

LENA. Oh, no. . . . No. . . . You're so . . . You're so sweet and good and . . . No, you didn't do anything wrong. You're really very good.

ABLE. Then why? . . .

(LENA *places her fingers over* ABLE's *lips as she guides him to the door.*)

ABLE. Will I see you tomorrow?

LENA. Why, of course. Why do you ask that? It's just one of my headaches. You know how I get headaches. What I need is a little rest.

ABLE. I don't like leaving you like this.

LENA. Able! I'll be fine.

(LENA *caresses* ABLE's *face again.* ABLE *kisses* LENA *and exits.*

Silence.

LENA *leans against the door.*)

LENA. (*Fighting tears.*) Oh, God. . . .

VEEDA. (*From the painting.*) Yes, do call on him. But I wouldn't take no bets he's got ears for you. Makin' it with your son gotta be one of those irreversible sins.

LENA. He's not my son.

VEEDA. Anything you say.

LENA. (*Massaging her head.*) I don't know what happened.

VEEDA. Just bet you don't. Well . . . You turned the child out, that's what happened.

(LENA *crosses to the bar.*)

VEEDA. Wrapped them hot thighs 'round that child's
      body. . . .
LENA. Shut up, Veeda.

(LENA *picks up the decanter. It is empty. She then picks up
the hidden bottle of cheap Scotch. She pours the Scotch into
her sherry glass. She stares at the glass and then decides to
drink the Scotch straight from the bottle.*)

VEEDA. That's right, girl, drink up, drink fast and wash it
      away. If you can. Lena Larsen, the woman with the
      passion box and death touch. What they call it? . . .
      Medusa touch? Yeah, that's what you got. Wipe 'um
      out every time.
LENA. Shut up.
VEEDA. See that poor child's face? How come you throw
      him out like that? He just know he ain't do the do
      right. That's sure to mess with his ego. He's at a vul-
      nerable age. Might mess with his manhood and wouldn't
      that be a waste? Really do put you in the mind of
      Roland.
LENA. Veeda! . . .
VEEDA. Boy, did you have that child goin'. Your head
      thrown back, you moanin' and groanin'. . . . (*She
      mimics* LENA.) You so . . . You so good. . . . My
      baby. . . . My sweet, sweet baby. . . .

(LENA *crosses to find the revolver.*)

VEEDA. Yeah, you done done it again, whippin' that sweet
      lethal passion box a yours on that child.
LENA. (*Pointing the gun at* VEEDA.) You shut your mouth.
VEEDA. Awwwww, Lena. . . . You not startin' up with
      this again? Go 'head, pull the trigger.
LENA. (*Strongly.*) You get your ass back in there. (*She
      drives* VEEDA *back to the frame.*) I'm sick of your
      mouth. Get in there. Move!
VEEDA. Hey, you ain't got to shove. I'm movin'. (*She steps
      back into the frame.*) Never resorted to violence be-
      fore. Believe you're over the edge this time.
LENA. Close that mouth of yours or I'll close it for you
      permanently.

VEEDA. Tell me, was it worth it? Was it good? Your head all thrown back. Your eyes rollin' in your head. His hands, lips. . . . You whisperin' . . . (*She mimics once again.*) You so . . . You so good. . . . My baby. . . .

(LENA *cocks the trigger.*)

LENA. Shut up!
VEEDA. My sweet, sweet baby. . . .
LENA. Shut up!
VEEDA. My sweet . . .
LENA. Shut up!

(LENA *pulls the triggers. She shoots* VEEDA. VEEDA *freezes in the original painting position.*)

LENA. Shut up! Shut up! Shut up! Shut up!

(LENA *pulls the trigger again. She crosses to the paintings of* ROLAND *and* FENDI *and shoots.*)

LENA. (*To the paintings.*) All of you. . . . Just . . . shut . . . up!

(*Silence.* VEEDA, ROLAND *and* FENDI *are frozen in their original positions.*)

LENA. (*Softly.*) Just shut up!

(*Silence.*)

LENA. Oh, God. . . .

(LENA *pans the room, the paintings. The lights begin a slow fade.* LENA *can be seen bringing the revolver up to her temple. The lights go to black.*

SOUND: *A shot from the revolver.*

SOUND: *A sensual saxophone solo.*)

CURTAIN

A FEW SOURCES ON BLACK WOMEN PLAYWRIGHTS

Plays by black women and critical materials on their work are scattered among various anthologies, books and journals. For those interested in further reading or research, the following list provides some useful sources, some of which include helpful bibliographic references.

ANTHOLOGIES

Baraka, Amiri (LeRoi Jones) and Amina Baraka. *Configuration: An Anthology of African American Women*. New York: Quill, 1983.

Couch, William. *New Black Playwrights*. Baton Rouge: Louisiana State University, 1968.

France, Rachel. *A Century of Plays by American Women*. New York: Richard Rosen Press, 1979.

Hansberry, Lorraine. *A Raisin in the Sun/The Sign in Sidney Brustein's Window*. New York: New American Library, 1966.

————. *Lorraine Hansberry: The Collected Last Plays*. Ed. by Robert Nemiroff. New York: New American Library, 1983.

Hatch, James V. and Ted Shine, Eds. *Black Theater USA: Forty-Five Plays by Black-Americans, 1847–1974*. New York: The Free Press, 1974.

King, Woodie and Ron Milner, Eds. *Black Drama Anthology*. New York: New American Library, 1971.

Locke, Alain and Montgomery Gregory. *Plays of Negro Life*. New York: Harper Bros., 1927.

Ostrow, Eileen Joyce, Ed. *Center Stage: An Anthology of 21 Contemporary Black-American Plays*. Oakland, Calif.: Sea Urchin Press, 1981.

Patterson, Lindsay, Ed. *Black Theater*. New York: Dodd, Mead & Company, 1971.

Richardson, Willis and May Miller. *Negro History in Thir-teen Plays*. Washington, D.C.: Associated Publishers, 1935.

Shange, Ntozake. *For colored girls who have considered suicide when the rainbow is enuf*. New York: Bantam Books, 1980.

Shange, Ntozake. *Three Pieces*. New York: St. Martin's Press, 1981.

REFERENCE AND CRITICAL WORKS

Davis, Thadious M. and Trudier Harris, Eds. *Afro-Amer-ican Writers After 1955: Dramatists and Prose Writers*. Dictionary of Literary Biography. Detroit: Gale Re-search Company, 1985.

Evans, Mari. *Black Women Writers (1950–1980): A Critical Evaluation*. New York: Anchor Books, 1984.

Freedomways (Lorraine Hansberry: Art of Thunder, Vi-sion of Light). Volume 19, Number 4, 1979.

Hatch, James V. and OMANii Abdullah. *Black Play-wrights, 1823–1977: An Annotated Bibliography of Plays*. New York: R.R. Bowker Company, 1977.

McKay, Nellie. "What Were They Saying? Black Women Playwrights of the Harlem Renaissance," *The Harlem Renaissance Re-Examined*, edited by Victor A. Kramer. New York: A.M.S. Press, 1986.

Miller, Jeanne-Marie A., "Images of Black Women in Plays by Black Playwrights," *CLA Journal*, XX, No. 4, June, 1977.

Tate, Claudia, Ed. *Black Women Writers at Work*. New York: Continuum, 1983.

Theatre Annual (Issue on: Women in Theatre). Volume XL, 1986.

2847